Marriage...

Falcon Whitelaw offered his services—as husband and stand-in father—to a damsel in distress and her darling daughter. *The Unforgiving Bride* was skittish about love, but this Whitelaw man could be very convincing....

Callen Whitelaw had one surefire way to soften up a rugged rancher out for revenge against her beloved clan.... *The Headstrong Bride* would marry him!

Zach Whitelaw chose his "convenient" wife for one reason only—to provide him with a brood of little Whitelaws. But no matter how many long, lazy days they spent in their marriage bed, *The Disobedient Bride* refused to get pregnant....

Dear Reader,

When I learned the bride trilogy from my HAWK'S WAY series, set in northwest Texas, would be reprinted, I sat down and reread the books for the first time since I wrote them. (I never read my books once they're published, because I can't resist the urge to keep editing, which isn't possible once they're in print.) The Whitelaws have become a real family to me, and it was a delight to look back at how the parents of future Whitelaw heroes and heroines met and fell in love.

I discovered that the timeless myths so evident in romance novels, including my own, are tremendously powerful. None of the three couples in my bride books marry because they're in love. It's only after they marry for other reasons—to save a child's life in *The Unforgiving Bride*, for revenge in *The Headstrong Bride*, and to get an heir in *The Disobedient Bride*— that they discover what true love is all about.

So meet the Whitelaws of Hawk's Way! Come along with me on a wonderful romance adventure. Sit back, put up your feet and get ready to laugh and cry and fall in love all over again.

Happy reading,

Joan Johnston

JOAN
JOHNSTON

Hawk's Way Brides

Published by Silhouette Books

America's Publisher of Contemporary Romance

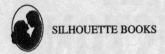 **SILHOUETTE BOOKS**

HAWK'S WAY BRIDES

Copyright © 2001 by Harlequin Books S.A.

ISBN 0-373-48440-2

The publisher acknowledges the copyright holder of the individual works as follows:

THE UNFORGIVING BRIDE
Copyright © 1994 by Joan Mertens Johnston

THE HEADSTRONG BRIDE
Copyright © 1994 by Joan Mertens Johnston

THE DISOBEDIENT BRIDE
Copyright © 1994 by Joan Mertens Johnston

Visit Silhouette at www.eHarlequin.com

Printed in U.S.A.

CONTENTS

Hawk's Way Family Tree

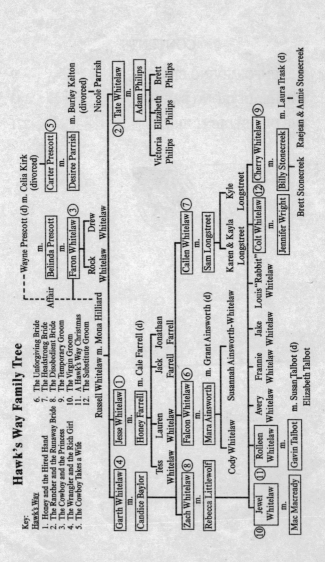

Key:

Hawk's Way
1. Honey and the Hired Hand
2. The Rancher and the Runaway Bride
3. The Cowboy and the Princess
4. The Wrangler and the Rich Girl
5. The Cowboy Takes a Wife
6. The Unforgiving Bride
7. The Headstrong Bride
8. The Disobedient Bride
9. The Temporary Groom
10. The Virgin Groom
11. A Hawk's Way Christmas
12. The Substitute Groom

THE UNFORGIVING BRIDE

This book is dedicated to all
single mothers who face disasters—
large and small—
and find a way to survive.

ACKNOWLEDGMENTS
I would like to thank St. Jude Children's
Research Hospital in Memphis, Tennessee,
for providing me with up-to-date information about
the symptoms and treatment of acute lymphocytic
leukemia and for answering all my questions willingly
and cheerfully. I'm afraid I represented the sick little
girl in my book so humanly to their representative that
I was asked, "Does your daughter have this disease?"
Thankfully, she does not.

I have taken some liberty in representing the material
given to me, but the symptoms, treatment and survival
statistics for this disease are accurately stated.

Prologue

Falcon noticed the woman right away, even though she was standing in the middle of a crowded sidewalk in downtown Dallas. She was not the sort of female who usually attracted his attention, being boyishly slim and merely pretty, rather than beautiful. But there was something about her that drew his eyes and held him spellbound.

He had barely begun to admire her assets—long, silky black hair whipped by the hot summer breeze, spectacular blue eyes and a tall, supple body—when he spotted the little girl at her side. The woman was joined a moment later by a man who slipped his arm around her slender waist and captured her mouth in a hard, possessive kiss. The little girl quickly claimed the man's attention, and he leaned down to listen to her excited chatter.

Falcon felt a sharp stab of envy that he wasn't the man in the quaint family picture. Not that he wanted kids, or wanted to be married, for that matter, but he would have given anything to be on the receiving end of the warm, approving look the woman gave the man as he attended to the little girl.

He was startled to realize that he knew the man. Which meant he could easily wrangle an introduction to the woman.

She's married.

Falcon didn't dally with married women. At least, he never had in the past. He pursed his lips thoughtfully. There was no reason why he couldn't meet her. Without stopping to think, he approached the trio.

"Grant? Grant Ainsworth?" Falcon inquired, though he knew he wasn't mistaken.

"Falcon Whitelaw!" the man exclaimed. "I haven't seen you in—it must be ten years!"

"Nearly that. Guess we lost touch after graduation from Tech," Falcon said with a smile as he extended his hand to meet the one that had been thrust at him. He forced himself to keep his eyes on his old football teammate from Texas Tech. But he wanted to meet the woman. He wanted to feast his eyes on her face at close range. He wanted to figure out what it was that made her so alluring.

"What have you been doing with yourself, Grant?" Falcon asked.

"Got married," Grant replied with a smug grin. "This is my wife, Mara, and my daughter, Susannah."

Falcon turned to greet Mara Ainsworth. He was sorry she wasn't one of those progressive women who shook hands with a man. He would have liked to touch her. She nodded her head and smiled at him, and he felt his stomach do a queer turn. He lifted a finger to his Stetson in acknowledgement of her. "Ma'am."

Because he knew it was expected of him, he lowered his eyes to the little girl. She was hiding half behind her mother's full skirt. Susannah had Mara's black hair, but her eyes were hazel, rather than blue. "Howdy," he said. "You're a pretty little miss. Almost as pretty as your mother."

The little girl giggled and hid her face completely.

From the corner of his eye, Falcon caught the flush of pleasure on Mara's face. He wanted to touch her cheek, to feel the heat beneath the skin.

"How old is your daughter?" he asked Mara. He needed a reason to look at her. His eyes lingered, cataloging each exquisite feature.

"Susannah's seven," Mara replied.

Falcon heard Grant talking, but he couldn't take his eyes off Mara. For a moment he thought he saw something in her open gaze, an attraction to him as strong as the one he felt for her. But he knew that was only wishful thinking.

Her lids lowered demurely so her lashes created two coal crescents on milky white skin. Whatever she was feeling, it was hidden from him now. Her lips parted slightly, and he could just see the edges of her teeth. He had to restrain a harsh intake of breath at the overpowering desire he felt to claim her mouth with his. He had never felt a need so strong or so demanding.

Falcon was aware that Grant was asking him something, but he only caught the last half of the sentence.

"...so if you're staying the night in Dallas, maybe we could get together and have a few drinks for old times' sake," Grant finished.

Falcon saw the quick flash of annoyance on Mara's face. Obviously she would rather have Grant to herself than share him with an old friend. Falcon started to give her what she wanted but realized that if he had a few drinks with Grant he could find out more about Mara, more about the state of their marriage. It looked happy from the outside, but if there were problems, maybe there was a chance Mara would welcome his attention.

Falcon hated what he was thinking. It wasn't like him to go after some other man's woman. But there was something about Mara Ainsworth that struck a chord deep inside him. If he had found her unattached, he might even have contemplated giving up his bachelor freedom. But it was folly to let himself even think about her so long as she was another man's wife.

By the time Falcon had come to the conclusion he ought to just get the hell away from the Ainsworths, he realized he had already invited Grant to have drinks with him at a bar near the stockyards.

"What brings you to town, anyway?" Grant asked.

"I'm here to buy cattle for my ranch."

"Didn't know you had a ranch of your own," Grant said.

"I inherited the B-Bar from my grandfather, my mother's father, about five years ago," Falcon replied.

Grant whistled in appreciation. "If I remember rightly, that's quite a spread."

Falcon hadn't done anything to earn the B-Bar, but he was proud of owning it. It *was* a big spread. He glanced at Mara to see if she was impressed. Most women were. But she was watching Grant. She had caught her lower lip with her teeth and was chewing on it. She looked worried about something. Was his rendezvous with Grant going to interrupt some previously made plans?

Falcon had grown up in a family where strong wills were the norm. He had learned that with determination and a little charm, he could usually get what he wanted. As a result, he wasn't used to denying himself anything. That had worked out fine, because there hadn't been anyone but himself to please for the past five years since he had inherited his grandfather's ranch. Suddenly he found himself wanting to take the worry from Mara's brow, even if it meant giving up the opportunity to quiz Grant about her while they were having drinks.

"Look," Falcon said, "if you all have other plans for the evening, I don't want to intrude."

Mara had opened her mouth to respond when Grant said, "No plans. I'll meet you at eight. See you then."

Falcon watched the gentle sway of Mara's hips as Grant led her away. She glanced back at Falcon over her shoulder and caught him staring at her. He felt himself flush, something he couldn't remember doing for a long, long time. He tipped his Stetson to her one more time. It looked like she wanted to say something to him, but Grant kept walking, his arm around her, and the moment was lost.

When the three of them were gone from sight, Falcon exhaled a long, loud sigh of regret. The woman of his dreams had just walked out of his life. He debated whether he ought to do something else tonight and leave a message at the bar for Grant that he couldn't make it. His feelings for Mara Ainsworth were dangerous. If he pursued the matter, he was asking for trouble.

But when eight o'clock came, Falcon was waiting at the Longhorn Bar. Five minutes later, Grant Ainsworth came in. There was a bond between teammates that extended beyond ordinary friendship, and Falcon was reminded of all the times he and Grant had tipped a brew after winning a difficult football game. He knew nothing of what had happened to Grant after college, but he intended to find out.

A country band with a wailing violin was playing up front near the dance floor, but Falcon had settled in one of the booths near the back, where the noise wasn't quite so loud nor the smoke so bad.

"What are you drinking?" he asked as Grant slid in across from him.

"I'll have a whiskey, neat," Grant replied.

Falcon gestured to a waitress wearing skintight jeans and a peasant blouse and ordered the drink Grant had asked for and another Pearl beer for himself.

When the drinks arrived, Grant held up his glass and said, "To pretty women."

Falcon grinned. "I'll drink to that." He took a sip of beer; Grant had finished his whiskey in a few swallows.

Grant slammed his glass onto the table and said, "That went down pretty damn smooth. I think I'll have another."

Grant gestured and had the waitress bring him another whiskey.

"You need any ranch hands for that place of yours?" Grant asked after he had taken a sip of the second drink.

Falcon was startled by the question. "You need work?"

Grant shrugged. "Been laid off recently. Could use work if you've got it."

Actually, Falcon was sure he had all the help he needed. But he thought of Mara and Susannah without food on the table and said, "Sure. There's always room for another hand."

Grant's shoulders visibly relaxed. He finished off the second whiskey and called for another. "You don't know what a relief that is. Mara was beginning to think I would never... But I've got a job, after all, so everything will be fine."

It was plain from the look on Grant's face that he and his wife must have argued over the matter. Falcon was happy to change the subject to what he wanted to talk about most.

"Where did you meet Mara?"

"Her father was foreman on a ranch in west Texas where I worked right after college. I took one look at her and knew she was the one for me. It took a little convincing to get her to say yes. But she did. We've been married for eight years now."

"Where have you been living?"

Grant looked sheepish. "Here and there around Texas. We've moved every year or so. Last job I had was in Victoria. We came to Dallas because I heard some ranches around here were hiring help."

Falcon frowned. Most cowhands were footloose and fancy free—when they were single. A married man settled down in one place and raised his family. He wondered whether Grant had willingly left all those jobs, or whether there was something he had done to get himself fired. He had seemed steady enough in college, but college was ten years ago.

Had Grant Ainsworth become a thief? Was he a bully?

Lazy? Incompetent? Cantankerous? Any of those faults would get him laid off in a hurry.

What had it been like for Mara to move around like that? Could she be happy with a man who was constantly losing his job? He recalled the adoring look on Mara's face when she had watched Grant with Susannah. Whatever Grant's shortcomings, Mara apparently still loved him.

"There are some houses on the property for hired hands. You're welcome to use one of them," he heard himself offer.

"I'd appreciate that," Grant said. Only he wasn't looking at Falcon when he answered.

Falcon was amazed and appalled when he realized that Grant was flirting with a pair of women sitting at a table across from them. He felt outraged on Mara's behalf. A man with a wife like her waiting for him at home had no business making eyes at other women. Suddenly Falcon didn't want to be where he was anymore.

"Look, I've got to be up early tomorrow. The drinks are on me—for old times' sake. I'll see you when you get to the ranch." Falcon threw a twenty on the table.

"There's no need—"

Falcon cut Grant off with a quick shake of his head. "Call it a celebration of your new job."

At the door to the bar Falcon glanced back and saw that the two women had already joined Grant in the booth. He scowled. Sonofabitch was cheating on his wife! Falcon felt a burning anger deep in his gut.

Falcon realized he just might have discovered why Grant had been let go from jobs so often. Suppose Grant played around with women wherever he went? That would certainly raise the hackles of the men he worked with and get him booted fast. Falcon grimaced. What kind of man had he just hired to work on the B-Bar?

Falcon thought of having Mara Ainsworth living on the B-Bar, in a house where he could see her every day. Knowing her husband didn't appreciate her. Knowing she loved the bastard anyway.

It was going to be hell.

Falcon had wanted to see Mara Ainsworth again, but he had never dreamed it would be at her husband's funeral. He stood at the back of a crowd of mourners shrouded in black, waiting for a chance to speak to her, to tell her how sorry he was that Grant was dead. And he was sorry, for Grant's sake. No one deserved to die that young. Deep down, in places where honesty reigned, he felt that Mara was better off without him. But he wasn't going to voice those feelings. He owed Grant that, at least.

But he couldn't forgive Grant for the utter senselessness of his death: his friend had been killed in a one-car accident the same night Falcon had met him in the Longhorn Bar. Falcon bitterly regretted leaving Grant with money for several more drinks. Obviously Grant hadn't sobered up before he got behind the wheel. It was a tragedy that happened all too often, and Falcon could only be grateful that there had been no innocent victims in the accident.

If Falcon felt guilty at all, it was because he coveted Grant's widow. Mara was free now. He could have her if he wanted her—after a decent period of mourning, of course. Even he wasn't blackguard enough to go after a grieving widow.

But he wanted her. More than he ever had.

Dressed in black, Mara had an ethereal beauty. The deep circles under her eyes only made her look more hauntingly attractive. He knew she couldn't have gotten much sleep in the past week since Grant's death. Susannah stood beside her mother looking bewildered.

Falcon had tried to see Mara when he first heard about the accident, but realized he didn't know how to find her. He had read an announcement of the funeral services and made plans to attend. That way he could talk to her and extend his sympathy. And find out where she planned to go from here.

Because he wanted to know where he could find her when she had finished mourning Grant Ainsworth.

The grave-side service had ended, and most of those gathered for the funeral had returned to their cars. Susannah had apparently gone with one of Mara's friends, because Mara was alone beside Grant's grave when Falcon approached her.

"Mara," he said.

It took her eyes a second to focus, but he knew the instant she recognized him, because her features twisted with loathing.

"How dare you show your face here!" she said in a harsh, bitter voice. "My husband is dead, and it's all your fault!"

Falcon was stunned at her accusation.

"You invited him to that bar! You got him drunk! And then you let him drive home!"

"I—"

"I hate you!" she said in a venomous voice. "I hope you rot in hell! I hope someone you loves dies a horrible death!"

She opened her mouth to speak, but all that came out was a low, ululating cry of pain. Her face crumpled in a mask of despair as she dropped to the grass beside her husband's newly dug grave. Her body shook with sobs of grief.

There was thickness in Falcon's throat that made it painful to swallow. He had never dreamed that she would blame him. How could she think he was responsible? He hadn't even been there when Grant left the bar. It wasn't his fault. She was wrong.

Not even in the farthest reaches of his mind had he planned to get Grant drunk and send him out to die in a fiery one-car crash. He had wanted Mara, it was true. But he had never wished Grant dead so that he could have her.

Small chance of his having her now. She hated his guts. She never wanted to see him again. She would as soon scratch out his eyes as look at him.

Falcon wanted to reach out to comfort her, to hold her in his arms and let her cry out her pain against his chest. He actually went so far as to touch her shoulder. "If there's ever anything I can do to help…"

The instant she realized who had touched her, she turned on him. He had never seen a woman's face contort in such fury and revulsion.

"Get away from me!" she hissed. "I don't need your kind of help. Go to hell, or go anywhere at all, but don't ever come near me again!"

He had backed away, stumbled over something, then turned and fled. He felt as though a tight band was constricting his chest. He couldn't breathe. He couldn't swallow. He felt like crying.

It was over. Mara was gone from his life before she had ever been a part of it. She hated him. She blamed him for Grant's death. He would never see her again.

But it would be a long time before he forgot the look of loathing toward him on Mara Ainsworth's face.

Chapter 1

One year later

Mara had tried every other alternative, and there was only one left. She had to swallow her pride and approach Falcon Whitelaw for the help he had once offered. Although, she couldn't imagine him even giving her a chance to open her mouth before he shut the door in her face. Mara shuddered when she remembered the awful things she had said to him, even if they were true.

But Susannah was sick, very sick, and she needed treatment that would cost thousands of dollars. Mara had applied to a number of agencies for help, and it was available, but only if she and Susannah left home and traveled to another state. Life was grim enough these days without leaving behind everything that was familiar.

On Grant's death, Mara had used most of his life insurance to buy a home for herself and Susannah. She had vowed never to move again. If there was any way to stay in Dallas, where they had finally grown roots—shallow ones, but roots, never-theless—Mara intended to pursue it. She had exhausted every other road to achieve her goal. There was only one left. She had to approach Falcon Whitelaw and ask him for money to help with Susannah's medical expenses.

Begging left a bitter taste in her mouth. But Mara was willing to humble herself in any way that was necessary to make sure Susannah got the treatment she needed. It was galling to have to approach the one man in the world she blamed for her current predicament. If Grant hadn't died in that accident, they would have had the health insurance he usually received as a part of his compensation. But Grant had been between jobs, so there was nothing. Instead Mara had been caught in every mother's nightmare. She had a sick child and no insurance to pay for medical bills.

Health insurance had been the last thing on her mind when Grant had left her widowed, and she found herself unemployed with a meager amount of life insurance and a child to raise. She had used the balance of the life insurance left after she bought the house to pay college tuition, believing that an education was the best investment for their future. It was a wise move, but had left the two of them exposed to the disaster that had occurred.

Mara hadn't even realized, at first, that Susannah was sick. In the months following Grant's death, her daughter had been tired and listless and seemed uninterested in doing the things she normally did. Mara had thought Susannah was merely grieving in her own way. Until one day Susannah didn't get out of bed at all. She had a high fever, and nothing Mara did could bring it down.

She took Susannah to the emergency room of the hospital and experienced the horror of watching her small, helpless child be hooked up to dozens of tubes and monitors. The diagnosis of Susannah's illness had come as a shock. Mara had sat stunned in the chair before Dr. Sortino's cluttered desk and listened with disbelief.

Acute lymphocytic leukemia.

"Children die of that," Mara had managed to gasp.

A pair of sympathetic brown eyes had looked out from Dr. Sortino's gaunt face. "Not as many as in the past. Nearly three-quarters of all children diagnosed with this disease today live."

"What about the rest?" Mara asked. "What about Susannah?"

"Our cure rate with chemotherapy is ninety percent. If that doesn't work, there's always a bone-marrow transplant to consider."

Mara had stared at him with unseeing eyes. *Chemotherapy.* She had never known anyone personally who had taken chemotherapy. But she had read enough, and seen enough on television, to know that chemotherapy made you vomit, and that your hair fell out. The thought of that happening to her precious daughter, the thought of all Susannah's long black hair falling out, made her feel faint.

"Mrs. Ainsworth? Are you all right?"

Dr. Sortino was on one knee beside her, keeping her from sliding out of the chair. She felt the sting of tears in her nose and eyes. "No, I'm not all right!" She fixed a blazing stare on the doctor who had been the messenger of such ill tidings.

"I'm angry," she spat. "I'm furious, in fact! Why Susannah? How did this happen? She's just a little girl. *She's only eight years old!*"

Dr. Sortino's eyes were no longer sympathetic. A look of pain and resignation had glazed his eyes after her vituperative attack. He rose and returned to his place behind the desk, putting a physical barrier between them that did little to protect him from her anger and despair.

"I'm sorry, Mrs. Ainsworth," he said. "There are as many as a dozen factors that may have been responsible for Susannah contracting the disease. We haven't done enough tests yet to make a guess on the precise reasons for her illness. But we can cure it...in most cases. You're lucky. Susannah has a tremendous chance of survival. With other diseases..."

He left her to contemplate her good fortune. But Mara didn't feel lucky. Leukemia was a serious disease. Her precious, wonderful daughter might die. "When do you start treatment?" she asked. "Will Susannah have to stay in the hospital? How will we know if it works?"

That was when kindly Dr. Sortino had started asking questions about insurance. That was when she had realized the enormity of the cost of treatment, and the hospital's inability to absorb another patient of this kind without a payment from some source.

"There are other facilities that can serve your needs better if you can't pay at least a portion of the costs up front," the doctor had said.

But those facilities were in another state.

Mara had tried buying insurance, but Susannah's illness was a preexisting condition and could not be covered.

"But I don't need insurance for anything else!" she had argued.

After the insurance companies turned a deaf ear, Mara tried the various foundations that provided assistance for children. And got the same answer. Help was available only if she was willing to go somewhere else to get it.

Mara knew she was foolish for clinging to the familiar, but she wasn't sure she could survive weeks, and maybe months, of living in a Ronald McDonald House in a strange city, all alone with only Susannah and her fears to keep her company. She needed a place that was home. She needed the support of the few friends she had made. And Susannah needed the normalcy of school and friends around her during her recuperation.

Her daughter was going to be one of the lucky seventy-three percent who were cured of the disease. Mara refused to consider any other outcome to Susannah's treatment.

But she needed money and needed it fast. Borrowing was

out of the question. She had just finished her first year of college, working part-time as a cook in one of the college hangouts. She didn't qualify for the sizable loan she needed without some security, and she hadn't enough equity in the house to do the job.

On the other hand, Grant had told her before he'd gone to the bar that Falcon Whitelaw was as rich as Croesus, that he had inherited a fortune from his maternal grandfather, including the B-Bar Ranch on the outskirts of Dallas. Falcon wouldn't even miss the thousands of dollars it was going to cost for Susannah's care. Besides, she was going to offer him something in return.

Mara had grown up at her mother's side and knew everything there was to know about keeping house for a rancher. She planned to trade her services as housekeeper to Falcon in exchange for his financial assistance in paying Susannah's medical bills. She feared she would end up indentured to him for a long time. Just the initial treatment was going to cost nearly $25,000.

Which reasoning all led her to the front doorstep of Falcon Whitelaw's B-Bar Ranch. She had to admit the ranch wasn't what she had expected. The terrain was flat and grassy, but long ago someone had planted live oaks around the house. It had the look of a Spanish hacienda, with its red tile roof and thick, whitewashed adobe walls.

Her hand was poised to knock, her heart in her throat. She swallowed both heart and pride and rapped her knuckles on the arched, heavy oak panel.

No one answered.

She knocked harder, longer and louder.

At last, the door opened.

Falcon had been out late carousing, and he had just dragged on a pair of jeans to answer the door, not even bothering to button them all the way up. They hung down on his hipbones and revealed his white briefs in the vee at the top. He scratched his belly and put one bare foot atop the other. He squinted, his eyes unable to focus in the harsh sunlight that was streaming in through the crack he had opened in the door. He thought better of trying to see and put a hand over his eyes, pressing his temples with forefinger and thumb in an attempt to stop the pounding inside his head.

"Who's there?" he muttered.

Mara stared in disbelief at the bleary-eyed, tousle-headed, unshaved face that had appeared at the door. "It's eleven o'clock," she said with asperity. "Are you just getting up?"

"Good God," Falcon said with a moan. He would never forget that condemning voice, not in a million years. Of all the days for her to show up at the B-Bar, she had to come now. He slowly lowered his hand and squinted painfully into the sunlight until his eyes had adjusted enough to confirm what his ears had told him.

It was Mara Ainsworth, all right. She was wearing that same derisive, accusing look she had worn at Grant's funeral.

Falcon considered shutting the door in her face. He didn't owe her anything. He had offered her his help a year ago, and she had refused it in no uncertain terms.

So what is she doing here now?

From the look on her face she had come to play Puritan temperance woman. He just wasn't up for the game.

Mara's belief that Falcon was an irresponsible care-for-nobody was reaffirmed as she eyed him from head to barefoot toes. Her nose wrinkled in disgust when the smell of beer assaulted her nostrils. He was drunk! Or rather, had been. He looked hung over at the moment.

"Are you going to invite me inside?" she demanded.

Falcon was a second late responding, and Mara invited herself in, since he was obviously in no condition to do it. She pushed past Falcon and walked through the arched doorway right into the living room, leaving him standing at the open door.

The house was dark and cool. The furniture was leather

and wood, large and heavy, the sort of thing the conquistadors must have brought with them from Spain. Navajo rugs were thrown on the red brick floor, and Mara found herself facing shelves full of Hopi Indian decorations. Arches inset along the walls held ornamental vases, adding to the Spanish flavor of the room. It was beautiful. It felt like a home. Which was odd, she thought, considering a bachelor lived here.

Without turning to face Falcon she said, "I need to talk to you." Mara surreptitiously rubbed her stomach where she had brushed against him. Her belly was doing strange things. He was an animal—that was why she felt this animal magnetism toward him. She hated the man. It was absolutely ridiculous to think she could be attracted to him.

She turned to face him, willing herself not to feel anything.

But she hadn't forgotten the powerful shudders that had rippled through her when Falcon looked at her the first time they had met. Something had definitely happened that hot summer day on the street in Dallas. She despised herself for what she had felt then. And it had happened again just now.

Animal magnetism, she repeated to herself. *That's all it is.*

Falcon shut the door with a quiet click and leaned back against it. He folded his arms across his bare chest, crossed one bare ankle over the other and stared at her. "I didn't think you ever wanted to see me again."

She flushed. The color started at the edge of her square-necked blouse and shot right up her throat to her cheeks, where it sat in two bright pink spots. "I...I didn't."

His eyes narrowed. "But now you do?"

She swallowed hard and nodded once.

"Well." He paused. "Well." Falcon didn't know what else to say. This was certainly an astounding turn of events. Just when he had convinced himself he could live without her, the woman of his dreams had shown up at his door. Of course, she hadn't exactly picked a moment when he was at his best.

Falcon didn't ask her to sit. He didn't want her to be any

more comfortable than he was. And he was downright miserable.

That didn't keep him from feeling the singular, consuming attraction for her that had struck him the first moment he saw her. And this time he knew he wasn't mistaken—she was feeling it, too. His lips curved in a self-satisfied smile. So, she was ready to admit the attraction she felt and had come to apologize for all those horrible things she had said to him.

Falcon gave free rein to the fierce sexual desire he felt for Mara Ainsworth. His groin tightened, and his blood began to hum. He refused to hide his arousal. Since she had invited herself in, she could just put up with the condition she found him in.

Mara was appalled at the blatant sensuality in Falcon's heavy-lidded stare. There was no hiding the bulge that was lovingly cupped by his butter-soft jeans. Even more appalling was her body's reaction to the prickly situation in which she found herself. She was dumbfounded by her gut response to Falcon's maleness. Her breasts felt heavy, and her belly tensed with expectation.

It was time to state her business and get out.

"I've come to get the help you offered a year ago. I need money. Lots of it."

Mara saw the shock on Falcon's face and hurried to finish before he could throw her out. "Susannah is very ill. She could die." She swallowed over the lump of pain that always arose when she said those words. "She has leukemia."

Falcon had dropped his lazy pose against the door and was standing now on both feet with his hands balled at his sides.

"When Grant died he was between jobs and we didn't have any insurance and I don't have the money for chemotherapy and I've tried to get it other places but they want us to leave Dallas and Grant said you have lots of money so you wouldn't miss it and I think it would be better for both Susannah and me if we stayed where we are. So can you help us?"

Falcon had taken several steps toward Mara during this

breathless speech. As he reached out to give her the comfort she so obviously needed, she took a step back away from him.

So. She wanted his money, but she didn't want him. That was blatantly clear.

"I'll work for you," she choked out. "I'll keep house, cook, clean, whatever you need. I know how to keep ranch books. I'll pay you back in service for every penny, I promise you that. I'm…I'm desperate. Please."

Falcon felt sick to his stomach. Mara, pretty Mara, had been reduced to begging. And she wasn't even asking him to give her the money. She was going to pay it all back. She didn't want to be beholden to him. Because she despised him.

It was there on her face every time she looked at him. She still blamed him for Grant's death. She was never going to forgive him.

So why should he give her the money?

Because there is a chance, just the slightest one, but a chance, that you might be responsible in part for her predicament. Falcon was shaken to the core by that possibility.

And that poor kid. He remembered Susannah's hazel eyes peeping out from behind Mara's skirt on the day he met her and the childish giggle before she hid herself completely from his sight. It was a shame for any kid to be sick, but it caught him in the gut to imagine that engaging little girl bedridden.

"Is Susannah…will she get well?" he asked.

"There's a good chance, a three-to-one chance, she'll be cured by the chemotherapy. But the hospital won't start treatments before I assure them I can pay. Can you…will you help?"

"Give me a figure. I'll see my accountant tomorrow and cut you a check."

"Thank you," Mara said.

He watched her take a step toward him, as though to hug him, to share the joy and relief she was feeling. Then she must have remembered who he was, because she stiffened and stopped herself.

"Thank you," she said again.

But she didn't look at him. She was looking at her hands, which were threaded together and clenched so hard her knuckles were white.

"I can start work right away," she said.

"That won't be necessary," he said in a harsh voice.

Her head snapped up, and her brow furrowed. "I don't understand."

"I'd go nuts with you stomping around here all self-righteous, watching every little move I make and raking me over the coals with those big blue eyes of yours. Thanks, but no thanks. You can have the money, but I'll dispense with your services, if it's all the same to you."

Mara was stung by the image he had painted of her. She wanted to fling his money back in his face, but she had to think of Susannah. She bit her lower lip hard and kept her peace.

"Are we finished with this talk?" Falcon asked irritably. "Because I have a headache, and I'd like to get some aspirin."

"I'll pay you back," Mara said quietly. "Somehow." She hurried to the door. It meant going past Falcon. He didn't move to get out of her way, and she shivered as their bodies brushed.

"Aw, hell. You're not going to get cooties if we touch."

"I didn't—I only—" she stuttered.

"Just get the hell out of here," he said in disgust. He opened the door and held it as she rushed through, dropping a slip of paper in his hand with a breathless "My address," and then slammed it behind her.

"Women! Who the hell needs them!"

He crumpled the paper without looking at it and tossed it on the floor. He wouldn't see her to give her the check. He would have his accountant do it. There was no question, though, about his helping her. He owed it to Grant, and to the little girl who was sick. He owed Mara nothing. He hoped their paths never crossed again.

Finally, at last, he and Mara Ainsworth were quits.

Chapter 2

"**Y**ou don't have the money."

"What?"

"You heard me, Falcon. I said you don't have the money to be giving a blank check to some bimbo."

"Watch what you say, Aaron. Mara Ainsworth is a lady."

"My apologies. That doesn't change your situation."

"Just what, exactly, is my situation?" Falcon asked.

"To be blunt, you've damn near run through your grand-father's fortune in the past five years."

Falcon was stunned. He stopped pacing the thick carpet in his accountant's high-rise Dallas office and sank into a leather-and-chrome chair. "You're kidding, right?"

"I wish I were," Aaron said.

"Why didn't you say something sooner?" he demanded.

"I did."

Falcon remembered a conversation or two when Aaron had warned him not to make some high-risk investments. Then there were the cars. And the parties. The trips to Europe. The fancy studs and champion bulls. And the gifts he had given to his lady friends. He hadn't thought it was possible to spend a fortune in just five years.

"How much have I got left?" he asked, still a little stunned by Aaron's news.

"Enough to keep the B-Bar afloat—if you're careful and give the ranch some attention. Not enough to be loaning thousands of dollars to some woman."

"Lady," Falcon insisted. "Mara is a lady."

"Lady," Aaron conceded.

Falcon dropped his head into his hands. He could always go to his family for help; his parents and his brother and sister had assets if he really needed a loan to help Mara. And he had two uncles and an aunt. But he would be too ashamed to admit to any of them that he had squandered his inheritance. He would never live down the humiliation. And he couldn't bear to see the look on his father's face if he disappointed him. His mother would hide the pain she felt at his failure, because she knew how hard his father could be on anyone who threatened her happiness—even, or especially, her children.

Falcon was the middle child of the Three Whitelaw Brats, as they had come to be known in the vicinity around Hawk's Way, the northwest Texas ranch where he had been raised. Falcon's father, Garth, had been a hard taskmaster, demanding honesty and responsibility and accomplishment from his two sons and daughter. But Garth Whitelaw had held the leash too tight, and all three of them—his elder brother, Zachary, and his younger sister, Callen and himself—had revolted.

They had formed a secret alliance, the Fearless Threesome, and protected each other, deftly covering one another's tracks when they were caught out in some prank. Not that they had been vicious or mean in what they had done, but they had been incorrigible, unmanageable, all three of them, daring anything and often finding themselves in desperate situations that required feats of bravado to escape.

They had been punished for their recklessness, but had re-

mained undaunted. As a child, Falcon's behavior had been as
wild and untamed as his Comanche forbearers. He hadn't im-
proved much over the years. At thirty, he was a maverick
who refused to be tied down to anything or anyone.

His siblings weren't much more settled. His sister, Callen,
was a black-haired, brown-eyed rebel who had defied their
father's attempts to direct her life by twice accepting marriage
proposals against his wishes—and breaking both engagements
when the man turned out to be the cad her father had told her
he was. Zach, with his coal-black hair and dark inscrutable
eyes, had become a recluse, a man who rode alone and didn't
seem to need or want a woman in his life.

Thanks to the Fearless Threesome, Falcon was used to escaping the consequences of his folly. Was it any wonder he
had been careless and irresponsible with his fortune? Only
this time, he didn't think he could ask Zach or Callen to help
him out of his trouble. Maybe it was time to grow up at last.
Maybe it was time to act like the dependable, reliable, trust-
worthy person his parents had raised him to be.

"Isn't there something I can do to help Mara and Susannah?" Falcon asked the man sitting across the desk from him.

Aaron chewed on his pencil, a habit that was apparent from
the series of teeth marks that already creased the yellow stem.
"There is one thing."

Falcon waited, but when Aaron didn't speak he asked, "All
right, what is it?"

"You could marry her."

"What?" Falcon leapt up and slammed his palms flat on
Aaron's marble-topped desk. He leaned forward intimidat-
ingly. "What purpose would that serve?"

"Thanks to your capable accountant, you have an excellent
health-care plan. You see, the insurance company wanted
your business for health coverage of employees at the B-Bar.
So I was able to negotiate a special clause in the contract that
allows you, as the owner, to cover your dependents—even for

a preexisting condition—as soon as you acquire them, in this case, by marriage.''

''That's incredible.''

Aaron smiled. ''I thought so myself when I wrote it into the agreement with the insurance company. You can marry Mara Ainsworth and have Susannah's medical expenses one-hundred-percent covered the next day.''

''I have to think about this,'' Falcon said as he rose and headed for the office door. He paused with the doorknob in his hand and turned back to Aaron. ''Are you sure that's the only way I can help?''

Aaron shrugged. ''You could always sell the B-Bar and give her the proceeds.''

Falcon grimaced. ''Don't be ridiculous.''

''I was being frank,'' Aaron retorted. ''Your choices are limited, Falcon. Let me know what you decide to do.''

Falcon left his accountant's office in a daze. He was dealing with a lot of emotions all at once, not the least of which was shame. What would his parents say, especially his mother, when she found out how profligate he had been with her father's bequest to him? And how was he going to face Mara Ainsworth and admit the truth? That he had managed to run through a fortune in five years of dissipated living. What would happen to Mara and Susannah if he couldn't provide her with the funds she had requested?

You could marry her.

How could he marry a woman who despised him? A woman who would never forgive him for making her a widow? A woman who shrank from his touch?

Unfortunately he had no choice. And neither did she, when it came right down to it. They would just have to make the best of it. It would be one of those marriages of convenience, where they shared the same name and the same house, but nothing else.

It would be a royal pain in the rear.

But it wouldn't last forever. Just until Susannah was out of deep water. Just until the crisis was over. He could stand being close to Mara for that long without touching.

He didn't linger and let himself come up with excuses why Aaron's suggestion wouldn't work. He jumped into his Porsche and headed for the address on the paper Mara had stuffed in his hand when she had raced away from the B-Bar yesterday.

He found her house on a shady street in an old, quiet neighborhood in Dallas. There were bicycles in the driveways and tire swings in the trees. The houses were two-story wood frame structures with picture windows and big, covered front porches. There was even one house with a white picket fence. It belonged, he discovered, to Mara Ainsworth.

He didn't see a car in the driveway, so he wasn't expecting her to be home. But he knocked anyway.

She opened the door wearing very short cutoff jeans and a Dallas Cowboys T-shirt. She was barefoot. And she wasn't wearing a bra. He knew because her nipples peaked the instant she set eyes on him.

He turned her on, but she hated his guts. It was just plain crazy. He had fought the attraction he felt, knowing it could lead nowhere. But it was clear to him, if not yet to her, that some powerful magnetism still existed between the two of them.

"Hello," he managed.

"Oh! I thought you were my neighbor, Sally. But, of course, you aren't."

Of course he wasn't. He stood there on the porch for a moment, waiting for her to invite him inside. When she didn't, he took a page from her book and stepped inside on his own. He heard the door close behind him.

"Where's Susannah?" he asked when she didn't immediately appear.

"She's still in the hospital."

"Oh."

Falcon looked around with a critical eye, wanting to find

something about Mara's home that he could dislike as much as she disliked him. The living room was done in quiet colors and simple Western patterns that were easy on the eye. She had a green thumb, because there were lush plants everywhere, bringing the outdoors inside. Plump pillows decorated the couch, and a cozy, overstuffed chair invited him to sit down.

Only, he knew better than to make himself comfortable. Once she heard what he had to say, she might very well throw him out. He turned to face Mara.

She was leaning against the door in much the same way he had done, but there was nothing relaxed about the pose.

"I didn't bring a check," he said.

She caught her lower lip with her teeth. "You changed your mind about helping us?"

"No, I didn't change my mind," he retorted irritably. "I don't have the money."

She snorted in disbelief. "You mean you choose not to loan it to me."

He began to pace, like a tiger in a cage. "No, I mean exactly what I said. I don't have the money." He paused in front of a natural-rock fireplace and leaned both palms against the mantel with his back to her. "It seems I've already spent most of my fortune. I only have enough left to keep the B-Bar in business."

"I'm sorry," she said.

He whirled, his eyes blazing. "I don't need your pity."

"I don't pity you," she said.

No, it wasn't pity he saw in her eyes. It was disappointment. And disgust. He felt a burning rage deep inside that he should be subjected to all this.

It wasn't my fault. I wasn't the one who killed Grant Ainsworth. Why should I feel responsible for rescuing Grant's wife and child?

If not for the situation he found himself in, it wouldn't have been anyone's business but his own whether he squandered his fortune.

"You could have told me all this in a phone call," Mara said. "Why did you bother coming here?"

"Because even though I can't give you the money I promised, there is a way I can help you."

He saw hope blossom bright and beautiful in her eyes. And dreaded the moment of disillusionment when he told her what he had to say.

"If you marry me," he announced, "Susannah will be covered by my insurance the day after we tie the knot."

"What?"

He thought she was going to faint, so he went to her, to help her. He stopped in his tracks when she backed away from him.

"I don't understand," she said.

"I thought I was very clear," he said in a harsh voice. "My insurance policy will cover any dependents of mine, even for a preexisting condition, the day after I acquire them. If you marry me, my insurance will cover Susannah's treatment."

"Marry you?"

"Yes, dammit, marry me! You don't have to sound so appalled at the idea."

"I'm not...appalled. I'm just...surprised."

Mara crossed to the overstuffed chair and sank into it. "I hadn't thought of getting married again."

"Especially not to the likes of me," Falcon finished for her.

Her brow furrowed. "I don't know what to say."

"Say yes."

She sought out his eyes with her own, and he could see the turmoil there. He knew he ought to let her refuse. Then he would be out of it, and the problem would be hers again. But the truth was, he wanted to be the one to rescue her. He wanted to redeem himself in her eyes. He wanted to earn her respect. He wanted a chance to prove he wasn't the good-for-nothing she thought he was.

"It doesn't have to be a real marriage," he said. "We'll have to live together, of course. But that shouldn't be a problem."

"I don't want to leave my house."

"It's just a house," Falcon argued.

"It's more than that," Mara said, eyes flashing indignantly. "It's a place where I belong, where I have friends. I can't give that up, too."

She bit her lip to keep from letting the whole of her tragedy spill out at him—namely, her fear that she might soon lose Susannah, as well.

He saw the tears that filled her eyes, ready to brim over. He knew she was going to reject him again, but he had to make the effort to comfort her anyway. He pulled her up out of the chair and into his arms.

To his amazement, she clutched him around the waist and pressed her forehead against his chest and began to sob. He tightened his arms around her and crooned words of solace. He didn't know how long they stood there, but when she finally stopped crying, one of his hands was tangled in her hair and the other pressed her tightly against him.

His throat felt thick. His chest ached. He would have given anything to be worthy of her. But it was too late. He had lived a profligate, self-indulgent existence. Now, without the other two-thirds of the Fearless Threesome to rescue him, he was finally going to have to face the consequences of his behavior.

He knew when she was herself again, because she stiffened in his arms. She didn't struggle to be free, but he knew that if he didn't let her go soon, she would.

"Marry me," he whispered. "I promise I won't do anything to make you uncomfortable in my home. For Susannah's sake. Marry me."

She heaved a ragged sigh that ended in a sob that she quickly caught with her fist. She lowered her hand and raised her tear-drenched face to his. "All right," she said in a hoarse voice. "I'll marry you."

She took a step backward, and he was forced to release her.

"I'll take care of getting the license," he said. "You'll have to get a blood test—"

"I'll take care of that on my own. When?" she asked.

"As soon as possible, don't you think?"

Her face looked ravaged. Her eyes were red-rimmed. But she faced him without flinching this time. "You tell me when and where, and I'll be there."

"I'll help you move your things—"

"I'll leave the house exactly as it is," she said fiercely. "It's my home, mine and Susannah's. When this travesty of a marriage is over—" she choked back a sob "—when Susannah is *well,* we'll be coming back here to live. Now get out! I can't stand to look at you anymore."

Falcon backed away to the door, unable to take his eyes off her. Mara hated him. And he was going to marry her. He told himself it was a sacrifice that he owed her.

But as he closed her door behind him, he couldn't help feeling regret, and even despair.

How the hell were they going to get through the next year together?

Chapter 3

It was her wedding day, and Mara felt trapped. This was not the perfect solution she had been searching for, not at all. But at least she didn't have to leave Dallas. She would find some way to keep Susannah in the same school, and she would be able to keep an eye on her house. But she had paid a high price for those small victories. She had to marry the man responsible for Grant's death.

Falcon had promised her it would be a marriage in name only, but in the same breath he had insisted they live together. She supposed there was some danger the insurance company could refuse to pay if they discovered it was a sham marriage, so it had to look real.

But it was a sham. A farce. A pretense. A mockery. She would be Mrs. Falcon Whitelaw. She would be married to a man she despised, a man so irresponsible he had run through a fortune in five years. She had to live in his house, make his meals, iron his clothes. *Be his wife.*

But she would never forgive him. What he had done was

unforgivable. And yet, she owed him something for the help he had given her.

Mara felt torn in half. Because there were other feelings she had for Falcon Whitelaw that had nothing at all to do with hate and scorn. She felt drawn to him in a way that was disturbing, to say the least. She had tried to deceive herself, to say that there was no substance to her attraction to the handsome rogue. But her body made a liar out of her every time she got near him.

So how was she going to survive living in the same house with him, seeing him every day?

"Are you ready?"

Mara was jerked from her thoughts by the words Falcon had murmured in her ear.

"It's time," he said.

"I'm ready." She turned to Falcon. He looked as grim as she felt. "Isn't there anybody you wanted to have here? Some family?" she asked him.

"No. You?"

"No. My parents are gone, and I haven't any brothers or sisters." But she knew Falcon had family. Grant had told her about the Fearless Threesome. Falcon must be missing his brother and sister about now. She wondered how he was going to explain all this to them.

As Falcon listened to the judge reading the words legally binding him to Mara Ainsworth, he was wondering the same thing. How was he going to explain a wife and child to his family? How was he going to explain this slapdash wedding, to which none of them had been invited?

He couldn't tell them the truth. But he didn't want to lie. Better to tell them half the truth. That he had met a very special woman, and that he and Mara hadn't wanted to wait to get married. He would promise to bring his wife to meet the family soon but explain that they had to stay in Dallas for the moment because Mara's daughter was sick and needed treatment at the hospital here. That ought to keep them at bay for a little while.

Then what?

He would worry about the future when it got here, Falcon decided. Right now he had his hands full dealing with the present.

He answered ''I will'' at the proper moment and watched Mara's face as she said the same vow. Her complexion was pale, and she had been chewing on her lower lip so it pouted out a little. He wanted to soothe the hurt. Before the thought got much further than that, the judge was telling him he could kiss the bride.

Falcon put his hands on Mara's shoulders, because he suspected she would retreat if he gave her the chance. He was watching her face as he lowered his mouth toward hers, so he saw the moment her eyelashes fluttered down. Her body was rigid beneath his hands, but her mouth…her mouth was soft and pliant beneath his.

Falcon had kissed a lot of women, but there was no time when he had ever felt like this. It was a reverent meeting of lips, and he cherished Mara, giving himself to her and imploring her to take what he offered.

For a moment, she did.

He felt, as much as heard, her tremulous sigh. She gave herself up to the kiss, her trembling body melting into his, her mouth clinging so sweetly that he thought his heart was going to burst with the joy of it.

Then she jerked away with a cry of distress that she quickly stifled. Her eyes, wide and wounded, stared at him accusingly, as though her surrender was all his fault.

Then he was turning away to smile at the judge—or at least to bare his teeth in a semblance of one—and shake the man's hand and receive congratulations. Falcon didn't risk putting his arm around Mara to lead her from the judge's chambers, but he walked as close behind her as he dared.

The judge knew his father, but had promised to let Falcon

break the news of his wedding. Even so, Falcon kept up the facade of wedded bliss until the door was closed behind him, because he didn't want any stories about the real state of his marriage getting back to his family. At least not before he had figured out how to explain things that didn't leave him in such a bad light.

Falcon opened the door of his Porsche and made sure Mara's calf-length ivory dress was inside before he closed it after her. They were on their way now to pick up Susannah, who was well enough to come home from the hospital until her induction therapy began. Funny name for it, Falcon thought, *induction therapy,* but that was what the hospital called chemotherapy used to induce remission. Susannah needed six to twelve weeks of treatment, which was scheduled to begin on Monday. With her condition stabilized, she was being allowed to spend the weekend with her family.

"How have you explained our wedding to Susannah?" he asked Mara.

A flush of color appeared on her ashen cheeks. "I told her we met and liked each other very much, so we decided to get married."

Falcon hit the brakes and almost caused an accident. "You told her *what?*"

"What did you expect me to tell her," Mara retorted. "That I was marrying you to get the money for her treatments? She's an impressionable child. I want to leave her some illusions about life."

"What's going to happen the first time she sees you cringe when I touch you?" Falcon demanded. "Or didn't you think she was going to notice?" he asked sarcastically.

"I…" Mara hadn't, in fact, thought any further than the wedding. She glared at Falcon. "I suppose I'll have to stop cringing," she announced.

"Great," Falcon muttered. "That's just great. What about our sleeping arrangements? How are you going to explain separate bedrooms to this precocious child of yours?"

"I'll be staying in a room next to Susannah," Mara said. "You'll be the understanding husband who wants me to be near my sick child."

Falcon snorted. "You've thought of everything, haven't you?"

"I wasn't able to think of a way to get out of marrying you!" she snapped.

Falcon slid the car into a parking place at Children's Hospital and cranked off the ignition. He turned to face Mara. "All right," he said, "let's get a few things straight before we go in to see Susannah."

Mara crossed her arms over her chest. "I'm listening."

Big concession, Falcon thought. "You're the one who wants Susannah to believe this marriage is real. I'm willing to go along with you."

This time Mara snorted.

Falcon ignored her and continued, "So I think we better set some ground rules. First, no more cringing, flinching or stiffening up like a board when I get near you. Can you handle that?"

Mara nodded curtly.

"Second, no more mudslinging, in either direction. Agreed?"

"That's fine with me."

He took a deep breath. "Third, you're going to have to allow me to show you some signs of affection."

"What? No! Absolutely not!"

"You're not thinking this through," Falcon said. "Won't Susannah be sure to make comparisons between the way you act toward me and the way you acted toward Grant? She'll know right away that there's something wrong if I never kiss you, if I never lay a hand on you."

Falcon watched Mara's face. He could see the struggle going on, the war she was waging. He saw the moment she conceded the battle. Her chin came up pugnaciously, and her hands balled into tight little fists.

"All right," she said through gritted teeth. "We'll do this your way." She turned to face him, eyes bright with unshed tears. "But don't push me, Falcon. Because I won't stand for it!"

There were things she had put up with in her marriage with Grant that she had decided in the year since his death she should never have tolerated. She wasn't going to make the same mistake twice. Better to lay down rules with Falcon now that would protect her later.

Falcon could have wished for more cooperation from Mara. At least she had been forced to put a door in the high walls that kept her separated from him. Falcon felt the first signs of hope he had known since he had agreed to this untenable situation. He would be able to hold Mara, to kiss her. Maybe, as she got to know him better, as he earned her respect, she would allow him to do more.

He would have a year to prove himself. Mara had told him that after Susannah had the chemotherapy treatments, her leukemia had to stay in remission for a year in order for her to be deemed past the first hurdle toward a cure. Mara and Susannah would be with him at least that long. And a year was a long time.

"I won't go beyond what I think is necessary to convince Susannah we have a normal relationship," Falcon said at last. He knew his idea of "necessary" signs of affection and hers were likely poles apart. But he wasn't about to make promises he couldn't keep. "Shall we go inside now and get Susannah?"

Falcon had forgotten how much Susannah looked like her mother. Her face had the same oval shape, the same strong cheekbones and short, straight nose. Her eyes were large and wide-set like Mara's. But he was shocked at the toll her serious illness had taken on Susannah. It was like seeing Mara pale and thin. His heart went out to the little girl the instant her eyes met his.

"How are you, Susannah?" he asked with a cheerful smile. "Do you remember me?"

Mara was sitting on the bed next to her daughter, and Susannah retreated behind her mother, peeping out at him shyly around Mara's shoulder.

"Your mother has some news for you," Falcon said.

Mara shot him a perturbed look, then smiled down at her daughter. "Yes, sweetheart. Falcon and I got married this morning."

Susannah looked curiously at Falcon. "Are you my daddy now?"

Falcon felt the floor fall out from under him. He obviously hadn't focused on all the responsibilities he was taking on. "I...suppose I am."

"Will you buy me a pony?"

"Susannah!" Mara exclaimed. "You shouldn't be asking Mr. Whitelaw to buy you things."

"Why not, if he's my daddy?" Susannah demanded. "Will you buy me a pony?"

Mara looked helplessly at Falcon, who shrugged helplessly back. Then he turned his attention to Susannah.

"Sure I will, pumpkin. What color pony did you want?"

Mara's lips pursed. "You're going to spoil her rotten."

"That's what fathers are for," Falcon replied. "Right, Susannah?" He grinned and tousled the little girl's hair affectionately.

Susannah beamed. "Right."

Falcon stopped what he was doing when it dawned on him Susannah's hair was all going to fall out when the little girl had chemotherapy. He kept the smile on his face for Susannah's sake, but he felt sick inside.

Mara saw Susannah's smile, the first one she had seen in weeks, and forgave Falcon for catering to her daughter. Nevertheless, she couldn't help resenting the fact that Falcon was able to give Susannah something that Grant wouldn't have been able to afford. She and Grant had barely been making ends meet, in fact. But she kept her mouth shut about how she felt. She had promised to curb her tongue for Susannah's sake.

Susannah had to ride a wheelchair downstairs, but the moment they reached the hospital exit, Falcon swept the little girl up into his arms. Mara didn't have time to feel left out, because Falcon slipped his other arm around her waist and pulled her close. A quick, warning glance kept her from pulling free.

Mara was glad she hadn't when Susannah reached out and grabbed her hand, so the three of them were completely connected. "Let's go home, Mommy," the little girl said.

"We're going to my house, if that's all right with you," Falcon said.

Susannah frowned.

"I live on a ranch," Falcon added.

Susannah's face brightened. "Will my pony be able to live with us?"

"Yes, he will."

"Is Mommy coming, too?"

"Wouldn't go without her," Falcon confirmed.

"All right. Let's go," Susannah said.

Mara marveled at how little effort it had taken for Falcon to convince Susannah that his ranch was a better destination than the home she had worked so hard to create for her daughter over the past year. But other than the doll Susannah had grasped tightly in her arms, and Mara herself, her daughter apparently had no attachments to the house in Dallas.

To Mara's amazement, Falcon turned out to be a totally charming companion on the trip to the B-Bar Ranch. He kept Susannah entertained with outrageous stories about himself and his siblings. The Porsche plainly needed to be replaced with a family car. Mara didn't relish confronting Falcon on the issue. Maybe he would realize the problem himself.

Falcon had just finished an anecdote when Susannah sighed

and said wistfully, "I wish I had a sister. Can you and Mommy get one for me?"

Mara exchanged a horrified look with Falcon, whose lips twisted in a wry smile.

"That's entirely up to your mother," he said, throwing the ball back into her court.

"Will you, Mommy?"

"It's not quite as simple as buying a pony," Mara said as she sent a cutting glance toward Falcon. "Why don't we wait awhile, until you're well. Then we'll see."

Mara saw Falcon's eyebrow arch at the way she had caviled. But she refused to take away any of Susannah's dreams, no matter how farfetched. Especially since there was no telling how much longer Susannah had to dream dreams.

That awful lump was back in Mara's throat, and she swallowed it down and forced a smile to her face. "Besides, you'll be too busy with your new pony to have time for a little sister right away."

"We're here," Falcon announced.

He unbuckled Susannah's seat belt and lifted her into his arms. "Come on," he said. "I want to show you your new home."

Mara followed, feeling forgotten, and though she wouldn't have admitted it, a little jealous of her daughter. Just when she thought Falcon was going to leave her behind, he stopped and set Susannah on her feet in the arch of the Spanish tiled entryway.

"There's a ritual that has to be observed," he said with a wink to Susannah.

Without warning, he swept Mara off her feet and into his arms. "I have to carry my bride over the threshold."

Susannah laughed. "Falcon picked you up, Mommy."

"He sure did!"

Mara was glad Susannah had bowed to Falcon's request in the car and was calling him by his name. It would have been sad to see Grant displaced so quickly by Falcon in her daugh-

ter's affections. But children, thank God, were resilient creatures, and Mara was glad Grant's death hadn't devastated her
daughter.

"Can you get the door, Susannah?" Mara asked. "If Falcon stands here too long, he just might get tired and drop
me."

Susannah laughed at the idea. "Silly Mommy," she said.

Falcon was surprised to hear the teasing quality in Mara's
voice. He was enjoying holding her, and he wished he didn't
have to set her down until he got her upstairs to his bed. Only
it wasn't his bed anymore. He had ceded it to Mara.

Susannah pushed the door open, and he followed her inside.
He managed to plant a quick, searing kiss on Mara's lips
before he set her down. She shot him a warning look, but
with Susannah present, there wasn't much else she could do.
Falcon figured all was fair in love and war, and this marriage
was sure to have a good deal of the latter.

"Welcome to your new home, Mrs. Whitelaw," he said.

The stricken look on Mara's face came and went so quickly
he might have missed it if he hadn't been watching her so
intently. But he did see it. He set his back teeth. So she didn't
want his name, either.

Falcon had never really desired anything badly that he
couldn't buy with money or have for the asking. Now he was
finding out what it was like to want something that was beyond his reach. What he hadn't known about himself until
this moment was how hard he was willing to strive to achieve
his wants. And, though it irked him to admit it, he wanted
Mara to want him with the same aching desire he felt for her.

It might take some time for him to find the right methods
to win her over, but he was determined to seek them out.
However, he was starting at the bottom of a very tall mountain
and he didn't think he was in for an easy climb. Still, when
he thought of the rewards to be had at the top, he was willing
to take the first step.

If he could only figure out what it was.

Right now he had to concentrate on getting the three of them situated in his house. He took Mara and Susannah upstairs to show them the master bedroom and the guest bedroom next door to it.

"I'm in the bedroom downstairs," he said. "That way we won't get into each other's way."

Mara had moved in her and Susannah's things the previous day and had worried about whether Falcon would take one of the other two upstairs bedrooms. She managed not to sigh aloud in relief that he had relegated himself to the downstairs area.

"We'll join you in a little while," Mara said. "I want to change clothes before I start lunch."

Falcon had been dismissed. He took one last look at his wife and new daughter before heading down the stairs.

They joined him an hour later in the kitchen. Falcon took a moment to admire his wife. She was wearing jeans that molded her hips and long slender legs and a plaid Western blouse that had the first two buttons undone so he saw a hint of her rounded breasts. She had rolled up her sleeves and had tied her hair in a ponytail that made her look like a girl again. He wanted to be the teenage boy that got her alone in the back seat of an old convertible and taught her all about the birds and the bees.

"I would have been glad to fix lunch," Mara said when she saw the table set and food waiting to be served.

"It was my pleasure," Falcon said. "It's just steak and baked potatoes and a salad." He grinned roguishly. "I'm afraid that's my entire repertoire."

Mara sat down in the chair he held out for her and watched with raised brows as he poured decanted red wine into a crystal glass.

"Wine?" she said. "At lunch?"

"It's a late lunch," he quipped. "And we did just get married," he pointed out.

Mara flushed and wasn't sure whether it was chagrin or

pleasure she was feeling. Maybe it was both. She could be excused for her confusion. This was, after all, a somewhat muddled situation.

Falcon poured some milk into a wineglass for Susannah. "So you can join in our toast to a happy life," he said.

Mara saw how pleased her daughter was to be included in the grown-up ritual. It appeared Falcon Whitelaw had a knack for pleasing females that she hadn't imagined.

Once they were served and Falcon had seated himself, he raised his glass for the toast he had promised. "To a long and happy life," he said.

Mara stared at him aghast. Such a toast might be appropriate for a newly wedded couple, but with Susannah sitting there, her life in the balance, it seemed particularly cruel. Falcon held his glass aloft, ignoring her wordless censure, demanding that she join him.

At last she did. "To a long and happy life," she echoed, clinking her glass against his and against Susannah's.

"To a long and happy life," her daughter said. Susannah grinned and drank some of her milk. "I'm hungry, Mommy. Let's eat."

That was a good sign. Susannah had been nauseous after the interim treatment she had received, and the doctor had given her a Benadryl injection to help counter the sickness. Apparently it was working.

"I was thinking that you might like to come see the horses in my stable after lunch," Falcon said to Susannah.

"Is my pony there?"

Falcon laughed. "Not yet. But I have a few colts and fillies that you might like to pet."

Susannah was beaming again. *How did he do it?* Mara wondered. Maybe the reason she was unable to make Susannah laugh was because she didn't feel much like laughing herself. So perhaps some good would come of staying with Falcon, after all.

"Do you want to come with us?" Falcon asked as he headed out the back door with Susannah after lunch.

Mara felt anxious letting Susannah out of her sight. But she didn't want to spend any more time with Falcon than she had to.

Misreading her indecision, Falcon said, "I'll take good care of her. I won't let her get hurt."

"Susannah's spent a lot of time around horses. She knows how to act." Her words came out sounding sharp and reproachful, and she wished them back. But it was too late. Falcon frowned and turned his back on her.

"We won't be gone long," he said as he let the screen door slam behind them.

Mara looked around at the mess in the kitchen and realized this was a way she could repay Falcon in part for the service he had rendered when he married her. There was more to be done in the kitchen than simply cleaning up after the meal. Falcon obviously hadn't had a housekeeper in a while. The floor needed scrubbing, and the cabinets were disorganized. There were other things she would be able to do when she had more time: curtains for the windows, flowers on the sill, cleaning the refrigerator and the stove. She would settle now for washing dishes and putting away leftovers.

Mara was just wiping down the front of the refrigerator when Falcon returned with Susannah. He had been gone, she suddenly realized, for most of the afternoon. Where had the time gone? She looked around her and saw a kitchen that sparkled. Her eyes shifted back to Falcon.

Mara sensed from the worried look on his face that something was wrong. Susannah had her head on his shoulder, and her arms were wrapped around his neck.

"I didn't mean to keep Susannah out so long," Falcon said. "She got a little tired. I'll take her upstairs for you."

But his eyes said, *Please don't leave me alone with her.*

In fact, Falcon was terrified. Without warning, Susannah had deflated like a balloon with a pinhole in it. One second she was patting the forehead of a pretty bay filly with four white stockings, the next she was hanging on to the leg of his jeans as though that was all that was holding her upright. Susannah had sagged into his arms when he picked her up, almost like deadweight.

He could feel her erratic breaths against his neck, and she had become unusually quiet. He was even more afraid of what Mara would say about Susannah's condition.

"We didn't do anything strenuous," he found himself saying to Mara. He waited for her to pull down the covers so he could lay Susannah on her bed. "One minute she was fine, and the next minute she was practically asleep on her feet."

"It wasn't anything you did," Mara said. "It's the disease. It saps her strength."

She took off Susannah's tennis shoes and covered her with the sheets and a quilt. The little girl was already asleep.

Mara turned to face Falcon and found herself wanting to smooth the furrow of worry from his brow. "She'll be all right again once she's rested."

When the shadows didn't leave his blue eyes, she reached out a hand to him. "It isn't your fault," she said in a quiet voice. "You didn't do anything wrong."

He seemed to notice suddenly that she was touching him. He stared at her hand, then turned his hand to thread his fingers with hers. "Come downstairs with me," he said. "We need to talk."

Mara felt the calluses on his hand, felt the strength of it and felt all kinds of other things that she had no business feeling. For a moment she resisted his gentle tug. Then she was on her feet and he was leading her downstairs.

He sat on the heavy Mediterranean couch of deep wine leather and dark wood and urged her down beside him. He slipped his arm around her and pulled her close.

Mara nestled her head under Falcon's chin and felt the lickety-split beat of his heart and the grip of his hand on hers. She didn't try to free herself or chastise Falcon for his presumptuousness. She knew he needed comfort, and she needed it too much herself to refuse it to him. They sat there for a long time in silence.

Without fanfare, without warning, dusk fell. The light coming in through the arched windows turned pale yellow and pink and orange. It wouldn't be long before it was full dark.

"I thought we were going to talk," Mara said.

"We are," he said. "I just needed this first."

"Me, too," Mara admitted.

"Is she going to die?" Falcon asked.

Mara felt the tears sting her eyes. "No."

Falcon tightened his hold on her. "Is that wishing? Or is that the truth?"

Mara told him everything she knew about acute lymphocytic leukemia. About the six to twelve weeks of chemotherapy to induce remission. About the ninety-percent cure rate for the chemotherapy. About the possibility of relapse, which could happen at any time, and which would require the entire chemotherapy treatment all over again.

"If she makes it for a year without a relapse, there's a good chance she'll be home free."

"And if the chemotherapy doesn't work?"

"There's always a bone-marrow transplant."

"And if that doesn't work?"

Mara tore herself from Falcon's embrace; it was no longer comforting. She rose and turned to face him with her hands on her hips, her feet widespread in a fighting stance. "What do you want me to say? That Susannah may die? The possibility exists," she said. "Are you happy now?"

He rose and faced her in an equally belligerent stance. "No, I'm not. How can you stand it, knowing what may happen?"

Suddenly all the fight went out of her. "I don't have much choice," she said, her eyes bleak.

"Mara, I—"

Falcon reached for Mara, to comfort her, but she whirled and ran. He didn't go after her. He wished he hadn't let himself get involved. He wished he had borrowed the money from someone to pay for the treatments Susannah needed. Because he didn't think he could stand by and watch Susannah Ainsworth die. Most of all, he didn't think he could bear to watch Mara suffer if her daughter didn't survive.

It was too late to back out now. He wanted Mara. And he had already given a piece of his soul to Susannah. He was bound to both of them by ties he hadn't even begun to imagine existed before they came into his life.

He would make sure Susannah had the best care possible, no matter what it cost. Even if he had to humble himself before his family to get more money to pay for it.

Chapter 4

Falcon had been married for two weeks, during which time Susannah had begun induction therapy in earnest. He made it a point to be at the house whenever Mara returned from the hospital with her daughter. He carried the child up to her bedroom from the van he had recently bought to replace his Porsche, holding her limp form in his arms while Mara arranged the bed. Then he settled her under the covers.

It was getting harder and harder to smile for the little girl. But Falcon forced himself to be cheerful. Mara's face was stark, her eyes bleak and worried. He didn't think so much solemnity could be good for Susannah.

"How are you feeling?" Falcon asked Susannah. He immediately regretted the words, but to his surprise Susannah lifted a flattened hand and tipped it back and forth like airplane wings.

"So-so," she said.

"Why ask when you know she's feeling sick?" Mara rebuked him.

"There's sick, and then there's sick," Falcon said. "Isn't

that so, Susannah?'' He brush her bangs away from her fore-hand and a hank of hair came out in his hand.

He turned stricken eyes to Mara, but found no comfort there. She looked as stunned as he felt.

Falcon sought a way to hide the scrap of hair from Susannah, but she saw it and took it from him, inspecting it carefully.

''My hair is falling out,'' she said matter-of-factly.

''It appears so,'' Falcon replied cautiously.

''Dr. Sortino says that's a good sign,'' she explained to Falcon. ''He says that means the medicine is working. I want to get a red hat, like my new friend Patsy wears. Is that okay?''

''That's fine, pumpkin,'' Falcon said. ''Your mom and I will see if we can find one.'' He started to playfully tug a curl that lay on Susannah's cheek and barely managed to stop himself in time. What if it came away in his hand? Susannah's disappearing tresses didn't seem to worry her, but he was still shaken by his recent experience.

Falcon tucked Susannah in and leaned over to kiss her on the forehead. As he did so he realized he was going to be devastated if chemotherapy didn't stop the disease. He had already started reading about bone-marrow transplants. They were horribly painful, and it was difficult to find donors. And they didn't always effect a cure. The statistics weren't encouraging. He couldn't imagine putting Susannah through it, knowing how much she suffered from the induction therapy.

When he stood up, he realized Mara had already left the room. That wasn't like her. Usually she stayed to read to Susannah after he was gone.

''I wonder what happened to your mom,'' he said.

''She left a minute ago,'' Susannah informed him. ''She was crying again.''

''Again?''

''She doesn't think I know, but I've seen her cry lots of

times," Susannah confided. "She thinks I'm going to die. Am I?"

Falcon was startled by such frank speaking. He wanted to reply "Of course not!" But that wouldn't have been honest. On the other hand, did an eight-year-old child deserve to hear an honest evaluation of her chances of survival?

Mara should be answering these questions, he thought.

Before he could answer Susannah, she asked, "What is it like to die?"

Falcon grinned ruefully. "You've got me there, pumpkin. I can't answer that. My suggestion is that you concentrate on getting well."

Susannah wrinkled her nose. "You never answered my first question. Am I going to die?"

Falcon didn't care if it was a lie. It was the only answer he was willing to give her. "No, pumpkin. You're going to be fine. But you have to rest and take care of yourself."

Falcon was amazed that Susannah accepted his dictum as truth. She closed her eyes and settled back against her pillow.

"Tell Mommy it's okay if she cries. I understand."

Falcon felt his throat swell with emotion. "I'll do that," he managed to say.

He got out of the room as quickly as he could, closing the door behind him.

He didn't have to search far for Mara. She was standing right there with her back against the wall, her chin on her chest, her arms crossed protectively over her breasts.

"Did you hear?" he asked quietly.

She looked up at him and nodded. Her eyes welled with tears. As he watched, one slid onto her cheek.

"I didn't know what to say," he confessed.

"You said exactly the right thing."

"I lied."

"*It was not a lie!* She's going to live!" Mara said fiercely.

Falcon slipped an arm around her shoulder and led her toward the master bedroom. "Susannah's liable to hear us," he warned.

Mara jerked herself free, and instead of going the rest of the way to her bedroom, headed downstairs. "Let's go where we can talk freely."

Falcon followed after her. It hadn't been an easy two weeks of marriage, but he and Mara had managed to remain civil to each other. He had a feeling their truce was about to end.

Mara marched all the way to the kitchen, where she found a glass and some ice and poured herself some tea. She drank half the glass and wiped her mouth with the back of her hand. "All right, let's get this over with."

"I don't want to fight with you," Falcon said.

Mara was filled with pent-up anxiety. If she didn't release it, she was going to burst. She slammed her tea glass down on the table. "You must be missing all those parties about now," she said. "All that late-night carousing...all those women—"

"Don't start," Falcon warned, grabbing her shoulders and giving her a shake. "I'll accept that you're overwrought because of Susannah's condition. That's no reason to take out your frustration on me."

Mara stared at Falcon, stunned at the accuracy of his statement. Dread and fear crowded her every waking moment, making it impossible to act normally. She shuddered at the thought of how she was behaving toward Falcon. True, she despised his irresponsible, devil-may-care attitudes. But if it hadn't been for his lighthearted teasing, his smiles and cajolery, she didn't think she could have survived the past two weeks. And there were so many more weeks to be endured!

She looked up at Falcon and let him see the remorse she felt. "I'm sorry," she whispered.

Her lips were trembling, her eyes liquid with feeling. Falcon didn't think, he acted on impulse. His mouth slanted across hers, and he thrust his tongue inside, meeting hers in a passionate duel. His hands slid from her shoulders across her breasts, and he heard her moan as he cupped their fullness.

Mara's hands slid around Falcon's waist and up his back, as she sought solace for the ache deep inside. She wanted to disappear inside him, to be absorbed into his being so there was no more Mara and Falcon, only one stronger being, more capable of surviving the awful uncertainty of the future.

"Falcon," she whispered in a ragged voice. "Please. Please."

Falcon picked her up and carried her to his bedroom. He kicked the door closed behind them and captured her mouth as he lowered her to the bed.

"Are you protected?" he asked. There was no sense bringing an innocent child into this convoluted situation. Later, if things worked out… But not now.

"Are you?" he demanded in a voice harsh with the need he was striving to control.

Mara nodded jerkily. "Hurry," she said. "Please hurry." It was a strange thing for a woman to ask a man who was about to make love to her. But Mara didn't want time to think about what she was doing. Nor did she want to give Falcon time to change his mind.

Mara wanted to touch his skin, to feel the warmth, the strength of him. She yanked the snaps free on his shirt and shoved it off his shoulders. She tested bone and sinew with her hands, then tasted with her mouth. She heard the zipper slide down on her jeans and felt Falcon pushing them down along with her panties.

Then she was naked to his touch and his hand was caressing her. His fingers slid inside her, first one and then another. She arched beneath him and bucked a little as the pleasure became too intense to bear. She bit his shoulder, hardly aware of what she was doing, only knowing that she wanted him, needed him. Now.

She reached for him and felt the hard bulge that threatened the seams of his jeans. He groaned as she cupped him in her hand and then stroked up and down. He unsnapped his jeans and shoved them down along with his briefs.

An instant later he was inside her. She moaned deep in her throat as she felt the hot, hard length of him thrust once into the welcoming warmth, then retreat and thrust again.

She lifted her hips in a primitive response to him, then reached for his mouth to mimic with her tongue his intrusion below. She gasped as she felt her body begin to convulse. Her fingernails left crescents on his flanks as she urged him deeper. She wrapped her legs around him and held him captive as he released his seed.

It was over too soon.

Mara felt the tears squeezing between her tightly closed lids. She was panting, trying to catch her breath, and failing. She felt totally enervated. And exultant.

And horrified.

What had she done? She shoved frantically at Falcon's broad shoulders, and he rolled over onto his back. He exhaled a deep sigh of contentment. Mara scrambled to her knees, pulling up her underwear and her jeans, which she realized had caught around her ankles. She searched for her shirt, meanwhile crossing one arm across her breasts.

"Where are you going in such a hurry?" Falcon asked.

"I...I have to get out of here," Mara said.

Falcon kicked his jeans the rest of the way off. Mara was appalled to realize that they hadn't even been able to wait long enough to get their clothes off! She chanced a glance at Falcon and was sorry she had looked. He looked smugly satisfied. As well he should be. She had practically fallen on him and dragged him to the ground. What on earth had she been thinking? She had just made love—no, no—she had just *had sex* with a man she despised!

She had been seeking comfort, and he had willingly offered it. The cad. The rogue. The cur.

"Don't bother seeing me out," she snapped, shrugging her way into her shirt.

He laughed.

She glared at him. "What's so funny?"

"You are. You can't pretend nothing happened, Mara."

"Oh yes I can!" She turned and marched out the door. At the last instant she was careful not to slam it. She didn't want to take the chance of waking Susannah.

All the way up the stairs Mara pounded her fist against the banister. "How on earth did I let that happen? I'm an idiot. I have to be out of my mind," she muttered.

But the truth was, she had never had such a devastating sexual experience with a man. She wasn't sure exactly what had happened, but she was terrified that she wouldn't be able to resist Falcon if he offered her a chance to repeat the encounter.

How the mighty had fallen.

It was time she reevaluated her relationship with Falcon Whitelaw. Maybe, if she looked hard enough, she could find enough redeeming features in him to justify a second look at the man.

It had been three long weeks since Falcon had made love to his wife—and he *had* been making love, even if she hadn't. Lately she looked sideways at him every time he got near her, as though she expected him to pounce on her and carry her off to his bedroom again. He wouldn't have minded one bit. But it was as clear as a pane of glass that she would fight him if he made the attempt. So he bided his time, waiting for the moment when she came to him.

Falcon needed to talk to someone about his feelings for Mara. Could he really want a woman this bad who went out of her way to avoid him? Was it asking for heartache to keep hoping she would forgive him—and herself—and work with him to make theirs a real marriage? Falcon had mulled the subject until he was nearly crazy but found no answers. Which was when he decided to approach his brother for advice.

Zach was the person closest to him, the person he had always turned to in the past when he needed a sounding board. He didn't want to leave Mara and Susannah for even the couple of days it would take him to visit his brother at Hawk's Way. So he called Zach and asked him to come to Dallas.

"What's going on?" Zach asked.

"I got married," Falcon confessed.

There was a silence on the other end of the line. "Who's the woman?"

"You don't know her," he said. "She has a daughter who's very ill. There were reasons... Look, I don't want to have to explain all this on the phone. Will you come?"

"I'll be there tonight," Zach said.

Zach piloted his own jet, so airline connections weren't a problem for him. Falcon made arrangements to pick him up at Dallas/Fort Worth International Airport.

Falcon realized he would just as soon not introduce his wife to his brother, or his brother to his wife. So he took Zach to a restaurant in town for dinner.

"Where does your wife think you are tonight?" Zach inquired as he folded the menu and set it beside his plate.

"Mara and I aren't accountable to each other."

Zach's brow arched in disbelief. "That's some marriage you have, baby brother."

"There are...complications," Falcon conceded.

"And?"

Falcon found it difficult to explain his marriage of convenience to his brother. Especially when Zach interrupted him to say, "I've never heard of such an idiotic reason to get married. You should have come to me for the money. Or gotten it from Dad."

His eyes narrowed and Falcon felt his brother's sharp perusal. "Unless you didn't really marry the woman just to help her out of her financial troubles. Is that it? Are you in love with her?"

Falcon flushed. Trust Zach to put his finger on the pulse of the problem. "I have feelings for her," Falcon conceded. He wasn't going to label them love, although they felt suspiciously like it. But only a fool would admit to love under the circumstance. "Unfortunately she hates my guts," he told Zach.

Zach hissed in a breath of air. "That's too bad. Any hope she'll change her mind?"

Falcon flashed his brother a devil-may-care grin that was tremendously hard-won. "I have some hope of it."

"So why did you call me?" he asked bluntly.

"I guess I wanted someone to tell me I *wasn't* an idiot to marry her," Falcon muttered.

Zach laughed. "Sorry I couldn't oblige you. Look, once the kid is well, you can get a divorce and forget all about the woman."

Falcon's lips flattened. "I don't want to forget about her. And the *kid's* name is Susannah."

"Well, well. Baby brother has grown some sharp teeth. If you feel so strongly, why don't you act on your convictions?"

"And do what?" Falcon demanded.

"Woo her. Win her love. Make it a real marriage."

"How?" Falcon asked in an agonized voice.

Zach took a sip of his whiskey. "I have a suggestion. I don't know if you're going to like it."

"I'm desperate. What have you got in mind?"

"Give her an ultimatum."

"What?"

"Tell her you can't be expected to live like a eunuch for the next year, and if she doesn't want you looking cross-eyed at other women, she can fulfill her marital duties."

Falcon flushed. "I couldn't put her in that position."

"Why not?"

"That wasn't part of the original bargain."

"So what?"

"You can be a ruthless, coldhearted bastard, Zach." He pitied the poor woman who ever fell in love with his brother.

Zach shrugged. "You asked for my advice. I've given it.

You're welcome to come up with your own solution to the problem.''

Maybe it wasn't fair to demand conjugal relations, Falcon thought, but perhaps he could merely *suggest* they start sleeping together. He knew from their one experience together that he and Mara were completely compatible in bed. It wasn't much on which to base a relationship. But it was a start.

"Thanks for coming, Zach," Falcon said.

"Don't mention it. When am I going to meet this paragon?"

"Not this trip," Falcon said. He didn't think he could stand to have Zach see the way Mara flinched when he got near her. It was one thing to admit to his big brother that he had problems, it was another to allow him to witness them in person. "If Susannah's induction therapy is successful we might be able to come for the family Labor Day picnic."

"I'll count on seeing you there." Zach threw his napkin down on his clean, empty plate. "If we're finished," he said wryly, "I think I'd just as soon fly back to Hawk's Way tonight. I can catch a cab back to the airport. I think you should go home."

Falcon rose and shook his brother's hand. "Goodbye, Zach. I think I'll take you up on that."

It wasn't that he thought Mara would be worried about him. She didn't like him enough to worry about him. But he wanted to be there to say good-night to Susannah before she went to bed.

"Think about what I said," Zach called to his retreating back.

Hell, Falcon thought, it wasn't likely he was going to be thinking about much else.

Chapter 5

"Is Falcon there?"

Mara tensed at the sultry sound of the female voice on the other end of the line. "Yes, he is," she answered.

"Who's this?" the female asked.

"This is his wife," Mara said with relish.

"Oh. Then I don't suppose he's free to fly to New York this weekend."

"That's entirely up to him," Mara said.

"Oooohh."

Mara could tell she had created confusion at the other end of the line. But really, did she have the right to dictate when and where Falcon went? She was his wife, but it was a marriage in name only. If he wanted to go traipsing off to New York with some sexy southern belle, who was she to say him nay. "I'll get him for you," she said as she set the phone down on the desk in Falcon's office.

She found Falcon in the kitchen with Susannah. "There's a call for you," she said.

Falcon picked up the wall phone extension in the kitchen.

Mara stood there listening, her arms crossed defensively over her chest. She knew Falcon must have a lot of old girlfriends, and she wanted to know how he was going to handle this situation.

"Oh, it's you, Felicia." Falcon turned his back on Mara and lowered his voice.

"Yes, I am married," he said. "Over two months ago. It was a very small wedding, Felicia. I didn't even invite my family!" he said in exasperation. "New York? This weekend?" He turned to face Mara, an incredulous look on his face. "My wife has no objection to my going? How do you know that?"

Falcon frowned. "She told you so?"

Mara shrugged with great indifference.

"No, I can't go, Felicia. I have responsibilities here."

Even from across the room Mara could hear the other woman's laughter and see Falcon's embarrassed flush.

"I know that's never stopped me before," Falcon hissed into the phone. "Things have changed since I got myself a family."

"I have a daughter, too," Falcon said. "She's eight. As a matter of fact, we have plans of our own this weekend. We're going shopping for a pony. So, I'm afraid I can't meet you in New York. Have a good time, Felicia. Goodbye."

Falcon slammed the phone down and had rounded on Mara in a fury when he noticed Susannah's wide-eyed interest. "You finish your lunch," he said to the little girl. "I want to talk to your mother in private."

He dragged Mara all the way to his office, which was across the hall from his bedroom, and shut the door with an ominous click behind him. Then he turned to face Mara with his legs spread and his hands fisted on his hips.

"How could you dare to suggest to Felicia that I'd be willing to trot off to New York? I'm a married man!" he snarled. "I take those vows seriously."

"It's a marriage of convenience," Mara corrected. "Plain and simple."

"Have I gone out *once* without you in the two months we've been married?" he demanded. "Well, once," he conceded, recalling his meeting with Zach. "But have I spent even one night away from home?"

"No."

"Then what makes you think I'd be willing to go carousing with another woman in New York? Did you *want* me to go?"

"No," Mara admitted in a small voice. She lifted her chin and said, "I...I thought you might need to be with a woman."

"And better anyone else than you," he said in a harsh voice. "Is that it?"

Mara dropped her chin to her chest. "I thought..."

"You didn't think!" Falcon accused. "Or you would have realized there isn't any woman I want except you!"

Her head snapped up, and her eyes widened in astonishment.

Falcon let her see the desire he felt for her, let his eyes roam her body voraciously. He should have done what Zach recommended. He should have come right home and demanded his husbandly rights.

But when he had returned from meeting Zach he had found Mara with Susannah in the upstairs bathroom. The little girl had her head bent over the toilet, where it had been for an hour. He had sat down beside Mara, and the two of them had stayed with Susannah until she had finally lain her head down in Mara's lap, exhausted. Falcon had carried Susannah back to bed and told her funny stories about his childhood until she had fallen asleep at last.

He had taken one look at Mara's face, at the terror and exhaustion, and known he couldn't ask anything from her that night. Nor had an opportunity arisen over the succeeding days and weeks. Falcon had faced the fact that his needs would have to wait. It was one of the first truly unselfish acts of his life.

Now he saw that his self-sacrifice had earned him nothing in Mara's eyes. She believed he was capable of abandoning her and Susannah for a weekend on the town.

"You must not think very much of me," he said, his brow furrowed with the distress he felt.

Mara realized now the mistake she had made. And why she had made it. She had heard that other woman's voice on the phone, and she had been jealous of her, and of every woman who had ever enjoyed Falcon's attention. Because she wanted that attention for herself.

Unfortunately, for both her sake and Falcon's, she had been too much of a coward to ask for it. He had not made one move toward her since the night they had made love, had not hinted by so much as a look that he wanted to repeat the experience. Meanwhile, she ached whenever she looked at him. Her body coiled with excitement when he merely touched her hand. She couldn't look him in the face for fear her feelings, which she was certain he didn't return, would be blatantly apparent to him. Obviously she had put him in an awkward position when she sought oblivion in his arms. Obviously he hadn't enjoyed it as much as she had. Obviously he hadn't wanted to repeat the experience.

It was easy to believe that he might have contacted Felicia, or that he might have planned to have Felicia call so Mara would let him go. Now he was telling her that she had been wrong. That he would prefer a weekend with her and Susannah to a weekend with a luscious femme fatale in New York.

"I'm sorry," she said. "I mistook the matter. I'll understand if you want to change your mind about spending time with me and Susannah—"

"Sometimes I could just shake you," Falcon said. He suited word to deed and grabbed her by the shoulders. "I burn for you, woman! Can you understand what that means? I want to be inside you. There isn't a moment when I don't remember what you taste like, what you feel like. I don't want another woman. I want you!"

His mouth slanted over hers, and he told her of his desperate need with his lips and his hands. It took a moment for him to realize that she was crying.

He let her go and stepped back, tunneling all ten fingers through his hair. "Hell, Mara. I'm sorry."

She closed her eyes and pressed the back of her hand over her mouth.

"You don't have to worry about that happening again. I can control myself. I'm not an animal."

He turned on booted heel and left the room, closing the door quietly behind himself.

Mara let out a tremulous sob. "Oh, my God. What have I done? And what am I supposed to do now?" she said to the empty room.

How could she want to make love to the man responsible for Grant's death? How could she let him hold her, love her, when she could not forgive what he had done?

More to the point, why was she finding it so impossible to let go of the anger she felt over Grant's death? It had been more than a year. Her feelings of bubbling hostility should have dissipated by now. But whenever she thought of Grant, feelings of vexation, of frustration and annoyance simmered to the surface. Until she could manage to quell those feelings, she would be better off keeping Falcon at arm's distance. For his sake, as much as hers.

Despite their altercation, Falcon was true to his word. He announced to Mara the next time he saw her, that the trip to the auction to find a pony for Susannah was all planned.

"We'll be getting there just in time to see the ponies auctioned, so Susannah shouldn't get too tired," he said.

"Come on, Mommy!" Susannah said excitedly. "Hurry up and get ready. It's time to go!"

Mara felt her spirits lift when she saw how happy and excited her daughter was. She quickly dressed in a Western blouse, jeans and boots and joined Falcon and Susannah outside.

Falcon was sitting on the edge of a tile fountain that graced the courtyard in back of the house, with Susannah in his lap. As Mara came up behind them she saw that Falcon had given Susannah a penny and was telling her to make a wish and toss the coin into the fountain.

"Will my wish come true?" Susannah asked.

"Who knows?" Falcon said. "This may be a magical fountain."

Susannah squeezed her eyes closed and tossed the penny. It landed with a plop that sent water back up onto her face. She opened her eyes and laughed as Falcon brushed the crystal droplets away with his fingertips.

Mara was moved by his gentleness with the little girl. "I'm ready," she announced. But a moment later she realized she wasn't the least bit ready to deal with the things Falcon made her feel.

She stood frozen as his eyes roamed her body. She felt warm everywhere his eyes touched her. She wanted to surrender to him heart and soul. She gritted her teeth against her wayward feelings.

Remember Grant, she admonished herself.

But the hate wouldn't rise the way it had so easily in the past.

That's because you know who's really to blame for Grant's death, don't you, Mara? And it isn't Falcon Whitelaw. Admit it, Mara. You're to blame! You knew what would happen, and you let Grant go anyway. It's all your fault! Your fault! Your fault!

"Mara? Is something wrong?"

Falcon's interruption silenced the accusing voice in Mara's head. She pressed a hand to her temple where her pulse pounded. "I'm fine," she said. "Shall we go?"

Falcon gathered Susannah in his arms and walked toward Mara. When he reached her, he slipped an arm around her waist and guided her toward the van. Their hips bumped, and she tried to free herself, but his hold tightened. She was aware of the warmth of his hand at her ribs, of a desire to be alone with him, when he could let that hand ramble at will.

You're crazy, Mara. You're out of your mind. How can you even think about making love to Falcon Whitelaw? He killed Grant!

No, *you* killed Grant.

Mara chewed on her lower lip, wishing the awful voice would go away and leave her alone.

Falcon saw the furrow on Mara's brow and wondered what was troubling her now. Maybe he shouldn't have let her know how he felt about her. Maybe she was concerned he would try to take advantage of their situation.

It perturbed him that Mara could think he might take by force what she did not willingly offer him. He had never forced a woman into his bed. Despite Zach's advice, he wasn't about to start now. But he didn't think there was anything he could say that would ease her mind. Every time he opened his mouth he ended up with his foot in it. Better to just let sleeping dogs lie.

At the auction Falcon nodded and tipped his hat to the several ranchers he knew, but he didn't approach them as he would have if Mara and Susannah hadn't been with him. He didn't want to have to explain a year from now about his absent wife and daughter. Instead he concentrated all his attention on finding just the right pony for Susannah.

It was quickly apparent that Susannah wanted a pinto.

"I like the ones with patches," she said.

It was up to him to find an animal she liked that also had both excellent conformation and a good disposition. It wasn't until near the end of the auction that he was satisfied with an animal that Susannah also liked.

"That one!" Susannah breathed with a sigh of awe. "Oh, please, Falcon, that one!"

The pony had a white face, with a black patch that ran

across his eyes. Falcon was having trouble deciding if the gelding was black with white patches, or white with black, it was so evenly divided by the two colors.

"I'm going to call him Patches," Susannah announced as she hugged the pony's neck after the auction. "You like that name, don't you, Patches?"

They were approached by one of the ranchers Falcon had seen earlier, Sam Longstreet.

"Howdy, Falcon," the tall, rangy man said, tipping his hat. "Are you going to introduce me to this little lady?"

He said "little lady," but his eyes were on Mara when he spoke, so Falcon knew it wasn't Susannah who had caught his interest.

Sam Longstreet and his father had a cattle ranch that bordered Hawk's Way. Sam was a little older than Falcon, maybe two or three years, but his face had more lines and his body was leaner, toughened by long days spent on the range. His sun-bleached chestnut hair was shaggy and needed a cut, and he hadn't shaved in the past day or so. Sam's boots were worn and his jeans frayed. Falcon wasn't sure whether that was because Sam didn't worry about appearances, or whether it meant hard times for the Longstreet ranch. Sam's father, E.J., had some business dealings with Falcon's father, although Falcon wasn't up on the exact details.

"How are you, Sam?" Falcon said. "I'd like to introduce my wife, Mara, and my daughter, Susannah. Mara, this is Sam Longstreet. Our families have been neighbors for generations."

Sam grinned. "It's a mighty big pleasure to meet you, ma'am. You're a sly one," he said to Falcon. "Haven't heard a peep out of your folks about you getting hitched."

"They don't know."

"I won't breathe a word to them," Sam said. "If that's how you want it."

"It's not a secret," Falcon said. "I just haven't found the right moment to tell them the news."

Sam grinned again. "Can I tell E.J?"

That was sure to put the fat in the fire. Word would get back to his father through E.J. that he had gotten married. "Give me a day to call my folks, then be my guest."

So, the moment of reckoning had come. He would have to tell his parents what he had done, and try to keep them from visiting the newlyweds before he had resolved his relationship with Mara.

Sam turned his attention back to Mara. "How did you hook up with this maverick?" he asked.

Falcon saw the consternation on Mara's face and knew she was trying to decide the best way to explain things to Sam.

"We met through an old friend of mine, a former football teammate at Tech," Falcon said. That was the absolute truth, and so much less than the whole story.

"Makes me wish I'd gone to Tech," Sam said, with an admiring glance at Mara. "Didn't make it to college myself." He turned his attention to Susannah, who was rubbing her own nose against the velvety soft nose of her new pony.

He squatted down so his green eyes would be at a level with her hazel ones. "My name's Sam," he said. "What's yours?"

To Falcon's amazement, Susannah didn't run and hide behind her mother. She answered Sam with a girlish, "My name's Susannah. This is my pony. His name is Patches."

Sam reached out to run a big, work-worn hand along the pony's jaw. "He's a mighty fine-looking pony," Sam agreed.

Susannah was wearing her red hat, but it was plain to anyone who looked closely that she was bald underneath it. Sam wasn't the kind of man to miss a detail like that. He exchanged a surprised look of sympathy with Falcon before he set his hands on his thighs and pushed himself back onto his feet.

He didn't ask questions about Susannah. Things hadn't changed so much in the west that a man could ask another man's business uninvited.

"Guess I'd better be getting along," Sam said. "I've got a new bull to get loaded up, and then I'm headed home."

"Be seeing you," Falcon said.

"Hope so," Sam said with a smile aimed at Mara. "Ma'am." He touched the tip of one callused finger to his battered Stetson, a mark of respect to Falcon's wife.

"What a strange man," Mara said.

"How so?" Falcon asked.

"He looks so…dangerous…and yet his eyes are so…kind. Which is the real Sam Longstreet?" she asked.

Falcon shrugged. "I don't know him very well, even though we lived close. He's older than me or Zach, and his father needed him to work on the ranch, so he never socialized much."

"Will he tell your family about us?"

"He'll tell his father, which is the same thing. But not before tomorrow. Which means I need to call them tonight."

"What do you think they'll say?"

Falcon had a pretty good idea, but he didn't want to burn Mara's tender ears. "They'll be happy for us," he lied.

"Come on," he said. "Let's get this pony home where Susannah can ride him."

But by the time they got home, Susannah's good day had gone bad. She was feeling sick and so tired that she could hardly keep her eyes open. Mara and Falcon put her to bed together with promises that she could ride Patches the moment she was feeling better.

"Are you sure the day wasn't too much for her?" Falcon asked as he and Mara left the room.

"The trip was a wonderful idea. It was only to be expected she would get tired," Mara said. "I don't think she would have missed it for anything," she said in an effort to take the guilty look off Falcon's face.

Falcon allowed himself to be assuaged by Mara's absolution. He didn't want to be responsible for making Susannah any sicker than she already was, and if Mara believed the day hadn't been too taxing for her daughter, he was willing to take her word for it.

"I'd like you with me when I make the call to my parents," Falcon said.

Mara followed him into his office and sat on the bench that ran parallel to his desk. Falcon sat down in the swivel chair in front of the oak rolltop.

"What are you going to tell them?" Mara asked.

"That I met a woman, and we got married."

"Won't they ask questions?"

"Probably."

"How will you explain…everything?"

Falcon grinned ruefully. "It depends on what they ask."

"You know what I mean," Mara said. "What will you tell them about *why* we got married?"

Falcon fiddled with his computer keyboard. "I don't know."

"Will you tell them the truth?"

"Not all of it," Falcon said. "They wouldn't understand."

"Why do you need me here?" Mara asked.

"They may want to say hello to you, to offer their best wishes," he said. They would want to do more than that, Falcon feared. They would want to know every last detail about Mara Ainsworth Whitelaw.

He dialed the phone number. It was answered on the second ring. His mother was breathless. She had apparently run to answer the phone. "Hi, Mom," he said.

"Falcon! We've been wondering what you've been up to. You haven't been in touch for *months!*"

"I've been busy," Falcon said.

"Surely not too busy to write or call your parents and reassure them you aren't lying dead in a gully somewhere," Candy Whitelaw chastised. "Now, tell me what prompted this call?"

His mother had never been one to shilly-shally around, Falcon thought. "I wanted to let you and Dad know that I got married."

"You what?" His mother called into the other room, "Garth, pick up the phone in there. It's Falcon. He's gotten married!"

Falcon heard his father's deep voice asking, "When did this happen? Do we know the bride? When are you bringing her here to meet us?"

"Is she there?" his mother asked. "Can we talk to her? What's her name?"

"Her name is Mara Ainsworth. She's standing right here. I'll put her on so you can say hello." Falcon handed the receiver to Mara, who looked at it as though it had grown fangs. At last she took it from him and held it to her ear.

"Hello?" she said tentatively.

"Hello, dear," Candy said. "I'm Falcon's mother. We're so delighted to hear the news. When did you and Falcon meet? When was the wedding? Oh, I'm so sorry we missed it!"

"Hello, Mara," Garth said. "Welcome to the family. When are we going to get to meet you?"

Mara wrinkled her nose at Falcon. She held her hand over the mouthpiece and said, "You rat! They're full of questions I think you should answer."

"It's nice "meeting" you at last, Mr. and Mrs. Whitelaw. I—"

"Call me Candy, please," Falcon's mother said. "And Falcon's father is Garth. Now, tell us everything."

"Thank you, Mrs.—Candy," Mara said. "I don't know where to start."

"Where did you two meet?" Garth asked.

"In downtown Dallas. I was there with my husband and daughter and—"

Mara cut herself off when she heard a gasp on the other end of the line. She looked up at Falcon and saw his eyes were squeezed closed. He was shaking his head in disbelief.

"I'm a widow now," she blurted into the phone.

There was a silence and then a relieved sigh at the other end of the line.

"I'm sorry to hear that," Candy said. "Oh, this is so awkward, isn't it, because if you weren't a widow you wouldn't be married to Falcon, and of course I'm glad Falcon found you, but not under such sad circumstances."

"I feel the same way, Mrs.—Candy," Mara said in a soft voice.

"Tell us about your daughter," Garth said.

"Her name is Susannah, and she's eight years old. She's been very ill lately, but we're hoping she'll be well soon."

"Is there anything we can do?" Candy asked.

"Pray," Mara said in a quiet voice.

"It must be very serious," Candy said. "Are you sure—"

"Susannah has leukemia. She's in treatment right now. We'll know more when the therapy is completed."

Again that silence on the other end of the line, while Falcon's parents digested the newest bomb dropped in their laps.

"Let me speak to Falcon," Garth said.

Mara handed the phone to Falcon. "Your father wants to talk to you."

"Dad?"

"What the hell is going on, Falcon?" Garth demanded in a harsh voice. "What kind of trouble have you gotten yourself into this time?"

"No *trouble,* Dad," Falcon answered in an equally harsh voice. "Mara is a widow and Susannah is sick, it's as simple as that. I'm not asking your approval of my marriage, Dad. I was only offering you the courtesy of telling you about it."

"We want to visit," Candy said.

"No, Mom. That wouldn't be a good idea right now."

"Why the hell not?" Garth said.

"Because I said so!" Falcon retorted, resorting to the words his father had always used to justify every order to his children. "We'll try to be there for the Labor Day picnic."

It wasn't much as peace offerings went, but it was all they were going to get. "Goodbye, Mom, Dad."

"Falcon—" Garth roared.

"Falcon—" Candy cried.

Falcon gently hung up the phone. "Well, that's taken care of."

"They didn't sound too happy," Mara ventured.

Falcon tipped Mara's chin up with his forefinger. "It's not their life, it's mine. If I'm happy, it doesn't matter what they think."

"Are you happy?" Mara asked, searching his face for the truth.

His thumb traced her lower lip. It was rosy and plump because she had been chewing on it again. "I'm not sorry I married you, if that's what you're asking."

She lowered her eyes, unable to meet his lambent gaze. But she didn't move away from him. Mara felt rooted to the spot. "You should have told them the truth," she murmured.

"Who knows what the truth is," Falcon said enigmatically.

Mara knew he was going to kiss her. She didn't try to escape the caress. Because she needed it as much as she believed he did. His mouth was gentle on hers, his lips seeking solace, not passion. She kept her mouth pliant under his, giving him the succor, the sustenance he sought.

When the kiss ended, she opened her eyes and was moved by what she saw in his.

He cared for her. He wanted her. And he despaired of having her. It was all there on his face.

Mara wished she could give him ease. But the past intruded and would not be silenced.

It had been easy to blame Falcon for Grant's death, even though she was more at fault than he was. Nevertheless, it was hard to let go of her feelings of rage and hate toward Falcon, however undeserved they were. Grant was still dead, and because of Susannah's illness—which was no one's fault at all—her life had been turned upside down.

There's a great deal of good to be said about Falcon Whitelaw, a voice inside her argued. *He's not a bad man, he just had a little growing up to do. He's wonderful with Susannah. And he makes your blood sizzle. Would it be so awful to give him what he wants from you?*

Falcon saw the conflict raging within her. She hated him. He tempted her.

He was the one who stepped back.

"Good night, Mara," he said.

"Good night, Falcon," she replied.

She didn't want him to go. She wanted him to stay.

Afraid she might do or say something she would regret later, Mara whirled and fled the room.

Chapter 6

"Where have you been?" Mara demanded.

Falcon was astounded to find Mara waiting for him in the kitchen. She had a cup of coffee sitting in front of her. He could tell it was cold, which meant she had been there awhile. He hadn't come home for supper, unable to face the thought of being near her and knowing he couldn't touch. He hadn't been far away, just in the barn, where he had worked soaping saddles that were in better shape than they had ever been, thanks to his restlessness. Was it possible she had been worried about him?

"I was in the barn," he said. "Working on my saddle."

"I thought something had happened to you. It's so late. You're usually in by dark."

"You *were* worried about me," Falcon murmured. "I'm sorry, Mara. I'll let you know where I am next time."

If anyone had told Falcon three months ago that he would have been willing to be accountable to *anyone,* let alone a woman, he would have slapped his knee at the jest and hurt his ribs laughing.

How the mighty had fallen.

Mara rose and crossed to the sink. "Susannah asked about you," she said, as though to deny her own concern.

"Is she all right?" Falcon asked anxiously.

Mara left the cup in the sink and turned to face Falcon. "The doctor thinks she may be in remission."

Falcon stared at her, stunned. Then he whooped and grabbed her around the waist and swung her in a circle. "This is fantastic!"

Mara held on so he wouldn't drop her. "Let me down."

Falcon set her down, but he kept his hands on her waist. He needed to hold on to someone, or he just might float off into space. "I can't believe this is happening. It's too soon. She's only been in therapy ten weeks."

"I know," she said. "It's…a miracle."

Falcon looked at Mara and wondered why she wasn't more excited. "You said *may* be in remission. Is there something you aren't telling me? When will we know for sure?"

"Dr. Sortino wants to do a spinal tap tomorrow. We'll know as soon as he gets the results from the test."

"Susannah hates those back-sticks," Falcon said. His hands tightened at Mara's waist. "They hurt."

"I know," Mara said. "Will you come with us tomorrow?"

It was the first time she had asked him to join her. The first sign at all that she needed him for anything other than his money. "I'll be glad to come with you."

She smiled for the first time since he had come into the house. "I'm glad you'll be there. Susannah has been asking when you're going to come to the hospital with us."

"She has?"

Mara stepped back, and Falcon let his hands drop. "She's very attached to you," she said.

"I'm attached to her, too," Falcon said.

"Well, that's what I waited up to tell you. Good night, Falcon."

"Mara, wait." Falcon didn't want her to leave. He wanted to hold her. He wanted to sleep with her in his arms. He thought of the ultimatum Zach had wanted him to give her— how many weeks ago had that been?—and knew he still couldn't do it. Not now. Not yet. Maybe if—when—they found out Susannah was in remission he could start making husbandly demands of his wife.

"What is it?" she asked.

"What would you think, if Susannah's feeling well enough, about going to Hawk's Way over Labor Day?"

Mara leaned back against the refrigerator and crossed her arms protectively around her. "Do you really think that's a good idea, for me and Susannah to meet your family?"

"You're my wife," he said. "And Susannah is my daughter."

Not for much longer.

The words hung in the silence between them. If Susannah was truly in remission, it would change everything. Mara wouldn't need him anymore. She would be able to move back to her house in Dallas with its covered porch and its white picket fence.

"I want them to meet you Mara. Even…even if things don't work out between us. I think you're a very special woman. I've felt that way since the first moment I laid eyes on you."

Mara flushed and shot a quick look at Falcon. "I was a married woman when you first met me," she reminded him.

Falcon's lips flattened, and Mara was sorry she had spoken. She had only meant that he shouldn't have been looking at a married woman that way. She hadn't meant to remind him of the catastrophe that had made her a widow. Falcon turned on his heel, and she knew he would leave the house again if she didn't do something to stop him.

"I've been doing some work in your office," she said as his hand reached the kitchen doorknob.

Falcon turned and glanced at Mara over his shoulder. "What kind of work?"

She gave him a lopsided smile. "Your desk was a little disorganized, and so was your computer filing system."

"You've been working on my computer?" He turned completely around and assumed a pose Mara was coming to recognize as his "I'm King of the Roost and Don't Give Me Any Backtalk" stance, his legs widespread and his hands fisted on his hips.

"I've been organizing," she said.

Falcon raised a skeptical black brow. "Organizing?" Lord help a man when a woman started organizing.

"Come with me, and I'll show you some of what I've done."

Falcon knew an olive branch when he saw one. He willingly reached out to take it. "All right. Lead the way."

Falcon had noticed little improvements around the house since Mara had moved in. Certainly her green thumb was much in evidence. There were potted flowers in the kitchen and trees in planters in the living room.

She had stuck patterned pillows on the leather couch to break up the somber expanse and rearranged nearly every vase into a different arched cubbyhole. The heavy curtains in the living room had been removed so the sunshine filtered in during the day, and gingham curtains had been added for color in the kitchen.

The whole house sparkled with cleanliness. She hadn't been kidding about her ability as a housekeeper. Which should have made him less nervous about her bookkeeping talents, but somehow didn't.

Mara hadn't completely rearranged his office. He could—and would—have complained if she had. She had been more subtle than that, making small changes, a book moved here, a file moved there. Of course, the spurs and halter he had been repairing had been relegated to a worktable in the pantry off the kitchen.

It wasn't until he sat down next to Mara at the computer that he realized what significant changes she had made in his bookkeeping system. She showed him how she had organized his files so he could see which stud had covered which mare, which cows had been inseminated by which bull. Amounts of grain that had been fed, and increase in weight on the hoof, were also calculated for his beef cattle.

"This is incredible! How did you learn to do this?" he asked.

"I told you I grew up at my mother's knee. I spent a lot of time looking over my father's shoulder, too," she said with a cheeky grin.

"I'm impressed. Why haven't you ever gotten a job doing this for some rancher?"

"I don't have a college degree," she admitted. "I had just finished my first year of school when I found out Susannah was sick."

Falcon was thinking she didn't need a degree to do his bookkeeping. But he could see that if something ever happened to him, she might need an education. "You should go back and finish," he said.

"I can't until I know Susannah is well."

"With any luck, we'll get good news tomorrow. I think you should plan to go back this fall, Mara. I can hire someone to take care of Susannah while you're in class."

"I already owe you too much."

"You don't owe me anything," Falcon said. "I've done what I've done because I wanted to do it. I wish you'd get it out of your head that you have to pay me back."

Falcon didn't breathe, he didn't move. On second thought, there was something she could do for him. She had presented him with the perfect opportunity to ask for what he wanted from her without giving her an ultimatum.

"There is something you can do for me," he said.

"What?" Mara asked.

He hesitated, then took the plunge. "I need a woman, Mara. You're my wife. I want to sleep with you."

She hissed out a breath, but didn't say anything right away.

He reached out and caressed her cheek with the back of his hand. Her eyelids slid closed. Her teeth caught her lower lip and began to worry it.

"I want to give you what you want," she said. "I know I owe you—"

Falcon jerked his hand away, and Mara's eyes flashed open. He rose to his feet and towered over her. The muscles in his jaw worked as he gritted his teeth. "If that's the best you can do, forget it."

She leapt to her feet and grabbed his arm to keep him from leaving. "I'm trying! I have needs, too," she admitted in a choked voice. "But I can't forget who you are. Don't you understand? I loved Grant. And because of you, he's dead."

"Grant was a drunk who killed himself in a car wreck!" Falcon snarled.

All the blood left Mara's face. "Who told you Grant was a drunk?"

Falcon stared at her, not sure what had upset her so much.

"Who told you Grant was an alcoholic?" she insisted.

"An alcoholic? Was he?" Falcon asked, dumbfounded.

Mara covered her mouth with her hand. She hadn't ever said the words aloud. Not to anyone. She had lived with Grant, realized he had a weakness, and tried to pretend it didn't exist.

Falcon grabbed her by the arms. "Are you telling me that you've blamed me for Grant's death all this time when you *knew* he had a drinking problem?"

"He didn't have a problem—"

"Tell me the truth!"

"Yes! Yes, I blame you. He was going to AA meetings. He had quit for almost six months before he ran into you."

"Is that why he lost all those jobs?" Falcon asked. "Was he drinking on the job?"

"I don't know," Mara admitted miserably. "He gave different reasons for why he was let go."

"And you never checked?" Facon demanded.

"I trusted him!" she said fiercely. There were tears in her eyes that betrayed the truth. The first time, or maybe the second, Grant had been able to fool her. But by the sixth or seventh time he was fired, she'd had no illusions left.

"How could you love a man like that?" Falcon asked, truly puzzled by her devotion to someone who must have caused her untold pain.

She shrugged helplessly. "He was a good father." *When he wasn't drinking.* "And a good husband." *When he wasn't drunk and chasing other women.*

Mara couldn't meet Falcon's intent stare and lie anymore. To him or to herself. It had been easier to blame Falcon than to admit Grant's weakness. Easier to blame Falcon than to admit her own culpability. Because, when all was said and done, she was responsible for Grant's death.

She had known he had a drinking problem. She should have watched him more closely. She should have gone with him.

Mara knew that sort of thinking was irrational. She had read enough since Grant's death, and learned enough in college psychology and sociology classes she had taken, to understand that Grant was responsible for his own behavior. But she couldn't shake her feelings of guilt. She should have been able to save Grant. And she had failed.

"It wasn't your fault," Falcon said in a quiet voice.

Mara's head jerked up, and she sought Falcon's eyes.

"He was an alcoholic. It was his problem. You aren't to blame."

"How did you know…"

"That you blame yourself?"

She nodded.

"Because I couldn't help thinking there was something I could have done to prevent Grant's death. Maybe if I'd noticed how much he was drinking…" Falcon thrust a hand through his hair. "Maybe if I hadn't left that twenty on the table… Maybe if I had stayed with him and made sure he didn't drive home drunk…."

"That's a lot of 'maybe's,'" Mara said.

"Don't I know it!"

"I feel the same way," Mara admitted. "I was his wife. I should have known better.

"After we left you that day, I begged him to call you up and meet somewhere, anywhere besides a bar. He said it was too late for that. He didn't know where to find you to make other arrangements. And he swore he wouldn't be tempted. He swore he wouldn't drink anything stronger than club soda. He had been sober for months before that night, so I believed him. I should have known he wouldn't be able to resist a drink when it was offered to him, especially since he wanted to keep his alcoholism a secret from you. I should have made arrangements to pick him up."

"What about Grant? Doesn't he deserve some of the blame for what happened?" Falcon asked. "Maybe more than *some,*" he amended.

Mara thought of all the ugly things she had said to Falcon, all the accusations she had heaped on his shoulders. "I owe you an apology," she said. "Some of the things I said…"

"Apology accepted," Falcon said.

Mara felt awkward. All her animosity toward Falcon had been based on his irresponsible behavior at the bar that had resulted in Grant's death. Bereft of antagonism, she wasn't sure how to interact with him.

"Can we start over from here?" Falcon asked.

"Can you ever forgive me—"

"Can *you* forgive *me?*"

Mara exhaled a ragged sigh. "I'm so sorry, Falcon. For everything I said. I was horrible."

"You were," Falcon agreed.

When her eyes widened in surprise, his lips curled in a roguish grin.

"Sorry," he said. "I couldn't resist."

"Behave yourself," she chided.

They were teasing each other, Mara realized. It was a start. A very good start.

Mara knew there was one way she could show Falcon he was truly forgiven. He had told her what he wanted from her. And if she was going to be honest, she wanted it, too. She reached out, her hand palm up.

"I'm tired," she said. "Let's go to bed."

Falcon arched a brow, but threaded his fingers through hers. "My room?"

She nodded. She didn't want to take a chance on disturbing Susannah. Or on having to explain to Susannah why she was suddenly sleeping with Falcon.

Mara felt unaccountably shy. "This feels strange," she admitted.

"I know what you mean," Falcon said with a rueful twist of his mouth. "I've been wanting to make love to you for weeks. Ever since—"

"Don't remind me," she said, putting a hand to one rosy cheek. "I was an absolute wanton."

"I didn't have any complaints," Falcon said with a grin. When they got to the living room, he tugged on Mara's hand and she followed him around to the couch. He pulled her into his lap and sat there holding her.

She laid her head on his shoulder and let her hand slide around his waist.

"I've been needing this," Falcon said.

"And not the other?" Mara teased.

"Oh, I want that, too. But it can wait."

Mara felt a pleasant sense of expectation. She had been afraid, when she had agreed to give Falcon what he wanted, that he would rush her into bed. She was glad to see he was willing to take his time. She sighed.

"What was that for?" Falcon asked.

"I was just thinking about how badly I've misjudged you."

"So I'm not an irresponsible ne'er-do-well?"

"You did fritter away your fortune," she said.

Falcon stiffened. There was that. He might not have murdered her husband, but he still was not the sort of solid person she might have chosen for a husband. Especially after the bad experience she'd apparently had with Grant. His arms tightened around her. He had done nothing over the past ten weeks to prove he would be a better husband to her than Grant.

Except he had stopped drinking and carousing and spending money like it was water. That had to count for something. He hadn't missed any of those things, either, Falcon realized. Nothing mattered as much to him as Mara. And Susannah. There had to be a way to convince her they belonged together as a family.

"I hadn't planned ever to marry again," Mara admitted.

He didn't want to hear this.

Falcon pressed a kiss to Mara's nape to distract her and felt her shiver. He kissed his way up her throat to her ear and teased the delicate shell with his tongue.

Her hand slid down to the hard bulge in his jeans. She traced the length of him through the denim with her fingertips. He drew in a breath of air and held it.

"Mara," he whispered in her ear.

"Yes, Falcon."

"Sweetheart, let's go to bed."

She didn't answer with words, just rose and headed for his bedroom, leaving him to follow behind her.

Mara knew she was asking for heartache. The more attached she let herself get to Falcon, the harder it was going to be to leave him when Susannah was well. The truth was, she was terrified of getting involved with another man. Falcon hadn't gotten drunk during the past couple of months, but that didn't mean he wouldn't revert to his former behavior sometime in the future. Grant had been sober for months at a time during their eight-year marriage. She didn't yet trust Falcon not to become another Grant.

There was still the awful uncertainty about whether Susannah would survive. And there were no guarantees Falcon wouldn't be claimed by an accident working on the ranch, or driving in his car. How could she dare make any kind of commitment to another human being who might be taken from her?

But, oh, how she was tempted to throw caution to the winds. The more time she spent with Falcon, the more feelings she had for him. He was funny and generous and gave of himself wholeheartedly. He was compassionate and caring. He was a scintillating lover. Such a man would make some woman a very good husband. He just happened to be hers at the moment.

She knew it had been unfair to expect Falcon to remain celibate during their marriage. She owed him tonight, at least. But she wasn't promising more. She couldn't promise more.

Mara stood at the foot of Falcon's bed feeling awkward, uncertain what to do next. Their previous coupling had been a frenzied thing, more an act of desperation than anything else. She had needed solace and forgetfulness, and Falcon had provided those things in lovemaking that was so passionate it had taken away all thought and left only feeling.

Mara didn't know what to expect now.

Falcon was also aware of how different their joining together was this time. He wanted to show Mara the tenderness he felt, as well as the ardent passion.

"May I undress you?" he asked.

Mara nodded, suddenly shy. Although she didn't know why that should be. He had seen everything before. But she realized, as Falcon slowly undressed her, admiring her with his eyes and his hands and his mouth, that there had been no time before to truly appreciate each other's bodies.

"I want to touch you, too," she told him.

He shook his head. "It would be too distracting. I wouldn't be able to enjoy what I'm doing."

As his mouth closed around a nipple and he suckled, she

surrendered to his ministrations. His hands caressed her skin, and the roughness of his callused fingertips raised frissons of sensation wherever they coursed.

Falcon tried to tell Mara with his hands and his mouth how much he adored her, how much she meant to him, how necessary she was to his very life. He wished he was better with words so he could tell her how he felt. Of course the word *love* never entered his head. He couldn't think such thoughts when he knew she hated him. But she had forgiven him. She had no reason to hate him anymore.

Mara was amazed at how her body responded to the touch of Falcon's hands, the feel of his lips on her skin. She experienced things Grant had never made her feel in eight years of marriage. How was she able to find so much pleasure in the arms of another man?

Mara stiffened imperceptibly, but Falcon was sensitive enough to her response to know something had gone wrong. She was no longer giving herself up to his caresses as she had been a moment before.

"Mara?" he murmured in her ear.

She gripped his waist tightly with both hands and for a moment he wasn't sure whether she was going to pull him close or shove him away. Then her arms slid around him.

"Hold me, Falcon," she said. "Make love to me."

"I will, darling. I am."

Falcon meant what he said. He was making love to Mara. But when he had her under him, and when he had brought her to satisfaction, he did not feel like shouting with joy. He felt like crying instead. Because he knew that what he was feeling for her was all one-sided. He had made love to her. She had submitted to having sex with him.

He tried not to let the despair overwhelm him. There was still time to win her love. There was still time for a happy ending.

He was torn, because as much as he wanted Susannah to be well, he knew her recovery heralded the end of his time with Mara. He would have to find a way, and soon, to convince Mara that she couldn't live without him.

Because he knew now he couldn't live without her.

Chapter 7

Over the months he had been forced to stay close to the B-Bar because of his responsibilities toward Mara and Susannah, Falcon had made an astounding discovery.

He liked being a rancher.

His skin had browned in the Texas sunshine, and a fine spray of sun lines edged his blue eyes. His hands had been callused before, but now they were work-hardened. His body had been honed by hard physical labor until he was a creature of muscle and bone and sinew.

He had made hard decisions, and most of them had turned out right. A recent visit to his accountant had confirmed what he already knew. His attention to the details of running the B-Bar was making a difference. Things functioned more smoothly. There was less waste. And the profit margin on the sale of his cattle and horses was higher. To add sugar to the pie, one of the risky investments Aaron had advised him against making had started paying huge dividends.

"If you keep this up, you're going to be rich again," Aaron teased.

Only, it looked like he wasn't going need any of his reacquired wealth to pay medical bills.

Susannah was in remission.

The induction therapy had worked more quickly and efficiently than even Dr. Sortino had hoped. It had only taken ten weeks for Susannah's white blood cells to register normal.

Falcon was amazed at what a difference good health made to Susannah's behavior. She sparkled, she fizzed, she had an absolutely effervescent personality. She was tremendous fun to be with. Falcon teased Susannah that she was so bouncy she was liable to take off some day and go right through the ceiling.

"I don't want to sit still ever again," Susannah said.

"Not even to eat supper?" Falcon had asked.

"Well, maybe for that," she conceded, stuffing a man-sized spoonful of mashed potatoes into her mouth.

When Falcon looked to Mara, to share the humor of the situation, he found her brow furrowed, her eyes dark and despairing. Despite Susannah's good health, Mara didn't appear happy. Falcon dragged her away to the living room after supper to find out what was bothering her. He settled her on the couch and sat down on the coffee table across from her.

"What's wrong?" he asked.

"I want to expect the best, that Susannah is out of deep water," Mara said. "But I can't help dreading the worst, that her good health is a mirage that's going to disappear if I take my eyes off her."

"You have to live for today," Falcon chided.

"I might have expected you to say something like that," Mara snapped.

Falcon flushed. "Once upon a time, I might have deserved that comment," he said. "Not anymore. I'm as anxious as you are to plan for the future." *With you.* "But there's no planning ahead in Susannah's case. She's either going to stay well, or she isn't. There's nothing you, or I, or all the worrying in the world can do to change that."

Mara's eyes were bleak. "You're right," she said. "I know you are. I just can't seem to shake this feeling…"

"Then Susannah and I will just have to do it for you." Falcon set out then and there to put a smile on Mara's face. He enlisted Susannah's aid. "Hey, Susannah," he called to the little girl.

Susannah popped up in the living room like a jack-in-the-box. "What is it, Falcon?"

"I say your mom is more ticklish than you are. What do you think?"

"Ticklish?" Mara said warily. "Who said anything about ticklish?"

Falcon grinned and approached her, hands outstretched, ready for serious tickling.

Mara jumped up and ran.

Falcon chased her.

When he caught her, he wrestled her to the floor and hog-tied her with his hands, like she was a new-born calf.

Mara was breathless, she was laughing so hard. "Falcon, stop! I just ate supper."

He leered at her like the villain in a melodrama. "She's all yours, Susannah. Have at her."

Susannah tickled her mother in the ribs and under the arms and behind her ears and on the soles of her feet.

Mara laughed so hard she howled. "Oh, stop," she cried through her giggles. "Oh, please, stop."

"What do you think, Susannah?" Falcon said. "Should we let her up."

"I guess so."

"Of course, this experiment is only half over," Falcon said, perusing Susannah with a speculative eye. "We haven't seen yet how ticklish *you* are."

Susannah screeched, "Help, Mommy!" but Falcon caught her before she had taken two steps and pulled her into his lap, where he began to tickle her mercilessly.

By that time Mara had recovered slightly, and she rescued her daughter. "I think there's someone here who needs a little of his own medicine," she said to Susannah.

"Yeah!" Susannah said as she launched herself against Falcon's chest.

Her attack knocked Falcon onto his back on the floor, and before he could recover, Mara had joined her daughter tickling his ribs.

Falcon was *very* ticklish.

He howled, he begged, he pleaded. "Please, no more!"

He could easily have escaped their attack at any time. He was bigger and stronger than both of them combined. But Falcon didn't want to escape. He loved being tickled by the two women in his life. He loved seeing their smiling faces and their eyes crinkled with laughter. Their chuckles and giggles and guffaws made him feel warm deep inside.

He let them tickle him until they were exhausted, until they fell onto the Navajo rug on either side of him and sighed with happy fatigue. He smoothed his fingers across the prickly crew cut that was all the hair Susannah had grown back so far. His other hand tangled in Mara's silky black tresses. He pulled them close on either side of him and closed his eyes and wished to be this happy the rest of his life.

But it was only a moment in time and not to be captured or held except in memory.

After that night, however, Mara seemed to let go of some of her fear. She didn't offer a smile often, but Falcon treasured every one. As Susannah regained her strength, she and Mara began riding out to meet him when he was working on the range.

The first time it happened, Falcon reached for his shirt and dragged it on over his sweat-slick body. But Mara seemed to find the dark hair in the center of his bronzed chest, and the droplets of moisture that slid down his breastbone, absolutely mesmerizing. So the next time he just left his shirt off and basked in the pleasure of knowing she found pleasure in looking at him.

Not that either one of them would have acknowledged the sexual tension that sparked between them.

Mara was more determined than ever that she and Susannah were going to return to her house in Dallas. It was safer not to get any more involved with Falcon than she already was. The sooner she escaped his home—and the temptation to succumb to his charm—the better. Now that Susannah was in remission, it was just a matter of marking time, to make sure the cure had taken.

On the other hand, Falcon was encouraged by the fact Mara sought him out when he was working—even though she carted Susannah along as a chaperon whenever she visited him.

Today, Mara had brought along a picnic lunch. They headed for the trees at one of the stock ponds and fought the cattle for enough space to settle down on a blanket and eat.

Falcon knew he would never get a better chance to broach a subject that had been on his mind since his parents had asked when they were going to meet Mara and Susannah. After they had eaten, and while they were lazing around on the blanket in the shade, he casually mentioned his family's annual Labor Day picnic.

"Ever since we've been grown and out on our own, it's been a way for us to get together once a year and exchange news. I've never missed one."

"Can we come, too?" Susannah asked.

Falcon blessed the child for her eagerness. "I'd like it if you did," he said. "I know my mom and dad would like to meet you," he said to Susannah.

"They would?" Susannah said, eyes wide. "Why would they want to meet me?"

"Because you're their first granddaughter." Falcon glanced

at Mara from the corner of his eye to see how she was reacting to his discussion with Susannah. Her lips were pursed, and she looked thoughtful.

"Can we go, Mommy?" Susannah asked.

"I don't know, sweetheart," Mara hedged.

"Please," Falcon said.

"Please," Susannah said.

"I suppose we can go—"

"Great!" Falcon said, cutting her off and preventing the qualifications he could see were coming.

"Great!" Susannah echoed, straddling Falcon's belly and jumping up and down.

Falcon rolled her off him so she was caught between him and Mara on the blanket. He had turned on his side, so he could see Mara's worried eyes.

"I'm not really your— And Susannah isn't actually your parents'—"

"Don't sweat it," Falcon said with a grin. "They'll love you. And they'll adore Susannah."

"Falcon, are you sure?"

"Do this one thing for me, please, Mara," he said.

"All right, Falcon," she agreed.

But he could see from the look on her face that she was anticipating disaster. He wasn't so sure she might not be right.

Falcon could feel his stomach knotting as they turned onto the road that led to Hawk's Way. The house he had grown up in was as impressive as ever, with its two-story antebellum facade, its railed porches and four towering white columns. The drive up to the house was lined with gorgeous magnolias, while the house itself was draped with majestic, moss-laden live oaks. It wasn't until he had returned home after leaving for the first time that he realized the house had been built more in the architectural style of the deep South than the typical Texas dogtrot home.

"It's beautiful," Mara said. She turned to meet Falcon's gaze and said, "I envy you growing up here."

"It's just a house," Falcon said. But he had a lot of happy memories here.

When they stopped the car in front of the house, they were greeted by an ancient man with long gray braids who was wearing a buckskin vest decorated with feathers and beads. His copper skin was deeply etched with wrinkles.

"Is that a real Indian?" Susannah asked, awed and somewhat intimidated.

"That's Charlie One Horse. He's got a bit of Comanche blood running through his veins. But I promise he's friendly."

Charlie One Horse, the housekeeper who had brought up the Whitelaw kids—Falcon's father and his aunt and uncles—after Falcon's grandfather had died, raised his hand, palm outward, with great solemnity toward Susannah and said, "How."

"Cut it out, Charlie," Falcon said with a grin. "You're scaring my wife and daughter." Falcon was aware of the pride in his voice when he introduced his family to the man who had been like another grandfather to him.

The old man grinned, exposing a missing eyetooth. "Howdy," he said, nodding to Mara. He turned to face Susannah who had retreated behind Falcon. "Sorry if I scared you, Susannah. My name's Charlie. I've got some chocolate chip cookies in the kitchen that I baked myself."

"You can make cookies?" Susannah said with a startled laugh.

"Best damn—" he caught Falcon's warning look and quickly amended "—darn cookies you ever ate. Come on and I'll let you taste one."

Susannah looked up at Falcon for permission and reassurance, which he gave. "I can vouch for Charlie's cooking."

"Only one, Susannah. You don't want to spoil your supper," Mara admonished as Charlie whisked her daughter away.

She turned to Falcon and asked, ''I didn't think she'd go anywhere with a stranger.''

''Charlie doesn't allow strangers in the house. Before he's through she'll be wearing feathers in her hair and war paint on her cheeks.

''Shall we go on inside?'' Falcon said. ''I'll come back for the luggage later.''

To Mara's surprise, there was no greeting party waiting for them in the foyer of the house, nor even in the parlor where Falcon led her.

''This is beautiful,'' she said as she observed the scarred antiques of pine and oak—all polished to a bright shine—in the parlor. An ancient map was framed over the mantel. ''Is this Hawk's Way?''

''Uh-huh.'' Falcon followed her to the stone fireplace so they could look at the map more closely. ''It shows all the various borders of Hawk's Way from the time my ancestors settled here more than a hundred years ago until today.''

''It's huge,'' Mara said

''It's not as big as it once was,'' Falcon said. ''When my elder brother, Zach, reached his majority, my father carved off a piece of the place and gave it to him for his own. Zach calls his portion Hawk's Pride.'' Falcon showed the lines that indicated the borders of Zach's ranch. ''You can see there's still plenty left for my father.''

Mara took several steps away from Falcon. She had been much too aware of the way his shoulder brushed against her back, aware of the feel of his moist breath on her neck, aware of *him.* ''Where is everybody?'' she asked.

Falcon grinned sheepishly. ''We're hours earlier than I told my folks we'd be here. I wanted to avoid exactly the sort of crowd at the door you were expecting.''

Mara smiled gratefully. ''Thank you.''

''Then you don't mind them not being here to greet you?''

''I'd give anything for a shower and a change of clothes before I have to meet anybody,'' she said earnestly.

"Your wish is my command." Falcon quickly retrieved Mara's suitcase, then returned and led her up an elegant winding staircase that ended in a hall with a row of doors on either side. "This is where the family usually stays when they come to visit. This will be our room."

Mara stopped in her tracks. "Our room? I thought…" Mara realized she hadn't been thinking at all. She had slept with Falcon in his room at the ranch, even though her clothes had remained upstairs in the room next to Susannah's. Obviously that facade of separation was not going to be maintained under his parents' roof. "We're staying in the same room?"

Falcon looked at Mara from beneath hooded eyes. "I have no intention of telling my parents the true facts of our marriage. They wouldn't understand. There's a king-size bed in this room, which is plenty big enough for both of us to sleep in without running into each other, if that's what you're worried about."

"Wouldn't it be better just to tell them the truth?" Mara asked.

"Why? What purpose would it serve? My mother would be hurt, and my father would be angry and disappointed. I haven't asked much from you, Mara. I'm asking for this."

For a man who didn't ask much, he had asked quite a lot lately. Mara had known there were pitfalls to this trip, she just hadn't known what form they would take. Now she did. Mara gave a gusty sigh. She supposed she should have expected something like this.

"All right," she said. "I'll play along with your charade." Some imp forced her to add, "But I expect you to stay on your own side of the bed."

Falcon grinned. "You can draw a line down the middle, if it'll make you feel any better. Come on in. This room has an adjoining bathroom, with a great shower."

Mara let him show her around the room, which she learned he had shared with Zach when the two boys were growing up. "His ranch is so close, he doesn't stay here overnight anymore," Falcon explained. "So I inherited the room."

"It's mine now," she said with a teasing smile. "Go away and let me get cleaned up."

"Are you sure you want me to leave?" Falcon asked with a lecherous grin, as he let her push him out the door.

"Absolutely," she said as she shut the door in his face.

Mara turned to peruse the room where Falcon had slept as a boy. The head and footboard of the huge bed were oak. There was an antique wardrobe along one wall and a copper-plated dry sink topped by a patterned pitcher and washbowl on another. An overstuffed corduroy chair with a rawhide footstool at its base was angled in the corner with an old brass standing lamp to provide light to read by. A small, round table held a selection of books secured between two bookends which, she was delighted to discover, were two pairs of pewter-dipped baby shoes. Falcon's and Zach's, perhaps?

The large, sheer-curtained window looked out over the front of the house, toward the long, magnolia-lined drive. There was no lawn to speak of. The prairie had been allowed to run wild.

Like the Three Whitelaw Brats, Mara thought.

It had never crossed her mind to consider how her marriage to Falcon would affect his family. Her mother had died when she was fifteen, and her father had been stomped by a bull he was trying to move from one pasture to another only a year after she married Grant. She had no brothers and sisters, no aunts and uncles.

Falcon, she was discovering, had more family than he could shake a stick at. Mother, father, sister and brother, aunt and uncles. That wasn't all. She had discovered on the drive here that he had numerous cousins who would all be arriving shortly.

Mara took a deep breath and let it out. Could she play the loving wife to Falcon in front of his family? She thought of everything Falcon had done for her and Susannah and knew she could. She need only remind herself of the laughter and joy Falcon had brought to a household that would otherwise have been mired in the somber reality of a life-threatening disease. Oh, yes, she could easily play the loving wife for him.

It occurred to Mara to wonder how much of the adoration in her eyes when she looked at Falcon would be an act.

Chapter 8

Mara had just stepped out of the shower and wrapped a towel around herself when the bathroom door opened without a knock.

"Who—"

"Omigosh! I didn't know anyone was in here!"

Mara stared at the young woman frozen in the bathroom doorway. She had wide-set dark brown eyes that danced with mischief and long black hair tied up in a ponytail with a ruffle of bangs across her forehead. She looked about seventeen. But if what Mara suspected was true, this was Falcon's twice-engaged and never-married twenty-eight-year-old sister.

"I'm Callen, Falcon's sister," the young woman confirmed with a welcoming smile. "You must be Mara."

"I am," Mara said.

Mara didn't know where to go from there. Callen didn't look like she was planning to leave anytime soon, and Mara was too modest to continue drying off in front of her.

Mara realized Callen was giving her a very thorough perusal. "Were you looking for something in particular?" she asked archly.

Callen laughed. "I'm afraid I'm too nosy for my own good," she admitted. "You're not at all what I expected."

"Oh?"

"Falcon's women in the past were…different," she said diplomatically.

Mara knew she should leave it at that. But her curiosity was killing her. "How so?"

"You're very pretty, but Falcon always had an eye for truly beautiful women."

Mara swallowed hard. "I see."

"Obviously Falcon found other things to admire in you besides your looks." Her brown eyes twinkled and she said, "You must have a very fine mind."

Mara saw the teasing smile spread on Callen's face and felt the startled laughter spill from her own throat. It was the first genuine, spontaneous laugh she could remember in months and months. "You *are* incorrigible," she said when she could speak again. "I like you, Callen. Now, what was it that brought you in here?"

"Oh. I was looking for a razor to use on my legs."

"In Falcon's bathroom?"

She shrugged impishly. "He keeps a package of disposable razors in here somewhere."

Mara gestured the other woman into the bathroom. "Be my guest. While you're hunting, I'll just dry off and get dressed."

She closed Callen inside the bathroom and quickly toweled herself off and grabbed clean clothes from the suitcase Falcon had left by the bed. She was wearing no more than a bra and underwear when Callen reappeared.

Callen was holding up a blue plastic razor and had a smug look on her face. "See? What did I tell you?"

"That's great." Mara reached for a turquoise squaw skirt and pulled it on, then added a white peasant blouse and a concha belt. Finally she pulled on stockings and added a pair of short leather Western boots. She shoved her hand through her hair in an effort to shake out some of the wetness.

"Do you need a hair dryer?" Callen said.

"Oh, are you still here?"

Callen sat down on the bed. "I was just wondering."

"What?" Mara said resignedly. Evidently Callen wasn't leaving until she was good and ready.

"What do you see in my brother? I mean, what was it about him that made you decide to marry him?"

His health insurance, Mara thought. There was no way she was going to tell Callen that. "You are nosy, aren't you?" she said instead.

"Uh-huh. You're avoiding the question."

Mara searched quickly for some attributes that would make Falcon seem good husband material. "He's fun to be with. He's good with my daughter. He's patient. He's—"

"Falcon?" Callen interrupted. "Patient?"

Mara nodded. "Infinitely. He's gentle and—"

"Gentle?" Callen interrupted again.

"Gentle," Mara repeated firmly. "And of course," she said with a look of mischief, "he has a *very* fine mind."

Callen laughed.

Mara watched as Callen's glance slid to the bedroom doorway. "Oh, hi, Falcon. How long have you been there?" she asked.

"Long enough," he said with a grin.

Mara turned beet-red. She fluffed her hair over her face and eyes to hide her embarrassment.

"I can see I'm de trop," Callen said as she looked from Falcon to Mara and back again. "See you at supper tonight, Mara." She gave Falcon a sucker punch in the stomach as she scooted past him. "You too, Falcon."

A moment later she was gone.

Falcon closed the door, shutting himself inside with Mara. "Well, well," he said. "I had no idea I was such a good husband."

''I had to tell her something,'' Mara said as she flung her hair back off her face. Her eyes flashed dangerously. ''I thought you wanted us to appear a happily married couple to your family.''

''I did. I do,'' he said soothingly. ''It's all right, Mara. You lied in a good cause.''

''I wasn't lying,'' she said quietly.

''What?''

''You heard me,'' she said, meeting his gaze. ''You are gentle and patient and kinder than Susannah and I have any right to expect.''

He noticed she didn't repeat her boast about his ''fine mind,'' which he had easily recognized for the euphemism it was. The proof was in the way her breasts stood peaked beneath her blouse, the way her cheeks flushed, the way her eyes observed him, dilated with passion.

He didn't wait for an invitation. He took the several steps that separated them and pulled her onto her feet. He slid one arm around and cupped her buttocks, pulling her tight against him. The other hand he tangled in her wet hair, drawing her close for his kiss.

He was gentle. Achingly gentle, even though what he wanted to do was ravage her mouth. And she responded, reluctantly at first, and then ardently, so he started to lose control. He thrust against her, letting her feel his need. He was having trouble drawing breath, but he didn't want the kiss to end.

There was one sharp knock and the door opened.

''Falcon, I—''

''Dad,'' Falcon managed to gasp. He kept Mara close, to hide the state of arousal they were both in.

''Doesn't anybody in this house believe in privacy?'' Mara muttered with asperity.

Falcon saw the rueful twist of his father's lips. ''Sorry for interrupting. Your mother wants to meet Mara. And Susannah is asking where her mother is.''

"Is she all right?" Mara asked anxiously, meeting her father-in-law's eyes for the first time.

She would have pulled from Falcon's embrace, but he kept her where she was with the slight pressure of his hand on her spine.

"She's fine," Garth reassured Mara. He focused on Falcon when he said, "We'll be waiting for you downstairs when you're finished with what you're doing."

Falcon flushed. He felt like a teenager caught necking on the front porch. "We'll be down in a minute, Dad."

When his father closed the door, he released Mara. She closed her eyes and groaned. "I have never been so embarrassed in my entire life. What must your father be thinking?"

"Exactly what we want him to think," Falcon said. "That we're a happily married couple."

"When you kissed me, did you know he was coming up here to get us?" Mara asked.

"Would it matter if I did?" Falcon said.

Mara sighed. "No, I suppose not." She had wanted to believe he found her desirable. But after what Callen had told her about his taste in women, she must be a very poor second choice. However, she had known for a long time she couldn't hold a man's attention for long. Hadn't Grant taught her that lesson? They had been married only six months when he started flirting with other women. It had been all of a year before she saw signs that he had taken another woman to bed.

Mara hissed in a breath of air. She hadn't thought for a long time about that night. About the humiliation she had felt when she had confronted Grant, expecting denial and getting none.

"A man needs a woman now and then," Grant had said.

"And what am I?" she had cried, her heart breaking in two.

"You're my wife," he said. "You don't have to worry about me leaving you, sweetheart. But there are itches I have that you can't scratch."

Mara's face had bleached white at the insult. *She wasn't enough woman for the man in her life.*

She had hidden her shame deep. She had been a good wife and mother, and Grant had praised her for those attributes. And he had come to her bed. But that hadn't stopped his trysts with other women. She had known the fault was somehow hers, not his. That if she was just more of a woman, he wouldn't be straying from her side.

Suddenly all those feelings of inadequacy came flooding back. All because her relationship with Falcon was changing.

When she had first married Falcon, she hadn't been worried about the issues that had caused such trouble in her marriage with Grant, because nothing about her marriage to Falcon was real. The normal expectations in such a relationship hadn't existed. Now she feared that history was going to repeat itself. Not that she had seen any signs of Falcon flirting, but if her experience with Grant was any guide, it was bound to happen eventually.

Only, it shouldn't matter to her what Falcon did, because their marriage was only a matter of convenience. Even if her feelings toward him were not as nonexistent as she could wish.

"Mara?"

Falcon had noticed Mara's pale features, the tense set of her shoulders, the way she worried her lower lip with her teeth.

"It's going to be all right. My parents won't eat you," he teased. "I promise they're going to like you.

"Even though I'm not like the women you've brought home before?"

"I've never brought a woman here before," Falcon said.

"Oh. But Callen told me about the kind of women you're usually attracted to," Mara said. "I'm not anything like them."

"Callen's too outspoken for her own good."

"I'm glad she told me. At least now I have no illusions about our relationship."

Falcon's eyes narrowed suspiciously. "What does that mean?"

"It means I know I'm not the kind of woman you would have freely chosen for a wife, and that as soon as it's possible, I'm going to release you from this marriage."

"Aw, hell," Falcon said, tunneling all ten fingers into his hair. "Look, Mara, the kind of woman a man carouses with and the kind of woman he marries are two different animals."

"You don't have to tell me that," Mara said quietly. "Grant explained the situation very thoroughly."

"What do you mean?"

Mara lowered her eyes so Falcon couldn't see what she was feeling. "I mean he explained how I was a good wife and mother, but he needed other women for…for his other needs."

"That bastard."

Falcon crossed to Mara and grabbed her by the shoulders and gave her a little shake. "Look at me," he commanded. When she had lifted her lids to reveal dark, wounded blue eyes he said, "I'm not Grant."

"You could be like him," she whispered. "I've seen you drunk. And that woman who called you—"

"Is that what you've been afraid of? That I'll turn out to be an alcoholic like Grant? Or a womanizer? I'm nothing like Grant! Haven't you learned that by now?"

"You drink—"

"A whiskey now and then," he interrupted. "Alcoholism is a *disease*," he told Mara furiously. "And I don't have it!"

"What about Felicia?"

"What about her?"

"Why would she think she could call and invite you for a weekend on the town if you hadn't encouraged her?"

"Felicia was a flirt of mine," he conceded, "*when I was*

single. I haven't even looked cross-eyed at another woman since I married you.''

"But you must have needs—I haven't— Grant always said—''

"I'm not Grant!" Falcon interrupted in a voice hoarse with rage. "You're the woman I want in my bed, the *only woman!*''

"But—''

"Don't say any more, Mara,'' he warned. "I'm leaving. Come down when you're ready. I'd give the whole game away if my parents saw us together right now.'' He turned and marched to the door, closing it with a heavy thunk behind him.

Mara was stunned by Falcon's outburst. Did she dare believe him? But what reason would he have to lie? And if he wasn't lying, what was she going to do about it? Did she dare trust him not to hurt her as Grant had? Did she dare let herself begin to love him?

She had to put such thoughts aside, at least for the moment. There was a job to do. She had to go downstairs and play the role of loving and contented wife for Falcon's family.

It was easier than she had expected it to be.

In the first place, Falcon's mother, Candy, was a dear. Mara could see how the Three Whitelaw Brats had gotten so spoiled. Candy was an indulgent and adoring mother, and she had her husband twisted around her little finger. Mara was amused at the solicitous treatment the tall, rugged cowboy gave his wife.

She had trouble keeping all Falcon's relatives straight. Honey and Jesse Whitelaw were there with Honey's two older boys from a previous marriage, Jack and Jonathan, and their daughter, Tess. Falcon's Aunt Tate was there with her husband, Adam Philips, and their two grown daughters, Victoria and Elizabeth. His uncle Faron Whitelaw and his uncle's wife, Belinda, had come with their two adopted teenage sons, Rock and Drew. It was a boisterous, motley and exceedingly noisy crowd.

Mara's main concern was that Susannah not get tired out. She watched her daughter carefully, but Susannah basked in all the attention she got from her cousins-by-marriage. Toward the end of the evening, after a supper that culminated in a food fight in the kitchen while the dishes were being washed, Mara separated her daughter from Rock and Drew and started upstairs with her.

"Come back when you've gotten her settled," Falcon's mother said. "We'll be gathered in the parlor in front of the fire."

Mara couldn't find a polite way to refuse. "All right."

Susannah was so keyed up, Mara wasn't sure she would ever get her settled. Her daughter's hazel eyes were feverishly bright and her cheeks were flushed. Mara pressed her hand against Susannah's forehead, fearing the worst.

Susannah shoved it away. "I'm fine, Mommy. Don't worry about me."

Mara forced herself to smile. "That's what mothers do best," she quipped.

Susannah bounced onto the bed and shoved her feet under the covers. "I can't wait until tomorrow," she said. "Drew said he'll take me riding. They have lots of ponies here! Can you believe it?"

"Now, Susannah, I don't know—"

"Please, Mommy. You have to let me go! Everyone's going!"

"I haven't been invited."

"It's just for kids. No grown-ups allowed."

At that moment Falcon stuck his head in the door. Susannah's room was across the hall from theirs, and would eventually be occupied by several other children. "Everything all right in here?"

"Falcon, tell Mommy it's all right for me to go riding tomorrow."

Falcon turned to Mara and solemnly repeated, "It's all right for me to go riding tomorrow."

"Not *you!*" Susannah said with a laugh. *"Me!"*

"Wasn't that what I said?" Falcon asked.

Susannah snorted in disgust. "Mommmmy! I want to go!"

"It really will be safe," Falcon reassured Mara. "The older boys and girls will take care of the younger ones."

Mara didn't have the heart to refuse Susannah. She pursed her lips ruefully. She had no business judging Candy's indulgent behavior toward her children. Look how lenient she was with her daughter!

"All right," Mara conceded. "You can go."

"Yippeee!"

"If you get a good night's sleep," Mara qualified.

Susannah pulled the covers up under her arms. "Turn out the light, Mommy, quick. I'm ready to go to sleep now."

Mara kissed her daughter on the forehead, using the opportunity to reassure herself that Susannah didn't have a fever. To her surprise, Susannah felt a little warm. "Susannah, are you feeling all right?" Mara asked.

"I'm fine, Mommy. Really, truly I am!"

Falcon crossed past Mara and pressed his own kiss to Susannah's brow. "Good night, pumpkin," he said as he turned out the lamp beside the bed.

He had left the door open, and he and Mara headed for the stream of light from the hallway. He closed the door behind them.

"I hope the other kids don't wake her up when they come to bed," Mara said. "She needs her rest."

"I'm sure they'll be quiet," Falcon said.

"As a herd of buffalo," Mara said with a sideways glance at Falcon.

He grinned. "You're probably right, but the only other choice was to put Mara in with us. I thought she would have more fun with the other kids."

And they would have the privacy that a newly wedded couple should want. He didn't mention that to Mara. She had already coped with enough friendly badgering from his family this evening to know he was right.

"How are you holding up?" he asked her as they headed back down the stairs. "My family can be a little overwhelming."

Mara shot him an arch look. "A *little* overwhelming?"

He grinned. "All right. They're a riot looking for a place to happen." He put a hand on the back of her neck and kneaded muscles that were tight with strain.

Mara groaned. "Lord, that feels so good!"

"Want to come back upstairs with me now? I give a killer back rub." And he was dying to give her one.

Mara hesitated, then shook her head. "I promised your mother I'd come back downstairs."

Falcon turned her to face him. He settled both hands on her shoulders and began to massage the tenseness he found there. He had the satisfaction of hearing Mara moan and watched as her eyes drifted closed in pleasure. "She'll understand if we both disappear," he murmured in her ear.

Excitement shivered down Mara's spine at Falcon's invitation. She was tempted! So tempted. She opened her eyes and saw him looking down at her, his eyes hooded, his nostrils flared. She knew what they would end up doing if she followed him up the stairs. In his parents' house. With his whole family waiting for them in the parlor.

"I don't want everyone leering at me tomorrow morning."

"They wouldn't dare—" Falcon grimaced. They would. He and Mara would be teased mercilessly. "You're right," he said, starting her back down the stairs. "Let's go join the multitudes."

Falcon seated Mara on the floor in front of the fire and settled himself behind her. His arms slid around her hips, and he pulled her close. They had arrived just in time to hear Candy finishing the story of how she and Garth had met and fallen in love, complete with fairy-tale ending.

"That's the most outrageous pack of bullsh—"

"Zach!" Candy admonished. "Keep your cynicism to yourself."

"I want to hear the story of how Falcon and Mara met," Callen said.

Mara stiffened. She hadn't expected this. She shot a frightened look over her shoulder at Falcon, who shook his head once, very slightly, to let her know there was no escape. To her relief, he was the one who undertook the task.

"It's really very simple," he said. "I was walking down the street in Dallas when I spied this absolutely stunning woman on the corner."

"You're kidding, right?" Callen challenged.

Falcon shook his head. "That's exactly the way it happened. Only, the next thing I saw was her daughter, and then a man joined her," he recalled.

A hush had fallen on the crowd.

"Who was the man?" Callen asked.

"He was an old friend of mine, a football teammate from Tech," Falcon said. "He was Mara's husband, Grant Ainsworth."

"I remember him," Garth said. "I met him in the locker room after one of your games."

What happened to him?

The silence was pregnant. Falcon said very matter-of-factly, "Grant was killed in a car accident. It was a year later before I saw Mara again, but I knew I couldn't let her walk out of my life again. I asked her to marry me, and she said yes."

"How romantic," Candy said with a sigh. "True love conquers all."

Falcon realized Mara was squeezing his hand so tightly her fingernails were cutting into his skin. He made himself smile at her. "I've been doubly blessed," he continued. "I got a daughter in the bargain."

"And a pretty little minx she is," Charlie One Horse contributed.

"Falcon told us Susannah has been sick," Candy said to Mara. "But she seems so well now."

"She has—had—leukemia. It's in remission."

"Thank God for that," Candy said.

The discussion shifted to Callen, and the fact that for the first time in years she didn't have a man at her side.

"And thank God for that!" Mara heard Garth mutter.

Mara watched Candy put her fingers over his mouth to shut him up and hiss, "Garth! Be good."

The evening wound to a pleasant close, as couples settled back together to watch the fire burn and to drink a glass of whiskey or brandy or some sweet liqueur. No wine drinkers here, Mara thought with an inner smile. But then, this was the frontier, where things were harder, the elements harsher and life was lived to the fullest.

She caught herself yawning and looked quickly to see if anyone had noticed. To her chagrin, Falcon's father was staring right at her.

"Time for bed," he announced.

She started to say, "I'm not tired" and realized she was. Falcon had to haul her to her feet. Her knees felt like jelly.

"Come on sleepyhead," he said. "We've got a big day tomorrow."

"We do?" Mara said. This day had seemed quite big enough.

"Picnic. Football. Frisbee. Croquet. We've got games to play."

Mara snickered softly. "That we have, Mr. Whitelaw. Games no one else even knows about."

Falcon swatted her on the fanny. "Save the cynicism," he said. "I get enough of that when Zach's around."

Mara undressed in the bathroom and put on a thick terry-cloth robe before she ventured into the bedroom. To her relief, Falcon was already under the covers. To her chagrin, his bronzed shoulders were bare.

She narrowed her eyes suspiciously. "Are you wearing anything under those sheets?" she asked.

"Pajama bottoms," he said.

"Oh. Well. That's okay."

"I'll be glad to take them off," he volunteered.

"Thanks, but no thanks." Mara turned off the light before dropping her robe beside the bed and slipping under the covers. She was aware that she wasn't alone in the king-size bed. It seemed to have shrunk. She could hear Falcon breathing, even believed she could feel the heat of his body.

"Good night, Mara."

"Good night, Falcon."

Mara stared at the ceiling, not the least bit tired.

Ten minutes later she said, "Falcon? Are you awake?"

"I am now."

"I like your family."

"They like you, too."

Mara shivered. But she wasn't the least bit cold. "Falcon?" she whispered.

"Why are you whispering?" he whispered back.

"I don't know," Mara whispered. "I don't want to wake anyone."

"I'm the only one in here," Falcon said, "and I'm already awake. Is there something you wanted to say to me, Mara?"

Mara heard the irritation in his voice and wondered what had caused it. "I guess not."

Falcon flipped the light on. He sat up and the sheet dropped to his hips. Mara's eyes shot to the expanse of bare flesh he revealed.

"What is it?" he demanded. "I'm awake, and you have my full attention."

"I was just wondering if you'd still be willing to give me that back rub."

"Why didn't you just say so? I'd be glad to." Falcon scooted over and ordered, "Turn over onto your stomach."

Mara did as she was told. Falcon quickly straddled her at

the waist and his hands came down firm and sure across her shoulders and began to massage the sore muscles there.

"How's that?" he asked.

"Mmmm," she murmured.

"How about getting this nightgown out of the way?" He pulled the thin straps of her silk gown off her shoulders and shoved the garment down below her waist, freeing her arms. "There," he said with satisfaction.

Mara had a sudden realization of what she had done. What she didn't understand was why she had done it. She knew where this encounter was heading, and she had to make up her mind quickly whether she was going to let Falcon make love to her.

There was no doubt he was ready and willing.

His hands caressed as well as massaged, and as her languor increased she knew her resistance was decreasing.

"Falcon?"

"Yes, love?"

Mara shivered again as he murmured the endearment against her ear.

"Would you like a massage when you're finished doing me?"

Falcon chuckled. "I would love one," he said. "Just as soon as I finish doing you."

She gasped as he slid his hands beneath her and cupped her breasts, teasing the nipples into tight buds with his fingers.

"Falcon?" she whispered.

"Why are you whispering again?" he whispered.

"Because I haven't got the breath to talk," she admitted.

For a long time, neither of them said anything. They spoke with their hands, with their mouths and with their eyes.

When Mara drifted to sleep, she was snuggled tightly in Falcon's embrace. She refused to question the right or wrong of what she had done. For now, he was her husband, and he wanted her. And she loved being with him. Maybe she had heard one too many fairy tales this evening.

Tomorrow was soon enough to let reality creep back in.

Chapter 9

A single rider galloped hell-bent-for-leather toward the Whitelaw mansion. He leapt from his horse before it had even stopped on its haunches and raced toward the crowd gathered under the live oaks in back of the house.

"Falcon!" Drew called. "Falcon!"

"I'm here, Drew," Falcon said, racing toward the teenager. "What's wrong?"

Mara was sitting at a picnic table with several of the other wives. When she heard Drew's cry she jumped up and ran toward him. "What's wrong?" she repeated only a moment after Falcon.

"It's Susannah," Drew said, his eyes huge and worried. "She's hurt. She fell off her horse."

"Oh, no!" Mara cried. "How bad is it?"

Falcon clutched Mara hard around the shoulders to keep her from seizing Drew's shirt and shaking him. "How is she?" he asked Drew.

"I couldn't tell," Drew confessed. "I left her with the others and rode back to get help. She seemed fine when we started out. We asked her if she could lope, and she said yes.''

''She's a good rider,'' Falcon confirmed.

''But she fell off!'' Drew said. ''We weren't even going very fast.''

''I'm sure you weren't,'' Falcon consoled the inconsolable boy. Falcon gave Mara a push toward his mother's already-outstretched arms and said, ''Keep her here.''

''I want to go with you!'' Mara said fiercely.

''Wait here,'' Falcon replied, his voice like granite. ''I'll bring her back to you. Call the family doctor and make sure he's here when I get back,'' Falcon told his father.

Garth nodded.

Mara let Candy lead her into the house. To her relief, Falcon's mother didn't ply her with platitudes like, ''I'm sure she'll be all right.'' They sat together in silence in the kitchen, each with a cup of hot coffee in front of her that neither touched.

It seemed ages before Falcon returned. He had Susannah in his arms.

''She wasn't hurt by the fall,'' he said quickly, before Mara had a chance to be frightened by her daughter's ashen complexion. ''At least, not more than a few scratches.''

''Then what's wrong with her?'' Mara demanded.

Falcon's blue eyes were bleak as a winter day. ''She has a fever. And her lymph nodes are swollen.''

Mara felt a chill slide down her arms. ''No. No!''

''I think she must have fainted. That's why she fell from her horse.''

''This can't be happening,'' Mara pleaded. ''Please, God, nooooo!'' she wailed.

''What is it?'' Candy asked her son.

Falcon's lips were pressed flat to keep them from trembling. He wasn't sure he could speak past the constriction in his throat. ''I think the leukemia is back.''

Falcon could say one thing for his family, they rallied

around in times of trouble. Zach flew the three of them back to Dallas in his private jet, while Callen promised to drive their car home for them. Garth phoned Children's Hospital to tell them to expect Susannah. Candy volunteered to pack their clothes and send them along with Callen.

The rest of Falcon's cousins and aunts and uncles promised to pray.

Falcon only managed to keep Zach from staying with them at the hospital by turning on his brother like a rabid dog. He bared his teeth ferociously. "Leave us be. We can handle this better alone."

What he really meant was *I don't want you to see me fall to pieces.* He felt like he was already in pieces. Mara wasn't in much better shape. He wanted to be alone with her somewhere in a dark place and put his arms around her and lay his head on her shoulder and comfort her and be comforted.

Zach settled a succoring hand on Falcon's shoulder, which was tensed hard as stone. "You don't have to go through this alone."

"Don't stay," Falcon said starkly. His eyes glittered with unshed tears. His throat had a huge lump in it. If his brother was there, if he had someone to lean on, he might break down completely. If he was alone with Mara, he would have to be strong for her. He would be able to stay in control.

Zach tightened his grip momentarily, then let go. "Call us," he said. "We want to know how Susannah is doing."

Falcon nodded. He couldn't manage any more speech.

Zach swept Mara up in a tight embrace, as though to lend her strength, then let her go. "She'll be all right," he whispered in her ear.

Mara whimpered, the sound of a suffering animal. "Thank you, Zach," she grated out. "I needed to hear that."

Even if she knew it wasn't necessarily true.

When they were alone together, neither Mara nor Falcon seemed to be able to reach out to the other. They sat down in chairs next to each other in the hospital waiting room, but they didn't touch.

At long last, Falcon broke the silence. "Even if it is the leukemia back again, that doesn't mean she won't eventually get well," he said, as though to convince himself.

"But she'll have to start all over with those awful treatments," Mara said in a low voice. "She'll be sick again. And lose the hair she was so pleased to be growing back."

Mara reached out a hand, and Falcon grasped it. They clung to each other in a way people do when they know there is strength and fortitude to be found in the other grasp. Mara raised her eyes and met Falcon's steady gaze. It gave her courage to face whatever was to come.

He isn't like Grant. He's nothing at all like Grant.

The revelation came to Mara in those few seconds like a star bursting and shedding great light. Grant had never been there for her when she needed him. He had never offered her strength. He had never been a rock to which she could cling in times of trouble.

Falcon hadn't reached for a bottle in times of trouble, nor sought out another woman. He had reached for her. He had come to her.

That wasn't the end of her epiphany.

Why, I love him, she marveled. Mara stared at Falcon as though seeing him for the first time. How had he come to mean so much to her? When had she started caring more for his pain than for her own? When had she started wanting him to love her back?

Her thoughts were cut off by the arrival of Dr. Sortino. Mara knew before he said a word that the prognosis was not good. She rose to her feet, still gripping Falcon's hand, and waited to hear what the doctor had to say.

"The leukemia is back."

Four words. Four frightening words.

Mara bit her lip to keep from crying. She pressed her face to Falcon's chest as though to escape what was happening.

There was no escape.

"We've got her stabilized," Dr. Sortino said. "We'll start the therapy again within the next few days. Don't despair," he said. "Children often have a relapse and then recover completely."

Mara lifted her head and stared at him with liquid eyes. "But some don't," she challenged.

"Some don't," he conceded reluctantly. "We'll have to wait and see."

"Can we see her?" Falcon asked.

"You can look in on her. She's sleeping now. The nurse will show you to her room."

He left then, without saying more. But Mara had heard quite enough.

"Hold me," she said to Falcon. "Hold me."

Falcon needed to feel the warmth of Mara in his arms. Because he was cold. So cold.

"She'll be all right," he told Mara. "She has to be."

But when they saw Susannah lying in the hospital bed, her face almost as white as the sheets, neither could manage an optimistic word. They grasped hands and held on.

"Your pony is waiting for you to get well," Falcon whispered to the sleeping girl. "And your mommy needs some more tickling," he said. "And I need you home to bounce around the house," he said in a choked voice.

He turned to Mara, and this time she took him in her arms and comforted him. His powerful body shook with silent sobs that were all the more intense because he fought them, even as they escaped.

Mara reached out a hand and touched her daughter's cheek. "Good night, Susannah," she whispered. Then, to Falcon, "Let's go home."

There was no question of staying in separate bedrooms. Falcon never let go of Mara's hand. He led her to his room and silently undressed her then undressed himself. He laid her on the bed and joined her there, twining their bodies together.

''I need you,'' he said.

Mara knew what he was asking. She gave herself to him, gave him the comfort and reassurance and love he needed, and took it in return. It was a gentle joining of two bruised souls who sought solace in each other's bodies.

Mara's heart swelled with love, and she gave Falcon a part of herself that she had kept hidden somewhere deep inside for long years—ever since Grant had told her she was not enough woman for him. For Falcon she could be more, was more, because he sought more from her.

Falcon lay beside Mara and realized that he felt far more than physical satisfaction. There had been a difference in their lovemaking this time, subtle but detectable. Mara had held nothing back. She had been lightning and fire in his arms, and he had found himself burning in her embrace. He knew now that what he felt for her was more than lust, or mere affection, or even admiration. He loved her, body and heart and soul.

He wanted to say the words. He needed to say them.

I love you, Mara. I want to spend my life loving you. I want you to have my children. Susannah needs brothers and sisters to play with. I'll make you both happy. I promise it.

But he didn't say any of those things.

She was already asleep.

During Susannah's second bout of induction therapy, any discussion of Falcon's and Mara's life together, their future, was held in abeyance. It was as though Susannah was the glue that held them together. Neither was willing to contemplate what form their relationship would take if something should happen and she should disappear from their lives. It might be too painful to remain together as a couple, because each would see in the other's anguished eyes a constant reminder of what they had lost.

In spite of that, their love grew. It happened in small ways, over many days.

They shared duties taking care of Susannah, relieving each

other when one had reached the end of his patience with the sick child's petulant whining on the one hand, or was unable to endure another moment of the little girl's tremendous persistence in the face of her debilitating illness on the other.

They spent their nights together making love. Neither spoke the words each privately thought. They told each other of their love in the only way they were allowed. Because there was no question of committing themselves to each other until—unless—Susannah recovered.

Mara made a point of getting up each morning with the sunrise, as Falcon did, and making him breakfast.

"I can do this myself," he said. "I know you're tired."

She traced the shadows under his eyes with a gentle hand. "And you're not?"

"Some sex goddess keeps me up half the night with her demands on my body," he teased.

"Remind the sex goddess you have to work in the morning, and I'm sure she'll leave you alone," Mara replied pertly.

Falcon pulled her into his arms and showered her face with kisses. "I'd rather miss the sleep," he said, snuggling his face against her hair.

Mara felt loved and cherished and appreciated.

"Get going, you've got work to do," she said as she shoved him out the kitchen door.

Sometimes, late at night, after he had made sweet love to Mara and she had fallen asleep, Falcon returned to his office. He wanted Mara to know she would be getting a husband who was financially responsible if she agreed to extend their marriage beyond its current artificial structure. He was planning for the future, something that hadn't interested or concerned him before Mara came into his life.

One night Mara awoke and found herself alone. She sought Falcon out and found him in his office.

"What are you doing here in the middle of the night?" she chided. "You need your sleep."

He was sitting in the swivel chair in front of his desk, and he circled it to face her. Because it had become second nature to find comfort in his arms, she settled herself in his lap and twined her fingers in his hair, pulling his face down to hers for a tender kiss.

"Now," she murmured against lips that were warm and wet against her own, "tell me what's going on. Are we in financial trouble? Do I need to go back to work as a short-order cook?"

"No," he said, perhaps too emphatically. "The whole reason I'm spending time at this desk is to secure our future together in a way that will leave you free to be home with Susannah." *And any other children we have.*

Falcon hesitated, aware he had crossed an invisible line. When Mara gave him no encouragement, he backed up again, into neutral ground. "I'm just making sure the ranch is run well and reinvesting what money I have in less risky ventures."

"You're a man who needs risk in his life," Mara said in a quiet voice.

"Not this kind," Falcon objected.

"Then let me see if I can provide another kind," Mara said, as she bit the lobe of his ear. Her hand slid across his naked chest and down toward the pajama bottoms he wore in case he had to check on Susannah during the night. He was already hard by the time her hand got to him.

"Mara," he warned. "It's nearly dawn. I have to get dressed and go to work in an hour."

"We've got a whole hour? That should be enough time for what I have in mind."

A moment later she was on her back on the floor of his office, and he was inside her. Their loving was stormy and tempestuous, full of risk, and she climaxed twice before he was finished and lowered himself, chest heaving, to the carpet beside her.

Falcon groaned. "I'm sorry, Mara. I didn't mean to be so rough."

She took one look at the love bite she had left on his shoulder and laughed. "I'm sorry, Falcon. I didn't mean to be so rough, either."

Once, during those weeks and months while their lives were on hold, Mara took herself back to the house she had bought because of its location on a quiet, tree-lined street where children played. She was amazed to see it was just an ordinary house. There was nothing particularly special about it. Yet, keeping this home was one of the reasons she had been willing to marry Falcon Whitelaw.

She let herself in and wandered through the house. It felt empty, despite the furnished rooms. She wondered what it was that had made this place seem so much a necessary part of her life. And realized it wasn't the house, but what it had represented. Permanence. A place of belonging where memories could be made.

This house wasn't a home. A home was where people lived and loved. Home was where Falcon and Susannah were. Home was the B-Bar Ranch.

Mara threw herself on the bed in her room and wept. For all the might-have-beens with Grant. What would their life have been like if only…? There, in the house where she had sought the happiness she had been denied in her marriage with Grant, she let go of the past. Her first love was dead and buried. He no longer had the power to hurt her.

The only question now was whether she had the courage to put aside her past fears and reach out and grasp what she wanted. It meant taking risks. She might be hurt again. She might not live happily ever after. It all came down to a matter of trust.

Did she trust Falcon Whitelaw—who less than a year past had been an irresponsible, carousing, ne'er-do-well—to offer her a future filled with happiness? Or would a lifetime with him be filled with trials and tribulation? Had he merely been on his best behavior for the months they had spent together? Would he revert to form once Susannah was well?

Mara sat herself down on the edge of the bed and dropped her head into her hand. There were no guarantees. She was going to have to take a chance. She was going to have to make up her mind one way or the other. Because she knew that the moment Susannah was out of danger—and she *would* be someday soon—Falcon was going to starting asking questions and demanding answers about their relationship.

And she would have to answer yes or no.

Chapter 10

"Hi, Mom. I'm at the hospital."

"Falcon? What is it? Is it bad news?"

"She's in remission."

"That's wonderful, Falcon!" his mother said. "Oh, I'm so glad for all of you!"

"Tell Dad for me, and Zach and Callen." Falcon didn't think he could handle talking to all of them. He was having trouble keeping his voice steady as it was.

"How's Mara?" Candy asked.

"She's fine."

"When will we see you again?" Candy asked.

"I don't know, Mom. Everything is pretty hectic right now. I'll call you again when things are more settled. Okay? I've got to go now."

"Goodbye, Falcon. Take care of yourself. Give our love to Mara and Susannah."

When things are more settled. Falcon wasn't sure how soon that would be. Certainly not until he had an answer from Mara about whether or not she was willing to end their sham marriage and start a real one. Although, since the day of Susannah's relapse, there had been nothing halfway about Falcon's commitment to his wife. Mara had given him hope that she felt the same way he did, but until the words were spoken, nothing was *settled*.

It had taken the full amount of time—Christmas had come and gone—for the induction therapy to work a second time. Even Susannah welcomed the "back-stick" that had resulted in the news that she was in remission again.

"We're going to take things a little slower this time," Mara gently admonished her daughter as they rode home from the hospital. "No more bouncing off the walls."

Falcon winked at the little girl. "You'll have to settle for bouncing on the beds," he teased.

Mara shot Falcon a warning look. She had almost lost Susannah the last time. She wasn't taking any chances with her daughter's health now that she had been given a second lease on life.

Falcon had different ideas about what was appropriate behavior for Susannah's present state of health, and during the next few weeks, the two adults were constantly at loggerheads over what Susannah could and could not do.

"You can't keep Susannah wrapped up in cotton batting," Falcon argued.

"I can, and I will!" Mara retorted.

"She's a little girl. She needs to run and play."

"What if she gets sick again?" Mara said, her heart in throat.

Falcon pulled her into his arms and rocked her back and forth. "We'll make sure she rests, but she has to be allowed to live as normal a life as she can, Mara."

Mara knew Falcon was right. She was being overprotective. "But I'm so scared," she admitted in a small voice.

"I'm here," he said. "I'll watch over you both," he promised.

It was as close to a declaration of love as he had ever come.

He wanted to go further. He wanted to say the rest. But Mara stopped him.

"I know you'll take care of us," she said. "But I wonder sometimes if it's fair of me to ask it of you. This isn't what you bargained for when you married me," she reminded him.

"But I—"

Again, she cut him off. "I don't want to think about the future. I want to do what you advised me once before. I want to enjoy today for what it brings and forget about tomorrow. Maybe when I know Susannah is going to get well, I'll think differently. But now...now life is too uncertain."

When she said things like that, how could he talk to her about their future together? But neither could he let what she had said pass without challenging it.

"Do you really mean to put your life on hold for however long it takes Susannah to get well? She won't be truly in the clear unless she stays in remission beyond the five-year mark. *Five years,* Mara. That's a long time."

"I know," she conceded. "When you put it that way, I know I'm being ridiculous. But I need a little time to start believing there will be a future for us—for me and Susannah."

He was achingly aware he was not included in her picture of the future.

"A year," she said. "If Susannah stays in remission a year, I'll let myself hope again. But it's too dangerous to believe in the future before then. You do understand, don't you, Falcon?"

He did. All too well. Mara wasn't going to make promises to him or to herself that she wasn't sure she would be able to keep. He wanted to say they could have a life together even if the worst happened, and Susannah died. But he discovered he couldn't voice even the possibility that the world might lose a free spirit like Susannah. She had become as dear to him as though she were his own flesh and blood.

* * *

To anyone watching from the outside, they appeared a perfectly normal, happy family over the months of winter that led into spring. In fact, Susannah quickly got well enough to misbehave. That created a whole new set of problems for Mara and Falcon. They were no longer merely caretakers for a youthful invalid, they were parents trying to raise a responsible, honest and self-sufficient child.

Falcon found himself sympathizing with what his own parents must have gone through with him and his siblings. Susannah had gotten used to being waited on and catered to during her illness. The first time Falcon insisted she pick up her damp towel and put it back on the bathroom rack, she responded as the spoiled child she had become.

"You do it," she said.

Falcon wasn't sure what to do next, but he wasn't about to let an eight-year-old order him around. "Pick it up, Susannah. Otherwise, you can go to your room and spend the rest of the morning thinking about ways you can help do your share in this family."

"You're not my father," Susannah shouted back. "You can't tell me what to do!"

Falcon stood stunned, appalled at the child's apparent dismissal of the role he had played in her life over the past nine months. Surely no real father could have been more kind or considerate, more loving or caring during her illness. But children, he was learning, can have short, selfish memories.

"Susannah Ainsworth! You apologize to Falcon this instant!"

Mara had overheard the entire conversation and was appalled at her daughter's devilish behavior. "You will pick up that towel and hang it back on the rack. Then you can go to your room and stay there the rest of the morning!"

"I'm sorry, Falcon," Susannah said in a petulant voice. Then she turned to her mother. "If I've picked up the towel," Susannah reasoned as she sullenly hung the damp towel on the rack, "why do I still have to go to my room?"

"Because you were rude and disobedient," Mara said.

"Why do I have to do what Falcon says?" Susannah complained. "He's not my real father."

Mara looked quickly at Falcon's face, which had hardened like stone, then back to her daughter. She was the one who had forced Falcon to remain on the fringes of her and Susannah's life. She was the one who wanted everything on hold until she was good and ready to move forward. She had created this situation, and the time had come for her to resolve it.

"Falcon *is* your father in every way that matters," Mara said. "He has the right to tell you what to do. And you have the duty to obey him and to treat him with respect."

Susannah turned wide, hazel eyes on Falcon. "Are you really going to be my real father?" she asked, her tone more curious now than belligerent. "Forever and ever?"

Falcon shot one desperate look at Mara, wanting to be able to say yes, and knowing that he hadn't the right.

Mara knew she had to make a decision. "Yes, he is," she answered for Falcon. It was easy, she realized, so easy to say yes to a lifetime with Falcon.

Their glances caught and clung for a moment. Mara almost gasped at the powerful emotions she saw in Falcon's eyes. She knew then she had done the right thing. She was committed to this man. For better or worse. For richer—and he was beginning to spend money like Croesus again—or poorer. In sickness—and there might be more of it for Susannah—and in health. It only remained for the words to be spoken between them.

Only, now that she had taken a step off the edge of a treacherous cliff, Mara was terrified that Falcon wouldn't be there to catch her.

"All right, you can be my father," Susannah said in the way children have of accepting momentous occasions with aplomb. "I'm sorry, Falcon," she said, this time with more contrition in her voice. She crossed to him and put her arms around his waist and said, "Actually, I'm glad you're going to be my father for real and always. I guess I sorta like you a lot." Then she looked up at him with an innocent, angelic face and said, "Do I still have to go to my room?"

Falcon swept the little girl into his arms and gave her a tremendous hug. "God, I love you, Susannah. I'm so glad you're my daughter for real and always." Then he set her on her feet and said, "And yes, you still have to go to your room."

Susannah grimaced. "All right, but if I stay in my room this morning, can we go riding this afternoon?"

Falcon shook his head at her persistence. He sent a questioning look to Mara as if to say, "All right?" When she nodded, he said to Susannah. "Sure. You use the morning to think, and we'll go riding this afternoon."

"Yippee!" Susannah said as she hopped, skipped and bounced away.

In an exaggerated motion, Falcon wiped his brow with his sleeve. "I have great respect for my parents when I see what they coped with from the other side of the fence."

"It isn't easy knowing the right thing to do or say," Mara conceded.

"Did you mean it, Mara? That I'll be Susannah's father for now and forever?"

Mara flushed. "Yes," she said in a whisper. "If you want to be."

"If I want to be? How can you even ask? I *love* Susannah." It would only take another breath to say *And I love you.*

Mara never gave him the chance. "I've got a lot to do this morning if I want to be free to ride with you and Susannah this afternoon," she said.

She backed up a few steps, then turned and almost ran for his office. She was like a skittish filly that had walked up to his hand to take the sugar he held out to her, but at the last moment had taken fright and run. Like the filly, he knew she would be back. Because once a creature had developed a taste for sugar, it was an irresistible lure.

It wouldn't be a bad thing to wait a little while and give his jumbled feelings time to sort themselves out. And give Mara time to realize that he would be there, waiting with his hand outstretched, whenever she was ready to move forward in their relationship.

At least the suspended animation in which they had lived for the past nine months was coming to an end. But Falcon wasn't taking anything for granted. He wanted the words spoken. He wanted things decided once and for all. And if he moved slowly and carefully enough, there was just the chance she would come to him today.

Just before lunchtime, Susannah came running into the kitchen. "Can we go riding now?" she asked. "Patches needs some exercise."

"What do you say, Mara?" Falcon asked. "Shall we go riding now, or after lunch?"

Mara finished wrapping the last of the sandwiches she had been preparing. "I've put together a picnic to take to the stock pond," Mara said. "But mind you, no racing!"

Falcon and Susannah raced the last few hundred yards to the stock pond, with Mara flying close behind.

"Whew! I have to admit that was exhilarating," Mara said with a laugh as she slid off her horse.

"I'm hungry," Susannah said. "Can we eat lunch now?"

"Sure. Untie the blanket from behind your saddle and I'll get the food." Mara began untying the saddlebags on her horse.

Falcon quickly relieved her. "I'll do this. You can help Susannah spread out the blanket."

All of them ate like they were never going to see food again. Replete, they settled back lazily on the blanket and watched the shapes on the ground made by the broken shadows of the leaves.

In a very short while, Mara and Falcon were treated to the sight of Susannah sound asleep on the blanket between them.

"She seems to tire so easily," Mara said as she chewed worriedly on her lower lip.

"Most kids her age take a nap, don't they? Or would if their parents could get them to slow down long enough. She's fine, Mara. Try not to worry so much."

"I do try!" Mara said. She rose from the blanket and walked a few steps away, where they wouldn't disturb Susannah's slumber.

When Falcon came up behind her and circled her waist, she leaned her head back against his shoulder. This felt good. This felt right. She wanted to stay married to Falcon. She wanted them to be husband and wife. But was that fair to him? What if she had trapped him by the things she had said this morning. What if he didn't want to stay with her and Susannah after all? She had to know the truth.

"I took advantage of the situation this morning," she said. "If you want out of this marriage, all you have to do is say so."

"Oh?"

Mara couldn't tell from that one quiet word whether Falcon was relieved or infuriated by what she said. But his hands had tightened uncomfortably around her.

"I can't breathe," she protested.

His hold loosened, but he didn't let her go. Neither did he speak. Maybe he did want out.

She continued, "When Susannah asked if you were going to be her father forever and ever, I said you would. But we've never talked about forever, Falcon. I made the choice for you. I know that's unfair, and if you want to be free of us, of both of us—"

He whirled her around and clutched her tightly at the waist. "Look at me, Mara."

But she couldn't. She was afraid.

He caught her chin between his fingers and forced it upward. He tightened his grasp and demanded, "Look at me."

He waited until she looked up at him before speaking again. His eyes were narrowed, his gaze fierce. A muscle worked in his jaw. This was not a weak man. This was not a man who would let her fall from a cliff. He would be there to catch her.

"I want to be Susannah's father," he said in a harsh, grating voice. "Very much."

"That means you'll also be stuck with me," Mara said with a breezy laugh that somehow got caught in her throat.

Falcon let go of Mara's chin and caught her by the shoulders. "I love you, Mara. I want you to be my wife, forever and ever."

Mara's heart soared when she heard Falcon's declaration of love. But she had to make sure he knew what he was getting into. "Are you *sure?*"

There was a silence that sent Mara's heart to her throat.

Falcon was shaken by Mara's third attempt to set him free. Didn't she hear what he was saying? Didn't she realize how much he loved her? There was only one thing that could possibly change his mind about staying married to her, and that was if she didn't want him. He needed to know that Mara loved him. He needed to hear the words. But he didn't dare ask her outright. What if she said no?

For the first and most important time in his life, Falcon found himself at a loss for words with a woman. "Mara, do you— Is there a chance that— Is it possible—"

"What are you trying to say, Falcon?"

From the blanket behind them a little voice piped up, "Falcon wants to know if you love him, Mommy."

"What?"

Both adults shot startled looks at the little girl, who was lying on her stomach with her head perched on her hands and her legs waving in the air.

"I thought you were asleep," Mara said.

"Well, I'm not," Susannah replied. "Do you love him, Mommy?" she demanded.

Mara flushed, and Falcon feared the worst. He tried to get the words past a constricted throat, tried to offer her the divorce she so obviously wanted. Fortunately he was too distressed to speak.

Because the next words out of Mara's mouth were, "Yes, Susannah, I love him very much."

Mara and Falcon exchanged glances that shouted hosanna and hallelujah, before Falcon pulled Mara into his arms for a possessive kiss. A moment later, Susannah was tugging on his shirt, demanding to be included in the family embrace.

"Love me too, Daddy," she said. "Me, too."

"You too, Susannah," Falcon assured the little girl. "I'll love you and your mommy both, forever and ever."

Falcon met Mara's eyes and they spoke without words. They might not have forever with Susannah. There were no guarantees of long life and happiness. But whatever time they had together, they silently vowed to live to the fullest.

"Let's go home," Falcon said. "I want to make love to my wife," he whispered in her ear.

"Yes," Mara replied in a soft voice. "Let's take our daughter and go home."

* * * * *

THE HEADSTRONG BRIDE

For Priscilla Kelley
Because the little things do matter

Prologue

"I'm so sorry about your father." Callen Whitelaw felt awkward offering sympathy to someone she hardly knew. At first she didn't think the grieving man was going to reply. When he did, he said one word in a ragged whisper.

"Thanks."

Callen tried to imagine Sam Longstreet crying with enough despair to make himself hoarse. She wanted to fold him in her arms and comfort him. But he was a stranger, even though he had been a neighbor all her life. She had known his father, E.J., better than she knew Sam, because E.J. had come to Hawk's Way often to spend time with her father.

"Is there anything I can do?" she asked.

"No." He hesitated a moment, then said, "Maybe there is. I have to go to Amarillo on business. Maybe you could meet me there, have dinner with me. I...I could use the company."

Callen was stunned by the invitation, which seemed to come out of the blue. Why would Sam Longstreet want to have dinner with her when he didn't even know her?

"Never mind," he said when she hesitated too long.

She caught his arm as he started to turn away. "Wait. Please. I'll be glad to meet you. Just tell me when and where."

He named a time and a restaurant, and then his attention was drawn by another rancher offering condolences.

Callen thought about the invitation during the entire drive home with her family, wondering what had compelled Sam to reach out to her. Once she was home, she asked her eldest brother, Zach, about Sam. Zach admitted to only a passing acquaintance with Sam. Her other brother, Falcon, hadn't come home for the funeral from his ranch in Dallas, but Zach said he could speak for both of them.

"Neither of us knew Sam very well," Zach said. "He was two years ahead of me in school, three years ahead of Falcon, so we didn't have any classes together."

Zach was thirty-four, so that would make Sam thirty-six, Callen figured. He had seemed every bit of that, his features chiseled by wind and weather, his striking green eyes webbed at the corners by the sun, his wide mouth bracketed by lines, his shaggy, chestnut hair streaked with blonde. It was a face aged by the hard life of a Texas rancher and by the grief that sat upon his brow.

"Sam wasn't too good with the books," Zach continued. "The football coach got tutors to help him pass his class work so he could play. He was a great running back, as I recall, but he pretty much kept to himself."

"Was he good enough to play professionally?" Callen asked.

"He hurt his knee in the state championship game. I guess he couldn't run fast enough after that to compete in college. He settled in to work on the Double L after high school, and as far as I know he never aspired to anything else. Why are you interested in Sam Longstreet, anyway?"

"He seemed so sad," Callen said.

"Stay away from him," Zach warned. "He's a saddle tramp with a rundown ranch."

"That's unfair!" Callen retorted in defense of a man she had just met. "Just because the Longstreets don't have as much money as the Whitelaws doesn't make Sam any less of a man."

"He's never going to amount to anything."

"How do you know?"

"If he was going to do anything with that ranch to improve it, he would have done it by now," Zach said.

"Not necessarily," Callen retorted. "Maybe he and his father disagreed about what ought to be done." Callen knew she had hit a sore spot with Zach, because he and their father often disagreed about ranching methods.

"You're speculating," Zach accused.

"You're just mad because you know I'm right," Callen shot back.

Her quarrel with Zach was loud enough to bring their mother, Candy, into the parlor from the kitchen.

"What's going on in here?" she asked.

"Callen's got herself into a snit over that good-for-nothing at the Double L."

"Sam Longstreet is not—"

"That's enough from both of you," Candy interrupted. "Zach, don't you have some business with your father in his office?" Once Zach was gone, she turned to Callen. "Now what's all this about Sam Longstreet?"

"I spoke to him at E.J.'s funeral," Callen said. "He seemed so alone, Mom, and so sad. I wanted to do something for him, but I didn't know what. He mentioned he was going to be in Amarillo on business and asked me to join him for dinner. I said yes."

Her mother arched a questioning brow but said nothing either to approve or disapprove of what Callen had done.

Yet Callen felt the need to explain herself. "I couldn't say no, Mom. I mean, there was something so peculiar about the way he looked at me. He didn't say much of anything, but I could hear him speaking to me with his eyes. It was so strange."

"Peculiar. Strange. Those are odd words to describe a man you've agreed to join for dinner," her mother mused.

"That's the problem, Mom," Callen said, shoving a hand through the dark bangs that hung slightly in her eyes. "I don't know exactly how to describe him. He seemed so sad. And lonely."

"I see. So you want to make him happy and less lonely?"

"Is that so awful?"

Her mother slid an arm around her waist and hugged her slightly. "Not if you keep in mind that what you're offering Sam Longstreet is friendship. Just don't let yourself tumble head over heels in love with a man who's too wounded to love you back."

Chapter 1

"I'm going to marry Sam Longstreet, and there's nothing you can do to stop me," Callen said to her father in a calm, brittle voice. Her brown eyes flashed with defiance. "What's wrong with Sam? He's a rancher, a close neighbor. Longstreet land has bordered Whitelaw land in northwest Texas for generations!"

Garth Whitelaw eyed his daughter, the youngest of his three grown children, with trepidation. She had been engaged twice, but never married. Both times, he had warned her she was making a mistake. Both times, she had disregarded his advice, only to break the engagements later when she learned the truth of what he had said. Now she was proposing a third prospective husband, this one as bad—maybe even worse—than the other two. Garth had learned that telling Callen no was like waving a red flag in front of a bull, but he felt so strongly that Sam was the wrong man for his daughter that he made his arguments anyway.

"Sam Longstreet will never amount to anything," he said. "He's a down-at-the-heels rogue with nothing to his name but a ramshackle ranch. At a guess, I'd say he's only interested in your money.''

"That's despicable!" Callen retorted. "How can you even suggest such a thing?"

"Because it's true," Garth replied in a steely voice. "You're an heiress, Sam's a dirt-poor rancher. He was lucky to get through high school, and he hasn't done anything since to educate himself. He's a loner, and he's lazy. The Double L is falling down around him. What can the two of you possibly have in common?"

"Sam's a wonderful man," Callen argued. "He's just had a lot of hard luck lately. His father made some bad investments that took all their savings. I'll agree Sam has been reclusive in the months since his dad died, but that sort of blow would be hard on anyone who loved his father as much as Sam loved E.J."

Garth probably missed E. J. Longstreet as much or more than Sam did. The two older men had been good friends. It was a shame what had happened to E.J., and Garth sympathized with Sam's loss. But that didn't mean he wanted Sam for a son-in-law. He couldn't imagine what his daughter found attractive about the rancher. He asked again, "What do you see in him?"

Callen hesitated a moment before she replied. "Sam needs me, Daddy. And I need him. He makes me feel…special."

Garth snorted. "I'm not saying what happens between a man and woman between the sheets isn't important. But you're going to find it mighty tough sitting across from a lazy good-for-nothing at the breakfast table for the rest of your life."

Callen's lips flattened and her eyes narrowed. "I didn't mean Sam makes me feel special in bed. I meant— Oh, what's the use! I'm not going to change your mind, and you're not going to change mine. I wasn't asking your permission to marry Sam, I just wanted to let you know we're going to be married and invite you to the wedding."

"I won't be there," Garth said flatly.

Callen's chin quivered. She gritted her teeth to steady it before replying, "That's up to you, of course." She started for the front door of the antebellum-style mansion that had been built more than a century before as the main ranch house at Hawk's Way. She paused at the front door, waiting, hoping her father would change his mind. Her heart sank as she heard his parting words.

"If you marry Sam, you won't have a job here anymore." Garth knew the threat was a mistake the moment the words were out of his mouth, but it was too late to take them back. Callen was the best cutting horse trainer he had. She wouldn't have any trouble finding another job. And he didn't want to lose all contact with his only daughter. Though it had been years since he had said the words to her, he loved her dearly.

Callen's shoulders stiffened, then squared, before she turned to face her father. "I hope you'll change your mind, Daddy. Because come Friday, I'm going to be Mrs. Sam Longstreet."

Callen headed for the stable to saddle her horse. She needed some time alone to think. The canyons and gullies of Hawk's Way had long provided a haven, a ready balm for her soul. Once in the saddle, Callen aimed her horse into the Texas sun. It felt wonderful on her face, and the wind brushed her bangs away from her forehead and lifted her shoulder-length black hair so it flew in the breeze. She relaxed her jaw, which she realized was still clenched.

She was furious with her father for opposing her marriage to Sam and equally terrified that he might be right. He had been right twice before. But Sam was different, not at all like the previous two men she had planned to marry. In the first place, Sam was a rancher. She had grown up on Hawk's Way, and there wasn't anything she didn't know about cattle or cutting horses. She and Sam had that in common, since he had grown up on the Double L. But she would have been

hard-pressed to name the specific things about Sam that made
her so sure they were right for each other.

When she had gone to dinner with Sam three months ago,
Callen had found herself utterly charmed by him. There was
something dangerous about Sam, about his moods and the
way he carried himself. And yet his eyes were so very sad.
And kind. That was the word she would have used to describe
his behavior toward her.

She could remember Sam's first kiss as though it had just
happened. He had walked her to her car from the restaurant
and stood there looking at her with eyes that spoke volumes.
The closest light came from the restaurant, and they stood
partly in shadow.

"You're beautiful," he said.

Callen had been told that before by more than one man,
but Sam made her believe it. He cupped one cheek with his
hand and brushed his callused thumb across her lips. She shivered at the touch. Her eyes had drifted closed as he slowly
lowered his head.

His lips were incredibly soft as he pressed them to hers.
He brushed them once, twice across her mouth before lifting
his head to stare into her eyes once more.

He'd left her wanting much, much more.

It was only the first of many excursions together. They
often went riding over Double L land and, if Callen were
honest, she had to admit the place needed work. Fences were
down, windmills screeched for want of oil, the barn needed
some sideboards replaced and the house—at least from the
outside—had seen much better days.

When she asked Sam about the rundown condition of the
Double L, he had replied, "It takes money to make repairs.
Not all of us are blessed with wealth."

Seeing how sensitive he was about the difference in their
economic situations, she hadn't brought up the subject again.

Their second kiss had come a week after the first, at a
moment when they had just stepped down to rest their horses.

She was caught by surprise because it was a kiss of hunger, and she hadn't seen the need in Sam's eyes until he reached for her and pulled her into his embrace. His body was large and hard, and she had felt enveloped by him—safe, secure, and very much wanted. His hands moved hesitantly over her body at first, barely touching, reverently touching, and finally claiming her. She felt breathless when he finally released her.

"Sam...please." It was a plea to finish what he had started.

Sam shook his head and, in a voice harsh with need, said, "No, Callen. It wouldn't be right."

"Why not?"

He smiled ruefully. "In the first place, I don't have any kind of protection with me."

She blushed furiously. She should have thought of that herself.

"In the second place, you deserve better. A soft bed and a lover who belongs to you, heart and soul."

She hadn't known what to reply to that.

"Come on," he said, lifting her into the saddle. "We'd better get back to the house."

They had been seeing each other almost daily for a month when she asked if she could see the inside of his house.

Again, Sam shook his head no.

"Why not?" she demanded, fists perched on hips.

"Because I wouldn't trust myself alone with you if there was a bed anywhere nearby."

Callen had been flattered but was so used to getting her own way that she didn't give up. She pressed herself close to Sam, feeling the way his body tensed and hardened. "I wouldn't mind, Sam," she purred in her most seductive voice.

"I would," Sam said as he caught her by the arms and moved her away. "You deserve the best, Callen. You deserve to be treated with respect."

Callen met Sam's gaze, her eyes wide with surprise. His words were what every woman wanted to hear, yet her brow soon furrowed in confusion. His ideas concerning courtship were so…old-fashioned. He had to know, since she had been engaged twice, that she wasn't a virgin who needed to be protected from the importunities of a forceful male. But Sam had apparently put her on a pedestal. She found it awkward to stay balanced there, knowing herself to be far less than perfect. But, oh, how good it felt to be so cherished!

Then the precious moment had come, just two days ago, when Sam proposed to her.

"I know I'm not good enough for you," Sam began.

She pressed her fingertips to his lips. How could he not be good enough when he made her feel so wonderful?

"You deserve better," he insisted. "But I'll do my best to make your life as happy as I can. Will you marry me, Callen? Will you be my wife?"

Her throat was so tight with emotion that she hadn't been able to answer right away. At last she said, "Yes, Sam, I'll marry you. I want to be your wife."

He kissed her then, tenderly at first and then hungrily, his tongue sweeping into her mouth and claiming her. He hugged her so tightly she squeaked with pain. When he released her, they looked at each other and laughed with joy.

His eyes glittered in the sunlight, and for a moment she was frightened at their intensity. She shivered, and he pulled her close, murmuring, "Don't be frightened, Callen."

Until Sam spoke the words, she hadn't realized how scared she was. But the look in his eyes urged her to trust him. And she did. Sam would never hurt her the way she had been hurt before. He would never allow himself to be bought off by her father, as her first two lovers had done. Sam would only love her and respect her and protect her.

Was it any wonder she had fallen in love with him? Was it any wonder that, when he had proposed, she had said yes? Her father had suggested that Sam was another fortune hunter. That he was lazy and poor and just wanted to marry her for her money.

Callen didn't believe it. Sam loved her. She would stake

her life on it. *Was* staking her life on it. Because, come Friday, she would be standing in front of a judge with Sam Longstreet by her side. And when the judge asked if she wanted to spend the rest of her life with Sam, she was going to say yes.

Sam Longstreet didn't want Callen's money, but neither was he marrying her for love. He had wooed her and won her with one specific purpose in mind: to get revenge on Garth Whitelaw.

Garth was the one who had convinced Sam's father, E.J., to invest his life savings in several ventures that had turned out to be swindles. Sam had been shocked to discover that Garth had led his father so far astray, since the two men had been friends for more years than anyone could count. His best friend's betrayal had made E.J. moody and morose. He had started drinking and rarely left the house.

Sam had tried to console his father when things were at their worst, but E.J. was inconsolable. After more than a hundred years, he would be the Longstreet who finally lost the Double L to creditors. Sam had come home from working on the range one day to find his father, whom he cherished, dead of a gunshot wound to the head.

He had nearly gone mad with grief.

He had sat for hours in the same room with his father's corpse, unable to move. The long hours he spent paralyzed had given him a lot of time to think. The more he thought about it, the more convinced he became that Garth Whitelaw had planned to dupe his father, knowing full well E.J. would lose his ranch. Then, when it went into foreclosure, Garth could buy the land for a pittance of its value and add it to Hawk's Way, thus replacing the several thousand acres Garth had given to his eldest son, Zach, on his twenty-first birthday. It was Garth Whitelaw's greedy desire to possess the Double L that was the direct cause of E. J. Longstreet's death.

On the day Sam buried his father, he confronted Garth at

the graveyard with his knowledge of the other man's perfidy. He waited until Garth was alone and approached him.

"This is all your fault," he snarled. "E.J. followed your advice and lost everything he worked for all his life!"

"I never—"

"Don't try to deny it," Sam said in a savage voice. "My father never invested a penny until he talked to you. Only this time you told him what would serve your purposes. This time you led him into a swindle. You knew how he felt about the Double L. You ruined him. You killed him as surely as if you'd held the gun yourself!"

Garth blanched.

Before he could retort, his daughter, Callen, reached his side. She was wearing her long black hair in a ponytail, with a fringe of bangs that made her look surprisingly young. Sam remembered her as a bothersome kid always trailing along behind her older brothers, Zach and Falcon, not that he and her brothers had had much to do with each other then or now. He noted in a detached way that Callen had grown up to be quite a beauty.

Sam watched as Callen looked up with adoring eyes at her father. Then he caught Garth's unguarded look of love for his daughter. At that moment the idea had come to Sam that here was one sure way to get vengeance on his enemy. Garth had stolen his father; somehow he would take Garth's daughter from him.

As Garth walked away, Callen looked up at him. "I'm so sorry about your father."

Sam checked the retort that he didn't need any Whitelaw pity, and said, "Thanks."

His face remained a thing of carved granite as he stared down at her. It dawned on him how easily he could have his vengeance.

Sam knew about Callen's two previous engagements. He knew her father wouldn't think he was good enough for her. All he had to do was make her fall in love with him. Father and daughter were sure to argue, and it would split them apart. Then he would offer to marry her, force her to choose between him and her father. Either way, she would lose. And, therefore, Garth would lose. His vengeance would be all the sweeter when he told Callen—if she chose him instead of her father—why he had married her.

Sam hadn't wasted any time beginning his conquest of Callen. He wasn't without charm, he simply chose not to employ it most of the time. There, at his father's graveside, he let his gaze linger on Callen's lips and then focus on her eyes. They were a warm, tobacco brown.

She flushed prettily. "Is there anything I can do to help?"

"You can meet me for dinner in Amarillo," he said.

When he turned his gaze back to Garth at the graveside, he was pleased with the frown he saw on the other man's face. He knew Garth wanted to warn him to keep his distance from Callen, but the older man kept his lips pressed tight as he whirled abruptly and walked away.

When all the other mourners were gone and Sam was finally alone in the tiny graveyard that held the mortal remains of generations of Longstreets, he stood near the cold headstone that marked his father's final resting place and made a solemn vow to avenge his death.

"I promise you, Dad, however long it takes, no matter what I have to do, Garth Whitelaw is going to suffer for what he did to you."

His courtship of Callen had been accomplished with surprising speed. He suspected she had felt sorry for him at first, and thus her barriers were all down. He had swept her off her feet with honeyed words and a few searing kisses. He hadn't bedded her, using old-fashioned morals as an excuse. His charade of respect and caring had worked even better than he had hoped. Within weeks she had fallen in love with him. When he proposed, she had accepted with tears of joy in her eyes.

The best part had been when Garth Whitelaw came to the

Double L with his checkbook open, asking how much Sam wanted to call off the wedding.

"I don't want your money, Whitelaw." Sam hadn't been able to keep from smiling. Garth was a fool to think he was going to be able to pay for his guilt with cash.

"I know you need money to keep the Double L from foreclosure. Tell me how much, and I'll loan it to you interest free," Garth offered.

"I don't want or need your help," he retorted. Truthfully, he was surprised that Garth had tried to buy him off with that particular offer. Sam figured the man must have had some other plan in mind to put the Double L in his debt. He wasn't going to fall for it.

"I want you to stay away from Callen," Garth said.

"She's a grown woman. She can make her own decisions."

"She's made her share of bad ones."

"And I'm a bad one?"

"The worst."

"Does Callen know you're here?"

Garth shifted restlessly, uneasily. "No."

A wicked grin split Sam's face as he relished Garth's discomfort. "Don't worry. I won't tell her you tried to buy me off."

Garth hadn't bothered thanking him, just stalked down the rickety stairs that led from Sam's sagging front porch, gunning the engine of his pickup as he headed down the dusty road.

So far, Callen had remained firm in the face of her family's disapproval. Sam had to admire her for that. He fought back the nagging conscience that told him it was wrong to hurt an innocent woman for the transgressions of her father. He was only doing what was necessary to avenge the wrong done to E.J. Garth Whitelaw hadn't given a thought to Sam's pain when he had ruined Sam's father. He quieted his conscience with the thought that when it was all over, Callen would still be alive. E.J. was gone forever.

The wedding was tomorrow. He wondered if Garth would find some way to stop it. He hoped the older man tried. It would surely put a wide breach between Garth and his daughter. It was a breach Sam intended to extend until father and daughter were totally alienated.

Sam swallowed the bitter bile that rose in his throat when he thought of the senselessness of his father's death. He needed the marriage to Callen to achieve his revenge against her father. It was important to guard against feeling anything for her. He had to bear in mind that Callen Whitelaw was just a tool he was using to achieve his goal of revenge. He had to forget about the softness of her skin, the sweetness of her kisses, the look of adoration and trust in her eyes.

Sam's lips pressed flat. When it came time to say his vows before the judge, he would do it. And crush the conscience that urged him to let the girl go free.

Chapter 2

Callen came alone to the county courthouse for her wedding. Her father had held fast to his vow to be absent, and her mother had refused to side against her father. Her brother, Falcon, couldn't leave Dallas because his wife, Mara, was pregnant and near term, and her brother, Zach, had told her plainly that she was making the worst mistake of her life, and he wasn't going to be a part of it. In a privileged existence that had been marked by periods of loneliness, Callen had never felt so alone.

As she paced the hardwood floor in front of the judge's chambers dressed in an antique lace dress, wearing an ivory felt cloche and carrying a pungent bouquet of gardenias, Callen wondered whether she was playing the fool. Was her family right? Was Sam actually a fortune hunter?

Callen glanced at her watch. Sam was late. For a half second she wondered whether he might not show up at all. Before that thought could take root, she saw him come through the imposing double doors of the courthouse. As glad as she was to see him, Callen couldn't help the feeling of foreboding that wedged in her throat and made it difficult to speak.

Sam walked right up to her, reached for her hands and took them in his. "You look beautiful," he murmured.

Unfortunately there was no way Callen could honestly return the compliment. In fact, she was sorely disappointed by Sam's appearance. "You didn't dress up."

Sam flushed. "No."

No excuse, no explanation, just no. His sun-bleached hair was shaggy and needed a cut, nor had he shaved for at least a day. His boots were worn, and his jeans were frayed. He looked like he hadn't slept for a week, and if he had, he'd done it in his clothes. The sun-lined face that had become so dear to her was carved in granite. And his green eyes, the kind, tender eyes that had made her fall in love with him, looked as hard as cut glass.

Callen shivered. Sam seemed a stranger. This was a side of him she had never seen. He was the saddle tramp Zach had named him, shady and disreputable. Two spots of heat rose on her cheeks when she thought of the scathing comments her father would have made if he had seen her bridegroom looking like this. Callen was ashamed and embarrassed by Sam's appearance. The thought flashed across her mind that she ought to run like hell from Sam, from this marriage.

She couldn't look at Sam, afraid he would see what was in her thoughts. Appearances shouldn't matter, she told herself. She had known Sam was poor. She had seen him unshaven in the past, in fact, had seen him in the same Western shirt and jeans he was wearing now. But that didn't ease her worry. She had expected Sam to treat their marriage, the ceremony at least, with the same reverence she felt. After all, they were beginning a new life together. If anything, Sam's appearance evidenced contempt for the ritual of marriage. Obviously she had mistaken his feelings on the subject.

What else are you mistaken about, Callen?

Callen fought back the voices of her father and her brother, both of whom had warned her not to marry Sam. She opened her mouth to tell Sam she couldn't go through with it and shut it again. She couldn't be wrong about Sam. She refused to be wrong about Sam. There must be some good reason why he hadn't taken the time to improve his appearance, an emergency on the ranch or some other disaster.

"Was there some trouble on the ranch this morning?" she asked.

"No."

"No cattle stampede? Brush fire? Pack of howling wolves at the door?" she teased.

"No."

She pursed her lips ruefully. "You overslept?"

"No."

She couldn't think of another reason that would explain Sam's careless appearance…and he wasn't offering one. She looked up into his green eyes, which softened slightly as he stared down at her, and waited for an explanation.

"I went to visit my father's grave," he said at last.

"Oh." Her shoulders relaxed. Of course. He was still grieving. He must have stayed at the small, fenced plot too long, and then not had time to remedy his appearance. Now that she examined Sam's face more closely, she saw red-rimmed eyes, a clenched jaw. Yes, he was definitely still grieving. It must be awful to know his father hadn't lived to see his only son marry, hadn't lived to know his grandchildren.

The thought of producing grandchildren brought a rosy glow to Callen's cheeks. She had thought a lot about what it would be like to lie with Sam, to grow large with his child, to hold a baby in her arms and have Sam smile at her, as they admired their child together.

Callen reminded herself of everything she had learned about Sam over the past three months. He was kind. He was considerate. He was charming. He was even handsome in a rugged sort of way. And his eyes made her feel cherished and loved. Or at least they had. Perhaps it was the memory of his father, the grief and the sadness, that had stolen the warmth from his eyes and made him look so harsh and hard when she had first seen him today.

She loved Sam for who he was, not for the outer trappings of the man, not for his wealth—or lack of it—but for the way he made her feel. She squeezed Sam's hands, raised her eyes to meet his and offered him a tremulous smile. "Come on, Sam. The judge is waiting."

"Your family?"

She swallowed over the lump in her throat. "They're not coming."

"Then it's just us?"

Callen nodded. Sam's lips pressed flat and his eyes narrowed. For an instant she wanted to flee, to save herself from Sam, from the possibility of a failed marriage. But it would be devastating to break a *third* engagement. She wouldn't be able to look her father in the eye. It was too late to back out now.

Callen took comfort in the thought that she knew Sam better than her father did. Sam would never hurt her. And if he did, her father would never hear of it from her. She would do whatever was necessary to make the marriage a good one. As one of the Three Whitelaw Brats, and with a lifetime of outmaneuvering and outsmarting two older brothers to her credit, she had developed the ability to rescue herself from the toughest situations. She loved Sam. Somehow, this was all going to work out.

She looked up at Sam, her heart in her eyes. There was a flash of some strong emotion on his face before he kissed her with a combination of tenderness and fierceness that left her breathless. The thought came to her, powerful and overwhelming. *I want to spend my life with this man.*

"Come on," Sam grated in a husky voice. "Let's go."

Sam felt like sobbing with relief—and disgust. He had done what he could to keep Callen Whitelaw from walking into disaster, but she hadn't backed away in time to save either of them. He led her toward the judge's chambers. It was time to take the next step on his trail of vengeance.

His eyes were red-rimmed because he hadn't slept. His conscience had smote him the day before the wedding, demanding that he free Callen from the devil's bargain he was about to make with her. He had tried desperately to think of a way to take his vengeance on Garth Whitelaw directly, without involving his daughter. But he couldn't think of anything that was as likely to cause Garth the same pain he endured himself as stealing someone he loved away from him.

In endeavoring to free Callen from the morass into which he had drawn her, Sam made a stunning discovery. He wanted her. Somehow during the course of winning her admiration, he had come to admire her, as well. She had a wicked sense of humor, a smile that flashed often enough to lift even his leadened heart, skin softer than silk, and lips as sweet as anything he had ever tasted. His groin tightened at the mere thought of bedding her. He suspected his desire for her had contributed to his inability to come up with another route of vengeance.

By the same token, because he had allowed Callen to get under his skin, it was going to be difficult to hurt her, as he must if he was going to achieve his goal of hurting her father. In the early hours of the morning, wretchedly alone, with the grief of his father's death making his stomach spin and his chest ache, he had come up with the idea of presenting himself to Callen in such a state of disarray that she would be the one to back away from him. He couldn't push her away; she was going to have to leave him of her own accord.

It hadn't worked.

Callen's family had sheltered her from the harsher facts of life, and with the confidence of the innocent, she had simply looked past the facade he had erected to shove her away and embraced the man she found beyond it. He sighed inwardly, damning her for making him want her even more, damning himself for being bastard enough to go through with his plan.

They had reached the door to the judge's chamber when Callen's eldest brother showed up. Sam eyed Zach warily, aware of the animosity on the other man's face.

Callen appeared delighted by Zach's arrival. "Zach! You came!" She let go of Sam's hand and flung herself into her brother's open arms.

Sam met Zach's narrowed eyes over Callen's head and knew the other man would do whatever he could to stop the wedding. Sam welcomed the coming fight with relish. He had wanted—needed—to hit out at the injustice of his father's death. With Garth unavailable, Zach Whitelaw made a very satisfying target.

"I'm so glad you changed your mind and decided to come," Callen said with breathless excitement. "I would have gone through with the wedding even if no one from the family came, but I'm so glad to have someone to stand beside me."

"I'm not here to support you," Zach said in a hard voice.

Callen stepped back, aware suddenly of the hostility that bristled between her tall, intimidating brother and the lean, dangerous man who would soon be her husband. Her heart sank. There was no way the two of them were going to be reconciled in the few minutes she had before the wedding. If it came to a choice, Callen knew she would go with Sam. That would surely make Zach even angrier.

Callen stared up at her brother. "Why did you come, Zach?"

Zach's eyes were on Sam. "To tell the sonofabitch you're getting set to marry that if he lays one hand on you, if he hurts you in any way, he'll have to answer to me."

Callen heard Sam's hiss as he took an outraged breath, felt his body stiffen, saw his stance widen for battle. She put herself between the two men, laying one hand on Zach's chest and the other on Sam's to keep them from coming to blows. "Please," she said. "Don't fight."

When she turned to Zach, she found no sympathy in his dark eyes, only scorn and anger.

"You're a fool to be marrying beneath yourself like this," Zach raged. "Take a good look at him, Callen. He's a disgrace."

When Callen didn't immediately turn back to Sam, her brother put a strong hand on her chin and forced her face around toward her bridegroom. Callen shook herself free as she heard Sam's growl of challenge.

"Let her go!"

"She's my sister. I'll do as I please."

"She belongs to me now," Sam retorted. "You damn well better leave her alone."

"The hell I will!"

"Stop it! Both of you!" Callen cried, shoving against two hard, heaving chests with the flat of her hands.

Zach continued his scorching castigation of her bridegroom without even taking a breath. His dark eyes burned as he held her gaze. "Think about who you're going to marry," he said ruthlessly. "Sam Longstreet barely made it through high school. He's got no dreams, no goals. Hell, all he wants is your money! He'll embarrass you in front of company because he looks like hell warmed over most of the time. Like now," he said, nodding with his chin toward Sam. "Is that the way a bridegroom ought to dress for his wedding?"

Callen looked, then lowered her eyes. She had been willing to disregard Sam's appearance, to excuse it. That was difficult with Zach standing beside her pointing out Sam's faults. She felt a flush of embarrassment, then a burning resentment toward her brother and, to a lesser extent, toward Sam for putting her in the position of having to defend something she had condemned herself.

"What Sam's wearing doesn't matter to me," she said stubbornly.

Zach grabbed her by the shoulders and turned her so she was facing him again. Her hand dropped away from Sam's chest, but she was aware of him standing behind her, of the leashed tension that sizzled and threatened violence.

Then Zach was speaking, his face so close she could see the temper smoldering in his dark eyes. "The man doesn't have any friends. You'll be all alone once you're living with him at the Double L," he warned. "Don't marry him, Callen. Put an end to this nonsense."

"I love him," Callen said in a quiet voice.

Zach pulled her into a protective embrace, almost crushing her with his strength. "God, Callen, what can I do to make you change your mind?"

"Nothing. I'm going to marry Sam, with or without your approval…or Daddy's blessing."

Zach's next words were spoken low in her ear so there was no possibility of Sam overhearing. "When you decide to leave him, when you recognize your mistake, you'll be welcome at my place."

He levered her away and into Sam's waiting arms. "Don't forget what I said, Longstreet. You harm one hair on her head, and I'll come after you." Then he stalked past Sam and out the courthouse door.

Callen stood there with Sam's arms wrapped comfortingly around her, hard-pressed to hold back the tears that threatened. The third time around she certainly hadn't planned on a lavish wedding. But she would have liked some of her family to be there, and she would have liked her groom to be a little better dressed.

She raised her blurred gaze to Sam's face and saw a flash of sympathy in his green eyes that disappeared so quickly she wasn't sure it had been there in the first place.

"Do you still want to marry me?" Sam asked in a taunting voice. "Or has your brother talked you out of it?"

Sam was giving her one last chance to back out, Callen realized. She searched his eyes for any sign of the affection he had shown her during their courtship. It seemed strangely absent. She felt frightened. What if her family was right, and she was wrong? She couldn't afford to make another mistake. But neither could she face the humiliation of crawling back home with her tail between her legs.

Stubborn pride kept Callen standing at Sam's side. She wasn't going to let her family talk her out of something she knew was right. Her relationship with Sam over the past three months had revealed the source of a vague discontent she had felt for years. She was thirty-two years old. She had yearned for someone to love, someone to love her. She wanted children, several of them, and she wasn't getting any younger. And she needed a home of her own, a place where she belonged. Sam had promised to fulfill those needs.

Furthermore, Sam had been a neighbor for years. If he had really been a fortune hunter, wouldn't he have come courting a lot sooner? He couldn't possibly have the sinister motives for marriage that her father and brother had suggested he did.

"Let's go on in." Sam put a hand to the small of her back and ushered her inside the judge's chambers. She wasn't acquainted with the judge, nor with the secretary and bailiff he offered as witnesses.

Callen heard nothing the judge said as he began the words of the ceremony. She was too caught up in remembering her family's accusations against Sam and her own reservations about what she was doing.

"For richer or poorer, in sickness and in health…"

He's a fortune hunter! He's only after your money!

Callen closed her eyes as a wave of nausea rolled over her. It was terrifying to defy her father, terrifying to ignore the warning signs that were all around her and follow her heart.

I love him.

That was the response that had silenced her father. That was the response that had silenced Zach. But was her love enough?

"Do you have a ring?" the judge asked.

Sam added a simple band of white gold to the diamond

engagement ring he had given her that had belonged to his mother.

Then it was her turn. She knew how much a rancher worked with his hands. A ring that wasn't simple would be a nuisance and likely wouldn't be worn. So she had bought him a plain gold band. She saw the flicker of surprise in his eyes and then what looked like pleasure as she slipped it on his finger.

The ceremony was over too quickly. The judge smiled at them and said, "You may kiss the bride."

Callen was ready for a quick peck on the lips. But Sam pulled her slowly toward him until their bodies were aligned and then lowered his mouth to claim hers. The kiss was thorough, and before he was done they were both breathing hard.

When she turned an eye back to the judge, his grin had broadened. He reached out to shake Sam's hand. "It's always a pleasure to see two people in love."

Callen noticed the smile on Sam's lips, but it never reached his eyes. Was it the mention of the word *love* that bothered him? Sam had never said the words to her, but he had shown her in a dozen different ways that he cherished her. Besides, she thought with a rueful smile, this was no time to be having second thoughts. The deed was done. She was Mrs. Sam Longstreet.

Sam was no longer smiling by the time they reached the steps outside the courthouse door. "Do you want to drive to the house together, or follow me in your car?"

"Do you have a preference?" She wanted him to say that he couldn't bear for her to be separated from him for a moment. She wanted to be romanced on her wedding day. Sam's response was too practical for her peace of mind.

"We'd only have to make another trip back for your car," he said. "Go ahead and follow me to the house." He turned his back on her and headed for his pickup, leaving her standing alone on the courthouse steps.

Callen noticed he hadn't called it a home.

She tried not to feel abandoned, tried to put the best possible face on the situation. But this wasn't what she had imagined. What had happened to the romantic swain who had swept her off her feet?

Callen pursed her lips thoughtfully. If she didn't stop seeing trouble everywhere, she was going to drive herself crazy. Things would work out. She only had to remember that she loved Sam. And he loved her, whether he said the words or not. She was married to Sam, for better or worse.

Unfortunately, when Sam carried her over the threshold of the Double L ranch house, she saw how bad *worse* could be.

Her father's description of Sam's place as a "ramshackle ranch" was very much on the mark, Callen realized. She had known the wood frame structure with its tin roof was old. But she wasn't prepared for what she found inside when Sam set her back on her feet after carrying her over the threshold.

"Well? What do you think?"

Callen searched for something nice to say. "It's...clean." Perhaps neat was a better word than clean. She eyed the dust that had gathered on every surface, the cobwebs in the corners. What furniture the house contained—and it was decorated Spartanly—was old and rat-bitten. There were no antiques here that had been lovingly polished to a high sheen like there were at Hawk's Way. Just secondhand junk.

No wonder Sam hadn't wanted to bring her into the house. There was nothing here that could be admired. Until this moment, Callen hadn't realized how luxurious her life-style at Hawk's Way had been, or how spoiled she had been by the comforts she had always taken for granted.

The condition of the furniture, of the house itself, suggested things had been going downhill at the Double L for far longer than the three months since E.J. had died. The place reeked of ongoing impoverishment.

Her father's words echoed in her head. *He's only interested in you for your money.* She shoved them back out again.

"It needs a little work," she said with a hard-won smile.

"But I'm more than willing to supply the elbow grease." She walked around the combination parlor and office excitedly pointing out the improvements she would make.

"First thing is to buy you a new desk. Then, a sofa placed just so in front of the fireplace, a couple of leather chairs—something comfortable with an ottoman for you—a few tables, lamps, some art for the walls, a carpet on the floor, and I guarantee you won't recognize the place."

"All those things cost money," Sam said.

Her smile broadened. "I'm rich. I can afford it."

He shook his head.

Callen felt a well of joy. *He didn't want her money!* Her father was wrong. She was moving toward Sam when his next words stopped her.

"We'll need that money to make back payments on the mortgage and to pay debts I've accumulated. I doubt there'll be much left for frivolities like furniture and rugs."

"What?" Callen was staring at Sam as though she had never seen him before. "I have plenty of money—"

He cut her off with a harsh oath. "It's not enough. I have a fairly good idea of the extent of your fortune. I'm telling you, it'll be eaten up by the cost of keeping possession of the Double L."

"Then we'll sell this place and—"

"No, Callen. This is my home—your home now. We're staying come hail or high water." In response to the shocked look on her face, he said, "Surely your father mentioned I was in financial trouble." His mouth twisted cynically. "You must have known how bad things are. The condition of the outbuildings, the fences that needed mending, the rundown condition of the house. You couldn't have been blind to all of it."

"I...wasn't...exactly." Only she had worn blinders, refusing to see reality, lost in a fog of euphoria: a fool in love. In one respect—Sam's need for her money—her father had been absolutely right. But she wasn't going to cry craven and run.

She loved Sam. And if he needed her money, he was welcome to it.

Callen lifted her chin. "Whatever money you need, you're welcome to spend. Use it how you think best."

Sam's eyes narrowed. He was astonished at Callen's generous offer. He had expected trouble when he told her he wanted to invest her fortune in the Double L. With the marriage still unconsummated, it was a sure way of goading her to run, to save herself from the fate he had planned for her. But her brown eyes had flared with a militant light and that stubborn chin of hers had bucked up. And she had offered him everything she had.

He refused to feel guilt or remorse, even though the pull of both made the skin stretch taut across his cheekbones. She had made a free choice to be his wife. She had stayed when she saw how rough things were going to be. Well, so be it. He had committed himself. It was time to get on with his revenge.

Chapter 3

"Come here, Callen."

Callen saw the fierce desire in Sam's eyes and felt an answering desire rise within her. Now that the moment was at hand, however, she was uncertain what to do. "It's broad daylight," she said with a shy smile.

"I want to see you when I make love to you for the first time," Sam replied.

A rush of pleasure and embarrassment painted Callen's cheeks a vivid rose. "There's not much to see," she murmured. Her breasts weren't anything to shout about, and while she had a narrow waist and a decent pair of legs, she was closer to cute than pretty, closer to pretty than beautiful. It would have been easier to do this the first time in the dark.

"Callen."

The single word was a command that compelled her to obey. She took the several steps that brought her near enough for Sam to reach out and pull her close. His arms folded around her possessively.

Callen felt safe, secure, treasured. Those weren't the feelings she had expected and, as it turned out, weren't the feelings she experienced moments later when Sam's mouth came down to capture hers.

Hungry. Unbridled. Ruthless. Sam demanded total surrender, and Callen was helpless to resist. The blood raced in her veins, sending heat and shuddering sensation throughout her body. Now Callen understood why Sam had kept his desire under control in the past. She was overwhelmed by feelings she had never imagined. His effect on her was devastating.

"Sam," she gasped. She clung to him, breathless and almost dizzy. She was shivering and couldn't seem to stop.

"Callen," he breathed in her ear. It was a plea. It was a promise.

He lifted her into his arms and carried her into his bedroom. It was darker there because heavy curtains covered the windows. She clung to Sam's shoulders as he leaned over and pulled down the covers on the bed, barely toeing off her shoes before he laid her down. She noticed the bed was made with fresh white sheets that had been tucked in with almost military precision. He had known he would bring her here. He had cared what she would think—about this, at least.

The sheets were cool, or maybe it was simply that she was so warm in contrast. He stood above her, his green eyes lit with a fierce, primitive light.

"Take off your clothes," he said.

Callen was caught unawares. She had expected him to do that for her, had anticipated it, in fact. He stood above her, arms akimbo, legs widespread, with that devouring look on his face, and waited.

She sat up and turned her back to him before lifting her hair out of the way. "Can you get these few buttons for me?" It seemed like an eternity before she felt the brush of his hands against her nape. She felt the sweep of air as her back was exposed and a moment later the touch of his mouth against her skin. A shiver of delight ran down her spine.

When he was nearly finished, Sam slid onto the bed behind

her. His hands slipped around to cup her breasts. She felt him exhale slowly as his hands shaped and molded the small mounds.

"You feel so good."

The sound of his voice rasped in her ear, sending another shiver through her. Her hands dropped to rest on his as she leaned her head back against his shoulder. "I've dreamed about this so often...."

"So have I," he confessed. "You feel so good, so right in my hands."

"There's not much there," she said with a wry smile.

"Enough. Plenty," he said as he turned her in his arms.

She gasped as his mouth latched onto one breast through the lace. She felt the nip of his teeth and laughed breathlessly. "Maybe I ought to finish taking this off."

He lifted his head and released her. "All right. Go ahead."

She was suddenly shy again. The unbuttoned dress slid off her shoulders, revealing the white silk camisole she wore. She rose on her knees and shoved the dress and a half-slip down, then sat and pulled them off over her bare legs. She hadn't worn nylons in deference to the June heat, so she was left in nothing but her silk tap pants and camisole.

She started to lower the straps of her camisole, but Sam reached out a hand to stop her. She followed his eyes downward and saw that her nipples had peaked beneath the silk. There was a damp spot near her right breast where his mouth had been. He lowered his head and suckled her through the cloth.

Callen groaned. She had never felt anything so exquisite. Her hands slid into Sam's hair, which was thick and silky to the touch, while her head arched backward in ecstasy.

Sam took his time removing the rest of her clothing. It was difficult for Callen to lie still under his sharp gaze once he had her bare.

"You're beautiful, Callen."

In that moment she believed she was beautiful, despite her

too small breasts and her straight black hair that refused to hold a curl and the spattering of freckles across her nose.

"I want to see you," she said, reaching up for the first of the buttons on his shirt. She had three unbuttoned when his patience deserted him. Callen laughed as Sam tore off his shirt, yanked off his boots and socks and reached for his belt buckle. He was naked moments later, and the laugh caught in her throat.

Whatever faults Sam might have had, his body wasn't one of them. Callen let her eyes roam from broad shoulders and muscled arms, down a chest that was furred with dark hair, past a washboard belly, to the curls that surrounded his arousal. His legs were long, his thighs sinewy and taut.

"You're the one who's beautiful," she managed to say.

He smiled.

Oh, what a wonderful smile it was! His white teeth flashed, and his eyes crinkled at the corners. She felt warm all over. Then came the laugh, up from his belly, past his chest and out of his mouth, a full, rich, happy sound.

She grinned. "What's so funny?"

"You thinking I'm beautiful."

"But you are," she insisted.

He snorted, a male sound of dismissal. "You're the special one, Callen." He sat on the bed beside her and let his callused fingertips stroke across her belly. "I can't believe you're mine."

Callen felt revered, cherished. She had done the right thing marrying Sam. She hadn't made a mistake. Sam couldn't touch her like this, hold her in his arms, stroke her mouth with his tongue in just that way if he didn't care for her.

He took his time loving her. His eyes constantly roamed her body, following where he touched. When he joined their bodies, making them one, he watched that, too. She had never been so aware of herself as a woman, never been so aware of the aching need to give everything she had to another human being.

Callen heard Sam's groan of agony and pleasure in the moment he thrust inside her, felt her muscles contract to hold him there. His hands lifted her buttocks as he made sweet, sweet love to her. She touched him everywhere she could reach, returning the caresses he had so freely given her. In her ultimate joy, she grasped his hair and pulled his mouth down to join hers as they cried out in exultation.

Afterward, she lay sated in his arms, breathless, her chest heaving. Their bodies were sweat-slick in the heat, and she realized suddenly that the house wasn't air-conditioned, that it was the breeze flowing from behind the curtains through the open windows that cooled their bodies. No wonder the curtains had been drawn, she thought. It kept out the hot sun. It was one more indication of the *worse* to go with the *better* in this marriage.

Right at this moment, Callen didn't have any complaints. She stretched lazily and felt Sam's hand slide down her thigh. It felt good, warm and rough against her skin. Sam was, quite simply, an incredible lover. She shouldn't have been surprised, but she was. She hadn't thought of him as the sort of man who dated a lot. So where had he learned to be so knowledgeable of a woman's needs in bed?

The answer to that question was easy, once Callen thought about it, though thinking at all was difficult with Sam's hand caressing her. A man as kind and considerate as Sam Longstreet would naturally be a good lover, because he would always be concerned about the other person's pleasure. She decided he deserved some thanks for his thoughtfulness. So she slid her hand along his naked flank, returning the caresses he bestowed upon her. She could feel the strength, the sinew and muscle that surrounded bone. She gave a little shove, and he rolled over onto his back.

"What's this?" he asked.

"I'm going to have my wicked way with you," Callen answered.

"By all means." His grin was far more wicked than anything she could have imagined doing to him. He lay still beneath her hands. Actually, not quite still. His body undulated beneath her onslaught, until he rolled her over beneath him and took up where she had left off.

They didn't leave the bed all day. It was full dark before either of them thought of anything except the delights to be found in the other's body. It was Sam's stomach that finally protested with a loud growl.

"I'm hungry," he admitted.

Callen snuggled closer. "Me, too."

"Who's going to get out of bed and fix supper?"

"I suppose I ought to," Callen said with a huge yawn.

"You're exhausted."

Callen heard the surprise and remorse in Sam's voice. She smiled to herself. "I hope you keep me this tired all the time," she teased.

She felt his body relax and heard his chuckle. "I might have gone a little crazy. I just never thought—"

He cut himself off and abruptly rose so that her hair, which was caught under his shoulder, got yanked hard enough to hurt. She cried out, then heard him swear as he stubbed his toe on the bedstead.

"Are you all right?" he called. Then, "Where the hell is the lamp?"

"I suspect it's where it's always been." Callen restrained a giggle as she reached out and snapped on a lamp beside the bed. She squinted her eyes until they adjusted to the light. When she could open them without pain, she saw that Sam was staring fixedly at her. She looked down and found there were small love bruises on her body where he had staked his claim. Her breasts were still flushed and rosy from their latest round of lovemaking. She quickly grappled for the sheet to cover herself.

"Don't. I…" He swallowed hard. "I like looking at you."

She forced herself to lie still. It was plain he wanted her again.

Fortunately—or unfortunately—his stomach chose that moment to growl again. He grabbed his jeans and stepped into them before heading for the kitchen in a hurry. "Stay where you are. I'll get us something to eat."

The first thing she did was jump out of bed and race for the standing oval mirror in the corner to see for herself how she looked. *Good Lord!* she thought. *That's what he finds attractive?*

Her hair was tangled beyond combing, her breasts were the same tiny size they'd always been, and she hadn't grown any taller. But a second look revealed the dreamy glow in her dark brown eyes, the heat beneath her skin that made her complexion pink and rosy, and the puffy softness of her lips where she had been thoroughly kissed. She looked like a woman who had spent most of the day making love with a man she adored.

She heard Sam returning, and scurried back to bed. Well, why not? If the man wanted to wait on her, who was she to complain? She was sitting up in bed when he entered the room, but she had chickened out and pulled the sheet up under her arms. There was such a thing as modesty, after all. She hadn't become a total wanton in one day. Had she? One glance at Sam's face, and she was afraid she had. She let the sheet fall and heard him gasp. He set the tray of soup and sandwiches on a dry sink across the room and came to her without another word.

The supper he had prepared sat forgotten.

When Sam woke, he felt disoriented. It took him a moment to realize the heat he felt came from another body snuggled up close. He eased himself away from Callen—from his wife—and sat up on the edge of the bed letting his eyes become accustomed to the dark. He wondered what time it was and sought out the alarm he kept next to his bed. The digital clock told him it was barely 10:00 p.m. It seemed much later.

He felt exhausted, but at the same time more rested than he had at any time since his father's death. He had reason to feel relaxed. His plan for vengeance had well and truly begun. He had taken the first steps to attach his wife's affections. Before he could take Callen away from her father, he had to be sure that if she was forced to choose, she would choose him. He had to be sure she was well and truly in love.

So he had made love to her as though she were the most precious of women. He had given her all of himself—or almost all. He hadn't given her his heart. He didn't love her. That would be a disaster and ruin his carefully laid plans. But he had created the illusion of love to the best of his ability.

It was only after that first incredibly powerful climax that he had realized the danger to himself. Yet he hadn't been able to deny himself the opportunity of making love to her again. She was all satiny softness and fiery desire. He hadn't been able to resist coming back for more. And more. He hadn't known he could want a woman like he wanted Callen. He was going to have to be careful. He had to remember at all times that his real purpose in marrying her was to cause her father pain.

Callen stretched and her foot reached out and stroked his thigh. "Come back to bed, Sam," she murmured.

He ought to get up and leave her now. He could feel the loose ropes binding him to her, even as he sought to bind her to himself. But he was the one in control. He could escape the noose whenever he chose, or use whatever means were necessary to cut himself free when the time came. He surrendered to the call and joined Callen in bed.

The next time he woke, it was dawn. Lately, because he couldn't sleep at night, he had dropped into bed exhausted at sunrise. But he had a mission this morning that had him out of bed the instant he realized what time it was. He had to make it to town, to the Stanton Hotel Café, where all the ranchers gathered early to drink coffee and listen to the stock and grain prices on the radio and compare notes before beginning the day. Garth Whitelaw would be there. And Sam had a few things to say to his new father-in-law.

The hotel had been built in the 1880s, and it still featured several of the original Victorian sofas in the lobby along with a Turkish carpet and some silvered mirrors in elaborate mahogany frames. The hotel café dated from the 1950s. It had a long service bar with stools that had red plastic seats and chrome backs. Someone had added trophy deer antlers on the walls, along with macramé wall hangings from the 1970s and a few pictures of the hotel when it had been in its prime.

Sam saw four ranchers at the far end of the bar. They sat in the same seats every morning. Garth Whitelaw was sitting on the stool closest to him, near the center of the bar. The stool next to Garth was empty, and Sam slid onto it.

He stared straight ahead, looking into the mirror behind the bar. He could see the faces of everyone reflected there. Sam noticed that he looked more than a little the worse for wear. He was wearing a hat that hid most of his hair, but it obviously needed a cut. He hadn't shaved and, to his chagrin, there was a love bruise under his right ear that Garth Whitelaw couldn't miss. Sam braced his elbows on the bar and ordered himself a cup of coffee from the waitress and proprietor of the café, Ida Mae Cooper.

The conversation at the bar had stopped. He let his eyes slide over three of the ranchers, daring any one of them to say anything. They each found something of interest to occupy themselves and avoided meeting his glance. When his green eyes met Garth's stony gray ones, he let his contempt show on his face.

"Offering some more good advice this morning?" Sam taunted. "You men might want to take what Garth Whitelaw says with a grain of salt. He tends to change the truth to fit his purpose."

There was an ominous silence as the men at the bar absorbed the insult.

Garth stiffened. He set down his cup of coffee and turned to Sam. "Are you calling me a liar?"

"If the shoe fits…"

Ida Mae sloshed some coffee into Garth's cup. "Don't want no fightin' in here, boys." Nobody could remember when Ida Mae hadn't been running the coffee shop. She had grown up on a ranch in the area, so she knew how to handle a rowdy crowd. Not that things got rowdy much these days. Only, Ida Mae could see that Sam had coming looking for trouble, and she knew for a fact that Garth was more than willing to give it to him.

"Why aren't you home with your wife?" Garth demanded.

A sneer cut across Sam's face. "I left her asleep in bed. She was plumb wore out."

"That's no way to talk about my daughter," Garth warned. "Or your wife, for that matter."

Sam was too intent on hurting Garth to care that he was acting in a manner that was totally alien to him. He would have killed any other man who spoke such a slur against his wife. But Callen wasn't just his wife, she was also Garth Whitelaw's daughter. She was part and parcel of his revenge. He was here to hurt Garth Whitelaw, not to protect his wife's name.

"I just thought you'd like to know I'll be going to the bank today to take care of my back mortgage payments," he said.

Garth's eyes narrowed.

"Can you believe it? Callen offered me her fortune," Sam said with a snide grin intended to raise the hair on Garth's neck.

"Why, you—" Garth started to rise, but was stopped by Sam's wagging finger.

"Uh-uh," Sam cautioned. "Ida Mae wouldn't like it if you messed up her place." He leaned closer and said in a voice not intended to be heard by the other men, "The Double L is lost to you, Whitelaw. Soon, your daughter will be, too."

"What the hell do you mean by that?" Garth shot back.

"Just remember what I said, Whitelaw." He rose, and Garth reached out to grab his arm. He yanked it free. "Stay away from me and my wife, do you hear?"

"I'll see my daughter—"

"She's not your daughter anymore," Sam said. "She's *my* wife. Stay away from the Double L, and leave Callen alone."

"If this is about E.J.—"

"You're damn straight it's about E.J.," Sam said, his face contorted in fury. "I want you to know what it feels like to lose someone you love and know they're gone forever."

"What the hell is wrong with you?" Garth demanded. "I had nothing to do with E.J.'s death."

"Nothing anyone can prove," Sam agreed. "But I know the truth. And so do you."

Garth shook his head in frustration and disbelief. "You're wrong, Sam."

"Just don't plan on seeing Callen again," Sam said baldly.

"I'll see my daughter when and where I choose."

"Not if I say no. I have some influence with my wife. She won't be working for you anymore, just so we have that straight."

Garth heaved a frustrated sigh. "I'm telling you again, I'm not responsible for what happened to E.J." He paused before adding sardonically, "And my daughter, as you will soon discover, is a woman with a mind of her own."

Sam already had some inkling of that, but he was determined to keep Callen so busy she wouldn't have time to miss her job—or see her father, even if she wanted to. "Just stay away from her," Sam repeated. "She's dead to you."

Sam whirled on his booted heel and stalked out of the café. When he reached the covered wooden porch outside the Stanton Hotel, he took a deep breath and let it out. He was not normally a vindictive man, and the outpouring of rage he had felt toward Garth Whitelaw had left him feeling drained. It was two hours before the bank opened, and he had just walked out of the best place in town for breakfast.

He thought of going home, and an image rose before him of Callen lying tangled in the sheets on his bed. Hell, he'd just go on home and get back in bed with her. There was plenty of time to come back into town later and pay the banker. He had accomplished what he'd set out to do. There was no reason why he couldn't go home and enjoy his wife...while she still was his wife.

Chapter 4

The first time Callen's mother called to invite the newlyweds to dinner, Callen accepted on the spot. She had been spending all her time fixing up the house, waiting to see if her father would relent and ask her to come back to work at Hawk's Way. So far, he hadn't budged an inch.

"Of course, we'll come, Mom," she said. "What time? We'll be there. Sam? Oh, I'm sure he'll be free. Don't worry, Mom. We're both looking forward to it." She had laughed at the cautious note in her mother's voice. Maybe her wedding hadn't been auspicious, but her marriage was everything she had dreamed it could be.

She was astonished, therefore, when Sam informed her he had made plans to take her out that evening.

"I was hoping to surprise you." He had a sort of sheepish look on his face that melted her heart.

"I wouldn't spoil your plans for the world," Callen said. After all, she didn't want to discourage any romantic notions Sam might have in the future. "I guess I'm not used to being married," she said, wrinkling her nose. "I'll have to get used to asking first before I make arrangements that include both of us."

Callen had called her mother with their regrets. The next time her mother called, about two weeks later, Callen said, "I'll have to check with Sam. Can I call you back later tonight?"

She had brought up the subject at dinner. Sam paused only hesitantly before he said, "Sunday dinner? I don't know why not. Sure, tell them we'll come."

Callen gave him a big kiss. "Thanks, Sam. It'll make my mom so happy. And I know you'll like my dad, once you get to know him."

Only, when Sunday came, Sam had an emergency he had to take care of that precluded going to Sunday dinner at Hawk's Way with Callen. Some fence was down along the south pasture, and his prize bull had wandered onto Abel Johnson's property. Abel didn't mind, but Sam hated giving away free stud service on his bull.

"I have to get him back right away," Sam said apologetically. "We'll have to have dinner with your folks another time."

Callen called and apologized to her mother. They set another tentative date for a week later. When the following Sunday came, Sam was sick with the flu. He looked awful, and Callen hadn't the heart to make him keep the dinner engagement with her parents.

When they had been married for three months, it came as a shock to Callen when she realized that she and Sam had not yet darkened the portals of Hawk's Way. In fact, she and her parents hadn't even crossed paths. It was easy to excuse the omission. She and Sam had both been incredibly busy.

Her time had been spent turning Sam's home—now her home, as well—into a charming, cheerful place by using lots of hard work and secondhand everything. She had managed to recover the couch with an Indian print in warm Western colors and was amazed at what a little polish had done to the furniture. She had bought paintings over the years, mostly by southwestern artists, which she had hung on the walls.

She discovered gallons of a pale yellow paint in the barn, which Sam confessed he had bought more than a year ago for the house. She took it to the hardware store and had it shaken up, and began painting the outside of the house. To her surprise, when Sam realized what she was doing, he stopped his repairs long enough to share the job with her. When they were done, she had stood arm-in-arm with Sam and admired the house.

"It looks so different!" she exclaimed. "It has a sort of rustic charm—"

"You mean, it doesn't look like a dump anymore," Sam interrupted sarcastically.

"You're putting words in my mouth," Callen protested. "I only meant that now I can see the care that went into building this place. Someone meant this house to survive for generations."

"It has. And it will," Sam said in a determined voice. He was silent for a moment before he said, "Thanks, Callen. I needed to see it like this. Like it can be."

He had gone back to his work mending the barbed-wire fence. She had refocused her attentions on the interior of the house. She replaced the heavy curtains in the master bedroom with vertical blinds from a discount store so she could still block out the sun during the hottest part of the day but enjoy the sunlight in the early morning and late evening. And she had pulled up the worn linoleum in the kitchen and found a beautiful hardwood floor, which she had refinished.

She spoke often to her mother on the phone, but it had become almost a reflex to refuse her invitations. There never seemed to be time. Callen wasn't sure how much of her reluctance to accept her mother's invitations lately was a result of being busy and how much was the result of her growing awareness that Sam didn't want to have dinner with her parents.

She wasn't sure exactly when she had realized there was a problem, but the signs were blatantly evident when she finally did. Sam reacted oddly to the mere mention of her father's name. Quite simply, his lips went flat and his eyes narrowed and a muscled jerked in his jaw. She could have gone alone to have dinner with her parents, but she didn't want them to think she and Sam weren't getting along. Because they were.

In fact, Callen had never been so happy. Sam was a dedicated and inventive lover, and he seemed to appreciate her efforts in the house. He was easy to talk to, and even though he seemed exhausted at the end of each day, he was never too tired to spend time with her. It was an ideal marriage. Except that Sam didn't seem to want anything to do with her family.

And there was something else. She couldn't quite put her finger on what it was, except she had noticed a certain reticence in Sam whenever she tried to make plans for the future, plans that included children. He said he had enough to worry about just solving day-to-day problems. He couldn't think about a family right now. And he was right. Still, it would have been nice to dream with him.

As much as it pained her to admit it, maybe Zach had been right about Sam lacking dreams and goals. For some reason Sam didn't want to think about the future. She didn't doubt that he loved her, even though he had never said the words. But she had become more and more certain over the past three months that he was hiding something from her. She was afraid to ask him about it, afraid to burst the bubble of happiness that surrounded her marriage.

Finally, she couldn't help herself. One night after supper, she blurted, "What's wrong, Sam? Why don't you want to have dinner with my family?"

He hesitated so long that she thought he wasn't going to answer her. When he did respond, he said merely, "You know how busy the past few months have been for both of us."

But she wasn't satisfied with that answer. "Did my father

say something to you…I mean, before the wedding?'' Callen held her breath. She couldn't believe her father would have had the nerve to approach Sam and offer him money to call off the wedding, as he had done with her two previous fiancés. But she could think of no other reason for Sam to dislike her father so vehemently. If anything, Callen would have expected Sam to despise Zach. After all, Zach was the one who had confronted Sam at their wedding. But Sam's anger didn't seem to be aimed in that direction.

The longer Sam hesitated, the more frightened she became that her father had offered him money. Suddenly she didn't want to know. ''Forget I asked,'' she said, rising abruptly and heading for the kitchen sink with a stack of dishes.

Sam followed her and wrapped his arms around her from behind. He nuzzled her nape as he said, ''What brought all this on?''

She sighed. ''You keep avoiding any contact with my parents. I wondered why.''

''It's very simple, Callen,'' he said in a quiet voice. ''I want you all to myself.''

She was afraid to believe him because it sounded so romantic and made her fears seem ridiculous. ''That's all?'' she asked. ''Nothing else? What about my father? Do you—''

''Let's not talk about your father. Right now, I just want to make love to my wife.''

He swept her into his arms, making her laugh at his impulsiveness. A moment later his mouth caught hers in a searing kiss, and then it was too late for thinking. She decided to let the future take care of itself. She was too busy loving Sam to worry about it.

Later, lying in bed beside his sleeping wife, Sam wondered how much longer he could manage to keep Callen separated from her father. It had been an exhausting exercise to keep an eye on Garth's movements and make sure Callen was away from the house whenever he visited. He had come twice to the Double L. Both times Sam had taken pleasure in sending him away without seeing his daughter.

"Where's Callen?" Garth had demanded the second time.

"In town shopping."

"I don't believe you."

Sam had made an open gesture with his hand, inviting Garth inside. To his surprise, the older man hadn't taken him at his word, shoved open the kitchen door and stalked inside.

"Callen? Are you here?" His call remained unanswered.

Sam could see Garth was surprised by the look of the place. Garth had visited E.J. often enough to know how they had lived. So he had to be aware of all the changes Callen had made. Even though Sam wasn't personally responsible, he felt proud of what Callen had accomplished. He had been amazed himself at the changes his wife had wrought. Quite simply, she had made his house a home.

It wasn't just the southwestern landscapes on the wall, or the lack of dust and cobwebs, or the shine on the furniture. It was the way she had rearranged the furniture so they could sit in front of the fire together. The way she made him comfortable in a chair before dropping to the floor in front of him and crossing her arms on his knees and resting her chin there while she talked animatedly about her day. The way fresh flowers found their way inside, along with sunlight and the evening zephyrs.

He wondered what Garth thought of all the changes. But he didn't ask. Instead, he said, "I told you she wasn't here."

"You can't keep her away from me indefinitely," Garth replied. "If this continues much longer, I'll just tell her what you're doing."

"Then I'd have to tell her why I don't want to see you. How you tried to bribe me out of marrying her." Sam relished the pinched look on Garth's face. He had the man where he wanted him. "Go away, old man. Your daughter is lost to you. Just like my father is lost to me. I hope you suffer, the way I've suffered."

Garth's face had whitened, the grooves around his mouth had deepened. But he hadn't argued, hadn't tried to defend himself again. He had simply left.

When Sam had found himself confronted by Callen this evening, he had considered telling her about the offer of money her father had made to him. That surely would have worked to alienate the two of them. But he had decided it wasn't necessary to hurt her that way. She would be hurt enough when she learned the real reason why he had married her.

Sam slipped an arm around Callen's waist and spooned her into his groin. He felt contented. Almost happy. Except that he knew all this was temporary. So there was a bittersweet quality to his life that made his chest ache and his throat swell. He wondered how long all the changes Callen had wrought in his life would last.

His personal life had undergone as many changes as his house over the three months of his marriage. Faced by Callen's boundless energy, Sam had found himself roused from a lethargy he hadn't realized had hold of him. At least he was sleeping at night, which made it easier to face a dawn that came too early, in his opinion. Sam hadn't even realized how lonely his life had been, until Callen filled his evenings with talk of her plans for the future.

He has no dreams, no goals.

Zach's words had come back to haunt Sam often in the first months of his marriage, and he had been forced to acknowledge the truth of them. There had been a time, long ago, when he had dreamed big dreams. He had imagined himself escaping the loneliness of his life at the Double L by playing football for a pro team, traveling and meeting fancy women and living the high life. He had been fast on his feet and determined to succeed.

But that dream had been blown away with the cartilage in his right knee. He hadn't been a good student and going to college for the sake of an education—rather than to play foot-

ball—hadn't appealed to him. After high school he had returned to what he knew—ranching.

He was a good rancher; he understood his business. But
with a whirlwind like Callen around, Sam realized just how
slow-paced his life with E.J. had become. It wasn't a matter
of being lazy, exactly. He'd simply had no reason to work
harder. He and E.J. had always had enough for their needs,
and their needs had been simple.

All that had suddenly changed with E.J.'s death. Callen was
a big part of Sam's reawakening. He couldn't imagine himself
lingering in bed after she was up and working. But even if
he hadn't married Callen, his life had been changed forever
by E.J.'s suicide. He had been jolted out of his lethargy by
the knowledge of how near he had come to losing the Double
L. The last-minute rescue provided by Callen's fortune had
made him realize he didn't want to live so close to the edge.
If that meant working harder, then he would work harder.

Sam smiled wryly. The fact of the matter was, it had been
necessary to work harder simply to get back to where he and
E.J. had been before E.J. lost his shirt to the various swindles
he had invested in. Thanks to Garth Whitelaw. Although Sam
still had possession of the Double L, it was a long way from
being a successful enterprise. He had begun to think and plan
what he could do to make the ranch more economically sound.

He had shared his ideas with Callen at first simply because
she seemed to expect him to converse with her in the evenings
when they sat in front of the fireplace. He wasn't really good
at making small talk, so he had hesitantly revealed his idea
to start training cutting horses. He was damn near as good
with horses as Callen, and it gave the ranch another source
of income besides beef cattle.

"That's a wonderful idea!" Callen had enthused. Her eyes
had twinkled with mischief when she said, "I'll just recom-
mend *you* to my friends who want their horses trained, instead
of Daddy."

"I don't want—"

Callen had bounced up from the floor and settled herself in his lap with her arms around his neck. "I can help, can't I, Sam? I won the junior cutting horse championship when I was sixteen, just like my mom. And I've been helping Daddy work with cutting horses since I was knee-high to a grasshopper."

"I'd planned to do the work myself."

"Of course you did," she said in a soothing voice. "Only now that you've got me, why should you have to do it all alone?"

Her words had tumbled into the deep well of loneliness he lived with and filled it up a little. He reminded himself not to get too dependent on Callen, since there was at least a chance that when the showdown came, when he forced her to choose between her husband and her father, she would choose Garth. But it had felt good to pull her close, to feel the pillow of her breasts against his chest, to feel her fingers twine around the hair at his nape, to feel her lips nuzzle his throat. His hands had tightened reflexively around her.

His conscience often warned him that he was doing the devil's work, that he would regret his efforts to take revenge against Garth Whitelaw in the way he had chosen. He fought his scruples by visiting his father's grave almost daily. Each grim sojourn stoked his righteous anger and multiplied his enmity. Those malevolent feelings festered inside him, and he had to work hard to keep the darker side of himself hidden from his wife.

He had seen in Callen's eyes that she knew something was still bothering him, even though she had recently allowed herself to be assuaged with the excuse that he just wanted them to have some time alone. Sometimes he wondered what he would say to her if she probed the situation further. But she had seemed content to let the matter rest.

Until today.

It had been a bad day all around. Sam had discovered two of his steers dead from eating crazyweed. A flash flood had taken out a whole section of fence. The valves on his pickup had finally ground to a halt and needed to be replaced. Then, when he got home, he had found the kitchen torn apart and no supper ready because Callen was repapering the wall.

"What the hell do you think you're doing?" he demanded.

"It's only remnants I found on sale at the hardware store," she said, apparently assuming the source of his anger was concern about the cost of what she was doing. "Isn't it pretty?"

For the first time, he looked at the paper. It had small, multicolored flowers on a white background. No man would be caught dead putting something like that on his kitchen wall. For the space of a heartbeat he wondered how he would be able to bear looking at it if she left him. The thought made him angry. Why the hell should he care if she left him? He didn't love her. Had never loved her. Would never love her.

"It's fine," he said flatly. And then felt like a worm because her face fell.

"You don't like it."

"I didn't say that. Hell, Callen, it's great paper. I just had a horrible day. And I'm hungry."

"Of course you are," she said, immediately stopping what she was doing to come and give him a hug.

He couldn't help himself. He hugged her back. Well, hell! What was he supposed to do? He had to make sure the woman kept on loving him, didn't he?

"I'll cook," he offered. "You're busy."

She wrinkled her nose and laughed at him. "I've tasted your cooking. Give me a minute and I'll have something ready for us. You've got time to finish writing out those bills that need attention." She turned him toward the kitchen door and gave him a little shove toward his study.

He stomped off to his office—which now contained an antique rolltop desk—to work on his books, something he hated because he could never get the numbers to come out right. It was a job E.J. had always done. Which only reminded him of how much he missed his father. Now he was forced to confront the computer in the study and all those numbers. He hated numbers.

It wasn't long before he could smell something good cooking in the kitchen. Shortly after that, Callen called him in to supper. He gratefully turned off the computer and headed for the kitchen. When he got there, he stood in the doorway and stared at the table.

The wallpaper mess had miraculously disappeared. There were flowers on the table, and she had lit candles. He didn't know where she had found the china, and he was afraid to ask. The table had a cloth and cloth napkins. He couldn't remember the last time he and E.J. had put a cloth on the table, and they hadn't used candles except when the electricity went out in a storm. He had complained once that all that special stuff wasn't necessary, but Callen had told him it was no trouble at all.

He sat down with a grunt of expectation, his nose lifting for the scent of whatever it was she had on the stove.

"I just broiled some steak, threw a couple of sweet potatoes into the microwave and steamed a little broccoli on the stove."

He wrinkled his nose. "Sweet potatoes?"

"Don't you like them?"

"At Thanksgiving. With lots of brown sugar and marshmallows."

"Try one. If you don't like it, I won't make it again."

He realized suddenly she had taken the meat of the sweet potato out of the shell, mixed something into it and stuffed it back in again. "What's in here?" he asked warily.

"Cheese and bacon."

Sam grunted doubtfully, but he took a bite and found it delicious. He didn't tell her liked it; he simply ate it all without further complaint. He had to admit that Callen was a good cook. The steak was rare, the way he liked it, and the broccoli was crisp, but not raw.

He looked up when he had finished to find her watching him expectantly. "Good" was all he said.

From the smile on her face a person would have thought he had told her she was the greatest cook in Texas. He felt guilty for his faint praise and added, "Really good."

"Are you feeling better now that you've filled your stomach?"

He thought about it a minute and chuckled. "I guess I am."

"Remind me to keep you well fed in the future," she said with a grin.

There it was again. *The future.* His irritation rose at the reminder of what he was doing with her...to her...and the words were out before he could stop them. "I'm not a child, Callen. Don't treat me like one."

He saw from the stunned look on her face that she hadn't expected him to lash out at her. The hurt look that followed a moment later made him feel guilty, because he knew she didn't deserve his criticism.

"What's wrong, Sam?" she said in a voice that was threatening because it was so serious. "I want to know. I can't live like this, knowing that something's eating you inside. What is it? Please, tell me."

At first he was terrified that Garth might have told her the truth. That she was going to create a showdown here and now. He realized in a horrified instant that he would do anything to keep her with him.

Even forego your vengeance?

He avoided answering the question, reasoning that she couldn't know the truth. Otherwise she would have confronted him with it. He met her gaze, which was dark and somber.

"Sam, please. Tell me what's wrong."

He rose so abruptly the ladder-back chair fell with a crash. "There's nothing wrong with me. I'm just not used to having someone around all the time asking me dumb questions!"

She jerked as though he had slapped her. And he had, figuratively. But the Callen he knew was full of guts and gumption, and she didn't disappoint him. She jumped to her feet and snapped right back, "I'm not *someone*, I'm your *wife*. And I only want to help!"

"I don't need your help," Sam said in a harsh voice, admiring her even as he pushed her away. "I have to handle this by myself."

"Is it your father? Are you still grieving?"

"I don't want to talk about this!" Sam said, heading for the privacy of his office. Damn, if the woman didn't get to the kitchen door before him and bar the way!

"You're not leaving this room until you tell me what's wrong," Callen insisted.

"Get out of my way, Callen."

"No."

He stood there a minute, trying to decide what was best. The solution to his problem was simple when it finally came to him. He turned on his heel and headed for the kitchen door that led outside. He slammed it on his way out.

It occurred to him much later that he was going to have to face Callen eventually, or end up sleeping in the barn. When it came down to it, he decided sleeping in the barn wasn't such a bad idea after all. Maybe a night spent on her own would convince Callen that his business was his own.

Actually, Callen spent the night sleeping quite soundly. Because, while she hadn't gotten Sam to tell her what his problem was, she now knew it hadn't been her imagination. Something serious was bothering him, other than the situation with her father. She was certain that Sam would have no choice except to confess. She wasn't going to give him any peace until he did.

Sam slept poorly in the barn. The hay in the loft was scratchy, and the wool blanket he had laid over it smelled of horse. It was also miserably hot. Sweat dribbled its way across his skin like many-footed worms. And he missed the feel of

Callen lying next to him. In the hours he spent lying awake, listening to the rustling movements of the animals below, he thought about his confrontation with Callen.

He was going to have to tell her something. Otherwise she was going to ferret out the truth. He didn't want that to happen. He crept back into the house at dawn only to find his wife already fixing breakfast. He shifted his eyes to the wallpaper and said contritely, "I'm sorry. I guess I owe you an explanation."

The fool woman dropped the spatula in the pan and walked right into his arms. She felt good and smelled sweet and her mouth was warm and wet and made his body go hard.

"I missed you," she whispered in his ear. She rubbed her cheek against his jaw and made a kittenish sound in her throat that drew his body up tight. "You need a shave, Sam," she said with a raspy chuckle. At the same time, her hands came up to caress his cheeks, and she sought his mouth with hers.

A moment later she jerked herself free. "The bacon!"

He watched her race back to the stove where the bacon had kept right on cooking.

She turned back to him with a grin. "It's perfect. Sit down and eat. Once your stomach is full, there'll be plenty of time to talk."

He took her at her word. The eggs were perfectly done, over easy with the yolks soft. The bacon was crisp, but not burned, and the toast was lavishly buttered. The coffee was hot and strong. She was a darn good cook.

She waited for him to finish his second cup of coffee before she reminded him that he had a confession to make.

"All right, Sam. It's time to talk. I want to know what's been bothering you."

He took a deep breath and let it out. He had to make this good. "I—I can't do the bookkeeping."

"What?" There was a blank look on her face. Clearly she wasn't expecting anything that simple.

"E.J. used to do it. I can't seem to get the numbers to come out right, but I can't afford to hire someone else to do it. Things are in a mess."

Her whole face lit up. "Why didn't you just say so? I can do the bookkeeping for you." She lowered her lids so he couldn't see her eyes. "I mean, if you want me to."

He hesitated, as though reluctant to agree. He hadn't realized he was going to be killing two birds with one stone. Not only had he put her off the scent about his "problem," but he was also going to be relieved of the onerous task of keeping the Double L books.

"I suppose that would be all right," he said gruffly.

She left her chair and sat herself in his lap, draping her arms around his shoulders. She looked deep into his eyes, until he was sure she would see the truth. But all he saw reflected back to him was her concern.

"Don't feel bad about the bookkeeping," she said earnestly. "Some people are inclined that way and some aren't."

He felt himself flushing. She was obviously aware that he hadn't been a good student. She had said, in as gentle and caring a way as she could, that it was all right if he couldn't handle the difficult stuff. She would do it for him.

Sam had known from the first grade that he and numbers didn't get along. Reading hadn't been any easier. It had been a struggle to keep up with his class work all through school. He had been the butt of a lot of cruel teasing, and he had grown a thick skin to fend it off. E.J. had kept him from feeling like a total idiot by reminding him that he grasped most ideas readily. Thank goodness he had been fast on his feet. That had given him self-esteem and a value to his peers.

But here it was again, that insidious feeling of inadequacy, just because he found numbers more than a mere challenge. Because he found numbers impossible to understand.

He felt like shoving her off his lap, but she forestalled him when she leaned her head on his shoulder trustingly and relaxed in his arms. She trusted him. She loved him. She didn't care that he couldn't figure numbers.

The crisis was past. They could go on as before.

He let the hurt go and held her close.

Chapter 5

When Callen brought up Sam's figures on the computer she saw right away why he hadn't been able to make them balance. Several of the numbers were juxtaposed. Instead of $312.42 for fence posts, as was stated on the invoice, Sam had inserted $321.24 on the computer. It was a simple matter, once she realized the problem, to correct the numbers and make them balance. She then wrote out checks and signed them.

It occurred to her that Sam's problem with numbers might have a source he hadn't recognized: dyslexia. Only, she couldn't imagine how he could have a problem like that and not have had it diagnosed a long time ago. The more she thought about it, the more convinced she became that Sam's difficulties in school might have stemmed from his inability to see numbers and letters as they appeared on the page.

She confronted him the next morning at the breakfast table with her suspicions. "Sam, do you have dyslexia?"

Sam stared at her as if she had accused him of having a social disease. "What?"

"Dyslexia. You've heard of it, I'm sure. Letters get jumbled up on a page when a dyslexic tries to read them. It's more common in males than females. I just thought, since you had so much trouble in school..." Callen's voice faded as Sam's features reddened. Was he embarrassed? Did he think she thought less of him because he had difficulty reading? It wasn't his fault. People were born with the problem. "I just thought you might have been diagnosed with it sometime in the past."

"I'm not sick, Callen," Sam said in a terrible, low voice. "I'm just not as smart as other people."

"How can you say such a thing!"

"Because it's true," he said flatly. "I've accepted it. So should you." He rose abruptly from the breakfast table and stalked toward the door.

She rose and started after him. "Sam! Wait! I only thought—"

He turned on her, a storm of emotions on his face. He grabbed her by the shoulders and shook her once. "Let it be, Callen. I've lived with the way I am for thirty-six years. It's a little late to be coming up with excuses for why I can't manage simple, ordinary addition and subtraction, don't you think? Accept it. I'm not smart. I never promised I was."

He paused a moment and a muscle jerked in his jaw before he said, "Maybe you should have listened to your brother. I never got past high school, and I was lucky to make it through that. You don't have to find excuses for me, Callen." And then, bleakly, "I know what I am. And what I'm not."

A moment later he was gone, and she was standing alone in the kitchen wondering what had gone wrong. She had never seen Sam so angry. Or so frustrated. She had never realized he was so sensitive about his education or his intelligence. He was wrong, of course. There was nothing stupid about Sam Longstreet. He was sharp as a whip. After what she had seen on the computer, she was willing to bet he was merely dyslexic.

Only, if he was, why hadn't someone—one of his teachers early on, or the tutors Zach said the football team had hired to help Sam pass his academic subjects—discovered the problem? More to the point, how was she going to get Sam to agree to a test to determine whether he had a reading dysfunction or not?

The problem got pushed to the background when Sam returned home hobbling later that afternoon. His face was ashen, and his body was trembling.

"My God! What happened?" Callen exclaimed as Sam lowered himself gently to a kitchen chair.

"I got stomped by a cow. Made the mistake of getting between her and her calf while I was repairing some fence. I managed to slide to the opposite side of the barbed wire, but not before she laid into me some."

"Why didn't you go straight to the hospital!" Callen exclaimed as she dropped to one knee in front of him. She reached up to unbutton his torn and dirtied shirt and hissed in a breath of air when she saw the growing bruises on his chest. "Sam, this looks serious," she said in a wobbly voice. "Please let me take you to the hospital."

"It's too expensive," he said flatly. "Besides, I've been through this before. I've got a broken rib, maybe two. The most a doctor can do is bind me up. I can do that for myself."

Callen was terrified that Sam might have internal injuries he wasn't aware of, or that one of those broken ribs might puncture a lung. "Please," she begged.

"No, and that's final." He tried to get up, but groaned and slid back into the kitchen chair. "You're going to have to bind me up. I can't do it myself."

"I can't—"

"I've got bandages I've used in the past. They're under the sink in the bathroom. Go get them."

Callen found several rolls of Ace bandages where Sam had told her to look and brought them back to the kitchen. Sam had slid his shirt off his shoulders. The skin was scraped raw in several places, and the bruising looked terrible. She bit her lip to keep from pleading with him again. In the short time they had been married, she had learned how stubborn he could be. There was no sense wasting energy arguing. She would bind him up, put him in bed and then get a doctor to come see him, whether he liked it or not.

The color was returning to Sam's face by the time Callen finished. "Do you need help getting to bed?"

"I think I can manage."

When he tried to get to his feet, he swayed dizzily. He reached out for her, and she slid herself under his arm to support him. "Just take it easy," she coaxed.

Callen eased Sam into bed and retreated to the kitchen to phone the Whitelaw family doctor. "I know you don't usually make house calls, Dr. Stephens, but Sam refuses to go to the hospital. I'm afraid he may have some internal injuries. Thanks. I'll be expecting you then."

Sam lay in bed staring at the ceiling, disgusted at having gotten himself into this situation. He didn't like depending on Callen for anything. He had to admit she had done a good job of binding his ribs. And he would have fallen flat on his face in the kitchen if she hadn't been there to catch him. But he already felt enough in her debt for all the work she had done around the house.

He had been a changed man since his marriage, rising earlier than he had in years and working late into the night. No matter how tired he was, he had always found time to make love to Callen. He had tried to convince himself it was all part of the plan. But he realized now he had done it because he had wanted to please and impress his wife. He had wanted to earn her respect. And now here he was stuck in bed, helpless, flat on his back.

He tried rising, but his ribs hurt him too much. He didn't have any choice but to stay where he was. He had just started wondering where Callen was keeping herself when he heard her talking to someone in the kitchen. His first panicked thought was that Garth had come to visit. He gasped at the pain when he tried to rise and fell back to the bed.

"Who's there, Callen?" he called out to her. His answer came in the form of a strange man in the doorway. One look at the black bag he carried, and Sam swore under his breath. He turned an accusing glance on Callen, who stared defiantly back at him. "I told you I didn't need to see a doctor."

"I have no desire to bury a husband I've just married," she replied tartly. "You'll let the doctor look at you, Sam Longstreet, if you know what's good for you."

Sam had to admire her daring, even if he deplored her tactics. He couldn't very well walk out on her this time, and so long as the doctor was here, he might as well get checked over. "All right, Doc. Go ahead and look. All you're going to find is a few busted ribs."

Sam couldn't stand the anxious look on Callen's face. "You don't need to stay," he told her.

"Just try getting me out of here!" she challenged with a spark in her eyes.

Sam turned his face toward the wall. She had him over a barrel and she knew it. Hell, it wasn't so bad having a woman hovering over him all concerned like this. In fact, it felt kind of nice to know she cared. "Do what you want," he said. But there was more resignation in his voice than anger.

Sam lay as still as he could under the doctor's poking and prodding, but more than once he wished Callen weren't there so he could let out the groans he had gritted behind his teeth.

"Broken ribs, all right," Dr. Stephens confirmed. "I don't like the looks of that bruising. Could be some internal bleeding. I'd like you to come to the hospital where I can do some more thorough tests."

"No," Sam said. "No hospital. No tests."

"Sam," Callen pleaded.

"No."

The doctor frowned. "If that's the way you want it, I can't force you to go. But I want Callen to check for tenderness in your belly here and here—'' he pointed out the spots to Callen with his fingertips ''—every couple of hours for the next twenty-four, and get you to the hospital quick if any tenderness shows up. Also, watch to make sure that bruising doesn't spread any farther downward.''

''Will he be all right?'' Callen asked.

''So long as he takes it easy until those ribs heal.''

''How long?'' Callen asked.

''No work for ten days, at least,'' the doctor said. ''Two weeks would be better. Otherwise you take the chance of aggravating your injury.''

Sam scowled. He already had more work than he could handle. This wasn't going to help things. He would get up when he was damned good and ready, no matter what the doctor said.

In that respect, Sam had underestimated Callen. She threatened dire consequences if he left the bedroom and brought his meals on a tray. Sam had never had anyone fuss over him in his life. At first he felt uncomfortable having her wait on him. He had done nothing to deserve Callen's concern, and if she knew the truth, she would be throwing bowls of soup at him, not serving them.

But, oh, how he relished the tender care his wife gave him! Callen crooned to him as she soothed his sweating brow with a cool cloth. She made delicious meals and served them to him with the newspaper, which she read to him while he ate, saving him the effort.

''Why didn't you tell me you were helping Jimmy Lee Johnson earn the money for a car?'' Callen asked him one afternoon.

Sam felt the heat in his throat rising toward his face. ''How'd you find out about that?''

''He came here looking for work. I thought he'd heard about your ribs, but he told me you've hired him to work for you every Wednesday.''

Sam was expecting Callen to complain about the expense.

He had opened his mouth to justify himself when she leaned over and kissed him hard on the mouth. He was too stunned even to respond.

''You are about the nicest man I ever met, Sam Longstreet. Not many men would hire a teenage boy to do work he could easily do himself and pay him money that he doesn't have, all to help that teenage boy realize his dream. Oh, I'm so proud to be your wife!''

She was gone a moment later, back to chores in the house. But the good feeling she had inspired—the simple pleasure of feeling good about himself—lasted the rest of the day.

Sam had hired Jimmy Lee because he had seen a lot of himself in the boy. Long ago he had eked out enough doing odd jobs for neighboring ranchers to buy his first motorcycle. It was sitting in the barn now. He hadn't ridden it in years, not since he had hurt his knee his senior year in high school. He had been forced to give it up while his knee mended. Somehow, he seemed to have outgrown it after that. He wondered if it would still run. Maybe when he was on his feet again, he would check it out.

Meanwhile, Callen only barely managed to deter her mother from coming over to help nurse Sam. ''He wouldn't be comfortable,'' she explained. ''He feels bad even letting me wait on him, Mom.'' It went without saying that going to her parents' home, even to attend their annual Labor Day picnic, was out of the question until Sam recovered.

To Callen's amazement and delight, her brother, Falcon, and his wife, Mara, ignored her warnings against company. They had driven to Hawk's Way from Falcon's ranch in Dallas for the Whitelaw's annual Labor Day picnic, and refused to leave without seeing Callen and Sam. They brought along Charlie One Horse, the ancient, part-Comanche housekeeper who had helped raise two generations of Whitelaws.

''Charlie!'' Callen cried as she grabbed him by his gray braids and pulled him close for a hug. ''I'm so glad you came to visit!''

She brought them all into the bedroom where Sam was propped up and paging through a stock magazine.

"Sam, I don't know if you've ever met Charlie One Horse. He's taken care of me since I was in diapers."

Sam shook hands and said, "Glad to meet you."

Callen was so excited, she barely gave them time to greet each other before she introduced her brother and his wife. "You know Falcon," she said, "and this is Mara, his wife."

"We've met," Sam said with a smile.

"You have?"

"Years ago," Sam said. "It's nice to see you again, Falcon. I'm sorry I can't get up, Mara. We weren't family the last time we met, so I didn't get a chance to hug you then. And now I'm stuck here in bed."

"I can fix that," Mara said with a twinkle in her eye. She leaned over and gave Sam a quick kiss on the cheek. She laughed at the possessive-jealous-chagrined look on Callen's face when she had finished.

"We brought some food from the picnic, since you couldn't come," Charlie One Horse said. He began to arrange a huge spread of food on a tray that he set in front of Sam on the bed.

"We came to celebrate the day with you," Mara said, "since you couldn't come to us."

"Callen and I will go get the drinks," Falcon said as he dragged her toward the kitchen. Once they were there, he turned to her and said, "What the hell's going on, Callen? Mom and Dad said they haven't seen hide nor hair of you since you got married. I don't think they believe Sam's really hurt."

"As you can see," Callen replied in an icy voice, "he is."

"That doesn't explain why the two of you haven't been to Hawk's Way to visit since you got married."

"You must have heard some of the awful things Daddy and Zach had to say about Sam before the wedding."

"So?"

"So, in time, when things cool off, we'll go visit."

"Why can't you go now, by yourself?" Falcon demanded.

"Because I won't go where my husband isn't welcome! What if Mom and Daddy hadn't liked Mara? Or didn't want to be bothered with Susannah, because she was sick with leukemia? How would you have felt?"

Susannah was Falcon's stepdaughter, Mara's daughter from a previous marriage. Her leukemia had been in remission for four years now. Another year and she would be home free.

Falcon grimaced. "I see what you mean."

"Tell Mom and Daddy you saw me, and I'm fine. And tell them Sam really does have broken ribs."

Charlie One Horse, her brother, and his wife didn't stay long, but Callen was glad they had come.

After they were gone, however, a wave of homesickness washed over her. She missed her parents. This separation was ridiculous. She became more determined than ever to make peace between her husband and her family.

Sam continued to be an irascible patient, but Callen could see he enjoyed being taken care of even though he grumbled about it. She knew because of the way his eyes lingered on her face as she sat beside him brushing a stray hank of hair from his forehead, the way he laid his hand gently over hers as she set the dinner tray before him, the way he pulled her down to kiss her lips, sending her pulse soaring as he lazily helped himself to deep, probing kisses.

Callen only managed to keep Sam confined to bed for nine days, but during that time she learned a great deal about needing and wanting and expectation. Because, although there was comfort to be found sleeping close to his warmth, and joy in his tender kisses, both of them knew it couldn't go beyond that.

Callen had been surprised at the strength of her unrequited desire. She had never realized how much she counted on the pleasure of making love with her husband at night. She had refused to let Sam exert himself until Dr. Stephens's prescribed two weeks were up, but she caught herself dreaming about the day they could resume their lovemaking.

Callen had decided to celebrate the occasion of Sam's recovery with a housewarming party. She hadn't forgotten Zach's accusation: *Sam has no friends. You'll be all alone.* The truth was, in the months since she and Sam had gotten married, not a single neighbor had come to call. Partly, Callen assumed, it was because their nuptials had been private, and they had sent no announcements. People didn't intrude on their neighbors in the West without some indication that the visit was welcome. Callen was sure that if she had given even a hint of wanting company, she would have had it.

This was confirmed when Callen began issuing invitations for the housewarming party. She discovered Sam was admired and liked by his neighbors. They had simply respected his wish to be left alone. If Sam didn't have close friends, it wasn't because his neighbors weren't willing; it was because Sam himself had discouraged the contact.

Callen was hoping the party would be the first of many, and that she and Sam would meet other young couples with similar interests who would become their friends. She hadn't counted on Sam's strenuous objection to any kind of gathering whatsoever.

"You've done what?" he exploded. "Why the hell would you do such a thing without asking me first?"

"First of all, because I didn't think you'd mind. And secondly, because I need friends. It wouldn't hurt if you had a few, as well," she added bluntly.

Sam glowered. "I don't need anybody."

"Of course not," she said with a sardonic twist of her mouth. "However, I would like to point out that if you'd had any kind of relationship at all with your neighbors you could have called on them to help out when you got hurt."

"I don't want to owe anybody anything."

"That's clear enough," Callen snapped back. "The truth is, we all need other people, Sam. Even you."

"I won't be at any party you decide to give."

"Fine. The party's off."

Callen headed toward the parlor from the bedroom in a huff. She didn't want Sam to see how shocked and hurt she was by his refusal. She had known what she was getting into when she married Sam. Her father and brother had both warned her what kind of man he was. *A loner. A man without friends.* She really hadn't considered what that might mean. She had seen in Sam only what she wanted to see. In love like she was, she truly hadn't minded the thought of just the two of them alone on the Double L.

Callen hadn't gone two steps before Sam caught her arm and swung her back around into his embrace. She immediately struggled for freedom, shoving against his shoulders and chest.

"Keep that up, and you're going to send me back to bed for another two weeks," he said with a groan of pain.

She stood frozen, her expression stricken. "What do you want from me, Sam?"

"I want you to listen while I apologize," he said in a quiet voice. He tipped her chin up with his forefinger and said, "Sometimes I can be a little unreasonable."

Callen arched a disbelieving brow. "You? Unreasonable?"

Sam chuckled as his arms tightened slightly around Callen. He hated the idea of exposing himself to all those people. He avoided crowds because he never showed well in them. But when he saw how disappointed Callen was, he conceded that enduring a housewarming party was little enough to give her in return for all she had done for him.

"We'll give the party," he said. "Invite anyone you want."

"Even my mother and father?"

Sam thought about refusing but realized there were ways to keep Garth from attending even if Callen issued an invitation. "Sure," he said. "Invite the whole family."

Callen's eyes welled. "Thank you, Sam. I will."

He fought off the stab of guilt clawing at his insides. The only way he could keep focused on his revenge was to remember how his father had looked when he had found him. Thankfully, Callen's voice jerked him from those grim thoughts back to the present.

"Maybe Falcon and Mara could drive over from Dallas again and bring Susannah and the baby."

"It would be nice to see them again," Sam said softly.

"Thank you, Sam," Callen replied with a shy smile. "I know you don't care much for company. I appreciate your willingness to give this a try."

Fortunately she chose that moment to kiss him, or Sam might have spoiled everything by admitting how little he was looking forward to the shindig his wife was planning.

Since it had been two weeks since Sam's injury, and they were in the bedroom, both Sam and Callen let themselves enjoy kissing and holding each other, knowing that their desires could finally be fulfilled.

It was amazing, Sam thought, how much he had missed those carnal sounds Callen made in her throat. He loved how she arched toward him, how she gave that little sigh as he sank himself into her to the hilt. He had forgotten the feel of her fingernails gripping his buttocks and the way her teeth nipped at his shoulder when she came.

Callen was astonished at how easily Sam could arouse her. How he knew just where and how to touch her so that she felt cherished and appreciated. She loved the way he kept his own desire leashed until she was satisfied and gloried in the unrestrained passion that caught him unawares so he cried out her name at the moment of climax. She lay beside him, her body heaving, feeling sated and happy.

Her hand drifted lightly across Sam's chest, her fingertips playing in the dark curls. "Are you all right?" she asked in a lazy voice.

"Mmm, hmm."

"I take that to mean you're fine," she said, feeling the

smile grow on her face. She reached up a hand to trace Sam's lips. He was smiling, too.

"I love you, Sam."

Callen waited, but Sam didn't say the words back. She had her hands on his lips, so she felt the smile disappear, felt the lips flatten.

"Sam?"

Sam knew the smart thing to do was say the words, even if he didn't mean them. Somehow, he couldn't do it. Callen deserved better. He wasn't going to lie to her any more than he already had. She had to know he admired her, that he was grateful for everything she had done to make his house a home, that he loved making love to her. Wasn't that enough without the words?

He kissed the fingertips she held against his lips, and when she would have withdrawn, he reached out to catch her hand and hold it there. "You're a very special woman, Callen," he murmured against her fingertips. "I've never known anyone like you."

It was the truth, but so much less than he knew she wanted to hear. He knew it was enough when he felt her relax against him. He ignored the voice that told him he needed her arms around him at night. He was a man who had never needed anyone.

Callen tried to tell herself it didn't matter that in four months of marriage Sam had never said "I love you." He had shown he cared in a dozen different ways, not the least of which was making love to her every night. They had their whole lives in front of them. She knew in her heart that someday the words would come.

She moved forward with her plans for a lavish housewarming party, inviting all their neighbors and her entire family. Mara and Falcon promised to come again and bring the baby, whose name was Cody, and Susannah. Both Zach and her parents had also agreed to be there.

When Sam heard that Callen's parents had accepted their

invitation, he made a point of seeking Garth out at the Stanton Hotel Café.

He walked up to the breakfast bar and said to Garth, "I want to talk to you. Privately."

Garth rose and the two men walked into one of the hotel meeting rooms that was empty.

"I got the invitation to your housewarming," Garth said when they were alone. "My wife and I are planning to attend."

Sam shook his head. "You're not welcome in my home." For the first time Sam saw pain flash across his father-in-law's features. He knew he ought to be gloating, but he found there was nothing to be proud of in what he was doing. He wasn't finding the satisfaction he had yearned for when he had set out upon this course. He forced himself to focus on the image of his father in death. That gruesome portrait produced the anger he needed to proceed with his vengeance.

"If you show up at my door," Sam threatened, "I'll make a scene the likes of which this county has never seen. I'll make damn sure everyone knows your part in E.J.'s death."

"You're bluffing," Garth said.

"Try me."

"I want to see my daughter."

"I want my father back."

The air sparked with electricity as the two men measured one another. At last Sam said in a guttural voice, "We don't always get what we want. Do we, Garth?"

Garth hadn't believed Sam could do it, that he could so effectively cut him off from contact with his daughter. But Callen had been a married woman for nearly four months, and he hadn't once seen or spoken to her. That seemed impossible to him, given the fact all he had to do was pick up the phone to talk to her or drive a few miles to be at her front door. But it was Callen herself who had asked both her parents to keep their distance. Garth had respected his daughter's wishes, never dreaming that so much time could go by without any contact between them.

He missed her. He wanted to see her, to speak to her, to reassure himself that she was as happy as Candy said she was from their conversations on the phone. "What if I come anyway?"

"If you insist on trying to get your daughter back, I'll give her back. In fact, I'll throw her out."

"You wouldn't do that."

"Wouldn't I?" Sam stared at Garth with eyes that looked totally merciless, with features that were as hard and unyielding as granite.

Garth knew from calls Callen had made to her mother that she was more in love with Sam now than she had been when they married. It would break his daughter's heart if Sam rejected her now. He couldn't do anything that might jeopardize his daughter's happiness. But he wondered how Callen could love this misguided and vengeful young man.

Much as Garth wanted to force a confrontation, he felt that waiting Sam out was a better alternative. Time was on his side. The chances of him running into his daughter in town or at church, or catching her on the phone, were very good. And after all, his ranch and Sam's bordered each other. There was always the possibility he would run into Callen on the range.

"You win," he said to Sam at last. "I'll find a reason to stay home from the party. I assume you have no objection if my wife attends?"

"None at all."

"If we're done, my coffee's getting cold." Garth left Sam standing alone in the empty room.

Sam wondered why he didn't feel more triumphant. He had won. He was keeping Callen and her father apart. If he wasn't mistaken, he had wounded his adversary. There had been suffering visible on Garth Whitelaw's face. He knew the expression because he had worn it himself. But he felt was no satisfaction in his accomplishment.

Sam knew what had marred his victory. It was the thought of the disappointment he would see on Callen's face when she realized her father wasn't coming. It was the knowledge of how unhappy he would be making his wife while he punished her father.

For a moment, a brief, flickering instant of time, he considered giving up his revenge. He considered forgiving Garth Whitelaw for his daughter's sake. He considered letting go of the past and grabbing for a future with Callen.

Then he saw his father in his mind's eye, lying in a pool of blood. And remembered the vow he had made.

"I promised you vengeance, Dad. And it's vengeance you'll have."

Chapter 6

Callen had several projects she wanted to accomplish before the housewarming party. First and foremost, she wanted to investigate further into whether Sam had dyslexia. A friend who was an elementary schoolteacher referred her to a woman who worked with dyslexic children. The specialist asked Callen to get a sample of Sam's writing for her.

Callen asked Sam to make up a list of his favorite foods. He was reluctant to write them down for her at first, but she insisted she was just too tired to write herself. She did her best to look weary when he eyed her suspiciously. He laboriously wrote a list, which she was surprised to see included a couple of dishes she had made for him since their marriage. The spelling was atrocious, and some of the words didn't make any sense at all. Callen was careful to keep her expression neutral when she took the list from him.

She met with the specialist and handed over Sam's list. "Is it dyslexia?" she asked anxiously.

The specialist, Mrs. Moran, smiled reassuringly. "It looks like a classic case. See? Some of the words are backward. For instance, *can* is *nac*. Are you sure someone hasn't told him before that he's dyslexic?''

Callen shook her head. ''I guess when he couldn't read, the teachers gave up on him. And knowing Sam, he would have hidden the problem as best he could. Is there something that can be done?''

''Oh, yes. Some very bright people have been dyslexic and performed exceptionally well. Einstein, for example. Sam can be taught to recognize words for what they are, even backward. But it takes practice. Do you think he would be willing to work with me?''

Callen smiled ruefully. ''The question is whether you'd be willing to work with Sam.''

''I've got Monday and Wednesday evenings open. I can come to your house, or Sam can meet me at the school. Some of the local service clubs have gotten together to sponsor a fund so my services are free to whoever needs them.''

Callen felt her heart racing with excitement. Her first inclination was to race home to Sam with the good news. Then she had second thoughts. What if he got angry when he found out that she had tricked him into giving her a writing sample? What if he didn't want any help dealing with his dyslexia? With the party only a day away she didn't want to start an argument with him. It would be soon enough to talk with him after the party about Mrs. Moran's conclusions and her offer of help.

''I'll be in touch with you,'' she told the specialist. ''And thank you very much!''

The day of the party dawned bright and sunny, and Callen was nearly bouncing with excitement like a teenager on her way to the prom. Sam had never seen her so euphoric. ''It's just a party, Callen,'' he said with a laugh after she tried putting both feet in the same leg of her jeans.

''I know. But it's the first party we've had as husband and wife. I want it to go well.''

"It will," Sam reassured her as he dragged her back across him on the bed and nuzzled her neck playfully. "You've got every detail planned, right down to how we're going to get everyone out the door after it's all over so we can come in here and make love."

Callen grinned. "At least I planned the best for last."

Sam chuckled, then pressed his lips to her throat and began to suck.

"Sam Longstreet, don't you dare give me a hickey!" Callen half shouted, half laughed. She shoved at his shoulders, but he held her tight in his arms. "I bought a new dress and it'll show," she warned.

Sam stopped what he was doing, but didn't let her go. "I want every man there to know you're mine," he said. "I want to put my mark on you."

"You're the only man I want," Callen said in a husky voice. "The only man I'll ever want."

Sam felt a lump of emotion in his throat. How had she become so precious to him? How could he have gotten himself into such an impossible dilemma? He couldn't give her up; he couldn't give up his vengeance. What was he going to do?

"I..." He couldn't say "I love you." It wasn't fair. Not when he was using her the way he was.

"You what?" Callen said in a teasing voice.

"I bought some fancy new clothes to wear tonight."

Callen sat up, her legs draped across his waist. "You did? Oh, Sam, that's great!"

"I didn't want you to worry that I'd turn up looking like I did at our wedding."

"I never thought—"

He covered her mouth with his hand. "You know damn well that's exactly what you thought," he said with a grin. "I couldn't miss the shaving cream you stuck by the sink, or the boot polish that turned up on the back of the toilet seat, or the fact that you've ironed every single one of my shirts for the past week. And I adore you for it.''

The words had come out before he had a chance to stop them. He didn't miss the startled look in Callen's eyes, or the way his own heart missed a beat when he said the words that were so close to what he knew she wanted to hear. He lowered his hand from her mouth, his gaze never leaving hers.

"Oh, Sam," she said. "Oh, Sam."

She was too choked up to say any more, and since his throat had closed like a vise, he used his hands and mouth to confirm what he had said. He cupped her breasts and felt the marvelous softness of them before mouthing her through the thin white T-shirt she wore. Her cry of delight made his groin tighten. Since he was naked under the sheets, it didn't take long before her jeans were off and he had her beneath him. He was lost in a world of pleasure so vast he wasn't sure he could ever get enough of it.

It wasn't until much, much later that Sam realized he hadn't used any protection. He had taken that responsibility from the first, because he knew the dire consequences that would result if he got Callen pregnant. This time he had been caught up in the powerful emotions of the moment, wanting and needing to show Callen how much he cared, how much he valued her. Birth control had been the farthest thing from his mind.

Sam couldn't imagine any other woman than Callen having his children. Only now was not the time. The game hadn't yet been played out. He told himself the chances of her getting pregnant were slim to none. But he felt his gut wrench when he realized that the possibility existed.

He forced it from his mind as he and Callen finished the party preparations together. She hadn't decorated the house so much as filled it with candles and flowers. She had polished every surface and vacuumed every speck of dust. Even he was impressed with the results.

He was quite literally stunned when he saw Callen's dress for the party. He had never seen her wearing anything so sophisticated or elegant. It was a black dress that molded her figure, cut just low enough to reveal a hint of cleavage, but not enough to really show anything. The back, however, was cut to the waist, revealing an expanse of skin so enticing he couldn't keep himself from reaching out to touch her skin.

"You're so beautiful," he said in amazement.

Callen blushed with pleasure at the look of admiration and pride in Sam's eyes. "Thank you, Sam. May I return the compliment?"

"I'm beautiful?" he said with a wry twist of his mouth. He looked down at the starched white tuxedo shirt and bolo tie he wore with a black leather vest and black trousers. "It's the clothes," he said flatly. "I look like one of those rhinestone cowboys that sit around drinking tequila in a bar back east."

Callen laughed, a tinkling sound that skittered down his spine and right back up again to catch him in the throat.

"It's not the clothes," she said. "Although I must say you're looking very fine tonight. It's you," she said as she eyed him from head to toe. "You really are quite a handsome man, Sam. I can't believe I never saw it before."

He felt himself flush at the compliment. She was looking at him as if she would like to eat him whole. Sam felt his body respond quickly and fiercely to her invitation. He kept himself a foot away from her, knowing that if he touched her they wouldn't be dressed to greet the guests that were due any minute. But he couldn't take his eyes off her, and he knew from her face that she was feeling the same need he was to wrap himself up in her and never let go.

They both jumped when they heard a knock at the door.

"Party time," Sam said, his voice harsh with desire.

Callen cleared her throat. "Shall we greet our guests together?"

Sam slipped an arm around her waist and drew her close. "Let's go."

The rest of the party was a nightmare for Sam.

He recognized their first guests as Tom Swan, who had been the center of the high school football team, and his wife, Julie. The two had been inseparable since sixth grade. Tom shook Sam's hand and greeted him with a friendly smile that Sam made himself return.

But Sam wasn't seeing Tom's smile or hearing his greeting. He was remembering the day in high school when he had overheard Tom talking to several members of the team in the locker room, while they thought he was in the shower.

"That Sam," Tom had said. "He sure can run! It's just too damn bad he can't read!"

He heard the boys he had thought were his friends laughing with hilarity at what a dumb jock he was. Oh, he had been a riot, all right. He could still feel the awful aching pain of that betrayal.

Looking into Tom's clear blue eyes, Sam knew his former teammate's opinion of him hadn't changed. Except now he couldn't run, either.

Tom was just the first of several of his high school football cronies that Callen had dredged up. It seemed people stuck around this part of Texas when they were born here.

And there was Janice Reese. She was the girl he had fallen head over heels in love with in sixth grade. He had followed her around for several weeks before she turned and confronted him.

"Why are you following me around, Sam?"

"I was just wondering, Janice, if you'd go to the Halloween dance with me."

She had wrinkled her nose at him in a way he thought particularly endearing. "What makes you think I'd go out with a dummy like you?"

He had been so shocked at the bluntness of her statement that he hadn't been able to come up with a good reason why she should want to spend time with him. He had backed away and kept to himself after that.

He wondered if Janice remembered that fateful encounter.

He had never forgotten it. He had known he had trouble with schoolwork, but had never associated that deficiency with anything lacking in himself. Until Janice had called him a dummy. It was amazing how that single sentence changed his perception of himself. He began to question himself, his intelligence.

He remembered asking E.J. if there was something wrong with him. But his father had reassured him that aside from having trouble reading and with figures, he was smart enough.

"Who was it figured out a way to get that windmill working again?" E.J. had said. "Who was it figured out the spring mechanism for the stall doors in the barn? Who was it figured out that mixing feeds would increase the yield of weight on the cattle? I could name a dozen other bright ideas you've come up with. You've got brains, boy. Never doubt it."

Only he had. It had come as a relief in seventh grade when he realized he could run like the wind. It had given him a way to excel at something. It had given him self-esteem. Until he had heard what the other boys really thought about him. It wasn't enough that he could run, when he couldn't read.

He had kept strictly to himself after that. He heard what his teammates said then. He was too stuck up to spend time with them now that all those universities had come courting, wanting Sam Longstreet to sign on the dotted line to play football. He had let them think the worst of him because there was no way he could tell them the truth.

And here they were, all of them in one place, smiling and shaking his hand and acting as if everything was perfectly normal. He felt sick to his stomach just being in the same room with them. They pretended like they didn't remember how it was. But he had never forgiven or forgotten their cruelty.

There was some respite from the horror of confronting his past. Surprisingly, it came in the form of Callen's two brothers, Zach and Falcon. Zach grudgingly shook his hand.

"I can see Callen's happy," he said.

"And that makes everything all right?" Sam asked.

"Just make sure she stays that way," Zach said.

Sam could see the respect in Zach's eyes, and the challenge. He couldn't help liking the other man.

Falcon greeted Sam with his arm around Mara, who was holding a blanketed baby. Susannah, her shiny black hair hanging to her shoulders, held trustingly to his other hand.

Sam remembered Susannah from their meeting years before. At the time, Susannah had been wearing a small red hat to conceal the fact that chemotherapy had made all her hair fall out. He could see the years had been good to her.

"You've got a good-looking family there," Sam said.

"Thanks," Falcon replied. "I don't have a free hand, or I'd shake yours."

"I can shake his hand, Daddy," Susannah said, suiting deed to word.

Sam bent down and shook the little girl's hand. "You probably don't remember me, but we met in Dallas about four years ago."

She frowned. "Yes, I do. You're the nice man with green eyes. I met you the day Daddy bought my pony."

Sam smiled. "I don't think I've ever been described so agreeably."

"You've done wonders with this place," Falcon said, looking around at the improvements, which he had missed seeing in his previous brief visit.

"All the credit goes to Callen. She's the one who worked the magic."

"Where is she?" Falcon asked. "I want to say hello."

"I think she's in the kitchen with your mother."

"Is Dad with them?"

Sam worked to keep his features even. "Your father couldn't come. Some kind of emergency at the last minute, I think."

"That's too bad. I think we'll try to find Callen, if you'll excuse us."

Sam looked around his parlor at the happy, smiling people and felt alone. He wanted to be with Callen, but he knew her family was with her now. He couldn't very well go in there and drag her away from them. He searched for someone, anyone he could comfortably converse with. His gaze stopped on Janice Reese.

As though he had summoned her, she walked toward him.

"I've been hoping I'd get a chance to talk with you this evening," Janice said.

"What have you been doing with yourself?" Sam asked. "I'm afraid I haven't kept up."

"I'm the librarian in town."

Sam smiled. It was more of a smirk. No wonder he hadn't seen her in nearly fifteen years. He wouldn't be caught dead in a library. It was full of books he couldn't read.

"I wondered where you disappeared to after high school," she said.

"Oh? Why is that?"

"I've had a crush on you for years. Ever since the sixth grade in fact."

Sam stared at her, stunned. "You called me a dummy!" he blurted. His face flamed.

She laughed sheepishly. "Isn't that awful? I can't believe I was so mean to you! I liked you a lot. I just…I was a stupid twelve-year-old." She smiled and said, "I'm sorry now I didn't track you down."

"Are you flirting with me, Janice?" Sam asked incredulously.

"Would it work if I did?"

"Nope. I'm happily married." What an easy lie that was to tell. He *was* happy. But for how long?

"That's what I thought. I could see the moment I caught sight of you and Callen together that you're in love with each other. I'm happy for you, Sam."

She lifted herself on tiptoes to kiss him on the cheek. To

keep her from falling when she lost her balance, Sam slid an arm around her.

At that moment Zach turned around and saw him. He watched Zach's eyes narrow and knew he had misconstrued the situation. Callen's brother was at his side before he could even steady Janice on her feet.

"What the hell do you think you're doing?" he raged at Sam.

"Mind your own business, Zach. This doesn't concern you."

"When my sister's husband has her arm around another woman who's kissing him in plain sight of all their friends, I'd say that's my business," Zach retorted.

"Nothing happened here," Janice began to explain.

"Keep out of this, Janice," Sam said in a curt voice. "Leave us alone, please." He gave her a little shove toward the other side of the room. Once she was gone, he turned his attention back to Zach. He could see there were already a lot of eyes on the two of them. The thought of explaining himself to Zach irked him, but he didn't want to make a scene and spoil Callen's party, so he said, "That was completely innocent."

"I'll bet."

"Janice was giving me a friendly kiss, and she lost her balance. That's all there was to it."

"You bastard. How long have you been seeing her?"

"What?"

"Everyone knows you had a thing for Janice Reese when you were kids. You mooned over her for most of junior high school."

Sam stared at Zach. He hadn't imagined he had been that obvious. He swallowed over the bile at the back of his throat and said, "I haven't seen Janice for fifteen years until tonight. And I didn't invite her, Callen did."

"You expect me to believe that?"

"It's the truth!" Sam shot back. "But then, you Whitelaws

aren't too big on honesty yourselves, so maybe you don't recognize it when you see it.''

"What's that supposed to mean?"

"Ask your father," Sam snarled.

Sam had forgotten discretion in the heat of the moment. He was suddenly struck by the silence around him and turned to find everyone staring at him and Zach. What he saw in their eyes made him furious. How dare they judge him! How dare they condemn him! Then he caught sight of Callen's stricken face in the kitchen doorway.

She looked embarrassed and ashamed. Of him.

And why shouldn't she be? They all knew what he was. Dressing up and putting on airs didn't change the fact he was dumb as an ox.

He shoved a hand wearily through his hair and turned his back on all of them. "Go home," he said quietly. "The party's over."

He heard shuffling and muttering behind him, heard Callen's voice thanking them all for coming. Heard her reassure Zach and Falcon and her mother that she would be fine. That she was in no danger.

Oh, but she was! She was deeply embroiled in his plan to ruin her father. He hadn't cared whether she got destroyed in the process. And now it was too late. She was going to be hurt. And there wasn't a damn thing he could do about it.

You could give up your vengeance. You could forgive Garth Whitelaw and go on with your life.

"Sam?"

He turned around and saw Callen standing not a foot away from him, her eyes filled with concern. Everyone else had gone.

He shoved his hand through his hair again. "I'm sorry, Callen."

"What happened, Sam? I thought everything was going so well. Why did you start a fight with Zach? Why did you ask everybody to leave?"

"Zach started the fight," he retorted. "And I asked them to leave because I didn't want them here."

"Why not?" When he didn't answer, she reached out a hand and laid it on his chest. "Please tell me, Sam. I want to understand."

He brushed her hand away because he wanted so badly to hold her in his arms when he knew he didn't deserve the love she offered him.

"Don't you see?" he said in an agonized voice. "They all knew."

A frown furrowed her brow. "Knew what?"

"About me."

She shook her head. "You're going to have to be more specific than that. Knew what about you?"

"That I can't read a third-grade primer. That I could barely get through high school. That I couldn't get into college if I tried. That I'm not smart." An agitated hand went forking through his hair again. "Hell. That I'm dumb as ditch water."

"You listen to me, Sam Longstreet! You *are* dumb if you think I'm buying that hogwash for one single minute. You're plenty smart. Your problem is you're stubborn as a mule."

"Oh, Callen." He drew her into his arms, unable to keep his hands off her another second, and hugged her tight. "Saying I'm smart doesn't make it so."

She freed her hands and cupped his face, forcing him to look at her. "There's nothing wrong with you that can't be fixed, Sam. The truth is, you have a reading disability."

"Callen—"

"Shut up and listen to me!" she said. "You have dyslexia, Sam." He started to let her go, so she slipped her hands around his neck and hung on tight. "I checked with a specialist. I gave her that list you made for me. You aren't dumb, Sam, you just see numbers and letters all jumbled up on the page. Einstein had dyslexia, Sam. It has nothing to do with intelligence."

His face flushed a ruddy color. "Callen..." He was afraid to believe what she was saying. Afraid to hope.

"You're a darling idiot, but you're *not* dumb," Callen repeated, looking earnestly into Sam's green eyes. "Mrs. Moran—she's the specialist—says she can teach you how to overcome your reading problem. I told her you'd want to try. Will you, Sam?"

"Callen..." His voice was hoarse and his nose stung. He felt like crying. "It's too late—"

"It is not too late! Mrs. Moran says all it takes is time and effort."

"I don't have the time," Sam said flatly.

"Make the time."

"I'm too old—"

Callen put her hand against his lips to shut him up. "You can learn to read, Sam. You can learn to add and subtract. It isn't going to be easy. And it might even be embarrassing at your age. But if your willing to make the effort, you can resolve a problem that's obviously been bothering you for a lot of years. I'll do whatever I can to help, but really, this is something you're going to have to do yourself."

Sam could hardly force the words over the thick lump of feeling in his throat. "What if I fail?"

Callen's arms tightened around him, and her lips pressed against his in comfort, in reassurance. "You won't fail, Sam. I firmly believe you can do anything you set your heart and mind to do."

Sam had to turn his head away so she wouldn't see the tears in his eyes. His voice was gruff with feeling when he spoke. "All right, Callen. If you want me to, I will."

She began pressing light, loving kisses all over his face.

"If we're done talking, I think it's time for bed," Sam said. "We can clean up this mess in the morning." He lifted Callen in his arms and headed for the bedroom.

He made love to her almost desperately. He wasn't sure

what was driving him. Fear. And elation. What if he could learn to read, after all?

He had listened to Callen's offer of help from Mrs. Moran as though it were no big deal. But deep down, in some secret hidden place where he had stuffed all the shame he had felt as a boy growing up, unable to do simple things like read or add a column of figures, a hard knot began to loosen.

Chapter 7

Once Sam started working with Mrs. Moran, his progress was astonishing. Even Callen was amazed at how quickly he mastered his reading disability. Not that it was easy. And it was embarrassing at times. Callen saw his frustration on occasion, when the words on a page simply made no sense to him. But with an objective in sight, Sam devoted himself wholeheartedly to learning.

Having tackled one challenge, Sam was ready for another. His hope of making the Double L into one of the finest cutting horse ranches in Texas was about to begin.

The first cutting horses arrived two weeks after the housewarming party. Sam and Callen worked together training a sleek quarter horse mare for a rich client in El Paso who wanted to give it to his daughter as a birthday present.

When they began to work with the mare, Callen saw a facet of Sam she hadn't known existed. He had an understanding of animals, a rapport with them, that was transcendent. She had great skill maneuvering a cutting horse; Sam became one with the animal.

"Why haven't you been training cutting horses all along?" Callen demanded when Sam stepped down from the saddle after working the mare. "You're absolutely brilliant!"

One corner of Sam's mouth cocked up in a self-deprecating smile. "You think so?"

"Absolutely! I've never seen anybody ride like that, and I've seen a lot of competitions in my day."

Sam shrugged. "I've always had an affinity to horses." He paused and added, "Animals don't care whether you know how to read."

"Oh, Sam." Callen stepped into his arms and hugged him tight.

"It doesn't hurt so much anymore," Sam admitted quietly. "I mean, now that I know what was wrong. I suppose it's going to take a while getting used to the idea of picking up a newspaper just like other folks and paging through it. And I don't imagine I'll ever take up reading for pleasure." He grinned charmingly. "But I won't ever feel like I'm less smart than another man, ever again. I have you to thank for that, Callen."

"Someone else would have pointed out the problem if I hadn't come along."

"No one else ever did."

How long, Sam wondered, would he have remained blind to the truth if Callen hadn't come into his life? In a matter of months she had turned his life upside down. If he held on to his goal of revenge, he might eventually ruin hers.

"Sam, I met a young woman when I was in the hardware store having some wood cut for shelves. She seemed really nice. Her name is Natalie Folsom. Her husband, Ted, is the new agricultural extension agent. I'd like to invite them to dinner."

"Are you asking me for permission, or telling me what you've done?" Sam asked.

Callen grinned. "You know me too well. Actually, I invited

them for Saturday night. I'm willing to call and cancel if you don't think it's a good idea.''

Sam sighed. He would probably never be a gregarious person, but it was foolish to let his past keep him from enjoying the present or the future. And Ted and Natalie Folsom weren't from around here. They knew nothing about him. ''I think it might be fun to have dinner with another couple.''

The Sam Longstreet who greeted the Folsoms at the door was the man Callen had fallen in love with. Only he was clean-shaven, had his chestnut hair trimmed above his collar, and wore polished boots and a pressed Western shirt and jeans. Callen hadn't let Sam's appearance keep her from falling in love with him, but she had to admit she felt proud of the man standing beside her.

Sam felt like a different man. It wasn't just his spiffed-up clothing and appearance. The difference came from the inside. He felt more self-confident, more sure of himself. Frankly, there wasn't anything different about him except that he knew now he was dyslexic. He had a learning disability, not an inability to learn. And he was making up fast for lost time.

Natalie Folsom was a curly haired redhead, with hazel eyes that crinkled when she smiled, and a smile that took up most of her face. She was petite and looked about seventeen, even though she admitted to twenty-four. Her husband, Ted, was only a few inches taller, but he had a muscular build. He wore glasses and had a receding hairline, but his face was open and friendly. He admitted to being a wrestler back in college ten years before, which made him a year younger than Sam.

They had nothing in common, Sam thought as the evening wore on, and yet he liked Ted. He was a good listener, and he made interesting comments when he spoke. Natalie was funny, and Sam loved seeing Callen laugh at her jokes.

Then Sam mentioned he had a motorcycle.

Ted's eyes lit up. ''You have a motorcycle? What kind?''

Sam grinned. ''Harley-Davidson, what else?''

''A Hog? Really? Me, too,'' Ted said. ''Can I see it?''

"It's in the barn, covered with a tarp. I haven't even looked at it for years."

"Then don't you think it's about time you did?" Ted asked.

The four of them traipsed out to the barn, and Sam pulled a dusty canvas tarp off his Harley-Davidson touring motorcycle.

Ted whistled. "What a beauty! You've had a lot of custom work done. I'll bet all this chrome sure shines up nice."

Sam reached out and slid a hand along the leather seat. "I'd forgotten how much I liked this machine." He had spent hours working on it, tuning it, shining it. He had been lost in a world of his own.

"Sam, I didn't even know you owned a motorcycle," Callen said. "When can I get a ride?"

"You want to ride it?" Sam asked in surprise.

"I'd *love* to ride it," Callen said with a sparkle in her eyes.

"How much work would it take to get it ready?" Ted asked.

Sam shrugged. "It shouldn't take much. I put it away clean."

"Then how about if we all take a ride next Saturday, let the wind blow in our hair and the bugs catch in our teeth."

Sam grinned at the picture Ted had conjured. "Sure, why not?"

"We can take along a picnic," Natalie said.

"And I know just the spot where we can go," Callen offered. "If this very late Indian summer cooperates. Who'd have thought it would still be warm this late in November?"

That night, as they lay in bed together after making sweet, sweet love, Callen laid her head on Sam's chest and slipped an arm across his waist and snuggled close. "Did you like Natalie and Ted?"

"Yeah. They're nice." Sam was feeling good. He couldn't remember a time when he had been this contented. He wondered what it was going to be like, having a friend like Ted.

It had been easy talking to the other man, easy to share stories about their Harley-Davidsons. And he owed it all to Callen. She was the one who had met Natalie and invited the other couple to supper.

"You don't mind getting together with them again?" Callen asked.

"Hell, no. I'm looking forward to it. I can't believe we're going to a picnic on motorcycles," Sam said, grinning in the dark.

"Me, neither," Callen said with a giggle. "It almost makes me feel like a kid again."

"I'll bet you were hell on wheels," Sam said.

"Wait'll you see me on Saturday," she promised.

"I can't wait," Sam said as he turned and kissed her.

He wanted her again. Incredible as it seemed, he was hard and ready. They were both already naked, so it was easy enough to lever himself over her, spread her legs with his knees and thrust into her.

"Sam." She moaned his name as she arched beneath him. "Oh, Sam."

He kissed her with joy, with thanksgiving, with the love he felt but could not speak aloud. He wasn't supposed to care. She was merely a means to his vengeful ends. But he showed her with his mouth and hands what he truly felt in his heart.

Sam spent every spare moment of the next week working on his Harley in the barn. Callen always knew where she could find him. Once they made love facing each other on the leather seat. Once, when she wore a skirt, he stripped off her underwear, then unbuckled his belt, unzipped his pants and took her standing up against the wall of the barn. Once he took her to the loft and laid her down on a blanket in the hay. They made love often, with joy in their hearts. Life seemed perfect.

Then Callen's mother called to invite them to Hawk's Way for dinner.

"Next week is the beginning of the Christmas season, and

it dawned on your father and me that we haven't seen much of you lately." The truth was, Callen and her father hadn't exchanged a word in nearly six months. "We'd both love to see you. Can you come?"

"I'll have to talk it over with Sam. But I'm sure we'll be able to come," Callen said.

"That's wonderful! We'll look forward to it. Call us when you know for sure."

Callen felt her stomach do a little twist when she hung up the phone. She had been so very happy before her mother reminded her that Sam and her father didn't get along. Well, she had tackled every other problem in her marriage with determination and conquered them all. What was one more little glitch? How difficult could it be to turn her husband and her father into friends?

"No," Sam said. "I'm not going to set foot in your father's house. Not now, not ever."

"Why not?" Callen demanded, her fists perched on her hips. "This has gone on long enough. I want to know what you have against my father."

Sam's lips pressed flat. He had known this moment was coming, that it would arrive sooner or later. He just hadn't expected it so soon. He met her brown eyes evenly and said, "Your father is responsible for E.J.'s death."

She got so deathly pale he thought for a moment she was going to faint. He reached out for her, but she flinched away from him.

"That's impossible. Your father committed suicide."

"Do you know why my father took his life?"

Callen frowned. "Not exactly."

"E.J. invested his life savings and every bit of capital we had for running the ranch in several get-rich-quick schemes. They turned out to be swindles. He lost everything. We were going to lose the Double L. He couldn't live with knowing he'd lost the only thing he had to pass on to me. So he killed himself.''

"I still don't see where my father fits into that picture."

"Your father advised E.J. to make those investments."

Callen shook her head no, slowly at first and then more vehemently.

"Shake your head all you like. E.J. never made a financial move in his life that didn't have Garth Whitelaw's stamp of approval.''

"My father wouldn't have advised E.J. into anything that wasn't legitimate. Not on purpose."

"Oh, he did it, all right. And I even know why."

"All right. Why?"

"He wanted Double L land to replace what he gave away to Zach on his twenty-first birthday.''

"That's ridiculous!"

"Is it? Think about it. How many times have you heard your father wish he had back the land he gave to Zach?"

Callen sucked in a breath. She had heard her father say exactly that over the years. He had given Zach thousands of acres of Hawk's Way land, in fact, about the same amount of acreage that comprised the Double L. And of course he missed the land, because it meant he couldn't run as many cattle, didn't have as much land to grow feed, didn't have the same lines drawn on the vast map of Hawk's Way that hung over the mantel in the parlor.

Her eyes widened in fright and horror. She didn't want to believe Sam's accusation. Refused to believe it. And was horrified to realize how much Sam must hate her father if he believed what he was saying.

"How could you marry me, thinking that about my father?" she asked in a quavery voice.

"I didn't intend to share you with him," Sam said. "I thought we'd never have to see him again."

"But he's my father!" Callen protested. "I love him. I could never stop seeing him!"

"Not even for me?"

Callen paced the room like a restless animal in a cage. "I love you, Sam. But I can't stop loving my father because I love you."

"And if you had to choose between us?"

Callen turned horrified eyes on Sam. "You wouldn't ask that of me. Surely you wouldn't!"

Here it was. The moment of truth. If he had done his work well, Callen would choose him over her father. Garth White-law would realize exactly what price he had paid for coveting Double L land. He had lost his chance to have the land. Now he would lose his daughter, as well.

"I am asking, Callen. I'm asking you not to go to dinner at Hawk's Way. I'm asking you not to see your father again."

Callen stood still, but her whole body trembled. "I'm going, Sam. What you're asking of me is unreasonable. I won't be forced to choose between my husband and my father. I love you both."

"You can't have us both," Sam said flatly.

"What do you mean?" Callen asked, wide-eyed with distress.

"If you go to dinner at Hawk's Way, don't come back here. You won't be welcome."

Callen laughed, a harsh, unnatural sound. "I can't believe what I'm hearing! And it's so funny. My father threatened nearly the same thing—that I would lose my job at Hawk's Way—when I said I was going to marry you. Sam—" She reached out a hand to him, but he stepped back beyond her reach.

"I meant what I said, Callen. The choice is yours."

Callen slept on her own side of the bed that night, hugging her arms to her body, unable to believe the impossible choice she had been given. She loved Sam more now than she had ever imagined possible. But she would die a little inside if she never saw her father again. She supposed she could concede to Sam now, and hope that he would change his mind later. But what if he didn't?

The next morning Sam noticed the air was almost as frigid as Callen's behavior toward him. "Good morning," he said as he sat down in the kitchen with a cup of coffee. One sip of the stuff had him screwing up his mouth at the bitter taste.

"I suppose if it gets any colder we'll have to call off the picnic on Saturday," he said.

"I'm not in the mood for a picnic anymore." Callen slammed his breakfast down in front of him.

The yolks on the eggs were broken and cooked hard, and the bacon was burned. Sam's lip curled. The woman sure knew how to make a subtle point.

She plopped down in the chair across from him and settled her fisted hands on the table in front of her. "Sam, we have to talk about this. You've got to change your mind."

"No." The eggs stuck in his throat. He washed them down with a sip of bitter coffee.

"Have you talked to my father? Did he give you any explanation of what might have happened?"

"I don't need to talk to your father. I know what I know."

"You're a damn fool, Sam," Callen accused, rising to her feet, "if you assume facts without knowing them."

Sam flushed. "I know my father, Callen. He wouldn't have done anything so foolhardy as investing on his own. He knew his limitations."

"So my father's to blame? Have you ever considered that your father may have made those decisions all by himself? That my father may be entirely innocent?"

Sam had refused to consider that possibility for several reasons. First, he knew how much his father had always relied on Garth Whitelaw to advise him on his investments. Second, if his father had made those decisions on his own, then it meant he was entirely responsible for losing his fortune, and that he had taken the coward's way out by committing suicide and leaving Sam to face the consequences alone.

Sam didn't want to believe that about his father. He needed to believe E.J.'s misfortune could be laid at Garth's door, along with the responsibility for E.J.'s untimely death.

"Do you want me to call Ted and cancel the picnic?" Sam asked.

Callen thought about it a moment. She had made up her mind to attend the dinner with her parents at Hawk's Way. If Sam held to his threats, she wouldn't be seeing him again after that. The picnic with Ted and Natalie might be the last one they ever had together. She wanted that memory to take with her.

"Tell them to dress warm," she said.

Sam couldn't believe that Callen was sticking to her guns. The dinner with her parents was the following Sunday. If he couldn't convince her to stay, he was going to have to let her go.

He was terrified of losing her.

He visited E.J.'s grave three times in the next week. He sat there with his back resting against the headstone and spoke aloud to his father, venting his frustration and asking for advice. He picked one of the fall flowers Callen had planted there and twirled it in his fingers. Then he began plucking the petals.

"She loves me...she loves me not...she loves me...she loves me not...she loves me. I really think she does, E.J. And I love her. I'm not exactly sure how it happened, but I think I've loved her for a long time. I don't know how I'll live without her. It's killing me to do this. But I don't know any other way to pay Garth back for what he did to you. And I promised you I'd give you that satisfaction, at least. It'll hurt him for sure if he knows Callen is suffering because of him. And I think she will, if I force her to stay away from the Double L.

"But, oh, God, Dad. I don't want to do it! It's tearing me apart inside. Tell me what to do! Tell me how to make everything come out right!''

There were no answers from the grave.

The day of the picnic dawned sunny and brisk. Sam produced a black leather jacket for himself and one for Callen. On the back in red lettering were the words Born To Be Wild.

''Where did you get this?''

He held it for her while she slipped into it. ''I bought it for you. I thought we might start riding together.''

She kept her chin down and her lashes lowered so he couldn't see her face as she zipped it up. Sam had bought this jacket when he thought they had a future together. If he didn't change his mind, this might be the only time she ever wore it.

Callen had ridden horseback all her life, so she knew the thrill of having a lot of horsepower between her legs. But when Sam revved up the Harley and she sat down behind him with her arms circling his waist, she knew what it was like to fly without ever leaving the ground. She felt the wind in her hair and smiled, knowing the chance she was taking that she would end up with bugs in her teeth. It was glorious.

It took a lot of trust to sit behind Sam and let him direct their course. She felt the power of the machine and the man who controlled it. She would have followed Sam anywhere, she realized. She knew he wasn't perfect. Far from it. But then, who was? Where it counted, when it counted, she knew Sam would always be there for her, loving her.

''Having fun?'' Sam shouted over his shoulder. The wind caught the sound and sent it in all directions.

With a helmet on, Callen heard nothing. ''What?''

''Having fun?'' he repeated.

''Yes. I don't ever want to stop,'' she hollered back.

''What?'' he shouted.

''Never mind,'' she said in a normal voice. ''I know the trip is almost over. I just want to enjoy what there is left of it.''

They ended up at the entrance to a deep canyon where there

must once have been water since several cypress and cotton-woods had grown there. The weather was brisk, but there was no wind, and the bright sun made it seem warmer than it was.

Callen spread a blanket and the two women put out a picnic fit for kings. "Come on, fellows," Callen called. "Time to eat."

Callen and Sam never referred to his ultimatum once all day. They chatted with their new friends and discovered that all of them like to do the Texas two-step. They made a prom-ise to go dancing together as soon as they could find a time when they were all free.

Sam and Ted talked about the weather and the price of cattle and whether interest rates were going to stay down or go back up again. Callen and Natalie talked about the weather and the price of food and whether health care reform would ever become a reality.

After lunch, when the sun was at its warmest, Ted and Natalie decided to take a walk down into the canyon.

"I'd rather rest, I think," Callen said.

Sam looked sharply at her. His Callen *resting?* It was un-heard of. "Are you all right?"

She smiled lazily. "I'm just fine. A little tired. I didn't get much sleep last night."

Sam knew at least one worry that might have kept her awake. "You two go on," he said to the other couple. "We'll wait for you here."

Sam set himself down on the blanket with his back against a cottonwood and patted his thigh. "You can use me for a pillow."

Callen scooted over so she could rest her head in Sam's lap. "Thanks, Sam."

They didn't talk. Both of them knew it would have meant arguing. By tacit consent, they were determined to enjoy these last moments together before all hell broke loose.

To Sam's surprise, Callen fell asleep only minutes later. He brushed her bangs away from her face, then smoothed his thumb across her cheek for the sheer pleasure of touching her skin. He wanted to hold her close and never let her go. He wanted to treasure her. He wanted to get his children on her. He knew he had created the tense situation between them, and that he had the power to end it.

Sam leaned his head back against the tree and stared up through the branches into the cloudless blue sky. How important was vengeance, anyway? An eye for an eye, a tooth for a tooth, the Bible said. He needed to see Garth pay for E.J.'s death. Needed to know his father's death had been avenged, so he could finally lay E.J. to rest. So he could go on with his life.

But what kind of life did he have to look forward to if he lost Callen in the pursuit of his almighty vengeance?

He convinced himself, sitting there under a leafless cottonwood, that in the end she would choose him over her father. After all, she loved him. And she wouldn't want to hear her father say "I told you so." She wouldn't leave him. She couldn't.

Sam hadn't realized he had fallen asleep until he heard the quiet murmur of voices. Maybe he hadn't slept so well himself last night. He slowly opened his eyes.

Callen was sitting nearby talking to Natalie. Ted was over by the cycles, polishing chrome. He realized Callen was talking about him, about their marriage. He quickly closed his eyes, curious as to what she would say.

"I can't believe you actually went through with the wedding," Natalie exclaimed. "If Ted had shown up looking like that, I'd have bolted for sure."

"Sam isn't the sort of man you should judge by appearances," Callen replied. "It's what's on the inside that really matters. He's kind. And hardworking. He makes me feel special. And he's so very smart."

Sam struggled not to wince at that. It was taking time for him to accept himself the way Callen insisted upon perceiving him. He remembered a boy struggling to make sense of confusion on a page. She saw a man with dyslexia who had accepted the challenge to read.

"And I know Sam will make a good father," Callen said.

"Are you by any chance expecting?" Natalie asked.

Callen didn't answer, and Sam held his breath. She must have gestured one way or the other with her head, but by the time he opened his eyes a slit, she had resumed speaking.

"There's only one problem with Sam," she said.

"What's that?" Natalie asked.

Sam clenched his teeth. Well, this was it. She was going to tell Natalie about their argument, about his ultimatum.

"He drives way too fast on that motorcycle!"

Sam exploded with laughter.

"Sam! How long have you been awake?" Callen demanded.

"Long enough," he said with a grin. He rose to his feet. "Come on. I think it's time we headed back. I'm going to need lots of time to get home before dark, if I don't want to drive too fast."

He held out a hand and Callen took it. He dragged her to her feet and into his arms and gave her a lusty kiss.

Callen struggled only a moment before she kissed him back. When they finally separated, she scolded him. "What will Ted and Natalie think?"

"That I like kissing you. And you like kissing me back."

Callen's cheeks were tinged with rose by the time Sam finished kissing her a second time. "It's getting dark, Sam. We'd better be heading back."

Sam saw the sun was on its way down. This idyll, indeed, the halcyon days of their marriage, were nearly over. Whether Callen left him, or whether she stayed, things would never be quite the same between them again.

Callen spent the entire week leading up to the first Sunday in Advent arguing with Sam, trying to convince him that he was being unreasonable. But he was adamant. On the Saturday before she was to have dinner with her parents, she brought out the big guns. She let the tears drip in cascades from her eyes, even though she knew she never looked her best when she was crying. Desperate situations required desperate measures.

The tears almost did him in. Sam was torn in two at the sight of Callen's tear-streaked face. He wanted to say the hell with it and let her go. Only he turned at that instant and spied a small stain on the hardwood floor where E.J.'s blood had soaked into the aged wood. He had covered the spot with a rug, but the rug had slid away to reveal the dark secret beneath it. His heart hardened. He had sworn vengeance against Garth Whitelaw. By God, he would have it!

At last the fateful day arrived. In the stark morning light, from the rumpled sheets he had shared with his wife the night before, Sam watched Callen dressing for dinner with her parents at Hawk's Way. ''So you're going, after all.''

''Yes.''

She looked awful, Sam thought. Her eyes were red-rimmed from all the crying she had done, and there were shadows under her eyes that told him she hadn't slept. Hell, neither had he. He wasn't about to miss a moment of what might very well have been the last night his wife spent in his bed.

''I don't want you to go, Callen.''

''Don't you see I have to, Sam? They're my parents. If E.J. were still alive, would you avoid him simply because I didn't like him?''

Put that way, his request did seem unreasonable. But the whole crux of the problem was that her father was the reason his father was dead. And if he wasn't able to keep Callen away from Garth, then he would have to put the other part of his plan into effect. He would have to do his best to make Callen miserable, and force Garth to live with the knowledge that he was the source of his daughter's unhappiness. He had to cut Callen out of his life. He had to divorce her.

Sam could see she was ready to go. ''If you leave this

house, don't come back," he said in a voice that sounded like
a rusty gate.

"You don't mean that," Callen replied in a calm voice.

Her eyes were full of love for him. He felt like a band was
tightening around his chest, cutting off his air. He stopped
breathing entirely when he heard what she had to say next.

"Because if I go out that door, never to return, so does
your son or daughter." Callen closed the bedroom door with
a quiet click behind her.

The silence was deafening.

An instant later Sam was out of bed and had his jeans on.
He zipped them halfway up and skipped the snap. They barely
clung to his hips as he headed after her. "What did you say?"

Sam caught Callen in the kitchen and dragged her back
around to face him. There were tears in her eyes again. He
hauled her into his arms and held her there. She was going
to leave him. He could feel it from the way she remained stiff
in his arms, unyielding.

He hadn't figured on a child. He had used protection every
time. Except that once. Just once. And there had been dire
consequences for his lapse.

Sam had a decision to make. Which was more important?
Vengeance? Or a lifetime with Callen and the child she carried inside her?

It was far easier to put the burden on her. He let her go
and stepped back. "Don't go, Callen. Please, don't go."

"I have to, Sam." The words were wrenched from her as
she turned and ran.

Sam let her go.

Chapter 8

Garth and Candy welcomed their daughter with open arms. They exchanged a look of concern over her head as they led her into the parlor to have a glass of wine before dinner.

"None for me," Callen said. "Water will be fine."

Candy poured a glass of sparkling water and added ice before she handed it to her daughter. "Sam isn't coming?"

Callen shook her head. She turned to look out the window and blinked back a tear before it could spill.

"I can't believe so much time has passed since you got married," Candy said. "We kept expecting to see the two of you here at Hawk's Way any day. Now it's nearly Christmas."

"Yes," Callen said in a voice that was commendably calm. She had already bought one of Sam's Christmas presents. She had signed him up for an audio book club, so he could listen on tape to all the books he had never read. "There was a lot to do on the Double L. Sam and I have been very busy."

Callen was a married woman and soon to be a mother herself. If she had learned anything in the months she had been

married to Sam, it was that there was no obstacle too great
to be overcome. Look at everything Sam had survived. Surely
there was some way to resolve this dilemma so they could all
have Christmas together.

"Is Sam treating you well, Callen?" her mother probed.

"Obviously her husband isn't treating her right," her father
muttered. "Otherwise she wouldn't look like death warmed
over."

"I'll thank you not to say anything disrespectful about my
husband," Callen said. "What goes on between Sam and me
is our business."

"I'm sorry he wasn't able to come," Callen's mother said.

"I'm just as glad he didn't," her father countered.

Callen rose and confronted her father. "I mean it, Daddy.
If you make one more remark like that about Sam, I'll leave."

"Please, Garth," Candy said. "Let's just have some dinner
and let Callen tell us what she's been doing since she and
Sam got married."

Callen saw the warning look her mother shot at her father
and was grateful for the help in steering her father away from
the subject of Sam Longstreet. But it was too much to hope
it wouldn't be raised again at the dinner table.

"So what have you and Sam been doing that's kept you so
busy you can't—"

"Garth."

Her mother's warning cut her father off and gave Callen
an opening to answer his question. She told them everything.
How Sam had needed her fortune to save the Double L from
foreclosure. How she had remodeled the house as best she
could using items she had scrounged, or bought at a discount,
or repaired with a little elbow grease and the sweat of her
brow. How proud she was of the result. How she and Sam
had painted the house together and how good it looked when
they were done. How Sam had come up with the idea of
training cutting horses and how successful they had been with
a mare intended for a girl in El Paso. How she had discovered

Sam was dyslexic, and how he was finally, at long last, learning to read.

Of the revelation about Sam, her mother said, ''That's unbelievable. I wonder why no one ever figured it out before.''

Because no one cared enough to find out the truth. Because Sam never let anyone get close enough to see how he was suffering because of it. Callen couldn't say that to her parents. They wouldn't understand. And really, it didn't matter now. She was there to love Sam, to care whether he was happy. That is, if he let her come home to him after she had finished this dinner with her parents.

She didn't tell them about the baby. She didn't want it to be used as a pawn in the battle she could see was coming. Nor did she ask her father about whether he was the one who had advised E. J. Longstreet into so many bad investments. She knew her father well enough to believe he hadn't done anything dishonest. If he had suggested some investments that turned out to be swindles, he had not done it knowingly. Besides, there was no way to change the past. What was done was done. It was Sam who had to forgive and forget.

Callen sought for a safe subject of conversation and found it. ''What have you two been doing with yourselves at Hawk's Way, now that all three of your young ones have finally flown the nest?''

Her parents exchanged a tender look. Her mother flushed. Her father grinned.

''To be honest,'' her mother admitted, ''we've had a sort of second honeymoon.''

''That doesn't mean we don't want to see our children as often as they can come visit,'' her father said.

''I'm glad for both of you.'' Callen ate the last bit of apple pie that Charlie One Horse had made because he knew it was her favorite dessert and shoved her plate away. ''I'm afraid I've got to go now.''

''Can't you stay and visit longer?'' her father said.

"I need to get home. There are lots of chores to be done. And I want to be sure I have time to cook supper for Sam."

Her parents walked her to the door, clearly reluctant to let her go.

"When will we see you again?" her mother asked.

"Soon."

"Don't make it so long next time," her father said gruffly as he pulled her into his arms at the door and gave her a hug. "I love you, Callen," he whispered in her ear.

Callen bit her lip to keep from bursting into tears. She couldn't remember the last time her father had told her he loved her. Callen hugged him hard. She peered up at him when he let her go. The skin was stretched taut over his cheekbones. He was getting older. There was more gray in his hair, and the creases beside his mouth were deeper. She glanced at her mother and saw there were lines around her eyes that she had never noticed before. Where had the time gone?

They were already grandparents to Falcon's stepdaughter and newborn son. Now they were going to have another grandchild. And she was going to have to find a way to convince Sam that their child needed its grandparents.

"Goodbye, Daddy. Goodbye, Mom," she said, giving them each another quick hug and a kiss. "Don't worry about me, please. I love Sam. And I'll find a way to make everything all right."

She was gone before they could ask her what she meant.

Callen drove back to the Double L as fast as her car could get her there. She parked in back and headed for the kitchen door. She turned the knob and shoved, but the door didn't budge.

It was locked.

She banged on the door. "Sam! The door's locked. Come on, let me in."

There was no answer. She couldn't imagine why the door was locked in the first place. They never locked the doors. It wasn't necessary. She raced around the house to the front door, thinking it might be open. It was locked, as well.

She pounded on it and shouted, "Sam! I know you're in there! This is ridiculous! Let me in!"

A quick check revealed his motorcycle was gone. So, he wasn't inside listening to her pound on the door, after all.

There was a key under the mat in front, and Callen stooped to see if it was there. It was. She picked it up and stood in the fading light of dusk and stared at it. All she had to do was put the key in the lock and open the door.

Why had Sam locked the doors, but left the key, she wondered, unless he intended for her to let herself in? But if he wanted her inside, why hadn't he simply left the doors open? Why had he made sure to be gone when she got home?

Callen felt a rising fury. If Sam was backing off from his ultimatum, if this was his idea of an apology, it fell far short of what was necessary. And if he was testing to see whether she dared to come inside after he had made it clear she wasn't welcome, he was going to be sorely disappointed. If Sam wanted to play games, she would show him how it was done. He would soon discover that a Whitelaw learned in diapers how to win.

Callen's lips twisted in chagrin. Of course, there was the small matter of where she was going to stay until Sam came after her with an apology on his lips. Returning to Hawk's Way was out of the question. She got into her car and headed down the drive away from the Double L without any clear destination in mind. Not that she could see anything anyway, for the tears blurring her vision.

When she realized several minutes later that she was on the road to Hawk's Way she pulled over to the side of the road and stopped. She refused to go home to her father. She didn't belong there anymore. She turned the car around and headed in the other direction.

She had only been to Zach's ranch a few times, but nothing had ever looked as sweet to her as his whitewashed Spanish-style adobe house. She parked the car in back and headed for the kitchen. She opened the unlocked door without knocking and stepped inside. Zach was sitting at the island bar in the center of the kitchen, finishing up a supper that looked like it had gone from the freezer to the microwave. He looked up when she appeared in the doorway, startled. He rose and took a step toward her.

Callen collapsed, weeping, into her brother's comforting arms.

He didn't ask her any questions. He didn't say "I told you so." He merely put her into bed in his guest room, drew the drapes to make it dark, closed the door and left her alone.

Sam sat with his back against E.J.'s headstone. Tears had dried on his cheeks. It was nearly full dark. He knew Callen must have come home by now and found the doors locked. He wondered whether she had bothered to look for the key and whether she had used it. He was afraid to go home and find out.

He had argued with himself for hours about whether he ought to simply go back to the house and unlock the doors and welcome home the best thing that had ever happened to him. In spite of all his threats, he knew he would welcome her with open arms if she came back to him. She had to know how he felt. But he had never told her that he loved her. He had never told her how precious she was to him.

Sam tried to remember what his life had been like before Callen came into it nearly nine months ago. Bleak. Lonely.

Lately it had been filled with laughter. Soon there would be a baby crying, bringing new life to the Double L. Unless Callen saw those locked doors and left. What if she didn't remember about the key under the front door mat? What if she didn't think to look for it?

He didn't know how he would live without her.

Sam jumped up and ran for his motorcycle. He lay low along the tank as the wind whistled around his ears. He felt the fear rise as he approached the house and saw it was still dark. He raced for the back door, yanked on it and realized it was locked. He pounded on it twice in frustration before he sprinted around to the front.

He saw the shine of the key in the last rays of daylight. It was sitting on top of the mat in plain sight. She had found it. But she hadn't used it.

Sam grabbed the key and jammed it into the lock. He turned the key and forced the door open, shouting as he hurried through the dark house.

"Callen? Where are you? Callen? Are you here? Callen?"

He turned on lights as he went until he had illuminated every square foot of the house. She wasn't there.

He walked back into the párlor and sat in the chair she had scrounged for him and put his feet up on the comfortable ottoman. There was no warm fire to greet him. There was no warm woman to hold in his arms. He leaned back wearily in the chair. He had never been so tired.

Where could she have gone?

To Hawk's Way, you fool. And you have no one to blame but yourself. You had a chance. You could have made a choice.

I did make a choice.

You made the wrong one.

I owed E.J.—

Do you think E.J. would have wanted to see this happen? Do you think E.J. would want his grandchild to grow up without its father?

She'll come back.

Better if you go after her.

She'll come back.

You're a fool, Sam Longstreet.

Sam tried to find some satisfaction in what he had done. His revenge was complete. But as he looked around his empty house, bereft of love and laughter, and thought of sleeping in his bed, empty and cold, and imagined a future spent

alone...vengeance suddenly didn't seem so important anymore.

It seemed a betrayal of the feelings he had for his father to
choose Callen over vengeance. But vengeance was a bitter
bedfellow.

Sam was torn in two. He couldn't think right now. He
closed his eyes and let blessed sleep claim him.

Callen pounded on the door. "Sam! Let me in! Sam!"

*The front door opened abruptly and Callen nearly fell in-
side. Sam caught her firmly by the shoulders and kept her at
arm's length. "You left this house, Callen. You're not welcome here anymore."*

*She laughed shakily. "Sam, this is my home, too. You're
my husband. I want to come in."*

"No, Callen."

*Callen was stunned. He had meant what he had said. He
didn't want her anymore. And all because she refused to love
one man more than another. Callen had too much pride to
beg. "All right, Sam. Have it your way."*

*She turned and walked toward her car. She got in and
gunned the engine, spitting rocks and dust as she headed
down the drive.*

Only she had no place to go.

"Callen! Callen!"

It was Sam. He was calling her back. He wanted her—

Callen bolted upright when she felt a hand on her shoulder.
Where was she?

"You were having a bad dream," Zach said.

Oh, my God, it had all been a dream! Callen bit back a
sob. The nightmare had seemed so real!

She looked around her, trying to orient herself. This wasn't
her bed. There was no comforting warmth lying beside her.
It all came back to her again with her eyes wide open. The
awful confrontation with Sam. His ultimatum. Returning

home to find herself locked out. Leaving the key where Sam was sure to find it and know she had chosen to leave him. Coming to Zach's house and collapsing in his arms.

"Oh, God."

"Are you all right, Callen? You cried out in your sleep."

It was still dark. She couldn't see Zach, but she could feel his arms close around her shoulders. She leaned her head against his chest and sighed. "I've made a mess of everything, Zach."

"You had some help."

"Yes. Sam isn't without blame. What am I going to do now?"

"Get a good night's sleep and go home tomorrow."

"It isn't that simple. Sam threw me out."

"He what?"

"He's got this crazy idea that Daddy is responsible for E.J.'s death."

"That's hogwash."

"He says Daddy pointed E.J. toward those investments on purpose, because he wanted him to lose the Double L."

"Why?"

"So Daddy could buy the Double L when it went into foreclosure and replace the land he gave to you."

Zach remained silent, and Callen's heart fell.

"I knew he wanted to buy some more land," Zach mused quietly. "But I thought he had Abel Johnson convinced to sell."

"You're not suggesting Daddy might have done what Sam's accused him of, are you?"

"No. Dad and E.J. were too close for that. I think if Dad had wanted E.J. to sell to him he would have come right out and asked."

"What if E.J. said no?"

"Then I think Dad would have looked elsewhere."

Callen sighed. "I thought the same thing. But Sam refuses

to believe me. And he refuses to listen to anything Daddy has to say.''

''Then I guess we'll just have to catch him and hog-tie him and make him listen.''

Callen laughed at the image Zach had conjured. ''Oh, I'd like to see you try.''

''You think I couldn't do it?''

''I think you'd have your hands full trying.''

''Seriously, Callen, what are you going to do now?''

''Can I stay here?''

''You're welcome for as long as you want to stay.''

''I'll have to find a place of my own soon,'' she said.

''You'll be no bother here.''

''Yes, but I have a feeling you may draw the line at hosting a squalling infant.''

She heard Zach take in a breath.

''You're pregnant?''

''Nearly three months.''

''Sam Longstreet is a fool.''

''Right now, I'd have to agree with you.'' Callen felt like crying.

Zach must have sensed it somehow because his arms tightened around her and he ruffled her hair. ''Don't worry, Callen. Everything will turn out fine. You'll see. First off, I'm going to see Dad and explain the situation. I may not be able to make Sam listen, but surely Dad can find a way to make him hear the truth.''

''Oh, Zach, I hope you're right.''

''You'd go back to him if he asked?''

''In a heartbeat. I love him, Zach. More than my own life. More than anything.''

''Then why aren't you at the Double L right now?''

''Because Sam has to realize he loves me the same way. Until he does, until he realizes that nothing is more important than our love for each other, it's better that I stay away.''

Zach eased her back down. "Get some sleep, Callen. We have a long day ahead of us tomorrow."

Zach didn't go back to his own bed. He dressed and left the house, arriving at the imposing front door of Hawk's Way a half hour later. He let himself in and made his way upstairs to his parents' bedroom. The door was closed and he knocked.

He heard the rustling of bedcovers inside and then his father's voice. "Who's there?"

"Zach."

His father and mother both appeared at the door a moment later. "What's wrong?" they said together.

"It's Callen."

"Is she all right? Has something happened to her?" his mother asked.

"She's fine, Mom. She's at my place, sound asleep in the guest room."

"If that bastard has done anything—"

"Hold on, Dad," Zach said. "You'd better be sure Callen doesn't hear you bad-mouthing Sam like that. She's likely to scratch your eyes out."

"What the hell is going on, Zach?" Garth demanded.

Zach turned to his mother. "I need to talk to Dad. Could you leave us alone for a little while?"

"There's nothing you have to say to me that your mother can't hear," Garth said.

"All right. I'll wait for you both downstairs."

It didn't take long for Zach to relate everything Callen had told him. Except the fact that she was pregnant. He figured she would rather tell them that herself. "So you see, Dad, you're going to have to make Sam listen to the truth."

"You don't think Sam's version of what happened is the truth?" Garth questioned.

"No, Dad. And neither does Callen. But I'm curious. Just what did happen?"

Garth sighed. "I believe I'll save that explanation for Sam. But I don't think he's going to want to hear it."

"When are you going to see Sam?" Candy asked.

"Is tomorrow morning soon enough?"

"I guess it'll have to be," Zach said. He rose with a stretch, and yawned. "I guess I'd better get back home and get what sleep I can. I'd advise you to do the same."

Once Zach was gone, Garth and Candy walked arm-in-arm back up the spiral staircase. They went through the motions of removing robes and returning to bed. Garth turned out the bedside lamp and pulled his wife into his arms.

But sleep wouldn't come.

"It wasn't your fault, Garth," Candy whispered in the dark. "There was nothing you could have done."

"I'm not so sure," Garth said. "He was my friend. I should have been able to prevent what happened. I should have done more. I should have done *something*."

"You did what you could. You did more than most. Don't blame yourself."

"Sam blames me."

"Sam needs someone to blame."

"What if he won't listen?"

"He'll listen. And he'll recognize the truth when he hears it."

"I hope you're right."

"Try to sleep, Garth. You'll need your strength tomorrow." Candy pressed her cheek against Garth's chest and let her hand twine in the hair at his nape. "You're a good husband, Garth, and a good father and a good friend. Don't ever doubt it."

"Thanks, Candy. I needed to hear that." Garth pulled his wife close. She was the treasure of his life. The light that burned bright in his soul. He hoped his children found the same wonder in their spouses that he had found in his.

Garth lay for a long time staring into the dark. He felt Candy's breathing deepen and steady into the rhythm of sleep. At long last, he closed his eyes and drifted into sleep.

Chapter 9

No doubt about it, Sam Longstreet was a changed man. And it was all the result of his marriage to Callen Whitelaw. Sam stood on his front porch, which no longer sagged, and looked around him. Not only had the rotting boards been replaced on the barn, but it had been painted a rust red. There were six sleek quarter horses in the corral, waiting to be worked. Two of those cutting horses belonged to the Double L. The rest were being trained for clients he had advertised for in quarter-horse journals. He had written the ads himself and read them when they appeared in the magazine.

He brushed a hand across his clean-shaven jaw and wiped the polished toes of his boots against the back of his jeans. There wasn't a piece of clothing in his drawers with a rip or tear, not a button missing on one of his shirts. He owed that to Callen, too.

In the distance he saw a windmill twirling like mad, but no screech of unoiled metal carried to him on the wind. He could see his cattle near the stock tank, munching contentedly on hay he had planted and reaped himself. He would be taking them to market soon, and because he was a lucky man, the price of beef was up.

The Double L had never been so profitable as it was now. He had made his mortgage payments the past few months with money earned by the sweat of his brow—and Callen's. He mustn't forget his wife when he was counting his blessings. Because she was the greatest one of all.

Sam knew what his wife had given to him. His ranch. His self-respect. Her love.

What had he offered her in return? Dishonesty. Duplicity. Deception.

He had never once told her his true feelings. Although, perhaps that wasn't surprising, since he had lied to himself almost from the first. He must have loved her even then. He couldn't remember a time when he hadn't. Only he had never told her. He had never said the words aloud. Not when she married him. Not when she made love to him. Not when she gave him back his ranch or offered him a chance to read and write when he thought such feats impossible. Not even when she made him believe there was nothing he couldn't do if he set his mind to it.

Had he made her happy, as he had promised he would on the day he proposed to her? He thought perhaps she was. Or had been, before he insisted on having his revenge against her father. If he had it all to do over again, he would do things differently. Oh, yes, he would. He would recognize the prize he had found in his wife and cherish her and protect her from anything that threatened her happiness.

He couldn't live the past again. But there was the always the future. Sam headed back inside the house for breakfast. There were no days off on a ranch. Despite everything, he had work that had to be done.

He wasn't hungry enough to cook himself a breakfast, settling for two cups of coffee while he stared out the curtained window in front of the sink. It was almost painful to be in this room without her. He wanted her here. Needed her here. Wished she were here.

Callen had lavished her attention on everything from the shiny hardwood floor to the new coat of paint on the cabinets to the flowery wallpaper. She had made the room hers, made it light and lovely. It wasn't a bachelor kitchen anymore.

Sam remembered a story Callen had told him about what it was like to grow up with two older brothers. They had gotten into so much mischief the neighbors had dubbed them the Three Whitelaw Brats. She was always tagging along behind them.

"But they didn't want me there," she said wistfully. "I was in their way. They had to be more careful when I was around—although I got hurt often enough even as it was.

"I grew up thinking I could do anything they could do. Mostly, I could. It wasn't until much later that I realized I didn't want to do all the things they were doing, that there were other things that interested me more. Only, if I did those things, I wouldn't have my brothers' company. I would have to do them alone.

"It's hard to believe that with everything I had at Hawk's Way, I could have been lonely. But I was. I was too much of a tomboy to get along with the other girls when I was younger, and by the time I realized I wanted to be just like them, it was too late. I couldn't seem to go along with the crowd. I was too much my own person.

"I spent a lot of time alone. That was what drew me to you at first, you know. I saw that same look of loneliness in your eyes. And I knew we could be friends."

"Why did you marry me, Callen?" he had asked.

"I wanted someone to love. I wanted to be loved by someone. And I wanted a home and a family of my own."

She had expected so little from their marriage. And so very, very much.

Sam's neckhairs stiffened when he heard a knock at the front door. That alone announced it wasn't a friendly visit.

He made his way through the house to the front door. When he opened it, he found Garth Whitelaw standing there.

"I want to talk," Garth said. "And I won't take no for an answer."

Sam hesitated before stepping back. "Come on in and say your piece."

Garth took a quick look around and saw that more improvements had been made since the last time he had been inside. The house had a warmth and coziness that proclaimed it a home. Unfortunately, his daughter was no longer living here. It was a situation he hoped to remedy.

Garth turned to Sam and found the other man's face unreadable. Which meant he didn't detect the loathing that had been there the last time the two of them had conversed. But there was no liking evident, either.

"I knew about those investments E.J. made," he began.

Sam's hands balled into fists, which he pounded against his thighs. "Damnation! I knew it! I knew you were to blame!"

"I didn't say I was to blame," Garth corrected in a terse voice. "I said I knew E.J. invested in those deals. He came to me and asked me what I thought. I advised him against it."

"The hell you did! If you'd told him not to invest, E.J. wouldn't have invested."

Garth shook his head. "That's where you're wrong. E.J. was sick, Sam. He had prostate cancer. He knew he was dying, and he wanted to leave you more than what he had. He was hoping to make a killing, since all those deals offered a substantial return. Only E.J. got burned. I think he was afraid to face you and tell you the truth." A muscle in his cheek jerked. "Just like I was."

Sam's face had bleached white. "You're lying." E.J. sick? E.J. dying of cancer? It was all so improbable. So unbelievable. Only, Garth's words had the ring of truth.

"I wouldn't have cared if he lost everything," Sam said in

a hoarse voice. "I wouldn't have blamed him. He didn't have to kill himself!"

"He was afraid of the cancer, Sam. I think that was as much the cause of what he did as losing his fortune." Garth sighed deeply. "I know it wasn't my fault, and yet I still felt responsible when I heard E.J. had killed himself. I felt I deserved whatever scorn you heaped on my shoulders. I should have interfered. I should have argued more against those investments E.J. made. I should have made him tell you about the cancer. Maybe then…"

Sam put out a hand to stop Garth's speech. "You knew E.J. as well or better than anyone. Do you really think you could have stopped him once he got an idea fixed in his head?"

"No. You're right. He was one stubborn cuss." Garth paused and added, "And you take after him. I came here today to tell you the truth. And to tell you you're a fool if you let Callen slip through your fingers. I haven't figured out why, but my daughter loves you enough to take your side against her own father. She threatened to leave my house if I said a word against you."

"She did?" That was news to Sam.

"I suggest you get yourself on over to Zach's place and get your wife and bring her home."

"I already have."

"What?"

At that moment a sleepy-eyed, tousle-headed woman came walking into the room. She walked right into Sam's open arms.

"Hi, Daddy."

"What are you doing here, Callen? Zach came over in the middle of the night to tell us you'd left Sam and were sound asleep in his guest bedroom."

"I had. I was." She shoved her bangs out of her eyes and yawned.

"Then, what the hell are you doing here?"

"Oh. Sam came and got me." She smiled a Cheshire grin and looked lovingly up at Sam. "He near pounded the door down. I guess that must have been when Zach was gone to Hawk's Way, because when I answered the door, Sam threw me over his shoulder and carried me away. It was very romantic."

Garth gawked. He couldn't help it. "You two are crazy."

"Crazy in love," Callen said as she stared into the warm welcome in Sam's green eyes. "It seems Sam can't live without me. And of course he wanted to be around while our child was growing up." She laid a hand on her belly, and Sam put his hand over hers.

Garth grinned as understanding dawned. "I'm going be a grandfather again? That's wonderful news, Callen." He leaned over quickly and kissed her cheek. He held out his hand to Sam. "Congratulations, Sam."

Sam took Garth's hand. "I'll take good care of her, sir. You don't have to worry about that. And about the other…"

"I should have explained everything sooner."

"I should have been more willing to listen."

It was as much of an apology or explanation as either man would ever offer. They shook hands once more before Garth stepped back.

"I guess I'll be going now. Does your mother know about the baby?"

Callen shook her head.

Garth's grin broadened. "I can't wait to tell her. You can expect her to call, I'm sure."

"Tell her to make it later," Sam said as his arms closed once more around his wife.

"I'll do that."

A moment later Garth was gone.

Sam scooped his wife into his arms and headed back toward the bedroom.

"Sam!" Callen exclaimed. "What are you doing?"

"I'm taking you back to bed, where I can make love to you to my heart's content."

"That sounds like a lovely idea."

Sam knew he had made the right choice, the only choice in retrieving his wife from her brother's house. He had sought vengeance against Garth Whitelaw to salve his own hurt. It wasn't what E.J. would have wanted. When it came down to a choice between having his wife and hurting her father, Sam had known what he had to do.

Callen had made her capture and capitulation seem romantic when she related it to her father. But it had been far more difficult to convince her to come home than Sam liked to remember. In fact, he felt lucky to have convinced her at all.

"Why do you want me back, Sam?" she had demanded.

"Because I need you."

"That isn't enough. I won't be used as a pawn to hurt my father."

He had swallowed hard and said, "I love you, Callen."

"Oh, Sam." She let one sob escape before she put a fist to her mouth to hold back the rest. "If you only knew how long I've waited to hear you say those words. But it'll tear me apart to love you, if it means letting you destroy my father."

"I don't want to destroy your father. Not anymore."

He had seen the hope in her eyes. "Really, Sam? Have you forgiven him?"

"I believe he's responsible for what happened to my father," he countered. "But I'm willing to forego my vengeance for your sake."

"That's not enough, Sam."

"What do you want from me?" he had asked bleakly. "I've chosen you instead of revenge. I've chosen love instead of hate. What more can I do?"

"Stop punishing yourself for what wasn't your fault. Forgive yourself for not knowing how upset and depressed E.J. was. Stop blaming yourself for your father's death."

"It wasn't my fault!"

"I know that," Callen had soothed. "And deep down, so do you. E.J. chose to die. He was the one who was responsible. Not my father. And not you."

"Callen…I…" She had been sitting in a chair in the kitchen. He had fallen on his knees in front of her as she opened her arms to him. He had clutched her tightly and felt her arms fold around him.

He had grieved then, the bitter tears cleansing away his anger and his guilt and, along with them, the need for revenge. He was whole once more.

He had picked Callen up in his arms, and she had clung to him, sitting close to him all the way home in his pickup. They hadn't made love last night, but had fallen asleep in each other's arms.

Then Garth had come this morning and explained about E.J.'s cancer. Sam would always regret the way his father had died. But he would be able to look back now without the terrible hate and anger that had colored the past months.

As he laid Callen on the bed and slipped in beside her, he pulled her close. "I love you, Callen. More than my life. More than anything."

"And I love you, Sam. I was just thinking…"

"What?" Sam asked as he nuzzled his wife's throat.

"I know you and Daddy would really like each other if you spent some more time together. So why don't we—"

Sam shut his wife up in the time-honored way, by covering his mouth with hers. He had the feeling he was going to spend the next few years going toe-to-toe with his bride. Which wasn't such a bad fate, when he thought about it.

"Sam—"

He kissed her again.

"Sam…"

And again.

"Oh, Sam."

"I love you, Callen."

Sam grinned as he kissed his wife. At least he had gotten in the last word this time.

Epilogue

"Sam, come quick!"

As a new father, Sam jumped two feet whenever he heard Callen call these days. Her frantic cry from the kitchen had him sprinting there to join her. "What's wrong? Are Karen and Kayla all right?"

His question was answered before he finished voicing it. His twin one-year-old daughters were sitting happily in their high chairs with cereal dribbled across their mouths, the trays of their high chairs and the floor.

"Come here and read this, Sam," Callen said, thrusting the local newspaper across the kitchen table toward him.

Sam took the paper without experiencing the knot that would once upon a time have formed in his stomach at the mere thought of confronting the written word.

"Look at that," Callen said, her finger thumping against the paper. "I can't believe any brother of mine could do anything so incredibly foolish."

Sam read the item Callen had pointed out to him.

Wife Wanted

Texas rancher seeks honest, responsible, compliant woman for wife. Must be capable of bearing children. Contact Zachary Whitelaw, Hawk's Pride, or phone 555-6748.

"Well, I'll be damned," Sam said with a chortle of glee. "That's one way to find a wife I'd never have considered."

"Do you see what that ad says?" Callen ranted. "*Compliant!* He might as well have said he wants a wife who'll kowtow to everything he says. The nerve!"

"Settle down, sweetheart. Your brother's a big boy. He knows what he's doing."

Callen snorted. "That'll be the day. The only comfort I have is that the whole idea is so ridiculous, so preposterous, that no sane woman will respond."

Sam threw the paper on the table. "I guess we'll just have to wait and see. Right now, I have more important things to think about." He drew his wife up into his arms. "You two close your eyes," he said to the little girls.

Sam lowered his mouth and gave his wife a lingering kiss, doing his best to ignore the giggles from the high-chair peanut gallery.

* * * * *

THE DISOBEDIENT BRIDE

This book is dedicated to my editor,
Melissa Senate, who knows when to push
and when to have patience.
Thanks, Mel.

Prologue

"**S**omething wrong, Miss Littlewolf?"

Rebecca surreptitiously wiped the tears from her cheeks and glanced up into warm brown eyes that were caught in a tangled web of crow's-feet. "I'm fine, Mrs. Fortunata. Just a little tired, I guess."

She and the short, rotund Italian woman had become friends because they both worked the graveyard shift at Children's Hospital. Mrs. Fortunata mopped and buffed the floors every night. Rebecca was a nurse for children with cancer.

The hospital cafeteria was nearly deserted. Rebecca's shift had ended a half hour ago, but she didn't have the will to get up and go home.

"You don't fool me," Mrs. Fortunata said. "Eyes red like that, you got a cold or you got a problem. Which is it?"

"Timmy Carstairs died tonight."

"You shouldn't let yourself care so much," Mrs. Fortunata gently chided.

"I know." A ragged sigh escaped. "I try to figure out which ones will make it, and which ones won't." Rebecca paused to swallow the huge lump in her throat. "I thought Timmy was going to be one of the lucky ones. He sure had me fooled." She tried to smile, but her lips wobbled dangerously.

Mrs. Fortunata shoved her mop into the nearby pail and wedged herself into the booth beside Rebecca. She took Rebecca's hand in hers and patted it. "Nice young thing like you oughta be headed home to a husband and kids of her own."

Rebecca tried for the smile again. And failed again. It was Mrs. Fortunata's life ambition to see her married and pregnant. Preferably in that order. "Maybe someday."

Mrs. Fortunata snorted. "You been sayin' that the whole two years I've known you. Why don't I ever see you with some nice young man? Ever since you kissed that Marty What's-his-name goodbye, you've been alone. You got something against men these days?"

This time Rebecca managed the smile. "No. I like men just fine."

"You haven't met the right man yet, is that it?"

Rebecca retrieved her hand and took a sip of lukewarm coffee to keep from having to answer. She had met the right man years ago. But she hadn't been the right woman for him.

"How're you gonna fill up your life," Mrs. Fortunata demanded, with flourishing gestures to emphasize her point, "if you don't find yourself a husband and have yourself some children?"

"I'd like to run a summer camp for kids with cancer," Rebecca replied. "If I could just figure out a way to finance it." The kids who were in remission needed a place where they could go and just be kids, but they often had special needs that couldn't be met by a regular camp experience. "It's probably never going to happen, but I can always dream."

"Everybody dreams. Only, you gotta do something to make those dreams come true. Me, I wanta quit moppin' floors someday."

"Why, Mrs. Fortunata, I thought you liked mopping floors," Rebecca teased.

"Tell you what. You get a camp for kids, you hire me to work for you. I quit moppin' floors like that." Mrs. Fortunata snapped two arthritic fingers together, or tried to. She gave up and made a flamboyant gesture that said it all without the snap.

"Meanwhile, you look here." Mrs. Fortunata reached into a pocket in the huge set of white overalls she wore and produced a ragged newspaper. She shoved it in front of Rebecca. "You need a husband. Here's a man who wants a wife. You give him a call. What do you say?"

Rebecca stared at the advertisement in the personals section of the Dallas newspaper.

WIFE WANTED

Texas rancher seeks honest, responsible, compliant woman for wife. Must be capable of bearing children. Contact Zachary Whitelaw, Hawk's Pride, or phone 555-6748.

Her eyes went wide with disbelief. "I know this man!"

"You do?"

Rebecca nodded excitedly. "My father was foreman of his ranch. I lived at Hawk's Pride from the time I was thirteen until I turned seventeen."

"Why'd you leave?"

"My dad died from a heart attack, and I used the life insurance settlement to go to college. There was no reason to go back."

"Now there is. You see this man. You tell him you want to be his wife."

"I can't do that."

"Why not?"

"He's already told me to get lost once. I don't need to be told a second time that I'm not wanted."

"Aha! So he's the reason you don't like other men!"

"I never said—"

"I see what you don't say," Mrs. Fortunata said. "You loved him. Fine. Don't let him get away this time."

"Mrs. Fortunata—"

"No excuses. You go see this man. You tell him you'd make a good wife."

"Look at the date on this paper," Rebecca said in desperation. "It's three weeks old. He's probably already found a wife."

"And maybe not."

"I just couldn't."

"What're you waiting for? You're gonna be an old lady all alone like me, you don't do something quick."

Rebecca laughed. "You were married for forty years before Mr. Fortunata died. You've got ten grandchildren!"

"My kids have moved all over the country. I don't see all those grandbabies so much as I'd like anymore. I miss them. You keep foolin' around, you won't even have grandbabies to miss!"

Rebecca laughed again. "All right. I give up. I'll go see him."

But it wasn't going to do any good. Zach Whitelaw had already told her to stay the hell out of his way. Of course, she had only been a kid of seventeen at the time.

Maybe he would be willing to take a second look at a mature woman of twenty-three.

Chapter 1

"I saw your advertisement for a wife. I've come to apply for the job."

Zach Whitelaw stared in astonishment at the woman dressed in a white T-shirt, jeans and boots on the other side of the screen door. "Becky? Is that you?" His lips slowly curled with amusement. He shoved the door open and said, "Come on in, kid."

"I'm not a—"

"Kid," he finished as he tugged on the waist-length black hair that had fallen over her shoulder. His grin broadened as he looked her over from head to toe. Their eyes met and his face sobered. "It's been a long time."

"Six years."

"Surely not that long?"

Rebecca nodded. She stood mute beneath Zach's perusal, but couldn't prevent the flush that turned skin that was a warm honey color—thanks to her Comanche forebears—a deeper hue.

"Nope. You're definitely not a kid anymore," he said at last. "What have you been doing with yourself?"

"I'm a nurse at Children's Hospital in Dallas."

"Figures," he said with a grin. "Last time I saw you a ragged-eared mutt was stumping along behind you on a splint you'd rigged up for his broken leg. Whatever happened to that mutt, anyway?"

"That 'mutt' is named Pepper," she said archly, "and I left him with friends in Dallas."

"Are you still rescuing every helpless critter that crosses your path?"

"I've had to cut back some," she conceded with a smile. "There's not much extra space in a one-bedroom condo."

"You had quite a collection of the walking wounded when you lived here with your dad." He chuckled. "Everything from a skunk to a snake."

"I could never stand to see anything in pain," she said without apology. "It's a major failing of mine."

"Must make it hard to work with sick kids," he said.

Oh, how perceptive he was. He always had been.

"Sometimes it is hard." More than sometimes, but she hadn't come to Zach for a shoulder to cry on.

Rebecca felt caught in the warp of time, unable to move in or out of the doorway. She had fallen madly in love with Zach at the age of thirteen. She had fantasized what it would be like to be kissed by him, to be held in his strong arms. She had hinted at what a good kisser she might become, if only she had someone to practice on. He had ignored the fumbling adolescent signals she had sent out and treated her like a bratty younger sister, letting her work with him. With amazing patience, he had taught her everything there was to know about ranching. But not a blamed thing about kissing.

Unfortunately, long before she was old enough to catch Zach's eye, he had fallen in love with another—much older—woman of twenty-two. She had thought she would die when Zach told her he planned to marry Cynthia Kenyon.

"You can't get married!" she had cried. "You can't!"

"Look, kid—"

"I'm not a kid, I'm a woman!"

He had laughed at her. Laughed! "Look, kid—"

"Don't call me that!"

"But you are a kid," he said gently. "Sweet sixteen and never been kissed. Wait a few years. Some man will come along and fall head over heels for you."

She had stared at him in horror. It dawned on her suddenly that he wasn't going to wait for her to grow up. He was going to marry Cynthia Kenyon and be lost to her forever.

"You're so stupid," she had gibed. "You don't know anything!" She had run then, searching for a place to hide, a place where she could nurse her pain alone.

Hours later, her father had found her in the loft of the barn. Her fondest memory of her father was the way he had comforted her that day. He had settled on his knees in the straw, folded her into his arms and held her while she cried, her body heaving with great wrenching sobs of terrible grief. When her body was exhausted, and she could cry no more, he had gently wiped away the tears with his bandanna.

"I know you think this is the end of the world," he said. "But someday you'll grow up and fall in love, and you'll realize this was just a childhood infatuation."

She had believed him. Or tried to believe him. But his words hadn't been much comfort to a vulnerable girl with a broken heart.

The next time she saw Zach, she had managed to stutter, "I w-wish you and Cynthia a l-lifetime of l-love and happiness."

He had put a brotherly arm around her shoulder. "That means a lot to me, kid." Then he had cuffed her chin playfully with his knuckles and let her go.

She hadn't gone near him for a whole week. Eventually, she had decided she might as well enjoy his company while she could. But things were never quite the same between them after that. She caught him staring at her more than once with an odd look in his eyes that made her uncomfortable.

It had been a sore test for her immortal soul when, two days before the wedding, Cynthia had been killed in a plane crash. Somehow she had managed to express the appropriate sympathy, but Zach had been inconsolable. She had held on to the hope, slight though it was, that he might turn to her in his grief.

He had not.

In all these years, and despite her father's promise that Zach would become a part of her past, she had never fallen out of love with him. She had dated occasionally and had even been engaged once. But Zach Whitelaw had been the standard by which she had measured all other men. She had backed out of her engagement because she had realized she was being unfair to Marty What's-his-name, as Mrs. Fortunata referred to him, by constantly comparing him unfavorably to Zach.

"Are you coming in, or not?" Zach asked.

"I'm coming in." She was momentarily shadowed by Zach's over-six-foot height as she stepped inside the kitchen of his adobe ranch house. He hissed in a breath as the tips of her breasts brushed against his shirt. They froze momentarily at the shocking contact. Zach reached out and took her shoulders in a tight grasp to separate their bodies. Nevertheless, a frisson of electricity continued to arc between them.

The attraction was there. It had been there since *the incident* between them when she was seventeen. At least on her side. She had no idea what Zach felt. It was because of *the incident* that she had kept her distance all these years.

"Those tactics won't work any better this time than they did the last," he said abruptly.

She looked up and found herself captured by eyes that were dark and dangerous. "I didn't mean to brush against you, Zach. It was an accident."

"Like the last time was an accident?"

He hadn't forgotten *the incident* any more than she had.

It had happened six years ago, before she left for college, but a full year after Cynthia's death. Zach had become a morose and moody man. She had wanted him to turn to her, to see her as the woman who could replace Cynthia in his mind and his heart. She had wanted him to marry her so they could be together forever. But he still didn't see her as a woman. So she had picked her moment and purposely tripped and fallen against him in the barn.

Their bodies had come into close, hard contact. She had reveled in his harsh intake of breath as her breasts pillowed against his chest. She vividly remembered the swirling dust motes caught in a golden shaft of sunlight, the pungent smells of hay and manure.

His hands had closed around her waist as though to push her away, yet he hadn't. Their faces had been close enough that she could feel his warm, damp breath against her cheek. But she had been the one who had to lift her lips to his.

She had been surprised by their softness. And disappointed when he jerked his face away. He had released her quickly and exhaled with a short huff. She had seen the evidence of his response to her in the tight fit of his jeans and smiled up at him. Her smile had faded when he failed to return it.

The look on his face had been terrible to see. His lips had flattened, and his eyes went cold. His hands balled into white-knuckled fists at his sides.

"Don't ever do that again," he said.

"Do what?" she asked with feigned innocence.

"Look, little girl," he said in a steely voice. "Don't play the tease unless you want to end up flat on your back with me on top of you."

She had flushed with embarrassment at such frank speaking. And tried again to deny her guilt. "I wasn't—"

"I like you, kid," he said quietly. "But I'm no good for you. Stay away from me."

She wrinkled her nose. "I'm not a—"

"Kid? You're seventeen. I'm thirty. Give yourself some

time to grow up. Then find a man who can love you, and settle down and have some kids of your own.''

"But you're the man I want!" she blurted.

His lips tilted on one side in a bittersweet smile. "I'll never love another woman, kid." His dark eyes turned merciless. "Just stay the hell away from me."

Seeing the same warning look in his eyes now as she had seen that long ago day, Rebecca put some distance between herself and Zach. At the sink she turned to face him again. "Why are you advertising for a wife, Zach? I would think you could have any woman you wanted just by asking."

"Actually, I don't want a wife."

"What?"

"I need a woman to be the mother of my children. I advertised for a wife so there'll be no misunderstanding that it's purely a business arrangement. Still want to apply for the job?"

Rebecca swallowed hard. "I see. That puts a new light on things." She had thought he was finally over Cynthia, but apparently not.

However, if this was the way he intended to acquire a wife, she would have to do her best to cope with the situation. She met all his qualifications. Or almost all. She was honest and responsible and would love having Zach's children. She had dismissed the *compliant* part of the ad. Zach should have known better than to write something like that in this day and age. But the "business arrangement" he had described raised questions in her mind.

"What about love?" Rebecca asked.

"What about it?"

"Don't you want a wife who'll love you?"

"It isn't necessary. In fact, it would be a nuisance, since I don't expect to love her back."

Rebecca had always fantasized that someday Zach would fall in love with her, and they would marry and live happily ever after. It was the stuff fairy tales were made of.

Zach had just announced he had no intention of falling in love with her or any other woman. Her brow furrowed in thought. He wasn't offering much, but it would take a harder man than the Zach Whitelaw she knew to resist all the love she planned to heap on him.

She gave him a brilliant smile and said, "I'm your woman, Zach. I'd be perfect for the job."

Zach laughed aloud. "Forget it, kid." He grabbed a bar stool from the center island, turned it around and straddled it. He crossed his arms on the stool's wooden back and grinned. "My advertisement was quite specific. You're not exactly what I had in mind."

"But, I—"

"Zach, there's another applicant at the front door who says—" The petite, dark-eyed, dark-haired woman stopped in her tracks at the kitchen door. "Becky! I didn't know you were here."

Rebecca gave Zach's younger sister a friendly smile. "Hi, Callen. You're looking great. I understand you're a new mother." She had caught up on all the local gossip at the Stanton Hotel in town where she was staying.

Callen laid her hands on her nearly flat abdomen. "I didn't know it showed."

Rebecca gave her a quizzical look. "I was talking about the twins, Kayla and Karen."

"Then you don't know about this one?"

"This one?"

She grinned. "Sam and I are expecting another child in six and a half months. This baby was a surprise with the twins only a year old, but it's very welcome."

"How is Sam holding up?" Rebecca asked.

"Sam's still in shock," Callen replied with a sheepish look. "It's a nice kind of shock, because we want a large family. But tell me about you. Are you just visiting, or are you here to stay?"

Rebecca shot a quick glance in Zach's direction. "That

depends on Zach. I saw his advertisement for a wife, and I've come to apply for the job.''

"Not you, too!" Callen said in disgust. "For the record, I disapprove of this whole business. Mom and Daddy aren't too keen on it, either. A man ought to marry because he's in love, not because he's decided it's time he had an heir and needs an appropriate brood mare. I can't believe you'd put yourself in the running. As much as I love my brother, he'd be hell to live with. And given his attitude toward women, he'll make a terrible husband.''

"I think he'd be fine husband material, assuming he got the right wife.'' Rebecca glanced quickly at Zach, at the lock of thick, black hair that had fallen on his brow, at the dark, inscrutable eyes in his finely chiseled face, at the high, wide cheekbones, and his straight nose and strong chin. It was an arresting face, and Rebecca had to force her eyes away from Zach and back to his sister.

Callen snorted and rolled her eyes. "You don't know my brother like I do. He's an arrogant, chauvinistic Neanderthal who hasn't been in a real relationship with a woman since Cynthia—''

Callen cut herself off. Apparently, even so many years after her death, Cynthia was a taboo subject. "I can't imagine what woman would want to attach herself to Zach for life!''

"Lucky for me I don't require a recommendation from you,'' Zach said with a lazy grin.

"Omigosh! I almost forgot. There's a woman in the living room who wants an interview, Zach. Is she number fourteen or fifteen?''

"Seventeen, actually.''

Rebecca was amazed and appalled at the number of women Zach had already rejected, but also encouraged. He must not be as ready to leap into marriage with a stranger as he professed.

Zach rose. "Duty calls.''

"May I come along?'' Rebecca asked.

"Why not?"

"I'm coming, too," Callen said. "I don't want to miss this," she said in an aside to Rebecca. "Wait until you see the kind of woman that's been replying to Zach's ad."

Rebecca wasn't sure what she was expecting, maybe a poor, plain, uneducated woman, who couldn't get a husband any other way. That would explain all those rejected applicants.

The woman sitting on Zach's saddle-brown leather couch was absolutely beautiful, self-assured, sophisticated and utterly relaxed. Rebecca felt her heart sink. No wonder Zach had laughed when she announced herself as an applicant for the position of wife. She was pretty and poised, but she just wasn't in the same ballpark as the beauty in Zach's living room. If this was her competition, she had her work cut out for her. She dropped into a pine rocker across from the couch and waited for the show to start.

"Hello," the woman said in a husky voice.

She even sounded sexy, Rebecca thought with dismay.

"I'm Zach Whitelaw," Zach said.

Rebecca didn't like the wolfish smile on his face as he ogled the woman.

The woman reached out a hand, which Zach took as he sat beside her on the couch.

"I'm Harriet Thomas."

The woman never took her eyes off Zach, and he seemed equally entranced. Rebecca cleared her throat loudly.

"I'm Rebecca Littlewolf."

Harriet never even glanced at her. Instead she said to Zach, "What would you like to know about me?"

"Zach's going to marry me," Rebecca said.

A flash of annoyance crossed Harriet's face. "I didn't know the position was filled."

"It's not," Zach said. "Cut it out, kid."

Rebecca wasn't intimidated by Zach's scowl. She had seen it plenty of times as a teenager, and the worst that had ever resulted was a severe tongue-lashing. "You do realize that Zach wants *lots* of children."

Harriet arched a finely tweezed brow. She turned to Zach, awaiting his response.

"That's true," Zach admitted.

"How many?" the woman asked.

"Three for sure, maybe four."

"I see." Harriet pursed her lips in a way that wasn't at all flattering. She stood abruptly and turned to face Rebecca. "He's all yours."

"I'll show Ms. Thomas out," Callen said with a wink at Rebecca.

"I can find my own way out."

Callen gestured toward the front door. When it had closed behind the woman, she turned back to the tension-filled room. "Oh, how I wish I could stay and hear the denouement in this little drama! But I've got a doctor's appointment, and if I don't leave right now I'm going to be terribly late. It was nice to see you, Becky," she said as she grabbed her car keys and headed for the door. "Good luck with my brother. You're going to need it!"

A moment later Rebecca found herself trapped in the rocker as Zach wrapped his powerful hands around each of the arms and leaned over to put his nose an inch from hers.

"This isn't a game to me, kid," he said in a feral voice. "I need a wife. And I intend to find one."

Rebecca swallowed over the sudden lump in her throat. "You've found her. I'm right here." She looked up at him, her heart pounding crazily, careful not to let the love she felt show in her eyes. Zach didn't want or expect love from a wife.

Zach suddenly stood and shoved all ten fingers through his hair. "It would never work."

Rebecca was startled by his response, which suggested he might have considered the idea. She leapt from the rocker and put herself directly in front of him, hands on hips, chin up, shoulders squared in a fighting stance. "Why wouldn't it work? Actually, if you think about it, I'm the perfect woman for the job. I know everything there is to know about a working ranch—you taught me yourself—and I'm familiar with every inch of Hawk's Pride. You know I'm honest and responsible." She flushed and said, "And I can provide a doctor's report to ensure I'm capable of having children."

She purposely didn't mention the *compliant* part, hoping he would forget about it. She took a deep breath and continued. "And I, more than any other applicant, know exactly why you don't want or expect love to be a part of the bargain." Meaning, she knew how much he had loved Cynthia.

When he didn't immediately refuse her, she let herself hope. When his teeth clenched, when the muscle in his jaw began to work, she felt a desperate sense of loss.

"Zach, just think about it."

"No, kid. And that's my final word on the subject."

He took one step before she managed to block his path with her body. "I refuse to accept that answer."

Zach grimaced. "That is exactly why you'd make me a terrible wife. There's not a *compliant* bone in your body."

"At least you know what you'd be getting," Rebecca argued. "You know me, Zach. You like me. Isn't that important?"

"Why do you want to marry me?" Zach demanded. "You've got your whole life ahead of you. What would you get out of an arrangement like this?"

Rebecca managed to keep herself from blurting *You!* Any hint of love would be the death knell to whatever hope she had of marrying Zach. She searched frantically for some reason Zach would accept and believe. And hit on the perfect response.

"Ever since I started working at Children's Hospital I've dreamed of starting a summer camp for kids with cancer. I could never afford that sort of thing on my own. If I were your wife, I could realize my dream here at Hawk's Pride."

His lip curled. "I see. So it's my money you find attractive."

"Well, you're not bad-looking, either," she quipped. One look at his face, and she knew she had better do some fast talking.

"The camp really is a wonderful idea, Zach." Her voice filled with enthusiasm as she warmed to her subject. "Hawk's Pride would be a perfect place to bring kids who've never seen a horse or a steer. We could teach them to ride horseback, or take them for rides in a hay wagon. It would be so good for them. If only you could see how hard they work just to stay alive, never mind to get well, you'd realize what a perfect reward a week at a working ranch would be."

Zach's eyes narrowed, as though to assess the truth of what she had said. He tucked his thumbs in his back pockets. "I suppose I would finance this camp of yours."

Rebecca nodded.

"How would you manage the four kids I want and a camp, too?"

"I'd hire good help."

"For the camp...or the kids?" Zach asked cynically.

"I'd be a good mother, Zach," Rebecca said seriously. "I lost my mother when I was born, so I know how much a child needs one. I'd give your—our—children all the love they could ever want or need."

Zach shook his head. "I don't know, Becky. I have to admit that camp idea sounds good. I've got a niece, Susannah—my brother Falcon's stepdaughter—who has leukemia. She'd love to go to a camp like the one you want to start. But it would be a lot of work."

Rebecca took great heart from the fact he hadn't called her *kid.* "I can handle it, Zach. Believe me, I'm the woman you're looking for. Admit it. I'm perfect for the job."

He eyed her suspiciously. "I haven't forgotten what you said when you were seventeen."

Rebecca couldn't keep the stricken look off her face. If she couldn't disabuse him of the notion that she still loved him after all these years, she might lose everything. She managed to put a ladle of scorn in her voice. "I hope you're not going to hold the foolish words of an adolescent against me. I might have been infatuated with you at seventeen, but I've grown up a lot since then."

"I've noticed," he said. "And I can't say I'm not attracted. I am." He took the steps necessary to close the distance between them. "I'd forgotten how green your eyes are, like spring grass. And I love the feel of your hair," he said as he fingered a handful of the silky strands.

"I'm attracted to you, too, Zach. In a physical way," she corrected hastily.

Rebecca laid a tentative hand on Zach's chest, near his heart. She could feel the hard muscle even through his Western shirt. Her hand slid up his chest and curled around his nape into untrimmed hair that was soft and thick.

She saw what was going to happen, waited for it, wanted it. He was going to kiss her. He watched her with dark, unfathomable eyes, until he was so close she was forced to lower her lids. He paused, a breath away, then touched his lips to hers.

Goose bumps popped up on her arms, and her knees buckled. Fortunately he caught her with an arm around her waist and pulled her close.

And deepened the kiss.

His tongue was hot and wet and came slow and deep into her mouth. She made an animal sound low in her throat and heard an answering growl from him. His arm tightened around her waist, and he cupped her behind and lifted her enough to fit their bodies intimately together.

She arched toward him, enthralled by his need for her. Her arms clung to his shoulders, while her mouth clung to his.

Suddenly she was standing by herself, chest heaving, legs wobbling, hands trembling. She stared, dazed, at Zach, who had backed up a good three feet from her.

"Well, I guess that's settled," he said.

"What's settled?"

"We'd be all right together in bed."

"Oh."

He tunneled splayed fingers into his hair. "I don't know, kid. This is so incredible. When I put that ad in the paper, I never imagined that someone I knew would answer it. I have to think about this."

Rebecca knew that if she gave Zach time to think, he would come up with a dozen excuses to reject her. "You won't find a better candidate than me, Zach. You'll be getting exactly what you want—a wife who'll marry you without expecting love and who'll give you children—without having to waste any more time looking. You have the added advantage of marrying someone you know, someone your family will accept and approve."

She saw Zach's eyes widen as he realized the truth of her pronouncement. According to Callen, Zach's parents disapproved of his method of choosing a wife. Marrying Rebecca Littlewolf, someone they knew, was bound to lessen their concern.

"Don't think too long, Zach. I have to return to Dallas in a couple of days."

"Then maybe I'd better make this decision right now."

Rebecca felt her heart begin to thud in her chest. Surely Zach could hear it, surely he knew how much she wanted to be his wife, and not at all for the reason she had told him.

"There are a few things we need to get straight first."

"Such as?"

"Don't delude yourself into thinking I'll fall in love with you. I won't. I'll never love another woman. Not after Cynthia."

Rebecca felt her stomach roll. "All right. What else?"

"I'm marrying because I want children. But I'm a man, and I have needs that I'll expect my wife to satisfy."

Goose bumps prickled her flesh at the thought of lying beneath him...above him...beside him in bed. "I'll be glad to satisfy those needs, presuming I'm the only woman who'll enjoy those pleasures," she said, answering his demand for sexual services with her demand for fidelity. "Anything else?"

"I'll expect you to devote yourself to the children first and foremost. In exchange, I'll see to it you get the financing and whatever other help you need for that camp you want for sick kids."

"Agreed."

"One more thing. If you're not pregnant a year from now, we get a divorce. After all, what I want is children, not a barren wife."

She sucked in a harsh breath, appalled at this unforeseen condition. "That's a cold-blooded thing to say."

He shrugged. "Take it or leave it."

For the first time since she had fallen in love with him at thirteen, Rebecca wondered if she was mistaken about Zach. The man she had found lovable could never have been so ruthless. Clearly this man was. What if she couldn't make him love her? What if Zach truly had become a heartless man? What if she spent the next year of her life falling deeper and deeper in love with him and then failed to become pregnant? Were the rewards to be had from marrying Zach Whitelaw worth the risks?

"If we divorce, I continue to run the summer camp here at Hawk's Pride, and you continue to fund it. I want that in writing," Rebecca said.

"No demand for alimony?"

Rebecca shook her head. "I told you what I want from this marriage." *Or almost all of what I want.*

"Given everything I've just said, do you still want to marry me?" he asked.

"I do."

It wasn't until Zach heaved a sigh of relief that Rebecca realized he hadn't been at all certain of her response. And that he seemed pleased by it. The grin that appeared moments later confirmed his feelings. "I guess we have a deal."

"How soon do you want to have the wedding?" Rebecca asked.

"Tomorrow. We can get Judge Smithers to officiate."

"No."

"There you go again, disagreeing with me," Zach said. "What am I going to do with you, kid?"

He gave her that same playful cuff he had administered when she was a girl of seventeen. She looked into his eyes, wondering what he saw when he looked at her. She wasn't the young girl who had left Hawk's Pride six years ago. She had a woman's needs, a woman's dreams and desires. She wanted much more than Zach seemed to be offering.

She had a moment's qualm, but fought it down. She wasn't going to lose the brass ring just because she hadn't reached for it.

"I have to give at least two weeks' notice at the hospital, Zach."

"All right, two weeks. Not a day more."

"Deal," Rebecca said, extending her hand.

Zach took it and pulled her close. "I'd rather seal our bargain this way," he said as his mouth claimed hers.

She felt his need and answered with her own. His strong arms, the ones she had dreamed about for so many years, closed around her, and he lifted her enough so that she felt his sure and certain arousal. His breathing roughened, and she heard a guttural sound of triumph issue from his throat.

It was going to be a rare match of wills, all right. Rebecca was gambling that she could tame the savage beast. She only hoped he didn't devour her before she got the chance.

Chapter 2

Zach wanted a woman. It wasn't the first time he had stared at the bedroom ceiling and denied his body's raging need. But tonight the object of his desire had a face and a name.

Rebecca Littlewolf.

It wasn't a bad thing to physically desire one's future bride, Zach thought. But he was surprised by the intensity of his need and at his inability to banish the tantalizing image of her green eyes and flowing black hair from his mind. He could imagine her eyes, lambent with passion, feel her silky hair draped over his naked torso.

Zach rose and paced restlessly into the living room, where a picture window overlooked the vast acres of Hawk's Pride. It was nearly dawn, and he could see the silhouette of rocky outcroppings that marked the entrance to a deep canyon on his property. He could see a windmill flying in the Texas wind and cattle feeding on the prairie grass.

On his twenty-first birthday, his father had given him this piece of property carved out of land that had been in the Whitelaw family for generations. He had looked forward to marrying and raising a family who would bring love and laughter into his life. That was all before Cynthia Kenyon.

Cynthia had been his first love and, filled with tales of his parents' romance told by the fireplace on long winter nights in his youth, he had fallen hard. She had moved in with him as soon as they were engaged. Two days before their wedding, he had discovered Cynthia in his bed with another man.

He had knocked the man unconscious with one blow; it had taken every ounce of self-control he had to keep from hitting her. He had carefully uncurled his knotted fists and shoved his thumbs into the back pockets of his jeans.

"Get out, Cynthia, and take that carcass on the floor with you."

"It didn't mean anything, Zach. He works for a New York modeling agency. He's going to offer me a contract. It has nothing to do with us."

It had amazed him that she could so cavalierly share her body with another man. And that she expected him not to care. "It means something to me," he said. "Get out, Cynthia. And don't come back."

"Don't do this, Zach," she pleaded. Big tears welled in her eyes and spilled onto her cheeks. "I love you. I made a mistake. Please, forgive me."

"Some things are unforgivable."

"I'm pregnant, Zach."

"With whose kid?"

He would never forget the look on her face, a mixture of confusion and fear.

"It's yours, Zach."

He didn't believe her. What man would have under the circumstances? She wasn't pregnant, or if she was, it wasn't his kid. He felt like a fool and an idiot. He had trusted her, and she had betrayed him. He didn't think there was any way he could ever forget the sight of her flesh joined to that of another man in his bed. He felt physically ill.

"Get out, Cynthia. And don't come back."

"All right, Zach, I'm going, but you'll be sorry someday. This is your baby I'm carrying, and I'll prove it. Then you'll pay. Will you ever pay!"

Cynthia and her lover had boarded a private plane headed for New York. It crashed shortly after takeoff, killing everyone on board.

Zach had asked the coroner whether Cynthia was pregnant.

"I'm afraid so, son," the man had replied. "I'm truly very sorry."

The guilt he felt over Cynthia's death had been bad enough. It didn't approach the horror he experienced at knowing a child—his child?—had died with her. There was no way he could ask for any kind of test to prove things one way or the other without revealing his doubt. So he grieved the baby's death. But he had always wondered whether she had made a fool of him in the end by making him mourn some other man's child.

It had been especially painful to see the tears in his mother's eyes, the haggard look on his father's face, when they heard the news of the death of their unborn grandchild. He had been too hurt, too humiliated, to admit to his family the possibility that the child wasn't his. Maybe it had been his. He would have to live with that uncertainty the rest of his life.

It had been almost impossible to graciously accept the sympathy offered to him on the death of his bride only two days before their wedding. Nobody knew of Cynthia's perfidy, and he didn't believe it would serve any purpose to expose her. The truth would certainly hurt her parents, who were good friends of his parents. He had simply gone into seclusion after her death and let people draw their own conclusions.

He must have loved her an awful lot to be so torn up.

Imagine losing your future bride and your unborn child at the same time. What a tragedy!

It must have been true love. He's been devastated by her death.

It wasn't only grief he had felt, it was bitterness, and a deep and abiding anger. Cynthia's prophetic words had come true. He would have to live the rest of his life with the consequences of throwing her out.

In the years after her death he had gone through women one at a time, testing them and finding them wanting. Flighty creatures. Dishonest creatures. Tantalizing, tempting, titillating creatures. He couldn't keep himself from looking at them with a jaundiced eye any more than he could keep himself from needing them to assuage his physical desire.

So why is a bitter cynic like you marrying a nice kid like Rebecca Littlewolf?

Zach heaved a mammoth sigh. What on earth had possessed him? He wanted to think it was a simple matter of expedience. He had interviewed enough women to realize he wasn't going to find the perfect wife through a newspaper advertisement. But he hadn't wanted to court a woman because that would have suggested he wanted affection to be a part of their relationship. Since he didn't intend to love his wife, he didn't think it was fair to expect her to love him.

And Rebecca Littlewolf was a known quantity. He had been a little surprised at her interest in using his money to start a camp. But it eased his conscience to know she had mercenary motives for marrying him. Money he could freely offer. Love was out of the question. It helped that she assumed, like everyone else, that he was still in love with Cynthia Kenyon.

It was an added bonus that he was physically attracted to Rebecca. He had been astonished at his body's instant response to the sight of her when she appeared at his kitchen door. Rebecca only came to his shoulder, but her body curved in all the right places. It was something he had noticed six years ago, although he had refused to act on his interest at the time, in spite of her invitation.

But there was more to like about Rebecca Littlewolf than her body. From the first day he met her, when she was a kid of thirteen, she had worn her heart on her sleeve. It had been a huge heart, for a kid, open to every wounded, needy or crippled being that crossed her path. He wondered how much of that openhearted, guileless girl remained in the woman she had become.

Zach shoved his fingers through his hair in agitation. At least he wouldn't make the same mistakes the second time around. He wouldn't set his heart on a platter for another woman. He refused to make himself vulnerable ever again to the kind of pain Cynthia had caused.

But he desperately wanted children of his own. By the time his thirty-sixth birthday had come and gone, he had realized that time was running out. Conceding that a wife was a necessary part of the family he craved, he had decided on an advertisement as the quickest way to interview the broadest range of candidates. He had been determined to make a rational, informed decision. He had wanted a woman he could admire and respect as the mother of his children, someone with whom he could live amicably. It was icing on the cake if he felt physical desire for her. In Rebecca Littlewolf he had found a woman who filled all his needs.

It took Zach a moment to realize that the soft thumping sound he heard was someone knocking at the back door. He sprinted to the bedroom, dragged on a pair of jeans over his briefs, and buttoned a couple of the buttons as he headed for the kitchen.

The morning sky was streaked with pinks and yellows that gave him enough light to see who was standing there.

"Hello, Zach."

"Come in, kid." As he had the previous day, Zach held the screen door wide for Rebecca Littlewolf. She stepped just inside and stopped.

"I didn't sleep much last night," she said. "I think we need to do some serious talking."

"Uh-oh." Zach hid his anxiety behind a grin, and gestured Rebecca farther into the kitchen. She crossed to the spot she had taken the previous day, in front of the sink. He didn't feel like sitting down, so he leaned against the center island and crossed his arms and his ankles. "What's on your mind?"

She let go of the strand of hair she had tangled around her forefinger and said, "I'm having second thoughts, Zach."

Zach felt a sudden lurch in his belly. He hadn't been particular about who his wife was before he had decided on Rebecca. Suddenly, he couldn't picture anyone else in the role. He found her lowered gaze and tucked chin enchanting. He wanted nothing so much as to lift that chin and kiss those eyelids.

"We shook on it, kid. As far as I'm concerned, it's a done deal."

"It isn't that simple, Zach."

"Why not?"

"Because of Cynthia."

He wondered exactly what she meant and was afraid he knew. "What about Cynthia?"

"I've been wondering whether, for the rest of my life, when you look at me, you'll be seeing her instead."

Zach snorted. "You don't look at all like Cynthia." She blushed a fiery red, and he realized she had taken his comment wrong. Her next words confirmed it.

"I know I'm not beautiful, like Cynthia, but—"

"Looks had nothing to do with my decision," Zach interrupted, unconsciously confirming her opinion that he found her wanting. "Look, kid—"

"I stopped being a kid years ago, Zach."

She shoved her hair behind her shoulders, revealing rounded breasts beneath a worn T-shirt that were proof of her point without the need for words. But he knew she wasn't making reference to her physical maturity. He conceded that he didn't know her as an adult. The woman standing before him was as much a stranger to him as any of the other candidates he had interviewed.

It was disconcerting to admit that he had been calling her

"kid" to keep her at a distance. At the same time, he had been using it as a term of endearment. The kid he had known was sweet and kind and had a heart of gold. He wanted to hang on to that memory of goodness as long as he possibly could. He had liked the kid he knew. It was hard to acknowledge those admirable qualities in the sexually attractive woman who stood before him. So "kid" it was...and would remain.

"All right, kid, let's hear it. What did you decide during your sleepless night?"

She took a deep breath and let it out slowly. "I was thinking maybe it would be better if we didn't get married."

"We had a deal."

"I'm not reneging on the deal, just changing it a little."

His eyes narrowed. "Changing it how?"

"I'm suggesting we live together, rather than marry right away."

"What purpose would that serve?"

"It might save us both a nasty divorce."

"Do you have any reason to believe you can't—or won't—get pregnant?"

She shook her head. "But that doesn't mean it will happen, either."

"I'm willing to take my chances."

"I'm not."

He grimaced. The teenage girl he had known and liked, the one who had marched to the beat of her own drummer with an army of three-legged, lop-eared, crop-tailed animals trailing along behind her, had grown into an equally obstinate and opinionated woman. She was playing with her hair again, which he recognized as a sign of nerves. He wanted to free her hands and take them in his own, to give comfort, to ease her fears.

He took a step toward her, and she extended her hand, the palm flattened in a signal to stop.

"Don't," she said in a breathless voice.

He took another step, and another, until the flat of her palm rested against his chest. Zach stopped then, because he had what he wanted. He could feel the heat of her, feel his heart pound beneath her trembling hand. She looked up at him with eyes that revealed her vulnerability.

She wanted him.

Zach swore under his breath. She had never been good at hiding what she was feeling, and she did nothing to mask the desire that glowed in her eyes. He had seen the look before in other women and knew she was a moment from surrender.

"Don't look at me like that, kid," he warned in a low, husky voice, "unless you mean what you're saying with your eyes."

She jerked her hand away and tucked it behind her. Her eyes blinked several times as though she were recovering from a trance. "I'm sorry, Zach. I didn't mean—"

He laughed, a rumbly sound deep in his chest. He reached out and folded her in his arms, rocking her back and forth several times. "Ah, kid, what am I going to do with you?"

"Why can't we just live together, Zach? I promise I'll marry you when—if—I get pregnant."

He shook his head. "That isn't good enough." He didn't—dared not—trust her. What if she no longer wished to marry him once she was pregnant? At least if they were married he would have some legal right to his child. But he wasn't going to put ideas in her head by mentioning his fears.

"It has to be marriage, kid. I don't want my child born a bastard, or left counting the months between our marriage and his birth."

"Don't you think *our* child is going to ask questions when *she* notices the nature of our relationship?"

"We'll be sleeping together. We'll be civil at the breakfast table. That's more than most marriages can boast," Zach said flatly.

Her brow furrowed. "I don't understand you, Zach."

"You don't have to understand me. That's not part of the

job description. All you have to do is keep your part of the bargain.''

She turned her back on him and stared out the window over the sink into the central courtyard. "I don't know, Zach."

He closed the distance between them and slipped his arms around her waist. She stiffened, then relaxed against him, into him. He heard her gasp as his palms flattened against her belly, but she didn't fight his intimate possession of her. He lowered his head and nuzzled the soft skin beneath her right ear.

She made a purring sound in her throat that caused his body to go hard. His hand slid down the front zipper placket of her jeans until he was cupping her. She spread her legs and arched into his hand.

"Zach."

A shudder reeled through him when she said his name.

"I...want...you so much." The words seemed forced from her and were followed by a guttural sound of pleasure.

"Marry me," he murmured in her ear. "Marry me and have my baby."

"Oh, Zach, you don't play fair."

His mouth suckled a tender spot on her nape, and she hissed in a breath of air.

Then he felt her hand on his thigh, high up, near his genitals. She wasn't playing too damn fair herself, Zach thought as his blood pumped, and his breath grew ragged. Soon she had both hands behind her, both hands cupping him, and he leaned into the pleasure, reached out for it, groaning in satisfaction at the way she touched him.

"No marriage, Zach. Not until there's a baby."

Abruptly he freed himself. He grabbed her by the shoulders and spun her around. His hands tightened on her shoulders as his eyes flashed with anger. "That sort of blackmail won't work."

He let her go and stepped back. "I have my reasons for wanting marriage first. I'm not willing to compromise, and

I'm not going to change my mind. That's the deal. Take it or leave it.''

For a terrifying moment, he thought she was going to leave it. She stared at the toe of her booted foot, dragging it back and forth several times across the brick-tiled floor.

''All right, Zach,'' she said at last. ''I think you're making a mistake.'' Her lips twisted. ''I think I'm making an even bigger one. But I'll marry you.''

''In two weeks?''

''Two weeks.''

''I'll have my lawyer draw up papers to guarantee funding for the camp. We can sign them before the wedding.''

''Have your lawyer send them to my lawyer first,'' Rebecca said.

Zach looked at Rebecca with searching eyes. The kid he remembered would have believed the best of him, not taken precautions against the worst. No, she wasn't a kid anymore, no matter what he chose to call her.

''Fine,'' he said. ''Anything else?''

''What time should I be at the courthouse?''

''Meet me at my lawyer's office at 3:00.'' He gave her an address. ''We'll go from there to the courthouse.''

She smiled in a way that was unutterably sad. ''I hope neither of us will be sorry a year from now for making this devil's bargain.''

''If you're having second thoughts, just don't show up at the courthouse.''

Zach was sorry the instant the taunt was out of his mouth. He was no longer willing to settle for just any woman. He wanted Rebecca.

''Goodbye, Zach.'' She crossed past him without looking back, her shoulders squared and her chin high.

Zach had no idea whether she meant goodbye until the wedding, or farewell forever. He opened his mouth to ask and snapped it shut again. He would burn in hell before he admitted to her that he cared, one way or the other.

For the next two weeks, that's just what he did.

Chapter 3

"Hi, Kid. Are you awake?"

"I am now," Rebecca mumbled, still half asleep. She checked the clock beside the hotel bed. "It's 5:00 a.m., Zach."

"Time to rise and shine, sleepyhead."

"Goodbye, Zach."

"Whoa, kid," he said with a laugh. "I wanted to let you know you're welcome to move your things in this morning. I'll be out working on the range, so you'll have the house to yourself. Kid? Are you there?"

"Sure, Zach. That sounds like a good idea."

"I could hang around if you need any help."

"I loaded the trailer. I can unload it."

"Okay, don't get your dander up. I'll see you later this afternoon, then."

"Goodbye, Zach." Rebecca dropped the phone into the cradle, groaned and shoved herself upright.

Her wedding day had arrived.

Rebecca was no more certain that she was doing the right

thing now than she had been two weeks ago. Mrs. Fortunata,
however, had been overjoyed.

"See? What did I tell you?" She dabbed at her eyes with
a hankie. "I can't believe you want me to be a camp counselor. No more mopping floors! I'm one lucky old lady. That's
for sure!"

It had felt good to make Mrs. Fortunata happy.

Rebecca winced at the thought of having to explain to Zach
that—without consulting him—she had hired Mrs. Fortunata—and expected him to pay her—to cook for them during
the months when camp wasn't in session and—also at his
expense—let her live in the counselor's suite in the girl's
bunkhouse year-round.

Mrs. Fortunata needed that kind of security in order to leave
her job at the hospital. And Rebecca had made up her mind
that, once she left the hospital, Mrs. Fortunata was never going to mop or buff another floor in her life.

It vaguely troubled her that she hadn't inquired whether
Mrs. Fortunata could cook. However, it had seemed a logical
assumption for a woman with that many kids and grandkids.
And even though Mrs. Fortunata had never held a position
exactly like the one Rebecca had offered her at the camp,
Rebecca knew she would be wonderful with the children.

She gnawed on her lower lip. She would just have to tell
Zach what she had done at a time when he would be receptive
to the idea.

As she drove under the black wrought iron archway that
spelled out *Hawk's Pride,* she watched for her first sight of
the whitewashed, Spanish-style adobe house that would soon
be her home. Wooden posts that served as ceiling beams pro-
truded at intervals along the high walls of the flat-roofed structure. She backed the rented trailer up to the kitchen door, but
instead of going inside immediately, followed the stone path
that led into the central courtyard.

The house, which was shaped in a square, had been built
around a moss-laden live oak that was twice as tall as the roof

and which provided a mantle of cooling shade. A latticed arbor near the sliding glass door to Zach's bedroom was draped with fragrant wisteria that hung down above a wooden swing big enough to seat two comfortably. The whole area was bounded by grass and flowers that created a delightful lover's bower. Rebecca couldn't help wondering if Zach had ever made love to Cynthia there.

She forced her thoughts away from Cynthia Kenyon. It would be too easy to let herself get eaten up with jealousy of a dead woman. But her stomach churned at the thought of what mementos of the other woman she might find in the house.

Rebecca let herself into Zach's bedroom through the sliding glass door. The blinds were closed, and it was dark and quiet and cool inside. Zach had a housekeeper several days a week, so there wasn't a speck of dust to be found on the tile floors, but a Western shirt had been thrown over the arm of a wooden rocker, and several ranch magazines lay on the floor beside the unmade four-poster bed. She could still see the imprint where Zach's head had lain on the pillow. From the tossed look of the sheets, he was a restless sleeper.

To her dismay, a picture of Cynthia Kenyon sat on Zach's dresser where he couldn't help but see it each morning when he awoke.

She was tempted to pick up the magazines and make the bed. And remove the photograph from Zach's dresser. She resisted the impulse, but exorcising the ghost of Cynthia Kenyon was high on her list of Things to Do When I Marry Zach.

"Hello? Kid, are you here?"

Rebecca froze when she heard Zach calling to her from the kitchen. She hurried from his bedroom, unwilling to meet him there. She nearly ran into him as they met in the archway to the living room.

"Oh, there you are," he said.

She laughed nervously and sidestepped her way farther into

the room, keeping her distance from him. "I thought you planned to be gone from the house."

"I took a break from fence mending on the chance you might need some help lifting boxes after all."

Rebecca looked at him closely for the first time and was struck dumb by what she saw. He had obviously been engaged in hard physical labor. A pair of worn leather gloves stuck out of his back pocket. His plaid Western shirt was open down the front and hanging outside his jeans, and his chest glistened with sweat. His Stetson showed a ring of dampness near the concha band, and the hair at his nape clung to his skin in wet curls. His boots were dusty, his jeans dirty and torn at the knee.

She wanted to touch him, to lay her hands on his slick skin, to taste the salt on his neck, to shove the hat off his head and feel the coolness of his damp hair and the heat of his flesh. She was amazed at the flood of purely sexual desire that made her knees feel weak.

"Zach."

"Oh, kid, don't look at me like that. Not now. Not yet."

Rebecca took a step toward him. She hesitated, remembering the picture of Cynthia in the other room.

Be careful, Rebecca. Oh, be careful. He's still in love with another woman, an inner voice cautioned.

But Cynthia was dead. Zach was hers now, and she wanted to touch him. She could tell from the fierce, possessive look in his eyes that he wanted her, too.

She took another step, and another, until only inches separated their bodies. She could feel his heat, smell the musk of hard-working man. She turned her face up to him and waited. Her body quivered with anticipation.

Zach stared at the woman before him. He had dreamed every night of finding her waiting for him like this. The reality slammed him in the gut like a fist. Her body called to his in a way that was as primitive as man himself. His genitals drew up tight, and he felt the blood pounding in his temples. He wanted her like he had never wanted another human being in his life.

Rebecca was helpless to move. She could see the threat of violent passion in Zach's taut face, in his tense body, and noted the flimsy leash by which he had it tethered. Her eyes fell closed in surrender.

His mouth was incredibly gentle when it touched hers. He came back for another touch, another taste, his tongue dipping slightly, then retreating.

She groaned. "More, Zach."

His mouth captured hers in another kiss, powerful with longing, hungry for satisfaction. Suddenly she had what she wanted, his arms crushing her, drawing her close. Her unbound breasts nestled against his hard chest, and she could feel and smell and taste him.

Her hands slid around his neck, and she arched toward him to feel the hardness, the strength of him.

"I have to touch you," he said, his voice raw with need. He ripped her T-shirt up over her head and made a sound of satisfaction when he caught sight of her naked breasts. He stopped for a moment and put her away from him and took his time admiring her.

She fought the flush of embarrassment at standing naked before him, and lost. She crossed her hands over her breasts and struggled to hide the panic she felt. What was she doing? What was she thinking? This was insane. They were going to be married in a few hours.

"Zach, wait. I...we..." She swallowed hard.

"It's all right, kid. It's only me."

Her glance shot up to meet his dark eyes. His facial muscles were rigid, his jaw clenched, his nostrils flared. But there was something in his eyes beyond the glitter of sexual need. Understanding? She lowered her gaze, confused by the feelings roiling inside her.

"I'm being silly," she admitted in a low voice. She tried for a laugh and failed. She took a deep breath and let it out before she lowered her hands and stood before him in jeans and boots and nothing else. Her body was trembling so badly she thought surely he must have noticed. Her chin came up, and she met his glance for the second time.

His eyes were dark and feral. Dangerous.

She fought the need to flee, to save herself from whatever was to come.

Slowly, reverently, his hands reached out to cup her breasts.

She hissed in a breath as his callused fingertips brushed against her nipples, causing them to peak.

"Incredible," he murmured. "So responsive. So very beautiful."

He lowered his head to suckle her.

Rebecca's knees threatened to buckle, and she grabbed hold of Zach's shoulders. She had never felt anything so exquisite. She thought she was going to faint.

She groaned and pleaded for what she knew not. "Zach, please."

He raised his head, and she saw the raw hunger in his eyes. It frightened her, and at the same time left her feeling exhilarated.

"What is it you want, kid?" he said in a voice harsh with unrequited sexual need.

That was the problem. She didn't know what she wanted.

He started to let go, but she put her hands over his to keep them pressed against her breasts. "Wait, Zach."

She had never seen a man want like this, never imagined the things she would feel. The feminine power. The powerful need.

She was afraid of what was to come. She had never done even this much with a man, and she trembled with expectation and with virginal fear. But there was something greater than the fear. Love. And need.

"I want you, Zach."

An animal sound issued from his throat as he lowered her onto the rug that covered the cool tile floor. He unzipped her jeans and yanked down her underwear before freeing himself. He shoved her knees wide apart and thrust inside her.

"Zach, wait—"

But it was too late. She hadn't realized it would happen so fast. She had underestimated the force of his desire, his hunger to be inside her. He had thought she was experienced and had acted accordingly.

Rebecca cried out sharply as he took her virginity.

Zach froze.

He raised himself the full length of his arms, but remained inside her. He looked amazed and confused. "You can't be."

"I'm not…anymore."

"I thought… You're twenty-three!"

"Could we discuss this another time?" She lifted her hips enough to make him groan.

"All right, kid," he said. "We'll talk later."

Rebecca could see the restraint Zach used to keep his need in check as he moved slowly, gently within her. His hand slid down between their bodies to caress her, and his mouth brought frissons of pleasure wherever it roamed.

"Your skin is like velvet," he murmured as his lips caressed her throat. "And your hair…I want to wrap myself up in it and get lost. I think…I think…"

Rebecca didn't want Zach thinking, because his thoughts might stray to another woman. She wanted the hungry sexual partner who had been so anxious to have her that he hadn't even waited to undress himself.

She began to touch him, tentatively at first, seeking places that would arouse his ardor. She tunneled her fingers into the springy curls that covered his chest and happened upon a male nipple that hardened as her fingertips played with it. She loved the feel of his skin, the hard muscle and sinew so different from her softness. She shoved his jeans down below his hips and heard him grunt with surprise and satisfaction as she indulged her curiosity and learned the shape of his lean flanks and buttocks.

When her fingers strayed to the area where his inner thigh joined his belly, he tensed. As she caressed him there, he hissed out a breath of air. When she laid the flat of her hand on him he grabbed her wrist and held her still.

"If you touch me there, I won't be responsible for the consequences," he warned.

Rebecca produced a "cat's got the cream" smile. And touched him there.

He gave a harsh groan and found her mouth with his. His tongue mimicked the thrusts of his body. His hand slipped between them, and Rebecca gasped as his thumb found a spot that was particularly sensitive. Her body tightened and stiffened as she fought the sensations Zach was producing with his hand.

"Let it happen," he murmured in her ear.

"I can't—"

His mouth took hers in a hard kiss, and she fought to catch her breath as her body tensed. Too much was happening. She felt her body slipping from her control, the feelings too intense to bear. She was reaching now for something, arching into Zach's body, her hips thrusting in rhythm with his, her mouth open and sounds coming out that would have appalled her had she not been so helpless to prevent them.

Her tongue met his in a duel of passion, while her hands slid down into the crevice between his legs, driving him over the edge.

She felt the warm spill of his seed inside her as her body clenched and went rigid. She heard his shout of exultation mixed with her own ragged cry of fulfillment. And then she felt his weight, hot and heavy as he relaxed his body onto hers.

Her hands slid around him as his head fell into the niche of her neck and shoulder.

His breath was warm and harsh in her ear, and she felt her own chest heaving with the effort to suck enough air to keep her alive.

"I'm too heavy for you," he said abruptly.

A moment later, he had her tucked against his side on the rug that had bunched beneath them, his leg over hers, their sweat-slick bodies joined from chest to hip, their heads lolling on the cool tile floor.

Rebecca was basking in an afterglow of wonder, when Zach brought her back to unrelenting reality.

"It's time to talk, kid."

"What is there left to say?"

"For a start, it would be interesting to know why you kept your virginity for twenty-three years and then couldn't wait another couple of hours for the wedding."

Rebecca was ashamed to admit the answer to Zach's query. Quite simply, she had been jealous of a dead woman. She played with the black curls that covered his chest, avoiding a response.

Zach wouldn't allow it. He put a forefinger beneath her chin and forced her to meet his eyes. "I'd like an explanation."

"There's a picture of Cynthia in the bedroom," she said in a quiet voice.

Zach stiffened. "And you were staking your claim?"

She peered at him from beneath lowered lashes. "Something like that. Did it work?"

"Cynthia can't compete or complain. She's dead."

"Then you won't mind if I put away that picture on your dresser," she retorted.

"Putting the picture away won't make any difference."

Rebecca felt the knot return to her stomach. It didn't matter whether she removed the photograph because the image of Cynthia would always be with him. So, perhaps it was better to leave it there until Zach was ready to put it away, along with his memories of his first—his only?—love.

Actually, Zach no longer needed the picture of Cynthia to remind him of her perfidy. Images of her face on the last day he had seen her had been permanently graven in his soul. But he used the photo to remind him that a woman couldn't be trusted. Looking at Cynthia every day for the past seven years had reinforced his distrust of women and kept him from letting himself get too deeply involved with one of them.

"Go ahead and get rid of it," Zach said.

"You do it. Whenever you're ready."

"All right."

But Zach didn't jump right up and run to the bedroom, as Rebecca had hoped he would. Instead, he said, "How about a shower?"

"Together?" Rebecca asked, startled—and intrigued—by the suggestion.

"Sure. Why not?" He was on his feet a moment later and pulled her up beside him.

They stripped where they were and walked naked down the hall to Zach's bathroom. Rebecca kept sneaking glances at Zach, admiring his lean flanks, his flat belly, and the genitals resting in a nest of dark curls. As his body hardened in response to her avid gaze, she wondered how on earth he had managed to fit inside her.

He met her incredulous glance and grinned. "If you see anything you especially like, feel free to help yourself."

"I like it all," Rebecca retorted, chagrined that he had caught her gawking. "But a hand wouldn't be very useful without an arm to guide it, and if I took a leg, you might have some trouble walking."

Zach laughed as he pulled her into his arms and nuzzled her throat beneath her ear. "I can see you're going to keep me on my toes, kid."

"Actually, I think I'd like you better flat on your back... with me on top of you."

Rebecca lowered her eyes, amazed at her own audacity.

Zach shot a surprised look in her direction. "Really? I'll be glad to give it a try...after we shower."

Rebecca had never had her hair washed by a lover, and she was amused by Zach's playful antics. Part of the excitement in playing with him was the knowledge that at any moment his touches could become caresses.

When they did, she was stunned by the strength of her response to him. For once she was glad to be so much smaller than Zach. He lifted her legs around his waist as they coupled, easily supporting her for the thrusts that led to the culmination of their desire.

Then they showered all over again. When they were done, he wrapped her in a towel and carried her to his bedroom. He joined her in his mussed-up bed, where they reminded each other in murmurs that they had to get to the lawyer's office by three, then promptly fell asleep.

Rebecca woke feeling warm and safe and realized she was snuggled deep in Zach's embrace. Then the hairs prickled on the back of her neck. She froze, and her heart began to thunder in her breast.

Someone else was in the room.

Rebecca clutched the sheet to her breasts as she sat up. Zach was slower to wake and let the sheets fall where they would as he shoved himself into a sitting position.

"What is it?"

"There's someone in here."

Zach looked around the room, then rose and moved toward the door. He looked out into the hall, then shut the door. He walked to the bathroom and checked, then checked the walk-in closet. He came back and stood before her with his hands on his hips. "There's no one in here but us, kid."

"There is!"

"Want me to check under the bed for green-eyed monsters?"

Rebecca flushed. "I didn't imagine it, Zach. There was someone here." She spotted the picture of Cynthia on the dresser over Zach's shoulder and froze.

Zach turned to look at what had caught her eye. He walked over to the picture, braced his hands against the dresser and dropped his head between his shoulders. "I don't believe in ghosts."

Rebecca leapt from the bed, dragging the sheet along with her. "I don't, either." But she had no other explanation for her strong feeling that there was another presence in the room.

He turned to face her. "You don't need the sheet. There's no one here but me."

Rebecca felt the heat skating up her throat. It was absurd to hide herself from him. He had already seen everything there was to see, and in a matter of hours he would be her husband. And he obviously wasn't shy about his nudity. She stubbornly tightened her hold on the sheet. "I don't usually walk around naked," she said primly.

He grabbed a corner of the sheet and began to tug on it. "I want to see you."

"Not now, Zach," she said in a whispered hiss.

"Why not now?"

Her eyes strayed to the picture on the dresser. The other woman stared back at her.

Zach reached behind him and turned Cynthia's photo around the other way. "Does that help?"

Actually, it did.

Zach kept tugging until he had Rebecca between his legs. He backed her to the edge of the bed, then turned and sat down and pulled her into his lap. "Cynthia was a part of my past. She's no threat to you."

"You're still in love with her," Rebecca accused.

"She's dead."

That didn't change what Rebecca had said. It was probably futile to argue the issue with Zach, but she wasn't willing to concede it, either. "Zach—"

His callused hand surrounded her nape and drew her head toward him so he could cover her mouth with his. She was still in a daze when he said, "Come on, kid. It's time to go get married. If we don't hurry, we'll be late for our own wedding.''

It didn't make much sense to argue with that.

Chapter 4

Zach's entire family was waiting for them on the courthouse steps—his parents, his siblings and their spouses and all their children. Rebecca felt a rush of butterflies in her stomach.

"I didn't know your family would be here."

"Couldn't keep them away. Mom and Dad didn't attend either Falcon's or Callen's wedding. I'm the last of the Three Whitelaw Brats to get married, so they sure weren't going to miss this one."

"Hello, Rebecca," Zach's mother said with a warm smile. "It's so good to see you again."

"Glad to see my son has a little sense, anyway," Zach's father said as he leaned down to kiss her cheek.

Rebecca found herself figuratively enfolded in the Whitelaw family's embrace. It felt good. It felt wonderful. Here was the family she had missed since her father had died. Here was the warmth and comfort she had been seeking all those years since she had left Hawk's Pride. She slipped her arm through Zach's. A man who came from a family with this much love in it couldn't have forgotten the feeling. He just had to be reminded, and it would all come back to him.

She suddenly felt a whole lot better about getting married. After the afternoon they had spent loving each other, she had every reason to hope their marriage would be successful. If she was lucky, she might already be pregnant.

Rebecca was glad, now that she saw how important this wedding was to Zach's family, that she had dressed for the occasion and insisted that Zach do the same.

She was wearing a soft off-white buckskin ceremonial Indian dress. It had a lovely pattern of colorful beads across the bodice and was fringed along the hem and sleeves. She wore matching knee-high buckskin moccasins. A beaded headband across her brow held her hair in place. The ceremonial dress had been worn by her mother when she was married, and by her grandmother before that, going back several generations. She had cajoled Zach into donning a black Western tailored suit with a white dress shirt, bolo tie and black boots.

Zach slipped a possessive arm around Rebecca's waist and began herding his family into the courthouse. "We might as well get on with it. Day's wasting."

Zach was surprised at the tightness in his chest and the ache in his throat when Judge Smithers began the legal ceremony. It wasn't a real marriage; it was simply a business arrangement. He realized now why Rebecca had seemed anxious at the thought of so much family present.

He was aware of his mother weeping quietly to his left, his father's arm around her shoulder. He could hear Callen and Sam's twins arguing over a doll and Callen's futile whispered attempts to shush them. He saw from the corner of his eye how his brother, Falcon held his wife, Mara and stepdaughter, Susannah close with an arm around each of them, and how Mara cuddled their son, Cody, to her breast. Susannah's leukemia had been in remission for four and a half years now. Six more months and the whole family could breathe a huge sigh of relief that she had made it past the five-year mark and was out of danger.

Having family here made what was happening more real. He had wanted the legal ties, but speaking vows to Rebecca with his mom and dad present made his throat close up tight. The surge of emotions was unexpected and unwelcome. He reminded himself that he wasn't marrying to get a wife, he had merely selected an appropriate mother for his children.

He felt Rebecca's hand trembling in his as he slipped a plain gold band on her finger. It dawned on him that his family was liable to raise quite a ruckus if he ended up having to divorce her in a year.

"You may kiss the bride," Judge Smithers said at last.

Zach caught his breath at the look in Rebecca's eyes when she turned her face up to his. A single diamond teardrop slipped from her eye. Before he could stop himself, he leaned down and kissed the tear away. Then he caught her chin with his hand and tipped her mouth up to his.

He kissed her lightly and released her, afraid to do more than that, afraid to claim her mouth with his, as he felt the strong desire to do. No sense planting any more false hopes in his family than were already rooted there.

"Congratulations, son." His father hugged him hard and then turned to take both of Rebecca's hands in his. "I know you're going to make Zach happy. I hope this marriage turns out as well as those of my other two children have. My best wishes for a long and fruitful life for both of you."

This was getting worse and worse. He watched with alarm as his tearful mother hugged her new daughter-in-law.

"Welcome to the family, Rebecca. I wasn't in favor of Zach's method of choosing a wife, but I'm so pleased that it brought you to him."

"Thank you, Mrs. Whitelaw."

"Please, call me Candy. Or Mom, if you wish."

Rebecca shot him a look of desperation, and Zach recognized her dilemma. To call his mom "Candy" would be to deny the relationship his mother so obviously hoped would develop between them. To call her "Mom" was to set everyone up for greater heartache if the marriage ended in a year.

Zach came to his wife's rescue, slipping his arm around her waist and pulling her snug against his side. "Thanks, Mom," he said, saving Rebecca from having to say anything at all.

"I've got a wedding cake and some supper at Hawk's Way for everybody," his mother said. "Will you and Rebecca come?"

How could he deny the look of entreaty in his mother's eyes? He fought the grimace and managed a crooked smile. "Sure, Mom. Becky and I have to make a stop by the house first, but we'll be there."

To Zach's mortification, his sister had brought rice for everyone to throw on the courthouse steps—only, it was birdseed instead of rice. It wasn't entirely inappropriate to observe that ritual of fertility, he thought. But it was one more indication that his family expected the marriage to thrive and prosper. He hoped and prayed it did.

He grabbed Rebecca's hand and ran for his pickup, dragging her behind, only to discover that Just Married had been scrawled across the back window with shaving cream, and a host of boots and cans had been tied to the back end.

He wanted to laugh and curse at the same time. Didn't they get it? It wasn't real. He had married for convenience. He didn't want all these trappings. They made him uncomfortable and forced him to confront the utter unfairness of the bargain he had made with Rebecca.

From the grim look on her face, she wasn't any more happy with the situation than he was.

Zach heard the shouts of laughter as he picked Rebecca up and practically threw her into the seat of the pickup before running around the hood and letting himself inside. He gunned the engine and peeled rubber as he left the cluster of well-wishers behind.

As soon as he hit the edge of town, he slowed down.

"Is there something you really want from the house, or was that a ploy to avoid your family for a little while longer?"

Zach sighed. "Was it that obvious?"

"It was to me. I don't think your family noticed. They have no idea, do they, Zach, about the truth of our relationship?"

"No."

Rebecca groaned. "I can't possibly call your mother 'Mom' under the circumstances. But I'm afraid otherwise I'll hurt her feelings."

"Then call her 'Mom,'" Zach said irritably.

"What if I don't get pregnant, Zach? What if this all turns out to be a farce?"

"We'll worry about that when the time comes. Right now, we just do what's necessary to get through the day."

Zach stopped at the house, knowing he had to pick something up or have his lie exposed. When he stepped inside the house behind Rebecca, he knew exactly why he would have come straight home if this had really been his wedding day. He caught his wife's wrist and stopped her just inside the kitchen door.

"Hey, kid."

His voice was low and vibrant, and Rebecca felt a shiver of expectation scurry up her spine. She turned as Zach tugged on her hand until she was facing him. His hand caught under her chin and lifted her face until she had no choice except to look at him.

"Hello, wife."

It had a good sound, a marvelous sound. "Hello, Zach." She caught the edge of a frown. Had he expected her to call him husband? She wanted to, desperately. But she had begun to realize that she needed to protect herself if she was going to survive the coming year. Zach had made the rules. She had to follow them. That meant keeping her distance emotionally to the extent it was possible. At least until she was pregnant. Then it would be safe to love him, but not until then.

He made a growling sound in his throat. "Lord, how I want you!"

"Now? But we have to get to Hawk's Way—"

He shook his head. "Not right away. Not for as long as it would take me to love you."

Rebecca felt goose bumps the size of eggs pop up on her arms at the thought of repeating what had happened earlier in the day. "Oh, Zach."

He didn't need more invitation than that.

"Let's get out of these clothes," he said.

Rebecca watched as Zach yanked off his boots, then grabbed for his bolo tie. In moments he was stripped bare. He was already aroused, and she was intimidated by the size of him.

She had dragged her dress off and quickly slipped out of the silk bra and panties that were all she had worn under the buckskin, but Zach was way ahead of her.

"Leave the moccasins on," he said in a sharp voice.

Rebecca froze. She was naked except for the headband and moccasins. Somehow she didn't feel self-conscious, not with the clear look of admiration in Zach's dark eyes.

He fingered the beaded headband and let his hand smooth down the length of her hair to cup her breast. "You look so beautiful...my very own Indian princess."

His eyes were heavy-lidded, his nostrils flared for the scent of her. He reached out and drew her close, sliding her into the cradle of his thighs. He lowered his head and touched his lips to hers.

This time Rebecca knew what to expect, or thought she did. Only, this time, Zach was in no hurry at all. He took his time kissing first one side of her mouth, then the other, before stroking the length of her closed lips with his tongue. She gasped, and his tongue slid inside, warm and wet and demanding.

His hands caressed their way down her back to her buttocks and then between her legs, forcing her to spread them so that he could reach her nether lips. Her knees nearly buckled as he slid a finger inside her. And another. His teeth caught on an earlobe and nipped until the pleasure turned to pain. He soothed the hurt with kisses.

Abruptly, he picked her up and carried her toward the bedroom. Only, to her surprise, he didn't stop there. He shoved open the sliding glass door and stepped out into the sunlight.

The arbor was as beautiful as she had remembered. The air seemed misted with the fragrant scent of wisteria. He laid her down in the cool grass and mantled her body with his own.

She grasped his forearms as he spread her legs with his knees, and gave a startled cry when he thrust inside her to the hilt.

"Are you all right?"

Her blood was racing, her pulse was pounding, but there were flowers overhead and birdsong and sunlight dappled by the giant oak. She was more than all right. "I'm fine, Zach. Oh, I'm very fine."

He slid his hands beneath her and supported her as he made slow, delicious love to her.

Rebecca began to writhe beneath the onslaught of his mouth and body. She returned the favor, nipping at his shoulder, kissing and touching whatever part of him she could reach.

Zach's control didn't last long.

Rebecca was watching his face, so she saw the moment when his eyes closed. He gritted his teeth and then groaned savagely as the pleasure flooded through him.

By then she was no longer watching him. Her eyelids had fallen closed as she threw back her head and gave in to the shudders of intense pleasure racking through her.

They lay together in that lovely bower for long moments afterward. Somehow, Rebecca knew Zach had never been here with Cynthia. For some reason, he hadn't wanted to make love to her in the bedroom. She was glad, because here there was no ghost to intrude on their peace.

"We have to get dressed," Rebecca said when she could breathe easily again. "We have to go to your mother's party."

"I hope you get pregnant soon," he muttered.

Rebecca recoiled. Zach's comment was like a glass of cold water in her face. It reminded her why he had married her, what one use he had for her, and the reason he had been so willing to make love to her. He wanted her pregnant. His expertise as a lover was a benefit to her, but her pleasure was not a primary reason for their coupling.

"I have to get dressed." Her words came out sounding sharper, more barbed, than she had expected.

She stood and felt embarrassed suddenly to be still wearing her moccasins. She turned and fled.

Zach had felt Rebecca stiffen in his arms and wondered what he had done to offend her. He hadn't intended to make love to her in such a frenzy, but once the idea had occurred to him, the need to touch her, to kiss her, to put himself inside her, had been overwhelming.

Instead of taking her to bed, where any sane man would have made love to his brand-new wife, he had carted her outside and laid her in the grass. No wonder she was upset. But he had realized, as he entered the bedroom carrying Rebecca in his arms, that he didn't want to make love for the first time as man and wife in the bed where he had found Cynthia joined with another man.

He turned onto his stomach in the grass and laid his cheek on his folded arms. He hoped Rebecca was already pregnant. He didn't want to get to know her any better—and he admitted he was curious about what kind of person she had turned out to be—until he was certain their relationship would be permanent. His family weren't the only ones who would suffer if there was a divorce. He knew it would be difficult to put experiences like this one behind him and forget Rebecca Littlewolf if she didn't conceive his child.

Zach returned to the house through the kitchen door, because Rebecca had locked the sliding glass door and he didn't want to cause a confrontation if he knocked and she refused to let him in. In the kitchen, he put back on his shirt, pants and boots, but left off his jacket and tie.

He found himself pacing the tiled floor as he waited for Rebecca to appear. He resisted the urge to go see what was taking her so long and called to her instead. "Hey, kid! Are you dressed yet?"

He stopped and stared when she appeared in the kitchen doorway. Her eyes were blotchy, and her nose was red. She had obviously been crying. The headband was gone, and so were the moccasins and the Indian dress, for that matter. She was wearing a simple print cotton summer dress with narrow straps that exposed her shoulders, and sandals that left her legs and feet bare. The dress was fitted to the waist and flared into a full skirt. She had gathered her hair into a ponytail so she looked all of seventeen.

His heart lurched.

It was as though he was seeing her for the first time as she really was. A young woman. Very pretty. Open and honest. When he met her glance, he realized the blind trust, which had been there as recently as this morning, was gone. Her green eyes were wary. Her chin trembled.

"I'm ready," she said in a hoarse voice.

"You've been crying."

"I... It's been a hectic day."

"It's not over yet. Are you sure you want to go to my mother's party?"

Her chin came up, and her shoulders squared. "Of course."

She still had gumption, Zach thought. At least that hadn't changed. "Let's go, then."

He stood back and was distressed to see that she shied away as she passed by him. He reached out to stop her. "What's wrong?"

"Nothing."

"I would never hurt you, kid."

She turned and looked at him over her shoulder. Her voice was low and vibrated with feeling. "You already have."

Chapter 5

Rebecca took a sip of coffee that burned her tongue and quickly set down her coffee mug. She glanced at Zach, who sat on the opposite side of the kitchen island. "It's that time of month," she blurted. Meaning, of course, that she wasn't pregnant and that they wouldn't be having intercourse for the next few days.

For the third month since she had married Zach, her period had come exactly on time. She risked a glance at Zach and found his expression as grim-lipped as she had expected it to be. She bit back an apology. It wasn't for want of trying that she wasn't pregnant. She and Zach made love at least once every day and sometimes twice. She had begun to look forward to those interludes, because otherwise, Zach avoided her company.

Her dream of making Zach fall in love with her had gone dreadfully awry. On the other hand, she was making tremendous progress on her camp for kids with cancer, which she had—quite cleverly, she thought—dubbed Camp LittleHawk. Zach had done everything she had asked to help make the camp a reality. Unfortunately, she had yet to fulfill her part of the bargain by providing the child he so desperately wanted.

"Maybe I should go see a doctor," she suggested.

"I think it's a little soon for that, don't you?"

"I don't know what to think," Rebecca replied irritably.

She had discovered that Zach never argued when he could get his way by completely avoiding a discussion of the subject. She watched him do it now.

"I noticed that both bunkhouses are finished," he said. "If I'm not mistaken that means you have everything in place for your camp to open. When does the first bunch of kids arrive?"

"Tomorrow," she said, her face lit by the excitement she felt. "We'll have an even dozen, six boys and six girls."

"I met your new assistant yesterday."

"Rowley? I know he'll be great with the kids. He always has a smile on his face," Rebecca said. "It also turns out that he was raised on a ranch, so he's comfortable around horses and cattle."

"He's got a broken arm," Zach said.

"Well, yes, that's true," Rebecca said. "But he's quite good at saddling horses one-handed."

Rebecca had first spotted Rowley Holiday hitchhiking along the highway into town with a saddle thrown over his shoulder. Of course, she had stopped to pick him up. At first, the young man had been a bit taciturn, but soon she had him talking about his life as a rodeo bronc rider. His broken arm was a bit of bad luck, he said, that was going to make things a little tough for the six weeks it took his arm to heal.

She liked his enthusiasm for his work and his willingness to shoulder life's burdens with a smile. The next thing she knew, she was offering him the job as camp counselor.

Like Mrs. Fortunata, Rowley had no credentials for the job. But it wasn't a conventional kind of camp. Although every child coming to the camp had cancer, they were all in remis-

sion or stabilized by treatment. She had arranged to have a
doctor on call, but the truth of the matter was, all she needed
was a pair of willing hands—or even one good strong one—
and an authoritative voice to direct the boys, while she and
Mrs. Fortunata took care of the girls.

"It's perfect," she had said. "You can spend some time
working for me and Zach and then hit the rodeo circuit
again."

"Oh, I don't know, ma'am..."

That was another thing she liked about the cowboy, his
courtesy. "You have to take the job, Rowley. Camp's starting
in a week. I had talked my husband into taking the job, but
he's awful busy with ranch business. You'd be doing us a
favor."

And of course, being the nice sort of man he was, Rowley
had accepted the job. She had brought him back to the ranch
and told him to make himself at home in the counselor's suite
in the boys' bunkhouse.

"Is there anybody else you've hired that I should know
about?" Zach asked.

"Nobody since Mr. Tuttle," Rebecca said.

"Thank God," Zach muttered. "And about Tuttle—"

Rebecca didn't want to argue with Zach about her newest
employee, so she jumped up and dumped the rest of her coffee
in the sink. "I've got to get moving, Zach. I'll see you tonight."

Zach felt the butterfly touch of her lips on his cheek before
Rebecca flitted out the door.

He left the kitchen a moment or two after her, headed for
the barn. He watched her fanny sashay across the yard, not
quite believing the upheaval in his life since the day three
months ago when they had gotten married. It had dawned on
him, finally, that Rebecca hadn't changed much at all since
the days when she had roamed Hawk's Pride with a menag-
erie of animals in tow. She was still bringing home strays.
Only she had graduated to the two-legged variety.

Besides Mrs. Fortunata, who insisted on cooking for them to pay her way until the first campers showed up—and was a passable cook, if you liked a lot of pasta—there was the cowboy with the broken arm, Rowley Something, whom she had hired as a camp counselor, and an arthritic old man, Mr. Tuttle—who couldn't close his fingers around a pitchfork, let alone lift a bale of hay—whom she had hired to muck out the stalls and feed the dozen-odd ponies she had talked him into buying for the camp.

It wasn't that he couldn't afford the salaries. He had started out with a sizable trust fund and had turned a profit with his ranch over the past fifteen years. He could easily be termed a wealthy man.

"But if you keep it up," he had warned Rebecca, "Hawk's Pride will become a Mecca for every freeloader in Texas with a sob story."

She had looked up at him earnestly and said, "I would never let anyone take advantage of your generosity, Zach."

How was he supposed to respond to a statement like that?

Hog-tied and buffaloed by a bit of female fluff, that's what he was. He had given up trying to stop her from rescuing the homeless, the helpless and the unhealthy. Her generosity of spirit was simply a part of who she was.

Besides, Mrs. Fortunata was a nice old lady, and Rowley had turned out to be a damned hard worker, even with one hand. And somehow, he had no idea how, Mr. Tuttle kept the stable clean and the ponies fed.

Zach watched from the barn, where he was saddling his horse, as Rebecca headed for one of the two bunkhouses—one for boys and one for girls—that had been built to accommodate the twelve pint-size campers. Rowley was working on a corral that would be used as a riding ring for beginners.

Zach pulled the cinch tight and lowered the stirrup but didn't mount immediately. He leaned his arms on the saddle and watched Rebecca talk animatedly with the broken-winged cowboy.

His marriage wasn't turning out at all the way he had expected. In the first place, he hadn't anticipated being so fascinated by his wife. Most of the time, he couldn't keep his eyes off her when they were in the same room together. Only last night, a tiny mole beneath her left ear had drawn his eye and his hand and finally his mouth. At breakfast, he had found himself imagining the feel of the delicate curls at her nape, the curve of her brow. Even this far away, he wasn't immune to her charm. He felt his stomach sift sideways as she gave the new cowhand a sassy smile.

If it had simply been a matter of physical attraction, he might have sated himself with her body long before now. But he had been surprised to discover that he liked Rebecca most when she was discussing her plans for the children who would attend Camp LittleHawk, or the people she encountered who only needed a little helping hand—which she was glad to offer—to get on their feet again. Her eyes laid bare a warmth and enthusiasm for life that drew him like a hot fire on a cold Texas night.

He worried that he might be letting his admiration for her get in the way of his better judgment. This wasn't a real marriage. She wasn't a real wife. Their relationship was supposed to be strictly a business arrangement.

Zach snorted. It never had been that, and he doubted it ever would be.

He felt an urgent need, however, to protect himself from the pain of another failed relationship. He had never seen Rebecca look sideways at another man, so perhaps she would never be guilty of infidelity. But he couldn't help the nagging feeling that he was just one more cripple—one with an emotional handicap, rather than a physical one—that she had chosen to rescue, and that, like the others, once he was on his feet again, she would move on to someone else.

Loving her would leave him vulnerable because she might never learn to love him back. Oh, he would be treated with courtesy and care, thoughtfulness and cheer, but that wasn't the same as being loved—body and heart and soul—was it?

The only way he knew to fight his growing attraction was to keep his distance from her. But every time he drew a figurative line in the sand, she adroitly, even nonchalantly, stepped over it. She was constantly coming to him to ask his advice. Did he think blue or green was a better color for the walls in the boys' bunkhouse? Should she start with ten campers or twelve? What kind of crafts did boys like to do? Did he think the private suite for the counselor in each of the bunkhouses was large enough?

Was it any wonder he felt a little anxious?

To make matters worse, while he wanted a child as much as he ever had, the little boy he imagined now had features and a smile that matched those on Rebecca's face. He hadn't expected it to matter which woman was the mother of his child. Suddenly, it did. He had no idea what he was going to do if Rebecca didn't get pregnant before the year was up.

He heard Rebecca laugh, and the husky, full-throated sound caused the hair on his arms to stand up. His eyes narrowed on Rowley, who stood with his hip angled in a cock-strutting pose and a winning smile plastered on his lips. He watched Rebecca lay a hand on Rowley's shoulder and saw Rowley bend his chestnut-haired head to listen intently to what she had to say. Then Rowley offered his hand to help Rebecca sit on a rail of the corral. Only his hand didn't come away once she was up there. It stayed, resting on her thigh.

Zach felt his stomach cramp. The streak of possessiveness he felt took him by surprise. This wasn't jealousy, it was something much more primeval, the response of a male animal whose claim on its mate is threatened by another male animal. He knew from bitter experience that an unwary man could have his woman stolen away from him.

Adrenaline flowed. Muscles flexed in readiness to fight.

Zach stalked toward the corral, his eyes never leaving the sight of the masculine hand on his wife. He wasn't seeing

Rebecca, he was seeing Cynthia in those last moments before he had thrown her out, her body slick with sweat, the sheets tousled around her and musky with the smell of another man. He didn't give Rowley any warning, just grabbed him by the shoulder, turned him around and hit him in the jaw.

"Zach! Are you crazy? What are you doing?" Rebecca scrambled down from the corral and dropped to her knees beside the fallen man. "Are you all right, Rowley?"

Rowley had his good hand to his jaw and was gingerly working it. "I think so." He looked up at Zach. "What the hell was that all about?"

"Keep your hands off my wife."

Rebecca rose and stood toe to toe with Zach. "What's wrong with you? Rowley didn't do anything."

"He was holding hands with you."

"That was perfectly innocent!"

"Yeah. Right," Zach said, his voice harsh with sarcasm.

"I think I'll leave you two alone to work this out," Rowley said, struggling to his feet.

"Don't leave, Rowley," Rebecca said. "Zach owes you an apology."

"Like hell I do."

"Apologize, Zach."

"I'll do better than that." Zach turned to Rowley and said, "You're fired. Pick up your things and be out of here before the end of the day."

Rebecca was furious. "Don't you move an inch, Rowley." She rounded on Zach. "This is my camp, and you have no right to fire my employees."

"This is my ranch, and if I say a man goes, he goes!"

Rebecca shoved a frustrated hand through her hair. "I need him, Zach. I can't manage twelve kids by myself."

"You've got me." It was only then he realized he had been hurt when she replaced him with Rowley. Rationally, he knew she had seen somebody in trouble and been unable to pass him by without offering a helping hand. But it was hard playing second fiddle to another man.

"I know you're there for me, Zach. Lord, I could never face the thought of doing all this without you. But I thought I had put you on the spot asking you to help. We can really use another set of hands."

"He's only got one that works," Zach snarled.

"Nevertheless," Rebecca said, obviously exercising a great deal of restraint, "please tell Rowley you want him to stay."

Zach inspected the cowboy through narrowed eyes. Rowley met his gaze steadily, neither apologetic nor confrontational. It wasn't the look of a guilty man.

So maybe he had gone off half-cocked. Maybe he had acted a little crazy. But Rowley had gotten the point. *Hands off my wife.* As long as that was understood, he was willing to make peace with the other man.

"I'm sorry I hit you," Zach said gruffly.

Rowley took the hand Zach offered. "Forget it, Boss."

"You're welcome to stay."

"Thanks."

"See, now. Was that so hard?" Rebecca said as she slipped her hand through Zach's arm and snuggled close. "I just know you two are going to be great friends."

Zach and Rowley exchanged chagrined expressions. Knowing Rebecca, they probably would.

Zach eyed the eight-year-old boy who stared right back at him with unblinking eyes. "You sure you want to do this?"

"Uh-huh."

He set the boy on top of the small pony and shoved the kid's tennis shoes into the shortened stirrups. He had already given instructions on how to rein the horse. He gave the brim of the boy's baseball cap a tug to make sure it was settled on his head. All the kids wore caps, he had noticed, because not many of them had hair. Chemotherapy had left them in various stages of baldness.

He met the boy's solemn, gray-eyed gaze and said, "Nothing to it, kid. Let your body move with the horse. If you run into trouble, grab hold of the horn."

"My name is Pete."

"All right, Pete."

Zach mounted his horse and looked back at the line of eight- to twelve-year-old boys mounted on ponies behind him. Rebecca had the six girls mounted in front of them.

"Everybody ready?" He met Rebecca's gaze, and she grinned and nodded.

He heard a chorus of "uh-huhs" and "yeahs" in reply. He noticed Pete, the last in line, was already gripping the horn.

"Let's ride." There were several excited giggles and one "Yippee!"

Zach waited for Rebecca to lead out the girls, then let the boys pass by him before he brought up the rear. He felt a swell of unwelcome emotion at the sight of the kids' faces as they rambled by him. Amazing how a simple thing like a ride on horseback made them so happy.

All except Pete. Pete wasn't smiling, and he had a death grip on the saddle horn.

Zach nudged his horse up beside the boy, who appeared smaller than his age. "You don't have to do this now, if you're not enjoying yourself."

"Yes, I do."

"Why is that?"

"I might not get another chance." He turned and looked Zach in the eye. "You see, I'm going to die."

Zach wasn't sure what to say. He knew Rebecca had medical histories for all the kids, but he wasn't sure whether they included a prognosis for recovery, and even if they had, he hadn't bothered looking at them. He had no idea whether Pete was speaking from knowledge or supposition when he said he was going to die.

"Hell, I mean, heck, we all die someday." Zach glanced guiltily around to see if Rebecca was close enough to hear the profanity he had uttered. He had promised her—crossed his heart—that he wouldn't swear around the kids. It was a hard habit to break. Where Pete was concerned, a little profanity didn't seem out of order.

Zach had never seen such a world-weary, cynical look on the face of a child. The eyes that met his were eight going on eighty.

"I'll be dead before Christmas," Pete said.

"Gosh, I hope not," Zach said.

"Yeah, well, hoping doesn't always help," Pete said.

Zach wasn't sure how much encouragement he should offer. Maybe Pete was right about his fate. But there were always miracles. He noticed the boy had relaxed in the saddle. "You're doing fine," he said.

"Yeah," Pete conceded. "This isn't as hard as I thought it would be." He shot Zach a self-deprecating smile. "I was afraid I'd get hurt. I sure don't want to end up dying any sooner than I have to."

"I see what you mean," Zach said. "We're falling a little behind. Think you can manage a trot?"

"Sure." Pete grabbed the horn and kicked his mount and quickly caught up to the rest of the kids.

Zach settled back into his position at the tail end of the line. He wished Rowley was doing this job, but the cowboy had stayed at the bunkhouse to organize some crafts for later in the afternoon. Kids like these needed to see a smiling face, and Zach was having a hard time keeping the frown off his.

"I'm taking the canyon trail," Rebecca called back to him.

"All right," Zach said. "Careful you don't end up taking the steep route."

The trail into the canyon forked soon after the descent. One trail was wide and easy to navigate, perfect for the campers. The other was narrow and took a lot of twists and turns. It was easy to miss the turnoff for the first trail and end up on the second.

"Did real Indians draw those pictures?" Pete asked when they passed some etchings on the face of the canyon wall.

"I haven't had an archaeologist out here, but I'd guess so. Some of the artists might even have been my ancestors."

"Or Mrs. Whitelaw's ancestors," Pete chimed in.

Zach raised a brow. "How did you know Mrs. Whitelaw's part Indian?"

"Oh, she told me so when I met her at the hospital."

It had not occurred to Zach that Rebecca might have previously met these children. If he had thought about it at all, he supposed she had passed the word about Camp LittleHawk through doctors who treated children with cancer. But of course she would know any kids who had been patients at Children's Hospital during the past two years.

"How long were you in the hospital?"

"I've been in and out for the past three years."

"You're in remission now, though, right?" It was a condition of attending the camp.

"Yeah. But it's not going to last."

"How do you know."

"I know."

Zach didn't argue. The kid probably knew what he was talking about.

He made an effort to treat the children—many on their first trail ride—as individuals, but he kept seeing them as a group. Without their hair, their faces were hard to distinguish. They all had the same haunted look in their eyes. Some were smiling, some were not. Only their noses were different, pug or pointed or tip-tilted, freckled or tanned.

He wanted to be anywhere other than where he was. It was painful to spend time with these children, to see them experience all this just like healthy children. Because they weren't healthy, and there was nothing he could do to change that. He felt tremendous respect for Rebecca and anyone else who was courageous enough to face sick children every day and pretend that everything was normal. That included his brother

Falcon, who had married a woman whose child was deathly ill from leukemia. At least Falcon's stepdaughter was well on the road to recovery.

When they arrived back at the ranch after the ride was over, he made of point of seeking out Pete's records. He had no idea what he would find. What he saw made no sense to him. *Acute myelocytic leukemia.* So, was the kid going to die, or not?

That night, even with his wife safely spooned against his groin and his arm securely around her, he found himself unable to sleep.

"Kid?"

"Umm."

"How could you stand to do it?"

"Do what?" she murmured, already half asleep.

"How did you nurse kids like…those kids."

She turned in his arms so she was facing him. He could see the paleness of her skin in the light from the moon that filtered through the open blinds on the sliding glass door, but otherwise her elfin features were masked in shadows. She snuggled her head into the crook between his shoulder and chin.

"You mean, kids with cancer?"

She didn't say "kids who might die" but he knew she understood what he meant. "Yeah."

He felt her shrug.

"You just treat them like kids, Zach."

"But…"

She leaned back, and he could feel her eyes on him in the darkness. "Is it Pete?"

"How did you know?"

"I saw you talking to him."

"I looked up his records. He has *acute myelocytic leukemia.* Is that bad?"

She sighed. "Kids with that kind of leukemia have a very low percentage of survival."

"How long has he been sick?"

"I first met him two years ago. His situation was more promising then. He had acute lymphocytic leukemia, and the disease went into remission. When he relapsed six months ago, he was diagnosed with the more serious cancer."

"He knows he's going to die."

"Most of them have faced that possibility."

"How can they smile? How can they laugh?"

"You mean, how can they keep on living, when life is so uncertain? They don't focus on the past or the future. They live one day at a time."

Just like me, Rebecca wanted to say.

"You knew it would be like this," Zach said. It was almost an accusation.

"I knew."

"I didn't believe you, you know."

"Didn't believe what?"

"That you wanted to marry me because of the camp. I thought you made all that stuff up on the spur of the moment."

Rebecca was grateful for the darkness that hid her surprise at his intuitiveness. "Why did you think I wanted to marry you?"

Zach chuckled. "You're going to think I'm an idiot. I believed you were still in love with me."

Rebecca held her breath. *Oh, God. Then why had he married her, if he didn't want a wife who loved him?*

"Now I see it really was the camp you wanted. And I can understand why. It's a good thing you're doing, kid."

"Zach, are you sorry that...I don't love you?"

He was silent for a long time. "I think maybe it's better this way. I don't have to feel so guilty, like I'm cheating you, not loving you back. What we have isn't such a bad bargain for either one of us.

"I respect you, and as you pointed out," he said with a grin that showed in the moonlight, "I like you. I can see you'll make a terrific mother. I don't think I could have made a better choice.''

She might have confessed the truth, if she had thought it would make a difference. But Zach hadn't said anything about loving her back. She felt like crying and swallowed over the painful lump in her throat.

Zach sought out her mouth in the darkness. She felt his desperation and wondered at its source. She offered him the only comfort she could. Her body melted against his. But there was no lovemaking tonight, not when there was no fertile ground in which to plant his seed.

He pulled her close and held her tight. Gradually his hold on her eased, and his breathing steadied, until finally she could tell he had fallen asleep.

Rebecca was wide awake.

She eased herself out from under Zach's arm and the leg he had thrown over her hip. She silently let herself out through the sliding glass door and wandered barefoot in the grass to the wooden swing, where she settled herself. It creaked slightly as she set it in motion with her foot.

Zach had given her a great deal of food for thought.

He had thought she loved him. And married her anyway.

Rebecca wished she knew more about Zach's relationship with Cynthia. The picture that had been in his bedroom the day she moved in still sat on his dresser. It hadn't moved a millimeter in three months. She was as determined now as ever that Zach had to be the one to put it away. But for the first time in months she held out some hope that he would.

Chapter 6

Rebecca was exhausted. She smelled of hay and horses, and it wasn't delicate female perspiration that trickled down between her shoulders but plain old hardworking sweat. She kept glancing over her shoulder at Zach, who was working on the other side of the barn, doing the same job she was, forking hay to the children's ponies.

She had sent Mr. Tuttle into town to buy supplies, insisting that she would rather fork hay than face the crowd at the supermarket. Zach had caught her doing Mr. Tuttle's job and joined her without a word of reproof. She had rewarded him for his forbearance and understanding with a beaming smile of approval. But the whole time they had been working, he hadn't said a word to her. Something was obviously troubling him.

She had a pretty good idea what it was.

Zach had been wearing a frown ever since he said goodbye to Pete. The two of them had spoken only briefly before Pete boarded a chartered plane that was headed back to Dallas with the dozen campers who had completed their week at Camp

LittleHawk. Whatever had been said had obviously upset Zach.

"Want to talk about it?"

Zach didn't answer, just kept forking hay.

Rebecca set her pitchfork against the door to a stall, crossed to Zach and touched him on the shoulder. He whirled at the contact and would have stabbed her with his pitchfork if she hadn't jumped backward. She lost her footing and landed hard enough on the cement floor to elicit a cry of pain.

Zach said a word she hadn't heard all week. He leaned his pitchfork against the wall and stalked over to stand towering over her.

"Are you hurt?"

"My hip…"

He dropped to one knee and with unexpected gentleness began massaging her hip. Rubbing the muscle as he went, he worked his way around to her buttock. "Is that better?"

"Much."

She watched his hand, mesmerized by its strength, by the feelings coursing through her at a touch that wasn't intended to be intimate. Suddenly, all movement stopped. Her glance shot to Zach's face. He was staring at her as though he were seeing her for the first time.

She reached up a hand to brush a curl from his forehead.

He flinched but didn't jerk away. His dark eyes smoldered.

She let her hand drop to her side and lowered her gaze to escape the heat of his. Abruptly, he stood and tugged her to her feet. For a moment she wasn't sure her hip was going to support her. She leaned into Zach and heard him hiss as her breasts came in contact with his chest.

His hands tightened on her wrists to steady her—and to separate their bodies. Once she had her balance, he let her go and took another step back from her. She peeked up at him from beneath lowered lashes.

The frown had become a full-fledged grimace.

Well, it was just too bad if he didn't like being touched.

He was in for a lot more touching before she was through. Then she remembered the frown that had been there earlier, the one that had caused her to approach him in the first place. "Zach, is something bothering you?"

He stuck his thumbs in his back pockets. "I don't know what you mean."

"You've had an awful frown on your face ever since you said goodbye to Pete at the airport. Did he say something to upset you?"

Zach gave a snort that was somewhere between derision and disgust. "The kid's dying, and he tells me he's looking forward to seeing me next summer. What was I supposed to say? Yeah, sure, kid, I'll see you next year. If you're still alive!"

Rebecca caught a glimpse of the anguish in Zach's eyes before he turned his face away.

"I can't handle this," he said quietly. "You'll have to hire another hand to help you with the camp. And keep those kids away from me."

He turned to leave the barn. He hadn't taken two steps before Rebecca planted herself in front of him, her fisted hands on her hips.

"Don't you dare walk away from me!"

Zach stopped, but his irritation was apparent. "Don't push me, kid."

"Push *you?* Do you think it's easy for *me* to work with those kids?"

He looked startled. "Isn't it?"

"Heck, no! The first year I was a nurse at Children's Hospital I spent half my time crying. Then I learned that crying didn't change anything. They kept right on dying whether I cried or not. I don't cry anymore, Zach, but the hurting has never stopped. I don't think the hurting ever goes away. But you learn to live with it. You learn to keep on going in spite of it."

Zach shoved a hand through his unruly hair. "So what made you come up with this insane idea for a camp?"

"Is it crazy to want to bring sick kids a little happiness? When I see the smiles on their faces, when I see the shine in their eyes, I feel so good inside that I'm able to deal with the fact that, for some of them, their time is short."

"It doesn't work that way for me. The little bit of joy can't make up for the pain. I quit, kid. Find another fool to do the job." He sneered. "Knowing you, that shouldn't be hard."

Rebecca paled at the insult, but stood her ground. "You can't quit, Zach."

"Watch me."

Zach brushed past her and was nearly to the barn door when one whispered word stopped him.

"Coward."

Zach turned, his eyes narrowed, his face white with furious disbelief. "What did you call me?"

"You heard me. Coward." Her voice was full of the scorn she felt. And the despair. If he didn't learn to deal with the fear of being hurt that was experienced by every person who made a commitment to care, the pain that was always a possibility when one person opened himself to another, his heart was never going to be free to love her. And her marriage was doomed.

"Go ahead, turn your back and leave. Sure, it's easier not to care, but you'll be left with an awfully lonely, terribly empty life. And I won't be a part of it."

Zach reached her in two strides, grabbed hold of her shoulders in a painful grip and shook her until she was dizzy. She knew the exact moment he realized what he was doing, because he stopped so abruptly her chin jerked forward and her teeth snapped together with an audible *snick*.

He released her instantly and stood before her, his chest heaving, his eyes feral, his nostrils flared. A muscle in his jaw spasmed as he gritted his teeth.

"I'm no coward," he said in a low, menacing voice.

''What else do you call a man who won't stand and fight?''

''Fight for what? To watch a lot of kids suffer? Forget it!''

Fight for us! she wanted to cry. *For our future together!*

''I guess I should have expected this,'' she taunted. ''It isn't the first time you've turned tail.''

''What the hell are you talking about now?''

''I'm talking about Cynthia.''

''She's not a fit subject for discussion.''

She reached a hand toward him but, much as she craved some connection, didn't actually touch him. She let her eyes caress him as her hands yearned to do.

''You're running from the pain of losing her, Zach. You have been for years. You're so afraid of getting hurt again that you won't let yourself care about anyone. That's why you really advertised for a wife. It was the most impersonal way you could think of to connect with another human being. No danger of caring. No danger of being hurt. Until you stand and face the pain of losing the woman you loved, accept it and move beyond it, you're never going to be over her.''

''I'm over her,'' Zach said bitterly.

''Then why is her picture still sitting on your dresser?''

Zach's mouth opened and shut again before he spoke. ''I'm no coward.''

''Prove it,'' she challenged.

''I don't have to prove anything to you or anyone else.''

''What about proving something to yourself?''

''I...'' Zach hesitated.

She set the flat of her hand on his chest near his heart. It was beating frantically. ''You can do it, Zach.'' Her heart leapt to her throat, making it difficult to speak. ''Don't quit now.''

''Hell, kid. I'll take the damned picture off my dresser.''

''That isn't enough, Zach.''

''What do you want from me?''

I want your love. But there was no way she could tell him

that. He had to figure it out for himself. "I want you to keep your promise to help me with the camp this summer."

A callused hand shoved its way through rumpled black hair. "Fine. I'll help with your damned camp. Are you happy now?"

"Yes."

"Can I leave without getting another arrow in the back?"

She managed a crooked smile. "Sure, Zach. I'll go with you. Mrs. Fortunata insisted on fixing supper again. Some kind of pasta, I think. It should be ready about now."

And I want to see Cynthia's picture—and her memory—finally laid to rest.

Zach never went near the bedroom until long after his wife had showered and gone to bed. They hadn't made love all week, but she had told him earlier that day, with a blush he had found enchanting, that they could resume lovemaking that evening. After the altercation in the barn, he wondered whether she would let him near her. Not that he had forgiven her for what she had said. There had been just enough truth in her accusation to hurt. But he needed her—the relief of her body, he amended—and he didn't think he could wait another night.

He had postponed going to bed, hoping that she would already be asleep. He had discovered over the past few months that if he kissed her into arousal, when she awoke she wouldn't be thinking of anything except making love to him.

But she wasn't asleep. She was turned on her side facing the doorway, and he could clearly see by the lamp she had left burning on his dresser, that she was awake. Slowly, methodically, he undressed himself until he was naked. He felt her eyes on him, felt the beginnings of arousal. But there was no invitation for him to join her, no sign at all that she would welcome him in bed.

He knew what she was waiting for. She wanted him to put away Cynthia's picture. She wanted him to face the pain of his loss and move past it. Hah! If she only knew! He hated Cynthia Kenyon and always would. Nothing was going to change that. He was glad she was dead.

Except, his firstborn child had died with her. Or maybe she had lied. Maybe it was some other man's bastard.

Zach picked up the picture and noticed his hand was shaking. He crossed to the closet door and opened it and stuck the picture facedown on a high shelf. He stepped back and closed the door. He leaned his forehead against the cool, lacquered wooden surface and held on to the knob for dear life.

He had no explanation for his labored breathing. And the shaking had gotten worse. His whole body was suffused with it.

"Come to bed, Zach."

He couldn't let Rebecca see him like this. He turned to tell her he wasn't ready for bed and saw her arms opened wide to him.

Like a honeybee that sees a particularly spectacular bloom, he was drawn to her. On uncertain legs he made his way the few steps it took him to reach the bed.

There was nothing sexual about the way he crushed her to him. He needed to feel close to another human being, to have the warmth of another body take the chill from his own.

He felt her hands against his face, in his hair, at his nape. Her touch brought fire, and yet the shaking grew worse.

"Oh, my darling. My sweetheart. It's all right. I'm here."

He heard her crooning to him, calling to him, and yet he seemed to sink farther into a deep abyss. He was so cold. He could feel himself shivering with it.

He burrowed his face against her throat, but he needed to be closer still, so he shoved her legs apart with his knees and thrust inside her.

She was warm and wet. He felt himself sinking farther into the well, into pitch blackness. There was nothing now but him and the promise of her.

And the pain.

It was the pain that made him tremble, the pain that sucked at him, drawing him deeper into the gloom.

His body drove into hers as he fought the pull of the darkness. He felt the sharp sting of her fingernails in his shoulders, her heels in his buttocks, dragging him back to the surface. He heard the guttural moans issuing from her throat and smelled the scent of her arousal as he fought his way back to her, to the light.

He felt his body tighten, felt the primitive urge to claim his mate. He could see the light a little way beyond him and fought his way toward it. His lungs heaved to bring him precious air, his body arched as it spasmed, and he cried out into the night as he spilled his seed into her.

He burrowed his head close and squeezed her tightly. He had fought the demons and won. He had found the haven he had sought. She was warmth and brightness. She was life and happiness. She was everything he had ever wanted.

Don't let yourself be fooled. Remember the pain. Feel the pain. If you feel the pain you won't be vulnerable to the dangerous clutches of love.

He held on to her, held her so tight he could feel her heart thumping erratically against his own, feel her ragged breath against his throat, feel the slickness of her skin as their sweat-streaked bodies lay intertwined.

"Thank you, Zach," she murmured.

"For what?"

She didn't say anything, and he knew she meant for putting away the picture.

"It doesn't change anything," he said brusquely. "I won't forget her. And I won't fall in love with you."

He felt her tense briefly before she relaxed against him.

"I went into this marriage with my eyes open, Zach. You don't have to keep reminding me how you feel."

But he had to keep reminding himself. It would be so easy to love her. It was so tempting to let down his guard. If he did, disaster was certain to follow. He had to keep reminding himself of that, had to keep himself from loving her.

When he woke the next morning, he looked automatically for the picture of Cynthia. It wasn't there. Like a drug addict, he needed his daily fix of hate and distrust, but it was difficult to manage without a face to focus on. He might have sought out the picture, taken it down from the top shelf of the closet to glance at it, except Rebecca's eyes never left him the entire time he dressed. He wouldn't give her the satisfaction of knowing he had been using the photograph as a crutch.

"I'll go start breakfast," he said at last, conceding defeat.

She crossed to him and slid her arms around his neck and raised herself on tiptoe to find his mouth. Her lips were soft and pliant and tasted like nectar.

"What was that for?" he murmured against her lips.

"Just because."

He read the understanding and approval in her eyes and felt…uncomfortable. He didn't want her feelings about him to matter. Pretty soon he would be doing things just to please her. That sort of behavior led a man down the garden path to danger…to disaster…to love.

"I'll join you in the kitchen in a few minutes, all right?" she said.

"Sure."

Once Zach was gone, Rebecca heaved a huge sigh of… relief…despair…she wasn't sure what.

He had actually done it. He had taken the picture of Cynthia off his dresser and put it away. So why didn't she feel more hopeful about their future together?

It was the desperation she had seen in him, in his love-making, that had left her feeling so disconcerted. He must have loved Cynthia even more than she had thought to be so distraught at giving up the chance to look at her picture every day. If he still loved another woman that much seven years after her death, maybe he really wasn't ever going to get over her. Maybe she had been a fool to marry him.

But she couldn't give up now. They had the whole summer ahead of them to work and play together. She was willing to bet that a flesh-and-blood woman could beat the pants off a ghost any day of the week when it came to loving a man.

He's mine now, Cynthia. Let him go.

Rebecca shuddered as a draft of cold air wafted across her face. She stopped and stood still as an eerie feeling rolled through her. She looked up and saw she was standing directly under an air-conditioning vent. That had to be the source of the draft. What a silly widgeon she was to imagine Cynthia haunting Zach's bedroom.

She didn't really believe in ghosts, but she couldn't shake the feeling that the other woman was still around. Maybe it had been that picture sitting there all these months. Maybe now she could relax and forget about Cynthia Kenyon.

There's no need for you to hang around here any longer, Cynthia. Zach belongs to me now.

The vertical blinds on the sliding glass door rippled.

Rebecca looked up at the air-conditioning vent and gauged the distance to the blinds. She pursed her lips and shook her head.

Naw. She didn't believe in ghosts.

She glanced back one more time at the bare spot on the dresser where Cynthia's picture had stood.

"It's a start, Zach. It's a darn good start."

Chapter 7

"I'm so glad you're home, Zach," Rebecca said. "Sam called, and your sister is in labor."

Rebecca watched the quick grin come and go from her husband's face. He was obviously happy for Callen and Sam, but also reminded by the imminent birth of the Longstreets' third child that after six months of marriage his own wife remained barren.

"I'm sorry, Zach."

"For what?"

"You know what."

"These things take time."

"Half of mine is gone."

"You don't have to remind me." Zach yanked off his Stetson and shoved a hand through sweat-damp hair. "How is that new wrangler working out?"

Rebecca saw how neatly Zach had changed the subject and conceded that perhaps it was better not to discuss what couldn't be changed with words.

"Campbell is wonderful. He doesn't pretend the kids aren't

sick, and he's careful to keep an eye out for any problems they might have.''

Campbell was a recovering alcoholic who hadn't been able to find a job anywhere in the county to support his wife and six kids. No one trusted him, including Zach, because he had fallen off the wagon so many times. Rebecca hadn't been able to resist his request for a job.

"He's sober now, Zach," she had argued. "And when I think of all those hungry children…"

Zach had known he wasn't going to win the debate, but he resisted giving in right away because he liked the methods Rebecca used to cajole him. It had been a pleasure at last to cave in to her entreaties for this latest lost soul.

"All right," he conceded. "Campbell gets one chance. I see him drunk and he's gone."

So far, Campbell had stayed as sober as a Baptist preacher in a dry county.

"At least that's working out," Zach said.

"Yes." Even if their marriage wasn't.

Zach had kept his promise to work with the children, but he hadn't let any of them get close again, not like Pete. He was courteous and helpful, a regular Boy Scout. But he dealt with the possibility of pain by closing himself off from feeling anything. It wasn't the result she had hoped for when she had blackmailed him into working with her the rest of the summer. One more week, and Camp LittleHawk would be done for the season. She didn't hold out much hope that Zach was going to change in the next seven days.

To make matters worse, she had failed to become pregnant. In most marriages, it would be ludicrous to worry that she wasn't pregnant six months after the wedding. With the one-year deadline Zach had set, she was conscious that time was running out.

"I think I have to see a doctor, Zach. At least to give us both some peace of mind."

"That's ridiculous."

Rebecca shook her head. "We know the problem isn't with you. After all, Cynthia was... You can certainly father a child," she finished quickly. "There might be something wrong with me. Something that never showed up during my regular checkups."

Zach closed his eyes. How could he admit to Rebecca that the problem might very well be with him? How could he explain that the child Cynthia carried might not have been his? There was no sense putting her through a bunch of tests if he was the one at fault. But maybe the problem was hers. Maybe it was better to let her be tested first, to make sure of her fertility before he questioned his own.

"All right," he said at last.

He watched Rebecca's shoulders sag as she conceded the necessity for tests. His stomach rolled. He couldn't make her go through that sort of thing by herself. Not when the problem might be his.

"We'll both go," he said.

"What?"

"I said we'll both go."

"But you—"

"Cynthia said the child was mine. There's some question whether it actually was."

She stared at him, her eyes filled with shocked disbelief. "How..."

"The day she died, I caught her in bed with another man."

"But..."

"So we'll both go see the doctor."

Rebecca didn't dare ask the thousand and one questions buzzing around inside her head. The look on Zach's face precluded questions.

"Maybe we'll have a chance to talk to a doctor while we're at the hospital waiting for Callen to deliver," Zach said.

"All right."

Rebecca couldn't quit staring at Zach during the drive to the hospital. He had fooled everybody! His parents, Cynthia's parents, his siblings, even she had believed he had been mourning Cynthia's death all these years. But would a man mourn the death of a woman who had been unfaithful to him? Would he mourn the death of a woman carrying a child he wasn't even sure was his?

If he hadn't loved Cynthia, what was it that had alienated him from love all these years?

Rebecca worried her lower lip with her teeth as she reasoned it out. He must have been hurt, humiliated even, by his fiancée's infidelity. No man would be likely to confess the truth.

So why had he kept Cynthia's picture where he could see it every day?

To remind him…of her betrayal.

Rebecca leaned back against the pickup seat and closed her eyes. She felt like a fool. All this time she had thought Zach was still in love with Cynthia, when he had actually been nursing his hate. Cynthia had torn out his heart and left a deep, vacant hole behind. Zach would never love again, because he had been burned too badly the first time. He would shut her out forever, the way he had shut Pete out when the boy got too close, because he couldn't take the chance that he would be hurt again.

Zach saw the tear slip down Rebecca's cheek and reached out to catch it. As his fingertips brushed her cheek, she leaned into his palm. "I know it must be hard on you to see Callen at a time like this. Especially when you haven't been able… when we… But she expects us to be there. She wouldn't understand why it's painful for us…"

"Oh, Zach, you wonderful, foolish man…"

"I suppose we don't have to go, but—"

She scooted across the seat and wrapped her arm around his waist. His arm slid naturally around her shoulders.

"It's fine," she said. "We'll go."

"Are you sure, kid?"

"I'm sure."

Rebecca tried not to breathe too deeply when they entered the hospital, but it was impossible to ignore the smell of disinfectant that permeated the place. In all the time she had worked at Children's Hospital she had never gotten used to it. The astringent smell evoked memories of children she had worked with who had gone home whole and healthy. And children who had not.

She followed a uniformed nurse with her eyes as the woman moved briskly down the narrow green—why were hospitals always beige or green?—corridor.

"Bring back memories?" Zach asked.

She smiled at his perceptiveness. "A few."

"Sorry you quit?"

She shook her head. "I like what I'm doing now a lot better."

"I suppose it beats seeing them sick in bed." Zach precluded her retort by grasping her hand and dragging her onto a crowded elevator. She glared at him, but forbore to argue in front of other people.

Zach held on to Rebecca's hand as a way of allaying his own nervousness. He wanted a child so bad he could taste it. He wanted to see the new baby...and he didn't. He wanted to be happy for his sister and brother-in-law, and yet he was so sick with jealousy that he felt a burning in the pit of his stomach.

It was every bit as painful as he had expected it would be to see the joy in Callen's and Sam's eyes at the birth of their son and know he had no child of his own on the way. It was every bit as difficult as he had known it would be to have the baby thrust into his arms and to feel the softness of its skin, to examine its minute fingernails and lush baby lashes and know the child belonged to someone else.

Worst of all was seeing the look of wonder on Rebecca's face as she held the baby close, to see her flush of embarrassment when the newborn rooted instinctively for her breast as she touched its cheek with her fingertip, and to see the longing in her eyes as she watched Callen nursing her son.

Rebecca looked up suddenly, and their eyes locked. A wealth of words was spoken, though none were said aloud.

I hope this will be us someday soon.

Oh, Zach, how I would love to have your child.

It'll happen. We just have to keep trying.

What if there's something wrong with me?

There's nothing wrong with you. You'll see.

What if it doesn't happen right away?

We have six months. That's plenty of time.

I love you, Zach. I've always loved you.

Zach felt the constriction in his chest, a sort of breathlessness caused by what he saw in Rebecca's eyes. She had never spoken of love, not once in all the months they had been married, except to deny it. She had not even said she cared, except for that one lapse when she had called him "darling" and "sweetheart." Only, he wasn't sure he hadn't imagined the words, because he had needed to hear them so badly at the time.

Could he be mistaken about what he saw in her eyes now? Did he want her to love him? Is that why he had projected an emotion where it did not exist?

Of course, she was always touching him. But he figured that was just a habit of hers. She also touched the children often, and the horses and the dog and the barnyard cats. He was no different. Rebecca was a sensual person. If wasn't her fault he reacted the way he did to her friendly pats and affable strokes and inadvertent brushing against him.

He reached out for Rebecca's hand again and, when he had it firmly in his own, said, "We have to be going now."

"Stay a little longer," his sister urged.

"We've got another group of kids, the last campers of the summer, coming tomorrow," Rebecca said by way of explanation for their early departure.

"I should be home in a couple of days. Promise you'll come visit then," Callen urged.

"We will," Zach promised.

"Promise?"

"Promise," Zach said, crossing his heart and holding up three Boy Scout fingers.

He had a death grip on Rebecca's hand and practically dragged her from the room. He wasn't even sure where he was going until he found himself in front of a doctor's door on the first floor in the administration wing of the hospital.

Dr. Elmo Bently. Obstetrics and Gynecology.

Zach stopped and turned to stare at Rebecca.

"We don't have to do this now, Zach."

"I think we do."

He knocked and when the doctor called out, he opened the door and pulled her inside.

"What brings you two here?" Dr. Bently asked.

"We want to be tested."

The doctor raised a brow. "Something wrong? One of you sick?"

"For fertility." Zach felt the heat stealing up his throat, but there was nothing he could do to stop it. He pulled Rebecca closer to his side.

The doctor frowned. "Either of you have any reason to suspect you're infertile?"

"Only that my wife hasn't gotten pregnant. And it isn't for want of trying," Zach managed to say.

The doctor chuckled. "Both of you sit down and get comfortable. I think we need to have a little talk."

The doctor asked a series of questions and listened as they answered.

"I'll do some preliminary tests if you insist," he said. "But it seems a bit early to suggest there's a problem with conception. The only possible problem I see is that you may be having intercourse too frequently. The body needs time to recoup, so there may be fewer sperm during subsequent ejaculations. You could try having sex every other day, instead of every day, and see if that helps.''

Rebecca wriggled in her seat at such plain speaking. But it was the first encouraging thing she had heard the doctor say. She looked sideways at Zach to see what he thought of this advice.

''All right, Doc, we'll cut back on frequency. But I still want us to be tested. When can we arrange to do that?''

''You can leave a sperm sample now, and I can see your wife in a couple of days.''

Zach plainly hadn't anticipated anything happening quite so soon, but he quickly recovered. ''The sooner, the better.''

Rebecca waited in the hall while a nurse took Zach to another area of the hospital. When it took longer than she expected for Zach to return, she wandered down the hall toward a modern computer information center that listed the location of all the wards. One stood out among the others.

Pediatrics.

She took the elevator to the second floor and, when she stepped off, turned away from the nurse's station as though she knew where she was going. In fact, Rebecca knew exactly what she was looking for. Several doors down the hall, she found it.

It wasn't a large room, probably because it wasn't a large hospital. There were eight beds, and each one held a sick child. She hesitated only a moment before stepping inside.

Her eyes were drawn to a girl about five years old. She wore a cast on her right arm and another on her right leg, which was attached to a pulley that kept it elevated. Her face was crisscrossed with tiny scabs that suggested she had probably gone through a car windshield. She was awake, but merely stared at the ceiling.

''Hello,'' Rebecca said.

The little girl turned big, curious brown eyes on her, but she didn't speak.

''My name is Rebecca. What's yours?''

"Jewel."

"May I sit down, Jewel?"

The little girl nodded.

"How are you feeling?"

"Are you a doctor?"

Rebecca smiled and shook her head. "No, just a visitor."

The girl sighed in relief. "Good. Because I'm tired of doctors."

"Seen too many of them?"

"Uh-huh."

"If you could go anywhere in the world this afternoon, where would you go?" Rebecca asked.

"Home."

Rebecca felt the sting in her nose that preceded tears and blinked quickly to keep them back. She had expected an answer like "Disneyland." How long had this child been here, anyway?

"How long have you been in the hospital, Jewel?"

"A long time."

"I'll bet your mommy and daddy come and visit you a lot."

"My mommy and daddy are dead."

Rebecca brushed a stray curl of plain, Mississippi-mud-brown hair from the girl's forehead while she tried to swallow back the huge lump in her throat. "That's too bad, Jewel."

"I had a brother, but he got killed, too. I just got hurt real bad." Her eyes brimmed with tears. When she blinked, one slid down her too-thin cheek.

"I'm sure someone out there will be glad to have a little girl like you come to live with them. Your grandma and grandpa? Or your aunt and uncle?"

She shook her head sadly. "There's no place for me to go. When I'm well, I have to go to a *father* home, I think it's called."

"A *foster* home," Rebecca corrected.

Rebecca saw the girl's eyes shift upward over her shoulder and turned to see who was there.

It was Zach.

"I wondered where you had gone. I took a wild guess, and lo and behold, here you are."

"I just wanted to visit," Rebecca said.

"Who's your friend?" Zach asked.

"Jewel, this is Zach. Zach, this is Jewel. She's been explaining that she'll be going to a foster home when she's well."

The little girl and the tall man solemnly shook hands.

"Hello, Jewel. It's nice to meet you."

"Hello. Are you a doctor?"

Zach smiled wryly. "No. I'm a rancher."

"Do you have horses on your ranch?"

"Lot of them. Ponies, too."

"I used to have a pony. My daddy and I...my daddy..." The child turned her face away and stared at the wall, clearly overwrought.

Rebecca touched the girl gently on the shoulder and said, "I hope you get well soon, Jewel."

If Zach hadn't taken her hand and pulled her away, she wouldn't have left at all.

Once they were far enough beyond the door that they couldn't be heard, Rebecca turned to Zach, her heart in her eyes. "Zach?"

"I know what you're thinking, and the answer is no."

"She doesn't have anywhere to go. In a week Camp LittleHawk will be done for the season, and it won't be starting again for months. It doesn't have to be forever. A foster home is just an interim step, until someone comes along who wants to adopt her."

"No."

"It isn't as though she's sick. She was injured in an accident. She's obviously well, or nearly well. She will be well."

"No."

"She's all alone in the word, no relatives, nobody. We can't turn our backs on her."

Zach huffed out a breath of air. "There would probably be a ton of paperwork to qualify as a foster home."

Rebecca's grin was blinding. "Oh, thank you, Zach. Thank you. You won't be sorry, I promise you."

"I haven't said yes."

"But you stopped saying no."

Zach chuckled. "You're impossible."

"And you love me for it," Rebecca said with a flirtatious look from beneath long lashes. She realized suddenly what she had said and quickly asked, "How did the test go?"

He couldn't meet her eyes. "First time I've done that since I was a teenager," he muttered.

She couldn't help the giggle that escaped.

Zach picked her up and hugged her tight. "Don't laugh. Your turn is coming."

Both of them sobered at the reminder that they had been unsuccessful in conceiving a child of their own. Zach set her down. "You can pursue the possibility of providing a foster home for Jewel. But be sure you understand we're talking about a temporary situation. If I'd wanted to adopt a kid, I could have done it a long time ago. Don't let yourself get attached to her."

He tipped her chin up to force her to meet his gaze. "Understand?"

"I can care for Jewel without getting emotionally involved. I proved that as a nurse. You don't have to worry about me."

He slid an arm around her waist and headed down the hall toward the elevator.

"Do you think they'll let us have her?" Rebecca asked.

"I think there's a pretty good chance of it."

"What makes you think so?"

"I know the head of social service in town. She owes me a favor for something I did for her in high school."

Rebecca arched a suspicious, inquiring brow. "What, exactly, was it you did for her?"

Zach grinned. "I think that's better left unsaid. Suffice it to say, if you want to foster Jewel, I'll do what I can to grease the wheels."

It was the least he could do. After all, for a welcome change she had consulted him before making a decision about helping somebody. Besides, he was willing to accept the homeless waif on a temporary basis for entirely selfish reasons.

He had discovered, quite by accident, of course, that his happiness depended more and more on Rebecca's state of mind. When she was sad, he felt bad. When she was happy, he felt good.

He gazed down into Rebecca's glowing face and grinned.

At the moment, he felt downright ecstatic.

Chapter 8

There was nothing physically wrong with either of them that should prevent conception. That was the official word from Dr. Bently. But another month had come and gone, and Rebecca wasn't pregnant. Thank goodness she had a million and one things to do to prepare for Jewel's arrival at Hawk's Pride to keep her mind off her troubles.

She had gone to visit Jewel every day during the month it had taken to qualify as a foster home and be assigned to care for the child. She had brought Zach along several times, arguing that it would help the little girl to adjust to living at Hawk's Pride if she knew the two of them better before she left the hospital.

Zach had grumbled, but he had gone.

And had no trouble at all talking with the little girl. In fact, once the two of them got started, it was hard to get a word in edgewise. When she asked Zach about it later, he grinned and said, "I have lots of experience."

Her blank look made him chuckle.

"You forget I've got three nieces. Falcon's daughter, Susannah, comes every year to spend some time with Mom and Dad, and I see her then. Also, I've spent more than a few evenings with Callen and Sam's twins.''

Her eyebrows rose.

''In case you're wondering, yes, I've changed my share of diapers and worn the baby powder to prove it. And 'Unca Zach' knows how to play airplane and horsey and motorboat.''

Rebecca had laughed at the image he conjured. Then the laughter had choked off, and her heart had leapt to her eyes as she met his gaze. She wanted to see powder on his nose from diapering their child. She wanted to hear a tiny voice calling him ''Daddy.'' She wanted to see him down on his hands and knees in the living room—and be there with him, a giggling child beside them.

She had torn her eyes away from his, because the look of wistful longing she found there was too painful to endure.

She had learned something else about Zach in those early visits with Jewel.

He was mush when Jewel turned those baby brown eyes on him and asked for something. Already the child had gotten him to promise her a pony, and let himself be wrangled into riding with her as soon as she was well enough to do so.

On one of those visits, Rebecca had realized that she was falling in love with Zach all over again. Or maybe it was for the first time.

Her feelings for Zach now were different, stronger, more certain than they had been all those years ago. While she had truly believed she loved Zach when she married him, she had never imagined the depth of feeling a woman could have for a man who cherished her with his body. Or the passion she would experience in the arms of an eager and inventive lover. Or the respect she could feel for a man who was kind and considerate and generous with his time and his money.

But in her wildest dreams, she had never imagined the well of emotion that was tapped when she saw Zach with Jewel.

She felt tender and soft, achy and raw. She wanted to give him a child of her body. Her love was a cup that once had been half-full but now was overflowing.

However, the problems in their relationship loomed large. *Zach didn't love her.*

Zach would divorce her if she couldn't conceive his child.

If she let herself think about it too much, she would end up crazy. It was better to live in the present and enjoy her life with Zach as much as she could.

At breakfast this morning, she had reminded Zach to be back by mid-afternoon so they could pick Jewel up at the hospital. She paced the kitchen like a tiger, awaiting his arrival.

The screen door opened, and he stepped inside. "I'm not late, am I?"

She glanced at her watch. "No. I guess I'm just a little anxious."

"You? Nervous? I've watched you face a dozen campers with a grin and a prayer. This is just one little girl."

"But she's going to be ours."

Zach's lips thinned, and his body tensed. "That's not precisely true. We're going to be taking care of her. For a little while."

Rebecca's chin came up. "Maybe so. But while she's in this house, we'll be standing in the role of parents. That's what foster *parenting* is all about. I thought you were committed to having Jewel here at Hawk's Pride, Zach. If you're not, maybe it isn't fair to bring her home with us today."

"I like the kid," Zach confessed. "She's got a lot of guts for somebody that young. I just don't want to set up any false hopes in you—or her—that any of this is going to become permanent."

"The social service lady already discussed this with Jewel. She understands we're only bringing her here temporarily, that they're looking for someone to adopt her."

"Poor kid," Zach muttered.

Rebecca slipped her arm through Zach's and leaned her head against his shoulder. "She's going to be fine, Zach."

"We'd better get going. She'll worry if we're late."

Jewel was sitting on the edge of her hospital bed waiting for them, her hands pressed between bony knees that poked out from beneath a short plaid skirt. Her face lit up when she saw them.

"'Becca! Zach!"

She shoved herself off the bed and gamboled toward them like a filly on newborn legs. It wasn't a graceful trip, because the limp in her right leg gave her an uneven gait. The bone had been broken in so many places that it hadn't mended perfectly. She was always going to have a slight hitch in her step.

Jewel gave Rebecca a quick kiss, then launched herself at Zach, who had no choice except to catch her.

Zach lifted the little girl high enough to make her squeal in mock terror, then settled her on his arm. The scabs were gone from her face now, and only faint pink lines remained. Eventually, even they were supposed to disappear. He couldn't help wondering what the kid's parents had been thinking when they named her Jewel. There was no sapphire or topaz or emerald in her eyes. They were a plain mud brown.

"Ready to go?" he asked.

"You bet! Can we go riding this afternoon?"

"Whoa, pardner! We have to get you settled in at the house first."

"Then can we go riding?" Jewel asked.

Zach laughed. "All right, Miss Persistence. We'll go riding later this afternoon."

"Yippee!"

Rebecca could see why Zach wanted a child so badly. He was a natural-born father. He was completely comfortable with Jewel, and the child responded to his openness by being equally free with him.

Jewel turned to Rebecca as Zach carried her outside and said, "Do I really have a room with a sliding glass door? Our house didn't have sliding glass doors."

As Rebecca buckled the child into the seat belt in the center of the pickup cab, Jewel said, "I can't wait to meet your dog with the raggedy ears. We had a dog, but he ran away and got lost. I always wanted a kitty, but my daddy was 'lergic."

The patter didn't stop. It didn't take Rebecca long to realize that the child was as nervous as she was. In fact, of the three of them, Zach was the least rattled.

Even he wasn't as immune to the excitement of the moment as he apparently wanted her to think. She caught him sneaking glances at Jewel when he didn't think the little girl was looking. He seemed intrigued and entranced by the child's effervescence. Rebecca couldn't help feeling a little envious. She would have given her eyeteeth to catch Zach looking at her like that.

In fact, Zach had been making a mental comparison between Jewel's stubborn determination and Rebecca's insistence on marching to the beat of her own drummer. The two of them—the girl and the woman—were remarkably similar in temperament. Perhaps that was what had drawn Rebecca to Jewel in the first place. Certainly, she had found a kindred spirit.

Once back at the ranch, they only took time for Jewel to change into jeans and boots before they headed for the barn. Jewel had insisted that the three of them ride together.

"I have some chores to do in the house," Rebecca said in an attempt to excuse herself.

"But you have to come! Pretty please?"

"Oh, all right." Rebecca ruffled Jewel's dishwater curls. "But don't think you're always going to get your way just by looking cute."

"That's the pot calling the kettle black," Zach murmured. He had noted with some amusement that Jewel was as good at wrapping Rebecca around her little finger as Rebecca was at manipulating him.

What he hadn't counted on was his inability to say no to the two of them when they ganged up on him.

"I think we should go down the narrow trail," Rebecca said as they approached the canyon.

"Isn't that a little dangerous? Especially for a first ride?" Zach asked.

"I've been watching Jewel, and she's an excellent rider," Rebecca said. "The narrow trail would be more fun."

"Can we?" Jewel pleaded. "Pretty please?"

Zach took one look at the two sets of pleading eyes, one a truly brilliant green, the other an ordinary brown, and gave in. "Just be careful and take it slow. I don't want to have to haul either one of you out of there."

Zach had to admit the narrow, zigzagging trail into the canyon was more fun, and Jewel enjoyed it every bit as much as Rebecca had suggested she would. When they reached the sandy bottom, they set out the simple picnic of ham sandwiches, potato chips and soda that Rebecca had brought along.

Rebecca watched as Jewel automatically handed Zach her bag of chips to open, then did the same with her can of soda. The little girl expected him to be helpful, to be there for her, and he was. Rebecca had to hide her smile when Jewel reached up with her napkin to wipe a dollop of mustard from Zach's mouth.

"Thank you," he said.

"You're welcome," Jewel replied.

Of course, when Rebecca got a little mustard on her lip, Zach didn't do anything as civilized as using a napkin to remove it. He leaned over and thoroughly kissed it off.

Her face was flushed when he released her at last. She was afraid to look and see Jewel's reaction.

To her chagrin, Zach winked at the little girl and said, "Spiciest mustard I ever ate."

Jewel laughed, and Rebecca gave up and joined in.

Jewel became drowsy soon after lunch and settled down on the blanket to nap. As soon as the little girl's eyes drifted closed, Zach pulled Rebecca into his lap and lazily kissed her. His lips played over hers, nipping her lower lip, then sucking on it, then teasing the edge of her mouth with his tongue. His hand closed over her breast, and his thumb brushed the tip, which instantly pebbled.

"Zach, what are you doing?" Rebecca asked breathlessly.

"Can't a man make love to his wife?"

"Not with a little girl sleeping three feet away," Rebecca whispered as she tried to stop his roving hands.

Zach wouldn't be deterred. His hand slid down between her legs to cup the heat of her. Rebecca had never seen him in such a playful mood. It was as though a younger, happier man had taken Zach's place. She wondered what had caused the change, but was afraid to ask for fear of spoiling the moment.

He nuzzled her ear and whispered, "I knew there was a good reason why I married you."

Rebecca looked at him quizzically. "Oh? What was that?"

"I have the hots for your body."

Muffled laughter bubbled from Rebecca's throat.

"And you're going to make an absolutely wonderful mother."

The laughter died. She sought out Zach's eyes. "Do you really think so?"

"Yeah. Anybody with a heart big enough to care for as many strays as you've brought home over the past seven months has to be a good mother."

"Zach…what if I don't get pregnant? What if—"

His fingertips touched her lips to cut her off. "No worrying allowed. We're on a picnic."

He laid her back on the blanket and slipped his hips into the cradle of hers. He rested his weight on his elbows and cupped her face in his hands. He made love to her mouth with exquisite gentleness, drawing out the pleasure, letting it build slowly, but steadily.

She bit back the moans that sought voice, because she didn't want to wake Jewel. Zach teased her and touched her until she was writhing beneath him. He pushed her to higher and higher levels of sensation. She wanted to beg him to stop, because there was no way they could consummate their love-making, and they both knew it. But she was enjoying herself too much and, if the hard length pressing against her hip was any indication, so was he.

When they heard Jewel begin to rouse from her nap, Zach bit her earlobe one last time and whispered, "Tonight."

It was an invitation and a promise.

"Tonight," she whispered back.

Of course, neither of them had counted on Jewel having an earache.

They had just put the little girl to bed and slipped under the covers themselves, when they heard a knock on their bedroom door.

Zach quickly pulled on a pair of jeans, cursing when he got them on backward. He barely had them on straight with a couple of buttons done when Rebecca, who had thrown a robe on to cover her nakedness, yanked the door open.

Jewel was standing there in a thin cotton nightgown, her head cocked sideways and her shoulder jammed against her left ear.

"Is something the matter?"

"My ear hurts."

Rebecca dropped down on one knee beside Jewel. She put a hand on the child's forehead. "I think she has a fever."

Zach called Dr. Stephens, the Whitelaw family physician, and got instructions over the phone on what to do to ease Jewel's discomfort. He relayed his instructions to Rebecca, who had already taken Jewel to her room and tucked her back into bed.

"Doc Stephens said if the pain doesn't go away in a couple of hours, or if her fever goes up any more, we need to take her to the emergency room," Zach explained.

"I'll stay with her," Rebecca said. "You go back to bed."

Zach felt awkward leaving Rebecca with the child, but there really wasn't anything more he could do. "I'll check on you in a little while," he promised.

As he made his way down the hall to their bedroom, he heard Rebecca's murmurous voice reading *Winnie the Pooh*.

Zach lay in bed awake—and alone—with nothing to do but think. The bed smelled of the musky perfume he associated with Rebecca, and his groin tightened in a totally natural, if untimely, response to her feminine scent. He told his unruly body to forget it. There wasn't much chance it would be satisfied in the near future.

"I think I've just experienced for the first time what it means to be a parent," he said aloud. He should have resented Jewel's intrusion, but somehow, he didn't. It was instinct, he supposed, the need to ensure the propagation of the species, that caused a parent to subjugate his own needs and desires to that of a defenseless child. It surprised him to realize that he had felt that primitive response to help and protect Jewel, even though she wasn't his own flesh and blood.

"Mother Nature's pretty sneaky," he concluded. He realized he was talking to himself again and shut up.

But it didn't stop him from thinking.

His mind wandered back to the events of the afternoon. He wasn't sure why he had felt so carefree, but he realized now that he hadn't thought once of Cynthia the whole day. That was a new record. The pain and humiliation of that failed relationship seemed very far away. Rebecca made life seem so easy to live. And she was so damned easy to love.

Not that he loved her, of course. Although, it might not be so bad if he did. Except there was a problem that had to be resolved first.

He had given Rebecca a one-year deadline to get pregnant.

Seven months of that year were already gone, and the lady was as regular as clockwork.

It wasn't safe to love her yet. Not if he might have to give her up in five months.

Are you crazy? Give her up? What the hell for? She's a great wife!

But I want a family, kids of my own.

Hell, kids grow up and leave you. A wife is forever.

I can get another wife.

One as giving as Rebecca? One who'll bring so much marvelous chaos into your life? I doubt it.

She's not the only woman in the world.

Face it. She's one in a million. And the lady lights your fire.

That was certainly true. He had enjoyed himself immensely on the picnic, especially toward the end, when he had been able to hold Rebecca in his arms and make love to her—without actually making love. The slow building of pleasure had been tremendously erotic. He had indulged in touching and tasting to his heart's content. He had felt her shiver of anticipation and known that in the dark privacy of their bedroom later that evening she would finally be his.

Only it hadn't exactly turned out that way.

Zach looked at the clock radio on the bedside table. He had been lying in bed for two hours wide awake. He hadn't heard anything from the other room in quite a while. He dragged his jeans back on and headed down the hall.

He pushed the door open carefully, so as not to wake Jewel if she was sleeping. It took him a moment to realize the bed was empty. His eyes quickly searched the room. The two of them were sound asleep in the wooden rocker in the corner, the child snuggled safe in the woman's arms.

He tiptoed over to the shadowed corner and stood staring down at them. The lamplight glowed on Rebecca's flawless skin, and on Jewel's faint, crisscrossed scars. Jewel's hair was a mass of short curls surrounding her face—such an ordinary brown to be so pretty, he thought. Rebecca's sleek black hair drew his hand, but he resisted the urge to touch, fearing to wake her.

Zach felt a sharp constriction in his chest. His throat closed up, and his nose stung. He couldn't remember the last time he had shed a tear for anyone or anything. But he felt like crying. Because he wanted what he saw, and he knew he would never have it.

Rebecca wasn't going to get pregnant. He wasn't going to be that lucky. He was going to be forced to choose between her and a child of his own. He could see it coming. He had imagined watching his children grow and prosper on Hawk's Pride for so many years, that he fought giving up his dream. He wanted children of his own.

But what if the price for children of his own flesh and blood was giving up Rebecca? Could he return to the empty life he had led before she came to fill it up?

He quietly backed out of the room.

Zach returned to his bedroom and shoved the sliding glass door open so he could hear the night sounds, so he could feel the evening breeze. The leaves of the live oak rustled, but otherwise the night was silent.

He stepped outside and looked up between the gnarled branches of the live oak at the star-filled sky. Generations of Whitelaws had watched those same stars. Maybe some had even stood under this same tree. He wanted to leave a legacy for the future when he was gone. He wanted to know a part of him survived when there were no mortal remains of Zachary Baylor Whitelaw on this earth. Was that so terrible? Was that so selfish?

Maybe not so terrible or selfish. But stupid, if it means losing Rebecca.

Zach sighed. It was premature to create problems where none existed. There was no reason why he had to make a decision now. There were months—five months—ahead of him when the situation might resolve itself. All he had to do was wait.

And pray.

Chapter 9

"We've found a family who wants to adopt Jewel."

"I see," Rebecca replied to the social service worker at the other end of the phone line. "When do they want to meet her?"

"This afternoon, if possible."

"I see."

"Would that be all right, Mrs. Whitelaw?"

"Of course."

"I'll let Mr. and Mrs. Proffit know that you'll be expecting them."

Rebecca set the phone down and turned to Zach, who was sitting at the kitchen island with a cup of coffee in front of him. Jewel was still sleeping.

"That was social service," Rebecca said. "They've found someone who may want to adopt Jewel. Mr. and Mrs. Proffit. They'll be coming to meet her this afternoon."

She sank onto a bar stool and dropped her head into her hands. "Oh, Zach, we've only had her three weeks!"

"This is what's best for Jewel, kid. She needs a mom and dad."

Rebecca's head jerked up. "What's wrong with us? She loves us, Zach. She won't want to leave."

"She's a child. She'll do what she's told."

"She'll be upset. She'll cry."

"She'll get over it."

"How can you be so heartless?" Rebecca demanded.

"I'm being realistic," Zach replied in a steely voice. "You always knew this arrangement was temporary."

"I didn't think they'd find anybody so soon." Rebecca's hands turned white-knuckled as she clenched them before her. "Or that I'd grow to love her so much."

She turned beseeching eyes on Zach. "Can't we keep her, Zach? Please?"

"She's not a lonely old lady or a down-on-his-luck cowboy. She's a growing child. She needs parents who can love her and provide her with a stable home."

"I love her. And if you'd let go of that stubborn pride of yours and admit it, you love her, too," she argued heatedly. "We don't have to let Mr. and Mrs. Proffit take her. We can give her a home, Zach."

"I don't want her!" Zach rose so violently that the stool skidded several feet, tottered and fell with a crash. "I want my own little girl. I—"

A whimper from the doorway cut him off. Zach felt a wrenching tear somewhere inside him when he saw Jewel standing in the doorway to the kitchen. She was still dressed in her nightgown, her hair in tumbled curls around her pinched white face. Her tiny hands were knotted into fists, and her chin trembled.

Good Lord, how much had she heard? Obviously, too much. And not enough. She had no way of knowing that his need for a child of his own had nothing to do with any lack in her. It was a fault in him, a pride of family that had been bred deep, and which he seemed unable to relinquish.

He exchanged a helpless look with Rebecca, whose face was nearly as pale with distress as the child's.

Zach quickly crossed to Jewel and bent down on one knee in front of her. When it appeared the little girl was going to turn and run, he took hold of her shoulders and held her in place.

"Jewel, listen to me."

"No! You don't like me! You don't want me here!"

Zach felt a sort of frantic fluttering inside. "Oh, Jewel, baby, I like you lots and lots. It's just…there are some nice folks who want to adopt you and make you their little girl forever and ever. Rebecca and I—"

"You don't want me." Her chin had sunk all the way to her chest. Her shoulders were slumped. The first tear spilled onto her scarred cheek.

"Oh, sweetheart…" Zach was torn in two. He couldn't say he wanted Jewel without offering hope that he and Rebecca might be willing to adopt her. But he didn't want to adopt her. There was nothing wrong with Jewel; she was a great kid. She just wasn't *his* kid.

He pulled the little girl into his arms and hugged her tight. There were tears in his eyes when he turned to Rebecca, completely frustrated, unsure what logical argument he could use to assuage the painful disillusionment of a five-year-old child.

Rebecca joined the two of them, and Zach opened one arm to pull her close.

"I promise to be good," Jewel sobbed.

"Oh, Jewel, you already *are* good," Rebecca crooned.

Zach couldn't say anything at all. His throat ached, and the muscles refused to work.

"It isn't that we wouldn't love to have you for our very own little girl," Rebecca said, "but…"

She met Zach's eyes, and he could see she wanted him to change his mind. But he had to draw the line somewhere. Otherwise, he was liable to find his house populated by homeless waifs. Jewel was lovable, but so were a lot of other kids. Slightly, but certainly, he shook his head no.

He flinched under the lash of scorn in Rebecca's eyes. It took every ounce of grit he had to hold to his convictions.

Rebecca's voice was calm, soothing, as she spoke to the distraught child. "There's a mommy and daddy coming to visit this afternoon who want you, oh, so badly, to come live with them. Wouldn't you like to meet them?"

"Noooooo," Jewel wailed. "I want to stay here. I don't want to go away. I love you."

She clutched at Zach's neck as she sobbed brokenly.

Zach saw Rebecca draw blood as she bit her lip to hold back her tears. He had to get away, or he was going to give in to them. He thrust Jewel into Rebecca's arms.

"I've got work to do. I'll be back this afternoon before the Proffits arrive."

Even far out on the range, all alone on horseback, Zach heard Jewel's pitiful voice in his head.

I don't want to go away. I love you.

And saw Rebecca's searing look of scorn.

He knew he had disappointed them both. He hadn't been the hero they had hoped for; he had been the villain.

That was the problem with being married to Rebecca. He was always trying to live up to her expectations of him. And often failing miserably. Over the past nearly eight months they had been married he had tied himself in knots trying to please her, to win a smile of approval from her. He suffered mightily those times when her glance told him he hadn't measured up.

Like now.

She had wanted a knight in shining armor to come to the rescue. He had acted like the evil magician instead, waving his wand to make the child disappear.

The truth was, now that he had some time to think about it, he conceded there was plenty of room at Hawk's Pride for one more. Who said they couldn't keep Jewel and have their own family, too? He had heard of instances where a couple who apparently couldn't conceive a child adopted one and then miraculously had their own.

He had learned from watching his brother, Falcon, that a man could love a child who was no relation to him as much as any father loved his own flesh and blood. It explained the pain he was feeling now at the thought of what his life would be like if Jewel wasn't a part of it. He would always worry whether she was warm and well-fed and happy.

He couldn't wait to get back to the house to tell Rebecca that he had a change of mind. He knew she would be pleased, and he hoped Rebecca and Jewel would forgive him.

He spurred his horse into a gallop and raced across the rugged countryside. Neither he nor his horse saw the rabbit hole until too late, and horse and rider both took a hard fall. Zach lay stunned for a moment, the air knocked out of him. As soon as he could, he rolled over to see how his horse had fared. The animal was back on its feet, but hobbling badly.

Zach shoved himself painfully to his feet and realized he had injured his ankle. He limped over to check his horse. The right foreleg wasn't broken, but the gelding had a bad sprain.

He had stopped swearing since the kids had shown up for camp, because he never knew when one of them was going to be around. But sometimes, nothing else expressed what he felt quite so well. And there were no kids here, at least a dozen miles from the nearest civilization.

"Damn it all to hell!" he muttered viciously.

There was no way he was going to get back to the house before the Proffits arrived. Oh, dear God. What if they took Jewel away with them? Rebecca would never forgive him. He would never forgive himself.

Rebecca was inwardly furious. Not only had Zach left her to handle a distraught five-year-old, but he hadn't returned as he had promised to deal with Mr. and Mrs. Proffit.

She greeted the couple cordially at the door. "Hello, Mr. and Mrs. Proffit, I'm Rebecca Whitelaw."

"Please, call us Dan and Susan," Dan said as the couple stepped inside.

They looked like very nice people, Rebecca thought. Dan was dressed in an expensive suit and tie, and Susan was wearing a designer dress and nylons. They were a little older than she had expected, maybe their middle thirties, but both of them were very attractive, what some might call "beautiful people."

"I thought Jewel would be here," Susan said.

"She's in her room. I hoped we might talk for a few moments first." She had no power to deny Dan and Susan if they wanted to adopt Jewel. Nevertheless, she felt a responsibility to ascertain what kind of parents they might be.

"Do you have other children?" Rebecca asked.

"No. We've tried, but we can't have children of our own," Susan said.

"I'm sorry." Rebecca had more empathy for their situation than she was willing to reveal. "Have you been trying to adopt for very long?" She had heard there were lengthy waits to find a child.

"We've only been looking for a year," Dan said.

Rebecca frowned. It sounded like they were shopping for a used car. "Would you like me to tell you a little about Jewel?"

"We'd rather meet her and make our own judgment about her," Dan replied.

"All right. Let me go get her."

Jewel was playing quietly in her room. She had been unusually, extraordinarily quiet ever since Zach had left the house. It was as though by being quiet she might blend into the woodwork, as though, by becoming invisible, Rebecca might somehow forget she was there and let her stay.

"Jewel, the Proffits are here. They'd like to meet you."

"Do I have to?"

Rebecca nodded. She held out her hand, and Jewel gripped it very tightly. When they arrived in the living room, Jewel wouldn't let go, so Rebecca walked past the Proffits, who were sitting on the leather couch, and settled herself in the pine rocker with Jewel standing between her jean-clad legs.

Before Rebecca could even make an introduction, Susan said, "She limps."

"And her face is scarred," Dan added.

"Jewel was in a car accident. That's how she lost her family."

"They didn't tell us about the limp," Susan said.

"Or the scars," Dan added.

"Will she ever walk normally?" Susan asked.

"She walks fine now," Rebecca replied between stiff lips.

"But she *limps!*" Susan exclaimed.

Rebecca felt Jewel stiffen. She circled Jewel's waist with her arm, to offer a bastion of comfort against the verbal onslaught of these rude, insensitive people.

"Will the scars go away?" Dan asked.

"They're hardly noticeable now," Rebecca managed to grit out. "In time they should fade until they're almost invisible."

"Almost?" Dan said, a frown on his face. He exchanged a look with his wife.

Rebecca felt sick. They *were* shopping for a child just like they would for a used car. And they didn't want one with any dents in the fender or scratches on the hood.

The couple rose abruptly. "I'm sorry we wasted your time," Dan said.

"Jewel isn't the right child for us," Susan said.

Rebecca couldn't believe her ears, couldn't believe they were saying these things in front of Jewel, as though she were made of chrome and steel and couldn't hear them perfectly well with her very human ears. She felt incensed at their cruelty.

Rebecca rose like an avenging angel and protectively shoved Jewel behind her. Before she could begin her tirade, she heard Jewel run from the room.

"Jewel, wait—" she called. But the little girl was gone. A

moment later Rebecca heard the screen door slam in the kitchen. Most likely Jewel was headed for the barn. She would catch up to her as soon as she finished with the Proffits, and try to undo some of the damage that had been done.

"You two don't deserve to have a child as wonderful as Jewel," she said fiercely. "She might limp, and she might have a few scars on her face, but that child has more love in her little finger than either one of you will ever know. Get out of my house. Get off this ranch. Get out of town. Because by the time I get through giving social services an earful, you won't find a child to adopt anywhere in this county!"

Rebecca didn't wait for them to leave before she headed toward the back door. When she got to the barn she was distressed to see that Jewel's pony was gone. The little girl couldn't heft the saddle, and it was still in place on the side of the stall. But she was perfectly capable of bridling her own horse and riding bareback, and indeed, the pony's bridle was gone.

There were dozens of ways a little girl could get hurt or lost on a ranch as big as Hawk's Pride. Rebecca didn't even have a clue where to start looking.

"Oh, Zach, where are you when I need you most?"

Zach was tired, hot, and hungry when he finally came limping down the dirt road to the main house. He had planted young live oaks the entire distance from the arched entry to the house when he first graded the road, and they provided welcome shade. He could see in his mind's eye the day when the approach to Hawk's Pride would be every bit as impressive as the magnolia-lined drive leading to Hawk's Way.

For the past several miles he had been composing his speech of apology to Rebecca and Jewel. He only hoped he wasn't too late.

Much as he desperately wanted to know how the interview with the Proffits had turned out, Zach headed for the barn first. Any cowboy worth his salt made sure his horse was taken care of before he attended to personal business. It was a habit bred in the West, because a man without a horse on the vast Texas plains could die walking to water. It behooved a cowboy, even in this day and age, to make sure his horse stayed healthy.

Zach had already unsaddled the gelding when a cowboy entered the barn. Zach started at the sight of the stranger, then realized it was Smitty, the man who had shown up on their back doorstep two days ago. And his newest employee.

He could remember thinking at the time that it was a good thing he had opened the kitchen door to the quiet knock instead of Rebecca. Because he took one look at the cowboy, at his worn boots and frayed jeans and dusty hat, and knew that Rebecca would have hired the man on the spot.

"Can I help you?" he had asked.

"I'm looking for a job."

"I don't need any hands right now." Which was the truth.

"I'm a hard worker."

"I don't doubt it. What put you out of work?"

"Oh. Well." A flush cheated up the cowboy's throat. "The boss and I didn't get along."

"I see." Probably a troublemaker, Zach thought. And felt relieved again that it hadn't been Rebecca who had answered the door.

"Man kicked his dog," the grizzled cowboy said. "Even a dog don't deserve that."

Zach had to agree. So maybe the cowboy wasn't a trouble-maker. "I wish I could help you, I just don't need any more hands right now." Especially with Camp LittleHawk disbanded for the summer. In fact, Rowley Holiday had taken off to join the rodeo circuit again.

"I'd be willin' to do just about anythin'."

Zach shoved his thumbs in his back pockets to resist the temptation to hire the man. "I just don't have any work," he said.

The man turned away, hesitated, then turned back. He

rubbed his whiskery jaw, then swiped his hand nervously along the leg of his pants. "You see, I got me a sick missus. Cancer. She's in the hospital gettin' chemicals pumped into her right now. I gotta have work to pay the bills."

Zach was certain he could have shut the door with a clear conscience if the man had mentioned any disease except cancer. He had a niece he had watched fight cancer, and he had spent the summer with kids ravaged by the disease. He told himself, when he offered Smitty a job, that he was doing it out of plain Christian charity, not because Rebecca had gotten him to thinking about how he had plenty and enough to share. Or because he knew how pleased and proud she would be of him for making "the right" decision.

In fact, when Rebecca heard what he had done, she gave him a look so tender, a kiss so sweet, that he flushed like a teenage kid asking for condoms at the drugstore.

His decision was vindicated now, because he needed someone to take care of his horse so he could get to the house, and here was Smitty available to help.

"Can I give you a hand, Boss?" the bewhiskered cowboy asked.

"Know anything about sprains."

"Sure do. Worked once upon a time at a racing stable. Got a poultice that'll do wonders. You just leave this cow pony to me. I'll take care of him.

"You better put some ice on that ankle of yours, too, Boss," Smitty said.

"I'll do that. By the way," Zach said as casually as he could, "have you seen Rebecca this afternoon?"

"Yeah. She was headed toward the canyon on horseback."

"Was Jewel with her?"

"Naw. She was alone."

Zach headed for the house. Maybe Rebecca had left him a note. Maybe there was some good reason why she and Jewel hadn't gone riding together. Maybe Jewel had gone over to play with Callen's girls.

And maybe the Proffits took her away.

Zach felt a chill of alarm when he entered the kitchen. It was so quiet you could hear nightfall coming. He let the screen door slam behind him and heard it echo through the house.

"Rebecca? Jewel?"

He limped his way down the hall to Jewel's room, afraid of what he would find. His heart was thumping crazily in his chest by the time he reached her doorway.

He made an audible sound of relief when he saw that her things were still there. He crossed to a chest and pulled the drawer open just to make sure. Her tiny T-shirts and flowered underwear were still there. Her favorite doll and her Pooh bear lay on the bed.

So where was she? And why wasn't Rebecca back from her ride? It was nearly dusk.

He headed back to the kitchen, grabbed the wall phone and called his sister.

"Hi, Callen."

"Hello, stranger. We haven't seen you guys since the Labor Day picnic. When are you going to bring Jewel and come visit?"

Zach felt his heart drop to his boots. He knew it was futile, but he asked anyway. "Jewel isn't there?"

"No. Don't tell me you've misplaced the child, Zach. That's a little careless even for you."

"Uh...I'm not exactly sure where she is. There were some people here this afternoon who wanted to adopt her."

"I know. Rebecca called me right after you left this morning. How did the interview go?"

"I don't know. I wasn't here."

Callen took an outraged breath, but Zach cut her off at the pass. "Before you start yelling at me, you should know my horse went down in a rabbit hole. The two of us had to limp our way back. I just got home a little while ago."

"Are you all right?"

"I'm fine. I just…I can't find Rebecca or Jewel." He shoved a frustrated hand through his hair.

"Shall I send Sam over to help you look?"

"I'll take a portable phone with me, and if I don't find Rebecca where Smitty said she was headed, I'll give you a call."

"All right. We'll wait to hear from you."

Zach wasn't truly alarmed yet. There was probably some perfectly logical reason why Rebecca wasn't back yet. And Jewel might be visiting some other friend. She might even be with his parents.

He had the phone in his hand dialing his parents' number when the screen door screeched open.

He turned with his mouth open to chastise Rebecca for not leaving him a note and froze.

Jewel stood in the doorway. Her forehead was scraped and oozed blood, her face was dirty and streaked with tears. Her lower lip was swollen almost twice its size.

"'Becca," she sobbed. "'Becca."

Zach was across the room in two strides and swept the little girl up into his arms.

"Where's Rebecca?" he demanded.

Jewel clenched his neck so hard she threatened to strangle him. "I'm so-or-ry. I'm so-or-ry," she sobbed. "Po-o-or 'Bec-c-ca."

Zach resisted the urge to shake her. The child was already hysterical, and violence was only going to make things worse. But he was terrified. Sorry for what? Why *poor* 'Becca? Where the hell was his wife? What had happened to the two of them?

Zach did his best to comfort Jewel, but he was shaking so hard himself it took him a long time, too long, to calm the little girl enough so she could speak coherently.

"Where is she, Jewel? Where's Rebecca?"

Jewel's chin trembled. Her mud-brown eyes sparkled with unshed tears.

"Jewel, please, where is she? You have to tell me. I have to go help her."

"You can't help her," Jewel said.

"Why not?"

"'Cause she's dead."

Chapter 10

Zach's heart missed a beat. His brain denied the words Jewel had spoken. The little girl had to be mistaken.

He set her on her feet and knelt beside her. "You have to take me to her, Jewel. Can you find your way back to where she is?"

"Her horse saw a snake and started bucking. She fell a long way down. I called to her and called to her, but she didn't answer me. I tried to get to her, but the trail doesn't go that way."

He brushed the curls away from Jewel's injured forehead. "How did you get so banged up?"

"Oh. My pony bucked me off, too, but I didn't fall into the canyon."

Zach could see it all, the two horses frantic with fear and with no room to maneuver away from the snake on that narrow, treacherous trail. Rebecca falling…falling. How far was "a long way down"? Maybe she was only injured. Maybe she had only been knocked unconscious. Maybe even now she was walking back to Hawk's Pride, wondering where the hell—heck—he was.

"You were a brave little girl to find your way back here all by yourself."

Tears welled in Jewel's eyes, and she shook her head. "I just got on my pony and told him to go home. He's the one who knew the way."

"Still—"

The child clutched handfuls of his jeans leg. "It's all my fault 'Becca got hurt. She told me I shouldn't have run away. She told me she would never have let those awful Poppet people take me away. But you said you didn't want me, and they didn't want me, either—cause I limp and I have scars— and I was afraid."

Zach dragged Jewel up into his arms and hugged her tight. "Oh, Jewel." How could anyone not want her? He knew now what her parents had been thinking when they named her. She was a jewel, all right, one more precious than sapphires or topazes or emeralds. And he would always treasure her as the priceless, irreplaceable gem she was.

It took him a moment to get hold of himself.

"We have to go find Rebecca," he said past the bullfrog-size lump in his throat. "Will you help me?"

"I'll try. What if I can't remember where she is?"

"Don't worry," Zach reassured her. "We'll find her."

He left the kitchen on the run, bellowing for help at the top of his lungs. People came on the fly from all directions.

"Rebecca's been injured somewhere in the canyon. I need someone to call 911 and get the paramedics on the way. Tell them we may need to airlift her from the canyon." If her back was broken. Or her neck.

"I'll do that," Mrs. Fortunata volunteered.

"I need someone to hook the horse trailer up to my pickup and load my horse and another for whoever comes with me. We'll drive to the canyon and go down on horseback."

"I'm on my way, Boss," Smitty said.

"I need someone to come with me to help…" He couldn't make himself say "carry her body," and said instead, "to help me climb down the canyon wall."

"I'll come," Campbell said.

Zach hurried back inside to doctor Jewel's wounds and wait for the call from Smitty that the trailer was ready.

The closer they got to the canyon, the more frightened Zach felt. What if Rebecca was dead? What if he never had a chance to tell her he loved her? Oh, dear God how he loved her! He had been pretending she was just like any other woman, that she could be replaced, because he was frightened of committing himself.

But there was no one quite like Rebecca. No one else would have dared to invade his house with her darling imps and homeless waifs…and make it feel so much like a home.

She had to be alive.

The trip down into the canyon was accomplished as quickly as was humanly possible within the bounds of safety. Zach had taken Jewel up behind him on his mount, and Campbell followed them. They were fighting time, because daylight was fast receding.

When they turned a bend, Jewel pointed down and shrieked, "There she is! Zach, I see her!"

She wasn't moving. Even from where he was, Zach could see blood on her shirt. He gauged whether it would help if they went farther down the trail before he tried climbing down into the canyon, but it bent in the other direction. He was going to have to go down from here to reach her.

He quickly lifted Jewel down, then dismounted and began rigging a rope to the horn of his saddle. He had done enough climbing on these canyon walls as a kid to know what he was doing. He quickly rappelled down the cliff wall, landing not far from Rebecca's body.

As he approached, she moaned.

He fought a gust of totally inappropriate, very relieved

laughter. She was alive! That was all that mattered. He bent down beside her, looking before he touched to see the extent of her injuries.

"Kid," he said softly, "you've really done it this time."

To his amazement, she opened her eyes and stared right at him. "Zach. I love you."

His throat ached. He knew why she had said it. Because she thought she was going to die. What a fraud she was, almost as bad as he was. "I love you, too," he said in a rusty-gate voice.

"You do?"

"Yep. Now shut up so I can see how badly you're hurt and get you out of here."

"Is Jewel all right?"

"Jewel's fine. She made it all the way back to the ranch by herself." He didn't think now was the time to tell her Jewel had thought she was dead. "Can you move your arms and legs?"

"Uh-huh. But I think my right wrist snapped when I used it to break my fall."

Her wrist was swollen to twice its normal size. "It looks broken, all right." He examined the cut on her forehead, which seemed to be the source of most of the blood. The head wound was less worrisome, now that he saw she was lucid. He looked at her eyes for signs of concussion, but didn't see any.

"Were you knocked out?"

"I must have been. It was early afternoon when I fell. The next time I opened my eyes, the sun was headed down past the rim of the canyon."

Zach took off his hat, shoved a hand through his hair, and pulled the Stetson snugly down. "I have to decide whether to move you myself or wait for the paramedics."

Rebecca struggled to sit up. "I can—" She winced and grabbed at her stomach.

"Something hurts?" Zach reached around her to support her back.

"I don't know. I must have bounced off a couple of rocks on the way down," she said with a halfhearted laugh. "Feels a little tender."

"Let me take a look." He undid her belt, unzipped her jeans and pulled the tails of her shirt up to take a look at her belly. It was horribly bruised. "Looks a little beat up." He touched her to see how tender she was, and she cried out with pain.

This looked serious, like maybe she was bleeding internally. Suddenly, the relief he had been feeling that she wasn't paralyzed or concussed vanished. She could die of injuries on the inside, injuries he couldn't see.

He took the time to wrap a bandage around her head to stop the bleeding from the cut there. Then he said, "If you think you could stand it, I'd like to rig a sling to get you out of here."

"Anything," she said. "I just want to go home."

"You're going straight to the hospital," Zach said. "And no arguments."

It was a sign of how bad her injuries were that she didn't make a fuss. In fact, in the thirty minutes or so it took him to get her up onto the trail, her condition deteriorated. She was unconscious again.

"Is she dead?" Jewel asked.

"No. In fact, I talked to her. She asked about you, and I told her how you came home to get help."

Jewel laid a palm on Rebecca's pale cheek and looked up at him. "Is she going to be okay?"

"She's going to be fine. We have to get her to the hospital, though, so they can make her well."

He had to get to the rim of the canyon for his cellular phone to work, but Zach had already decided that Rebecca needed to be airlifted to the hospital. It was the hardest thing he had ever done to watch the helicopter lift off without him.

It took too long to get the horses loaded back up, to drive back to the ranch, and then disconnect the trailer from his pickup so he could head for the hospital.

"Can I come?" Jewel asked.

"No, you have to wait here with Mrs. Fortunata."

"But 'Becca needs me!"

"You can go visit her when she's better," Zach promised.

"But she might die! Like my mommy and daddy died!"

"A hospital is no place for children," Zach snapped, his patience gone. "I have to go. Be a good girl, and go find Mrs. Fortunata."

He turned his back and headed for the cab of the truck. He didn't see Jewel climb into the back of his pickup and hide under a tarp.

Zach parked the truck in the hospital lot and hadn't gone two steps when he felt a small hand insinuate itself between his fingers.

He grabbed hold and turned to find himself staring at a mulish expression every bit as stubborn as anything he had ever seen on Rebecca's face. "How the hell—heck—did you get here? Damn—darn it, Jewel, what am I going to do with you?"

"I *have* to see 'Becca."

Zach didn't have time to take her home now. Grim-lipped, he tightened his hold on her hand and dragged her along with him. "You can sit in the waiting room. But I don't want to hear a peep out of you. Understand?"

"Uh-huh."

Once inside, Zach headed for the closest desk with someone behind it.

"Your wife is in the operating room," the admitting nurse told him. "She had internal injuries that required surgery. The surgeon will come see you when he's finished. There's a waiting room on the second floor."

Jewel was as good as her word. She was quiet as a mouse. But she never left his side, and she was with him every step he took. When he insisted that she stop tagging along behind him, she sat in a chair in the corner and followed him with her eyes. It was as though he was her last connection to Rebecca, and if she let go, she would lose everything.

He understood how she felt.

Zach was surprised when Callen and Sam arrived, although he shouldn't have been. Word passed quickly on a country grapevine. His family had always rallied to each other in times of trouble. His mother and father arrived shortly thereafter, and he had a call from Falcon, asking about Rebecca's condition.

"I don't know anything yet," Zach said. "They're still operating."

"Are you all right?" Falcon asked.

Zach remembered another time, years ago, when he had gone to the hospital with Falcon when his stepdaughter, Susannah, had become very ill, and they had feared it was a relapse of her leukemia. He had wanted to stay and provide a comforting shoulder for his brother. Now he realized why Falcon had sent him away. If he had that shoulder available, he might very well cry on it. And he couldn't afford to fall apart. He had to stay strong for Rebecca. And for Jewel.

"I'll be fine," Zach said. "As soon as I know Rebecca's going to be all right."

"Ask Mom to give me a call when you know something. We'll be praying for you."

"Thanks, Falcon."

It was late when the doctor finally arrived, his surgical greens dotted with dark patches of sweat. Zach recognized him as a guy who had been a couple of years behind him in high school. If he just thought a minute, he would remember the doctor's name. Only his brain was a little jumbled right now. He just couldn't think.

A volunteer had come in and turned off several of the lights, so the room was basked in shadows. Sam and Callen had gone home to put their children to bed, and his parents had retreated to the hospital cafeteria for a quick cup of coffee. Jewel, who had refused to leave with Sam and Callen, and Zach were alone in the waiting room.

When the surgeon approached Zach, his expression was grim. Zach's knees threatened to give way, but he wanted to be standing when he heard what he could see was going to be bad news. "Ted Slocum," the doctor said, holding out his hand.

Zach took it. "I'm Zach—"

"I know who you are, Mr. Whitelaw."

Zach didn't even realize Jewel had joined him until he felt her tiny hand close around his. He gripped her fingers and found as much comfort as he gave.

"Is she... How is she?" Zach asked.

"She had serious internal injuries. We couldn't stop the bleeding."

All the blood drained from Zach's face. "She's not—"

"She's alive," the doctor hurried to reassure him.

"Thank God." Zach's eyes closed momentarily in relief. "Oh, thank God for that."

"Her condition is stable, and I expect her to make a complete recovery. But I had to take out her spleen. And her uterus."

It took a moment for the doctor's words to sink in.

No. Oh, no. Poor Rebecca. Oh, poor Rebecca. Zach felt numb, but he knew the pain wasn't far off. It was like the time he had been stomped by a Brahma in a college rodeo. For a moment he had simply lain breathless in the dirt. Then he had tried to draw air into his lungs, and a fierce, searing pain had cut across his chest. He fought off the moment when he would be forced to confront the reality of the doctor's pronouncement, the moment when the pain would start.

"We wanted a family, you know. Three kids, or maybe four. Now you're telling me Rebecca can never have any children. It's..." He felt his self-control disappearing as a blinding rage took hold of him. "It isn't fair, goddamn it! This just can't be happening. Rebecca will... She... Rebecca... Oh, God, how will I ever tell her?''

"I'm sorry, Zach. There was nothing else I could do." The surgeon reached out a hand in comfort, but Zach shrank away from his touch. The doctor turned and headed for the door.

"When can I see her?" Zach called after him.

"She'll be in recovery for a while. I'll have a nurse send for you when she's conscious."

Zach sank into the nearest chair and dropped his head into his hands. He bit his lip to hold back the wounded cry that sought voice, but the awful, wrenching sound escaped his throat and echoed in the room.

He realized now the choice had been made long ago. He could not give up Rebecca. That did not keep him from grieving the loss of his never-to-be-born children. Or the loss of the children Rebecca would have loved the way she loved all helpless living creatures who crossed her path. A tight band gripped his chest making it nearly impossible to draw breath. The emotional pain of this catastrophic event was every bit as bad as the physical pain had been all those years ago.

Two tiny booted feet appeared beside him. He felt a hand patting his shoulder in comfort.

Jewel leaned close to his ear and said, "Don't cry, Zach. 'Becca's gonna be okay. The doctor said so."

He lifted his head from his hands unaware of the tears on his cheeks. "I know, Jewel. It's just..." She was too young to understand the devastation he felt at the doctor's other news.

"Are you sad 'cause 'Becca can't have any babies?"

He had underestimated her. Again.

"Yes, I am."

She played with a frayed spot at the knee of his jeans where it had gotten caught on some barbed wire. Her hand stilled and she looked up at him. "If you want, I could be your little girl."

Zach felt a rush of emotion. How vulnerable she looked,

waiting for his answer, her heart right there in those wonderful, unforgettable mud-brown eyes.

He swallowed past the thickness in his throat. "I'd like very much for you to be my daughter, Jewel."

Her gap-toothed smile was slow in coming, as though she couldn't quite believe her ears. Then she launched herself into his open arms, which closed around her.

"Oh, 'Becca will be so glad!" she said. "She told me not to worry, that she'd give you a good talking to, and that you'd change your mind," she admitted with youthful naïveté. "Only you changed your mind all by yourself!"

Zach smiled ruefully and let himself bask in the little girl's grin of approval. Oh, Jewel was her mother's daughter, all right. He was going to have his hands—and his heart—full with the pair of them. Thank God.

Zach surreptitiously swiped the tears from his eyes when he spotted his parents returning to the waiting room. "The doctor's been here, and Rebecca's going to be fine," he said.

"Only she can't have any babies," Jewel piped up.

Zach saw the look of shock and sympathy in his parents' eyes and knew he couldn't stay and talk with them right now. He wanted—needed—to see Rebecca.

"Will you keep an eye on Jewel? I'm going to see Rebecca." He didn't wait for an answer. As the waiting room door closed behind him, he heard Jewel saying, "I'm going to be Zach and 'Becca's little girl."

He smiled. That ought to keep his parents busy for a while.

Zach got directions from a nurse to the private room where they had moved Rebecca. There was a light at the head of the hospital bed that illuminated her face, but the rest of the room was cloaked in shadow. Her eyes were closed, but they opened when he sat down next to her on the bed.

"Hello, kid," he said.

"Hello, Zach."

"How do you feel?"

"Like a horse kicked me in the stomach."

She reached down to her stomach and gingerly touched it. She frowned as she felt the staples in her skin that the doctor had used to close after surgery. "Zach?"

He reached for her hand and brought her knuckles up to his lips. "The doctor had to do a little surgery."

"How little?"

"He took out your spleen."

She heaved a sigh of relief. "Oh, is that all? I think I can do without that."

"And your uterus," he said in a quiet voice.

She snatched her hand from his and winced at the pain caused by the jerky movement. "What did you say?"

"Your life was at stake. The doctor had no choice. He had to remove your uterus." It hurt, oh, how it hurt to see the stricken look on her face.

"No!" she cried. "It's not fair. Oh, Zach, it isn't fair! I wanted to give you children. I wanted—"

He pulled her awkwardly into his arms, trying not to hurt her as he maneuvered her head against his shoulder. He kissed away the hot tears spilling from her eyes. "It doesn't matter, kid. It doesn't matter to me. I'm just so glad you're alive. I love you so much—"

"But—"

"Nothing else is as important to me as you are."

"But—"

"I don't know how I would go on living if anything happened to you."

"But—"

"I love you—"

Rebecca clamped a hand over Zach's mouth. With every word he had said her heart had lightened. It was a blow to realize she could never bear children, but she was more concerned now with what that information meant to Zach. "You said we would get a divorce if I wasn't pregnant in a year. Are you saying you've changed your mind?"

She removed her hand to let him speak.

The silly man nodded vigorously and said, "Uh-huh."

Her eyes narrowed. "You only married me to have a mother for your children."

"Uh-huh."

"But I can't have any children now."

He shook his head. "Not true. In fact, if I'm not mistaken, you've already got one."

She stared at him a moment before understanding dawned. "Jewel? Oh, Zach, are you really willing to adopt Jewel?"

"The kid insists on staying. I couldn't very well throw her out, could I?"

Rebecca smiled through her tears. "Oh, Zach… We'll have a houseful of kids, I promise."

"I'd bet on it," he said with a chuckle. "I'd be a fool not to bet on it! I could make a fortune betting on it."

She laughed, and he lowered his head to capture her laughter with his lips. It was like coming home. His heart thumped a little faster. He might have lost this chance at happiness. He was reaching out now with both hands to love and life. And children. His and Rebecca's children. He wondered who they were, where they were right now, and by what mysterious means they would find their way to his doorstep.

"How many, Zach?"

"What?"

"How many can we have?"

"Oh, Lord," he said with a groan. He should have seen this coming. "Four. Altogether. Not one kid more, Rebecca. I swear I can't handle more than that."

"All right, Zach. Four."

Zach eyed her suspiciously, then shook his head in resignation and pulled his wife close. It was going to be more. He would bet on it. He could make a fortune betting on it. And he would likely need the fortune to feed everybody.

Zach grinned.

"What's so funny?" Rebecca asked.

"I'm just happy." Zach pulled her close. "I'm just a very happy man."

Epilogue

Seven. Zach hadn't imagined being the father of seven children after ten years of marriage, but he was surviving the experience amazingly well. Jewel was fifteen now, and blessed with two sisters and four brothers. Only one of the children had been a newborn when they adopted him. Colt was seven now and hell on wheels. You weren't supposed to have favorites, but he would always have a special fondness for Jewel, who was the first child to steal his heart, and for Colt, who had known no other father before him.

The other children had all been older when he and Rebecca adopted them, but they were equally precious to him. The other two girls, Frannie and Rolleen, were nine and seventeen now. The other three boys, Rabbit and Jake and Avery, were eight and twelve and thirteen, respectively. Of course, Rabbit's name wasn't really Rabbit, it was Louis. But they had discovered he loved raw carrots and lettuce and all sorts of vegetables, so Jewel had given him the nickname, and it had stuck.

Fortunately, they had a lot of help. Mrs. Fortunata and Mr.

Tuttle had fallen in love and married years ago, and the two of them were like another set of grandparents for the children. Thanks to Rebecca, there were always extra hands around the ranch. Some of the Camp LittleHawk kids had even come back to work at the camp and become friends.

Like Pete. Who had beaten all the odds. He was eighteen now and had been a camp counselor last summer. He was heading to college in the fall. He wanted to be a paleontologist, of all things. He said it was the Indian drawings in the canyon at Hawk's Pride that had gotten him interested in the subject.

Zach watched Rebecca edge through the sliding glass door and step into the courtyard.

"Why are you sitting out here all alone in the dark?" she asked.

"It's quiet out here." Which a houseful of kids was not. Ever. Zach opened his arms, and Rebecca settled in his lap on the wooden swing and snuggled her head against his chest. "I was just thinking what a lucky man I am," he said.

"We are lucky, aren't we?"

"Umm." With so many kids, it wasn't always easy to find a private moment with his wife, so he relished this one. He shoved the hair back from her nape and kissed the softness there. She still lit his fire, all these years later, and he felt the slight tension in his genitals as he took the weight of her breasts in his palms.

Rebecca made a kittenish sound in her throat. "You aren't sorry, are you, Zach?"

He was too busy kissing her throat to answer.

"About having so many children, I mean, and not any of them your own."

He raised his head abruptly and dropped his hands from her breasts. He turned her so he could take her face between his palms. He was irritated at having to stop his lovemaking to settle something that he had thought was settled long ago.

"Let's get this straight once and for all. These children are all mine, legally, morally, and every other way. I love them all. I'd give my life for each and every one of them. They're Whitelaws, through and through.

"And I bless the day you came into my life and became my wife. I won't say living with you is easy, because it isn't. There are times I don't think I can be the man you expect me to be, but I keep trying because I love you.

"Which isn't always easy. Because it isn't natural for me to be as open and generous as you are. And sometimes there are so many strangers working around here, it's hard to know who's who.

"But I wouldn't give up one single frustrating, exhilarating, mind-boggling minute of the past ten years."

"Oh, Zach, I'm so glad you feel that way." She fiddled with the collar of his Western shirt. "Because, there's this girl—"

"No. Absolutely not."

"But you just said—"

"Seven is enough. We agreed when your brought Rabbit home that he was the last. I'm forty-six, Rebecca. Forty-six-year-old men don't go around having kids."

"But Cherry is fourteen, Zach. She won't be any trouble at all. Or, maybe only a little."

Zach groaned.

"It seems she has this attitude problem and has been skipping school. Her foster parents finally gave up on her. She's in a juvenile detention center right now, but if we—"

"All right."

"—agree to be her—"

"I said all right."

Rebecca threw her arms around Zach's neck and kissed him all over his face. "Oh, Zach, thank you so much."

Rebecca opened the first two snaps on his shirt and slipped her hand inside to rest it against his chest. "You have the biggest heart of any man I know. And I love you, very, very much."

Eight wasn't so many, Zach thought. But this was absolutely the last one.

Next time he was putting his foot down.

*   *   *   *   *

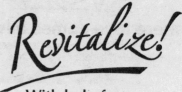

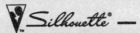

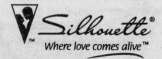

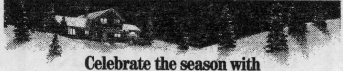

Silhouette Books cordially invites you to come
on down to Jacobsville, Texas, for

DIANA PALMER's
LONG, TALL TEXAN
Weddings

(On sale November 2001)

The LONG, TALL TEXANS series from international
bestselling author Diana Palmer is cherished around the
world. Now three sensuous, charming love stories from
this blockbuster series—*Coltrain's Proposal, Beloved* and
"Paper Husband"—are available in one special volume!

*As free as wild mustangs, Jeb, Simon and Hank vowed
never to submit to the reins of marriage. Until, of course,
a certain trio of provocative beauties tempt these Lone Star
lovers off the range...and into a tender, timeless embrace!*

You won't want to miss
LONG, TALL TEXAN WEDDINGS
by Diana Palmer, featuring two
full-length novels and one short story!

Available only from Silhouette Books at your favorite retail outlet.

Silhouette®
Where love comes alive™

Visit Silhouette at www.eHarlequin.com

PSLTTW